Everybody loves Stella Cameron!

"Stella Cameron leaves you breathless, satisfied . . . and hungry for the next time!"

—Elizabeth Lowell

"Sizzling, sexy, and sensational!"

—Jayne Ann Krentz

"Stella Cameron writes an exciting, fast-paced and very sensual novel—just the kind of book I love."

—Linda Lael Miller

"Stella Cameron works magic with our hearts and casts a seductive spell."

—Katherine Stone

"Stella Cameron's books are filled with wit, grace and sizzling sensuality."

—Anne Stuart

"Her narrative is rich, her style distinct, and her characters wonderfully wicked."

—*Publishers Weekly*

"Stunning!"

—*Romantic Times*

"Dazzling and refreshing!"

—*Affaire de Coeur*

Turn the page and discover for yourself
the incomparable magic of Stella Cameron!

The Best Revenge

Stella Cameron

Zebra Books
Kensington Publishing Corp.
http://www.zebrabooks.com

ZEBRA BOOKS are published by

Kensington Publishing Corp.
850 Third Avenue
New York, NY 10022

Copyright © 1998 by Stella Cameron

Zebra and the Z logo Reg. U.S. Pat. & TM Off.

First Printing: February, 1998
10 9 8 7 6 5 4 3

Printed in the United States of America

For Kate Duffy

*The writer who insists all editors
are redundant hasn't met Kate.
Thank you for being my "remote ears and eyes!"*

Prologue

Glad Times, Georgia

"You just keep your filthy, lyin' mouth shut, Rae Faith. Hear?"

Rae sat on the floor in the hot, windowless room she shared with the baby. With her back against the thin door, she felt vibrations from every stumbling move Willie Skeggs made in the single room that was cooking, eating, and living space on the other side of the door.

Baby Ginny whimpered. Rae cradled her high on her shoulder and made little love noises. Willie got real mad if Ginny cried, and that made Rae scared, especially when Willie was drunk. Willie was drunk tonight. Again.

"Hear?" Willie shouted. "I asked if you heard me, girl. No more lyin' to your mama. No more tellin' her I done things when I didn't." He pounded on the door.

Rae wedged her feet against the bottom of the old trundle bed where she and Ginny slept. The bed, with its threadbare patchwork quilt, and two wooden crates where she kept clothes, her own and the baby's, were the only furniture.

The baby let out a gurgling cry that screwed up her pretty pink face. Rae loved Ginny so much it hurt her heart to think about it. A good kind of hurt.

"Rae! You leave that snivelin' brat in there and get out

here. You're a big girl now. Seventeen years old, for cryin' out loud. You gotta take care of your daddy now."

Rae breathed harder, yet felt more breathless. "You aren't my daddy," she said very softly to herself. "I don't know my daddy, but you aren't him."

"Rae Faith. Your mama told you to take care of me, didn't she? Answer me." More thumping on the door. "Get out here before I come in and get you. Your mama's gone and left me again. I'm lonely, Rae Faith."

He was starting to whine. A bad sign. Once the whining started, the rage was only minutes away.

Ginny nuzzled her soft face against Rae's neck. Hungry again. Rae needed to go get a bottle, but that would mean getting within grabbing range of Willie Skeggs.

She felt so sick she could vomit. Mama had left hours ago to go dancing in Atlanta. Rae had been hiding out ever since. She hadn't eaten since breakfast when she'd scrambled an egg in bacon grease and stacked it between two slices of Wonderbread. Wearing only his shorts, Willie had then been stretched out on the bed he shared with Mama, asleep, several empty beer bottles scattered around the second bedroom in the cabin. His straight blond hair needed a wash and hung over his face. Beard stubble darkened his slack jaw. Rae had watched him while she gulped down the congealed egg and damp bread, and while she warmed a bottle for Ginny. Mama had been out all night, and Rae had known there would be another fight when Betty Skeggs came home and Willie woke up.

Tangled in a grimy sheet, one of Willie's long legs had trailed off the bed. Mama never stayed home long enough to make that bed, and Willie sure wouldn't do women's work. Willie was tall and muscular, but going to fat 'cause he didn't do anything but lie around the cabin all the time. When he splayed his legs like that, Rae couldn't help seeing up inside his loose shorts, seeing things she didn't want to see, but couldn't help staring at.

Then she'd looked at Ginny and thought how that sweet baby had come from there. From there and from her gentle sister, Cassie. Willie had always called Cassie "droolin' idiot," but he'd done things to her whenever Mama was out, and made Cassie pregnant. And now Cassie was dead five months from the seizure she'd had when Ginny was born. Cassie had been eighteen.

"I'm countin' to ten, Rae Faith." Willie's words ran together. "You get out here. Now. *One.*"

Five months Cassie had been dead. She wasn't an idiot, Rae thought defensively. Cassie had got brain trouble from hitting her head when she was real little. That made her kind of slow, but gentle-slow, not stupid-slow. And Willie Skeggs had watched Cassie grow up and get breasts. He'd started going after her then. Cassie got big breasts, not like Rae's small ones. The two sisters were different like that. Cassie had grown into a beautiful, curvy, blond young woman while Rae just got a bit taller, and what Mama called "dark and secretive." Willie Skeggs hadn't looked at Rae while Cassie was alive—or not until she got too big with Ginny anyway.

Then he'd begun trying to get Rae alone. And he'd made it a few times; but he'd always been too drunk, and she'd always been too quick.

"Rae Faith," Willie wheedled, and Rae could tell he'd put his mouth to the crack between the door and the jamb. "Come on out and let me be nice to you, Rae Faith. I got somethin' for you. Time you had a little fun. You spend too much time holed up in that cupboard of a room like that."

Experience had taught her that argument only inflamed him. Her best hope was that he'd get tired and go fall on the bed.

"Your mama's treatin' me mean," Willie said, his breathing heavy. "She don't give me what I need no more."

Rae opened her mouth to say her mama paid for the beer Willie was drinking, but clamped her teeth together just in time.

"She doesn't let me feel like a man. You know what I mean, Rae Faith. A man's gotta be allowed to be a man, or he ain't nothin'. Come on out, little honey, and let Willie be a man with you. You know you're ready. More'n ready."

He wanted to do that to her. Like he used to do to Cassie every day after their mama left for work at the broiler plant. Willie never even bothered to close the door when he used to take Cassie in there. He'd said he wanted Rae to see how much Cassie enjoyed it so she'd know he wasn't hurting her sister.

At first Cassie cried. Willie would hit her then, but he still did it to her.

Later Cassie went without being told, and sat on the bed all quiet—waiting.

Rae's eyes stung and she blinked. She ought to have been able to stop Willie from doing that to her sweet sister.

"Speak to me, Rae Faith!" He had to shout to make himself heard above music coming from a car parked outside the cabin next door.

Her skin prickled. Willie was mad now.

"Answer me. Tell me you're comin' to keep me company."

Ginny started to sob. She swallowed air and hiccuped, and her face turned bright red. Beneath Rae's hand she could feel that the baby's diaper needed changing. The smell of ammonia hung in the close air. Ginny should have been changed some time ago.

"Betty said she's not comin' back this time." Willie was crying. Sometimes he cried, but only until he drank some more and got angry some more. "She's left me, Rae Faith, and she knows I can't do for myself with this bad back of mine."

Ginny reared backward and screamed.

"Shut her up," Willie said. "Shut her *up*." He threw a shoulder against the door and it rattled.

Rae's heart beat harder and harder. "Go away," she said. "Ginny's got a fever. She needs to be quiet."

"She shoulda died with her idiot mama."

"Cassie wasn't an idiot," Rae cried. "And Ginny's your—" She mustn't say it.

The screaming grew louder. The baby's body was hot, and she writhed.

"Willie," Rae said in a deliberately calm voice. "I need to get Ginny some water. And I want to give her a cool bath. She's real hot, Willie. Why don't you go to bed?"

"I'm gonna do that." He laughed, and burped. "I'm gonna do that, and you're gonna come with me, sweet thing. Time I gave you something real nice to think about."

He wanted to do that to her, that thing he used to do with Cassie. The thing he and Mama did after the fighting, and before Willie fell drunk asleep and Mama went into the cramped bathroom to soak in the tub.

Rae had listened to girls at school laughing together about it, and she'd watched boys talking about the same thing while they eyed the girls. The boys she could understand. They would be like Willie who couldn't get enough, but Rae tended to think none of the girls would do it willingly, not if they knew how ugly it was. Some girls did get pregnant and have babies. Rae couldn't believe they did it again after that.

Sammy Joe Phipps had tried to put a hand up Rae's shirt once. Rae slapped him so hard he looked like he was going to cry. He never tried it again. Nope—she wasn't having anything to do with any of it if she had her way.

Thunderous banging on the door set Ginny to screaming.

"Get your skinny ass out here," Willie yelled. "I'm gonna show you who's boss, and it ain't you, little girl. Little girls was put here to drive men crazy. It's up to men to show 'em how they've only got one thing that's any good and it's between their legs."

"Hush," Rae said, hating how her voice shook. "You're upsetting the baby and she's sick, Willie."

The door hammered against her back. Rae's knees started to buckle. She opened her mouth, and the air hurt her throat.

Willie gave the door another shove and bent Rae's knees some more. Her bottom inched along the linoleum.

Willie's fingers forced a way around the edge of the door.

Rae shifted Ginny to her other shoulder and cast about, silently begging for the Lord to show her a way out to safety. She'd have left for good before, only there had been Cassie who needed her, then Ginny. She didn't know how she'd take care of Ginny if she went now, but she'd just have to find a way.

Willie grunted, and put his weight on the door. His dirty fingernails dug into the wood on Rae's side. "You're tryin' my patience, Rae Faith. All I want is to show you a good time, but I'm losin' my temper, I tell you."

"Mama's coming home soon," Rae said, breathless. "You were asleep when she left. She said she'd be back by two. It's almost two now."

"Lyin' *bitch*," Willie said, and in a lull in the music from outside, Rae heard him pour more beer down his throat. "Both of you. Both lyin' bitches. Mother and daughter. I oughta walk out and see how you get on without me. Lyin', no good bitches. Like mother, like daughter. My daddy always warned me about that. S'true. She's out there now. Puttin' out for some no-good who's tellin' her lies. She was always a sucker for them pretty lies."

Rae tried to cover her ears.

"Tell her she's sexy and she can't open her legs fast enough. Never mind if she's got a husband at home who needs her."

Ginny's screams ripped through Rae's head. She jiggled the baby faster and faster, but the screams only got louder.

Sweat ran down Rae's neck and between her breasts and shoulder blades. Her thin cotton tank top and shorts were soaked.

A crashing blow hit the cheap wood above Rae's head. With a splintering sound, Willie's right hand smashed through.

Rae's scream joined Ginny's. She stared upward and saw bloody gashes well on the protruding fist.

"Christ," Willie shouted. He tried to yank his wrist back, but shrieked when frayed slivers embedded in his flesh.

Rae felt the moment when he turned crazed.

The door pummeled her back, scooting her forward until her knees folded, and Ginny was crushed between Rae's thighs and her chest.

Rae searched frantically for something that might help. The only solid implement within reach was a big old flashlight that had once been painted orange, but was now mostly coated with rust.

To reach the flashlight, she had to give up her spot on the floor.

Holding Ginny tight, Rae shifted to grab the flashlight.

The instant her resistance left, the door flew open with such force it ripped from its hinges and crashed over the trundle bed. Naked to the waist of his jeans, Willie lay spread-eagle on top.

"Help me," he yelled. "Help me, bitch. Get this door off of me."

"You're on the door," Rae said. She felt tears on her face. They must be Ginny's. "I've got to see to Ginny."

When she made to climb past Willie, he kicked at her with a silver-toed boot, and she shot backward.

"Help me." He gasped aloud, and panted, his hand still trapped in the door. "I'm bleedin' to death."

She had to think, to do things really carefully. "It's okay, Willie. You stay real still. If you don't, you're going to bleed worse."

"Make the goddamn hole bigger. Put the brat down and help me, will ya?"

"Sure I will," Rae said soothingly. Her teeth chattered. Ginny stopped crying and shuddered, banging her face against Rae's sharp collarbone. "I'm going to go into the kitchen and find something to help you with."

"Like hell," Willie spat out his words. He turned his head to see her, and she saw tears running from his reddened eyes. "You think I'm as stupid as that droolin' idiot sister of yours was? You'd leave me here. Put down the brat and hold this door still."

She'd got through high school, Rae thought, her head beating inside. Done it early. Even with Mama wanting her at home, and Willie demanding she look after him, and Cassie when she was alive, Rae had graduated. Not with the gown and stuff. There hadn't been money for that. But she had the certificate hidden under the mattress on the trundle part of the bed. Right under Willie Skeggs' no-good body, and the door.

"You listening to me?" He cried openly now, and sobs tore sounds from his throat. "I'm bleedin' to death here."

The diploma was her treasure. And the transcript that showed she'd had a 3.6 grade point average. The principal had asked if she was going to college. He'd been kind, and smiled at her. She never told anyone how hard it was to do her homework. She wanted to go to college. Maybe she would one day.

"Rae Faith!"

Why was she thinking about all that stuff now?

Because it was time to do something about it, that's why. For Ginny and herself. And in memory of sweet Cassie, who never had any chance at all.

"I'm going into the kitchen," Rae told Willie firmly.

Once more she started to climb over him.

Once more he kicked at her, and this time he connected. Rae crumpled to the brown linoleum, barely managing to keep her grip on Ginny.

"Hold the goddamn door steady," Willie said.

The slam of the outside screen door silenced him. Ginny sniffled.

"Now you're for it," Willie said, drawing his lips back in

a grimacing smile. "Your mama's home. In here, Betty baby. Come and see what your pet did to her daddy."

An unshaded overhead light in the main room of the cabin showed piles of newspapers on the couch where stuffing bubbled free from rings worn open over springs. Unwashed dishes littered a table wedged between the couch and the end of the counter by the sink.

"Betty," Willie called. "Come here, sweetcakes."

After a few moments' hesitation, Betty Skeggs' high heels tapped a fast track to the destroyed doorjamb. She took in the scene, looking from Willie lying on top of the door, to Rae cowering against the wall with Ginny clutched in her arms and blood from Willie's kick seeping down her shin.

"What's happenin' here?" Like Willie's, Betty's accent was pure Tennessee, which was where they had lived before leaving in the middle of the night for some reason Rae had never been told—or dared to ask about. "What's wrong with your leg, Rae Faith?"

"She went for me," Willie said, starting to pull his arm back, then howling and slumping down again with his face hidden. "Wouldn't do what I told her. Ran in here and slammed the door when I came after her. I tried to stop the door from hitting me, and my hand went right through."

"Liar!" Rae couldn't close her mouth. She stared at him. "He was breaking the door down, Mama. He wanted to do it to me like he did to Cassie."

Betty Skeggs wasn't a small woman, but she was strong. She leaped across her husband's legs in a single stride and her closed fist connected with Rae's jaw so hard, Rae's head snapped up and she heard something crack.

"You teach her, Betty. You show her, honeycakes." Willie slid sideways to kneel on the floor. "She's a devil. Needs teachin'. Get me free of this and I'll make sure she never opens her mouth like that again."

With pain exploding in her brain, Rae concentrated on

holding Ginny. The baby had shrieked, a shocked shriek that rose into fresh, hysterical cries.

"What d'you think you're doing with that flashlight?" Betty said. She took a handful of Rae's long, dark hair and pulled her head sideways. "You're no good. Your father was no good. I thank God you're no child of mine. Don't know why I ever dragged you along with me."

Rae held the hair closest to her scalp and tried to free it from Mama's fingers. "I'm yours, Mama." She never wanted to hurt her mother, her flamboyant, sometimes mean, sometimes affectionate mother. "Don't say I'm not yours. We're all we've got. Remember how you used to say that before him." She looked at Willie.

"Smack her mouth, Betty," Willie said, gingerly working his wrist out, inch by inch.

Betty brought her face close to Rae's. The baby squirmed between them. "You aren't mine, I tell you." Stale liquor loaded her breath. Green shadow clung in the laugh lines around her blue eyes. Navy blue mascara clumped her lashes together and smeared to her cheeks. "Your daddy—Windy, we called him. He blew in. He blew out. Never stayed long, and one day he blew out and never came back. Only he left you with me. And I was dumb enough to be sorry for you, scraggly little thing that you were."

"Betty," Willie moaned.

"But Cassie was my sister," Rae said, her thoughts running together. The cabin was so hot her clothes could have been wet tissue plastered on her skin. "You always said sisters had to stick together."

"You had the same mother. So Windy said. Cassie wasn't his kid, but you were. Left the pair of you."

"But I thought—"

"Don't matter what you thought," Willie moaned, dragging the door with him as he managed to sit on the edge of the bed. "Betty's got a soft heart. Sure wasn't for the puny relief money they give for a couple of brats. Right, doll? But

I wouldn't have let you be taken advantage of if you'd told me the way of it."

"Not even to get your hands on Cassie's big boobs?" Mama said.

Rae closed her eyes and whispered, "Don't."

"Grow up." Mama's lipstick was gone, and she turned the corners of her full mouth down. Everything about Mama was full, including her thighs beneath the short skirt of her fringed denim shirt. That's why men lined up for a little of her time, so she said. Her body and her brain—that's what they wanted, Mama said.

"Goddamn you, Betty," Willie said suddenly, explosively. "Shut your fuckin' mouth and help me, will ya?"

Betty stared at him for a long time. Very slowly, she took off a red shoe with a four-inch heel that made her well over six feet tall. "Sure I'll help you, Willie," she said, and brought the heel down on the door, breaking away more of the wood—and gouging Willie's arm at the same time.

He opened his mouth, but no sound came out. His sallow cheeks turned gray and his eyelids lowered.

Blood gushed.

Betty raised the shoe and struck again.

More blood pumped, but she'd freed Willie. She pulled out his hand and picked up the door as if it weighed nothing. Rae watched, mute, as Mama carried the door through the cabin and hurled it outside.

When she returned, Willie was clasping the wounds in his arm and blubbering. He glared at Mama, then at Rae. His eyes narrowed on Rae, and he said, "It's her fault. She came from trash and she acts like trash. Violent trash. She's got to be taught a lesson, I tell you. Then she's gotta be made to do what we need here."

Mama stood with her hands on her hips. "Get out," she told Rae. "Go. Now. While Willie's not up to doing nothin' about it."

Confused, Rae stared at the woman she'd known as her

mother for all her remembered life. "Go where?" she asked in a small voice.

"Anywhere," Betty Skeggs said. "I gotta take a pee. Go before I get back. And take the brat with you."

Rae watched her go and heard the bathroom door close.

"Not so fast," Willie said with a sneer. "I got a little something I promised you first."

Rae rushed for the door, but despite his wounds, Willie was faster. He tore Ginny from her arms and threw the baby onto the mattress. "Take off your shorts," he said, advancing, wiping the blood from his wrist onto his flabby gut.

"Mama," Rae shouted, but the sound was silly, small. "Let me go, Willie. Mama'll be mad if you touch me."

"You heard her, girl. She ain't your mama. Take 'em off." While he approached, he unsnapped the waist of his jeans and unzipped them. Then he reached for the elastic waistband of Rae's homemade shorts.

Ginny began to slip from the bed.

"Help!" Rae called. "Please help us!"

Willie laughed and gathered her tank top in his fist. The fabric started to give at the side seams. Willie twisted, managing to push his knuckles into her nipples as he did so.

"Mama," Rae shouted brokenly. "Ginny's falling off the bed. She'll hurt her head like Cassie did."

"Too bad you ain't got what Cassie had," Willie said, using both hands to squeeze her breasts. "They'll do. And what else you got'll do just fine. All the same to me."

Rae heard Betty's voice before she saw her. "Sonuvabitch," Betty Skeggs said in a hissing tone. "I told you what I'd do to you if you tried it again."

"Ah, give it up, Betty," Willie said, pushing a hand inside Rae's shorts. "She ain't nothin' to us except what she's good for. Go get some sleep for that lovely face of yours. I'll be there soon enough."

Then Rae saw Betty. The woman jumped on Willie's back like a big kid going for a piggyback ride. And with short nails broken from long hours working over the carcasses of chickens, she clawed at Willie's eyes. He released Rae and bucked, and grappled with Betty's fingers. His blood smeared her hands and his own face.

With a huge heave, he swung her around his body and threw her to the floor. Then he was upon her, beating her with his fists, not caring where his blows landed.

Betty tried to fend him off, but she was no match for Willie Skeggs when he didn't have a door on his arm.

Rae retrieved terrified Ginny and set her in one of the crates filled with clothes.

"Stop it, Willie," Rae said, plucking at the waistband of his jeans. "Stop. You're hurting her."

"I'm fuckin' killin' the bitch," he said, and punched Betty again, this time in the stomach. And he landed another blow to her belly, and another.

Betty retched, and blood ran from the corner of her mouth.

"No, Willie," Rae cried.

He wasn't listening. Betty still fought, but weakly now. She tried to find some place to hold Willie's bare chest, his pumping arms.

When she fell back, Willie wrenched her skirt up, revealing that Mama wasn't wearing panties. He slapped her face, and finished opening his jeans. While Mama made awful noises and choked up more blood, Willie concentrated on getting his thing inside her.

Rae knew she was going to throw up.

She retrieved the flashlight she'd dropped.

Willie began to move over Mama, whose chin sagged toward her shoulder. Her eyes were closed.

"You've killed her," Rae whispered.

And soon he'd kill her, too, Rae thought, and then Ginny, sweet Ginny.

Rae gathered up the baby and reached into the trundle, beneath the mattress, until she felt the envelope. She pulled it out and stuck it inside her tank top with Ginny pressed against it.

She could do it. She had her diploma. The principal said as long as you graduated and kept your nose clean, you could be what you wanted to be. One day Rae would go to college, but first she'd make money and look after Ginny for Cassie.

Creeping, she made her way around Willie, who sweated and grunted over Mama's limp body.

Once outside she could vomit, but not here, not while she needed to get away.

Carefully, Rae stepped into the other room and rose to tiptoe.

And yelling, howling like an animal, Willie Skeggs came after her along the floor. He grabbed her ankle and brought her down. Somehow she kept hold of Ginny, held her close and safe.

"Now you, bitch. That one's no good. Won't be no good till she sobers up. Then she's gonna learn who's boss. First I'm teachin' you, though."

Ignoring the baby, he found the waist of Rae's shorts once more, and pulled.

Rae lifted her right arm, and brought it down.

The heavy, rusty old flashlight hit the base of Willie's skull with a sound like breaking open a coconut with a hammer.

Rae threw the flashlight away.

Willie fell, facedown on the linoleum.

He didn't move again.

"Mama," Rae whispered, crawling to the woman. "Mama, help." Mama didn't answer. Her eyelids fluttered, but that's all.

With Ginny held in one arm, Rae shuffled to Willie and felt his neck the way she'd seen them do on TV. She couldn't feel anything.

She'd killed him.

So shaky she thought she'd fall over, Rae got to her feet. They didn't have a phone, so she couldn't call for help. Not that anyone would come out here. Even the police were afraid of the gangs in Glad Times.

She knew what she had to do.

In a corner of the kitchen, Mama kept plastic bags from grocery shopping. Rae gathered some and filled them with clothes for her and Ginny. She took a couple of baby bottles, a carton of milk, some cookies, and a box of disposable diapers. What was left of the loaf of Wonderbread joined the rest of the supplies, as well as a shriveled apple and a bunch of spoiled bananas. Several crumpled bills and some change lay on the kitchen counter. Rae scooped the money into the pocket of her shorts.

She checked Mama and Willie one more time. They were the same, except Mama moaned, and muttered.

Fingerprints.

Locating the flashlight, Rae pushed it in with the clothes. If the police questioned her, she'd say she was scared and ran away with the baby. Before then, she'd lose the light. Everyone knew Betty and Willie Skeggs fought a lot—they'd think this had been one more of their fights. Except Mama—who wasn't Mama—would probably send them after the child she'd never wanted.

Rae made her way through the heated darkness, through the straggle of mean cabins where music blared and people shouted, to the road.

To the west lay Atlanta. Rae had been there a couple of times. She didn't like it. Mama always got drunk there, and met men.

The way south led to Savannah. She'd read about it, and it sounded nice. She'd go that way, and maybe find some place where she could get a job with her diploma.

Rae started walking. The handles of the plastic bags cut into her elbows, but she didn't care. It was hot, but there was a little breeze, and Ginny wasn't crying anymore.

Sooner or later she'd get a ride with some trucker, and

she'd pray he was a good man. Couldn't be so much worse than the man she'd left behind.

Rae lengthened her stride, and bounced Ginny the way she liked to be bounced.

She'd be okay. Ginny would be okay.

Rae Faith was a good girl who'd kept her nose clean.

She would forget the man on his face on the dirty floor, and the woman who said she'd never wanted her anyway.

Rae Faith was a good girl who'd kept her nose clean.

She kissed Ginny's cheek, and checked to make sure the diploma was safe in its envelope beneath her own tank top.

One

"If I was that man of yours, I wouldn't leave a pretty little gal like you all alone like he does. No, siree. Not me. I'd be afraid some smooth-talkin' fella who knows his way around a woman would step right up and help her forget all about her husband."

Rae smiled at grizzled Jo Purdy, and Fats O'Lean, and the rest of the afternoon assortment of elderly loafers outside Loder's General Store, Diner, Post Office, and Up-to-date Beauty Shop. Sparring with the resident characters who lined the store windows on both sides of the door was an almost daily event, but on this August day she was too hot.

Rae was also too tired. And she was worried.

"Nothing to say for yourself, Rae Maddy?" Jo said, showing off his three artfully arranged and wobbly brown teeth. "Reckon I must be wearin' you down with my charm, huh? How's about you and me doing a little dancin' tonight?" Tipping his sweat-stained Braves cap over his bright, but watery eyes, Jo wriggled his skinny, eighty-something rump on the wooden bench.

His buddies guffawed.

Rae summoned another smile. "I'd never keep up with you, Jo. A spry, fancy-footed young sprig like you? Nope.

I'll have to pass and leave you to someone who's more woman than I am."

Picking a path across creaky boards on the wide veranda fronting the store, Rae heard the ensuing chuckles, and the slaps that landed on Jo's back, and was grateful for the diversion she'd created.

She pulled open the sagging screen door and stepped into the thick, muddle-scented air inside Loder's.

Before she let the door close entirely behind her, she fiddled with the shoulder strap of her purse and pretended to be adjusting a buckle. She fiddled, but she scanned the opposite side of Decline's main street, called, aptly, Main. Main was also the only street of any consequence in Decline.

Pickups, mostly carelessly parked, formed a dusty battalion in front of Skeeter's Bar. Rae could hear laughter rolling out of the bar in gusts, laughter and the steady beat of the only two kinds of music played in these parts: country, and western.

Two o'clock in the afternoon, hot as Minnie Loder's griddle around noon on a Sunday, and so serene Rae's skin crawled. Just another normal day in Decline. Only it wasn't normal, and Rae knew it. In the town that had been her haven for the best part of ten years, she felt a deadly threat. For the first time. Through all those years she'd kept alert, kept watching the papers, even done a little detective work once, but there had never been any hint of trouble. None with her name on it.

She was itchy. Worried about John being late back from his business trip up north. John was in refrigeration sales and traveled all over. He never stayed home more than a day or two, and he was often late; but he always came back to spend hours just being inside the house he called his haven, with the woman he called his sanity. Quiet, easy-going John, whose one requirement of her was that she be there, in their pretty house out of Decline, when he did show.

Deadly threat?

Threat, nothing. When John got back she'd tell him all about it, and he'd tell her there was no need to worry.

John was three weeks late. He'd never been that overdue before.

Twice, she'd seen the stranger twice. Once when she'd dropped Ginny off at school that morning. Once around noon when she'd looked up from a table in the reference section of Decline's tiny library. Each time the man had met her gaze calmly, then looked away as if disinterested. Rae wasn't fooled. A tall, leanly muscular man with dark curly hair just the wrong side of too long, a hard mouth just the wrong side of irresistible, and narrow gray eyes cold enough to freeze a person from the inside out—after they made her tremble— a man fitting that description was following Rae Faith Maddy.

Men like that didn't wander around Decline. This was a town people passed through, or, like Rae, used for what little it could provide when they didn't feel like going into Savannah.

Rae's breath caught somewhere around her throat.

He was there. Not in front of Skeeter's, but leaning against the side of a dark green Land Rover parked to the left of the bar, near Doc Piney's place.

Rae looked at him.

He looked right back.

Why me? A wild, probably self-destructive urge to rush across the street and demand just what he thought he was doing all but propelled Rae forward.

She lowered her eyes, went inside Loder's, and let the screen door slap shut behind her.

The heat was at its mighty worst. Overhead fans moved air with monotonous, just-opened-the-oven results. Rae passed up the general store—which no one was minding— and walked through an archway and down a single step into the post office. Mrs. Minnie Loder, wrapped in clean, daisy-covered cotton, and obviously fresh from the Up-to-date

Beauty Shop, sat in her faded canvas chair with her feet propped on a stool. There wasn't a Mr. Loder, and he was never mentioned.

"You're late, Rae," Minnie said. She grinned, and her round cheeks all but closed her shiny brown eyes. "Maybe that husband you reckon you got finally paid a visit?"

Rae ignored the loaded and nosey question. "I was held up at the library. They got in all the stuff I ordered." But, as usual, she'd had to use it at the library because they didn't hold with people taking materials on loan away from the building.

"What was that kind of book you said you was writing?" Minnie asked. Minnie always asked.

"Novelization of a movie," Rae said patiently. "Do I have any mail?"

Minnie swung her considerable feet to the floor and heaved upright. "Guess I'll have to check." Minnie always said that, too.

Rae waited while Minnie went behind the counter and poked in one of the numbered cubbyholes on the wall.

The sound of a hair dryer droned from next door where Sue Ellen, and whatever girl was currently in training, dealt with the heads of most of the inhabitants of Decline. Pineapple was the shampoo and spray scent of the day, but it didn't quite mask the aroma of lunches-gone-by from the diner at the very end of the building.

Minnie riffled through several pieces of mail she'd removed from Rae's box. Rae wished John would relent and agree to a regular rural delivery. He said this was safer, and more anonymous. He said he worried about her because he couldn't be with her most of the time and didn't want anyone having an excuse to stop by the house—or to know anything about their business.

Many times Rae had pointed out that having someone put their mail in a box by the highway didn't constitute an opportunity for a social visit, and that they had nothing to hide anyway, but he was adamant. John asked so little of her, she didn't have the heart to insist.

"Looks like you got another statement from that fancy Atlanta bank," Minnie said, sniffing, and turning an envelope over. "And one from the bank in Savannah. Never knew anyone who felt they needed more'n one bank, except you, Rae."

A show of irritation would only slow the process of getting her hands on her property. Rae knew, because she'd once lost her temper and spent ten minutes mopping Minnie's tears.

"Lots of people like to have more than one financial institution," she said, hoping she sounded patient.

"This one here's a big one. Wonder who's sending you big, brown envelopes. No return address, neither." Minnie examined the offending piece of mail. "Puts me in mind of one of them bomb things."

"I wouldn't worry. Ordinary people like me don't get letter bombs." Rae looked over her shoulder and through the window. The Land Rover was where it had been. The man wasn't.

She set her front teeth precisely together. She wanted her mail. She wanted to get home. She wanted Ginny with her, and the doors locked. And she wanted John to get back—just long enough to give her confidence a jolt. John was good at that.

"Why would you write other people's stories rather than your own?" Minnie asked, tucking the mail between her arm and her comfortably round bosom. Minnie was somewhere in the uncertain years between early and late fifties.

"It's work-for-hire," Rae said, repeating what she'd told Minnie on many occasions. "It pays well, and mostly I like it."

"Why wouldn't you write your own stories? No ideas?"

Explaining further was pointless. "I expect that's it." Any discussion of her aspirations as a writer wouldn't mean anything to Minnie.

"John's been gone a long time, hasn't he?" Minnie asked. Rae heard the screen door whine open, and rattle shut, and the solid thud of boots on boards. "Sounds like business is picking up," she said, smiling. "I'll get out of your hair."

Minnie smiled back and poked at her tight, frosted curls. "What d'you think? Sue Ellen persuaded me the color's flattering. Makes me look younger, she says."

The footsteps crossed the store, heading for the post office.

"You ought to do something with that hair of yours," Minnie said, when Rae didn't answer.

"I think Sue Ellen's right," Rae said hurriedly, overcome with a premonition about the approaching customer. "Very becoming. You should have her do it like that all the time."

"Oh, not me," Minnie said, hitching her bottom against a ledge. "I think change is good for a body. That's why you should have Sue Ellen do something about that hair of yours."

A heavier footfall meant the latest customer had stepped down into the post office.

Only with supreme willpower did Rae stop herself from turning around.

"Wouldn't you like a new look?" Minnie said. She nodded to whoever had come in—and her eyes lingered, and lingered. "Oh, it isn't as if your hair isn't pretty enough. But it's . . . *predictable.* That's the word. Why, I remember when you showed up here all those years ago and took a room with Buelah."

"I really ought to be going," Rae said with a sensation that her back was being thoroughly examined.

"You were all arms and legs and a lot of black hair. Pale like you'd never seen the sun in your life."

"If I could have—"

"Of course, Buelah being a teacher, she always did think it was her job to take care of youngsters. She sure took care of you."

"Buelah is a wonderful lady," Rae said, growing so tense her jaw ached. "I've got to be going, Minnie."

"Afternoon," Minnie said, nodding at the newcomer. "Something we can do for you, mister?"

"Maybe."

Rae looked at the floor. He had a still, dark voice. How appropriate.

"What would that be?" Minnie didn't rattle easily.

The man came to stand beside Rae. She knew it was him, the one from outside the school, and at the library, without looking any higher than the soft, many-times-washed jeans he wore over scuffed, but expensive brown ropers. He tapped an equally expensive, camel-colored Stetson against his thigh. The man might be lean, but he wasn't too lean, no sir. Those legs were made for all kinds of things—including a sideways stare from a woman who knew a good pair of male legs when she saw them.

Legs weren't an issue here.

Being followed in broad daylight was an issue.

She should be grateful it *was* daylight.

She should get out of here. Now. "Minnie. I'll take my mail, please."

"Why, Rae Maddy, shame on you," Minnie said, outrage heavy on every word. "Is that any way to greet a stranger? Why, here in Decline we're known for our hospitality. This is a friendly place, mister. I don't know what's come over Rae here. What can I do for you?"

The mail could wait. Rae turned to leave—and came face-to-face with the "stranger." He looked at her. Hard. The cool, gray eyes were naturally narrow, and his nose would be described that way, except for a slight detour high on the bridge where he must have met something awfully hard sometime.

Rae's hair might be black. The stranger's was blacker, and she'd been wrong in her first assessment. It was more than a little past acceptably long.

"Excuse me," Rae said. Standing between stacked crates, he didn't leave any room for simple escape.

"Surely, ma'am," he said. "Don't let me chase you off. I

just wanted to ask if there are any mail boxes available for rent."

"You bet there are," Minnie said, her glee at finding a new customer evident. "You moving in around here, then?"

"Maybe."

A man with a big vocabulary.

"You'll like it," Minnie said. "Interesting people in Decline. Rae here's a writer. Writes other people's stories. From movie stories. If that makes any sense. Make any sense to you, mister?"

He hadn't moved his eyes from Rae's. "Maybe."

"I'm Minnie Loder," Minnie said, oozing warmth. "This is Rae Maddy. She's married to John Maddy—not that most of us would know him if we saw him."

"Minnie—"

"They've got the sweetest little girl. Ginny. Well, she's Rae's. John adopted her. Isn't that right, Rae? Isn't that what you told me?"

A nerve flickered in the stranger's left cheek. "Dallas Calhoun," he said. "Pleased to meet you both."

Rae's skin burned, so did her temper. Later she'd have words with Minnie about this episode.

"Where you moving in, then, Dallas?" Minnie asked.

"Still deciding."

"What line you in?"

"Land." If his mouth ever slipped out of tight gear it could just become irresistible.

"Working it?" Minnie asked. "You a farmer?"

"Buying and selling it," the man responded. "Here, let me hand this lady her mail so she can get about her business."

"Surely," Minnie said and, to Rae's astonishment, put her mail into one of the man's large, outstretched hands. "I was just telling Rae how she ought to change that hair of hers. Hasn't had a change since she came to Decline, and that's got to be—"

"A long time," Rae said. "Thank you. I wish you joy in Decline, Mr.—"

"Dallas. Just call me Dallas."

The man took a nonchalant look at the four envelopes he held, and gave them to her before stepping aside. Tilting his head, he eased his hat back on and tipped the brim in a casual salute.

Rae walked from Loder's. She wanted to run but wouldn't give Mr. Maybe the satisfaction of seeing just how badly he'd unnerved her.

Outside again, she ignored comments from the regulars this time, and didn't stop walking until she climbed into the white Chevy pickup John kept telling her to replace.

She wasn't shaking. Rae was proud of that. Coping with the kinds of things that reduced most people to jelly came naturally. She smiled a little. A lot of time had passed since she'd given Willie and Betty Skeggs more than a passing thought. She gave them one now. The way they had introduced her to hell had one advantage, it made a woman tough to terrorize.

Rae put her mail on the seat beside her and backed the truck out. When she drove away she saw a face at the window in the post office. *"Dallas. Just call me Dallas."*

She might not be shaking, but Mr. Dallas Calhoun had made a profound impression on her, and not the kind of impression that made for deep, dreamless sleep.

Rae wished she could go and get Ginny right now. Buelah Wilks, who taught music at the school Ginny attended in Southville, a town twenty minutes by car from Decline, liked to drive Ginny home. A spinster, Buelah had perfected a crusty countenance. Rae knew that countenance was tissue thin, and nonexistent when it came to Rae or Ginny. To Buelah, Rae was the daughter she'd never had, and Ginny the granddaughter.

Rae could never bring herself to deprive Buelah of her special times with Ginny. When Rae had arrived in Decline, where the trucker who had given her the latest ride dropped her, she'd gone to Buelah's door in desperation, having read the woman was looking for a boarder. She didn't have a penny left from the few dollars she'd taken before leaving Glad Times. All she could do was ask for a place to stay for a while against the promise of sending the rent as soon as she was settled somewhere and had a job. Buelah had taken in two strangers, one a baby, after asking only one question. "Can I trust you?" And she'd accepted Rae's answer with not another word, and later convinced her to stay in Decline.

Buelah's house had been home to Rae and Ginny until John Maddy persuaded Rae that she didn't have to be in love with him to marry him.

The pretty red brick house John had bought for his little family nestled in a fold of land five miles out of the center of Decline.

After a last check in the rearview mirror, and being reassured by the empty highway behind her, Rae turned onto the driveway that wound between rows of live oaks draped with Spanish moss. The house was old, so were the trees. Rae loved the place.

She parked the Chevy at the side of the ranch-style house and rolled down the window. She picked up the envelopes, shuffled the one from a bank in Atlanta and the one from a bank in Savannah to the back, and grinned. Minnie Loder was something else. If there were still "Hello Girls" manning party lines in Decline, Minnie would be pushing and pulling the plugs, and making sure there were no secrets in the town.

The third piece of mail came from a construction firm John dealt with on some projects up north. The fourth envelope, the large, heavy manila one, was addressed to Rae in a vaguely familiar hand.

No return address.

Atlanta postmark.

Rae took a breath and blew it out slowly. Would she ever

stop looking for problems? Even though she didn't *shake*. She smiled again, this time at herself, and tore open the envelope.

Inside was a large sheet of heavy paper folded in from each corner and taped where the points came together to form a package.

Rae took another breath, and held it this time. With a thumbnail, she popped the tape.

Bills, bundles of bills held together with rubber bands, poured into her lap.

Hundred-dollar bills.

Lots of hundred-dollar bills. How many? Dozens? How many dozens?

The sweat on Rae's back had little to do with the heat. She picked up a fistful of bills, and another, and another, and stared at them, uncomprehending. From the very bottom of the envelope slid a pair of keys on a wire ring.

She swiveled in her seat to look up the driveway behind her. No sign of a green Land Rover.

Closing her eyes, she worked for the calm she'd learned to draw around her when the going got too difficult.

Not one bad thing had really happened.

John was late, later getting back than he'd ever been before; but, as they said, bad news traveled fast, and she hadn't heard any.

An expensively dressed, too good looking man had shown up in a few places where she'd also been. Big deal. So what?

And she had a few thousand dollars in used bills lying in her lap . . . and there was a note tucked into the rubber band around one bundle.

Rae pulled out the note, unfolded it, and read:

> *Rae, honey: Keep a chunk of this and put the rest in the safety-deposit box. Not the one we usually use, the other one. In Savannah. I had you sign the card, but you didn't have a key, remember? Now you've got*

*both keys. Take care of them. And don't forget the box
is in the name of Rae Faith.*

At the time she hadn't understood why John did that. She
still didn't. The thundering of her heart sent blood pounding
at her eardrums. She felt sick, and her head ached.

*I never planned for things to turn out this way.
Maybe that's the trouble, I didn't do enough planning.
Don't get scared, my friend. You've been my best
friend, you know. That's what I needed you to be, and
you were. You were always there for me to go home
to, friend. We never had much time, but that time was
worth whatever it took to get. Thank you. Seems too
little to say, but I never was great with words—like
you are.*

*Stay calm. Don't talk to anyone about me. If they
ask, I've been home and left again. Don't say I've made
contact in any other way. And you never did know
where I went when I was away. Tell them that if they
ask.*

John was in trouble. Rae's sweat turned icy. She felt numb,
and helpless. But she had to help John, she had to.

There were only a few more paragraphs to the note:

*You've got your own bank account. Don't use all
this money unless you have to. You won't need it, but
keep it for emergencies. And keep writing those books,
Rae. You're good. You already make a good enough
living to get along if you have to. In the safety-deposit
box you'll find other things you can cash in as you
need more money. You and Ginny will never want for
anything.*

*The house is in your name, and it's paid for. There
are bonds in Ginny's name for when she gets older.*

For school. She's got her mama's brains. Make sure she goes to school, Rae.

Be careful. Remember, whatever happens, whoever comes along asking questions—not that I think anyone will—but if they do, you don't know anything. Get the money into the box and burn the envelope, and this note.

Rae, you have nothing to worry about. And you don't owe anyone any explanations.

Damn, but this hurts. Thank you for being the best thing that ever happened to me. I only wish you and I could have been together before . . . well, before I got involved with people who made it impossible to go back. Kiss Ginny and tell her I love her. Make sure she knows she mustn't talk about me to strangers. Not to anyone. She's smart. She'll understand.

I'm sorry, honey. Learn to forgive me, okay?

Love, John

PS: Rae, honey, I know I told you love wasn't an issue, only trust, but I have loved you in my way, and I've always been so proud of you

Very carefully, Rae laced her fingers together on top of the money.

John wasn't coming back. Ever.

Her hands shook.

Two

The light went out in the third window to the left of the front door. Probably the child's room.

Dallas Calhoun lounged against the branchless trunk of an old slash pine. Once darkness had fallen, he'd parked the Land Rover beside the highway and walked onto the Maddy spread.

He lounged, but every muscle was tensed and ready to move.

The woman had been a surprise. She should have been flashy, obviously sexy—provocative. Tough. Dallas considered. She should not have been slender, attractive in a quiet way—and dignified.

What he had to do would be a whole lot easier if the lady was a painted tramp who advertised what she had for sale with every swish of a hip.

He smiled a little at that, and bent to tear a blade of grass. He stuck the grass between his teeth and continued to mull over his next move.

Hell, appearances deceived all the time. Dallas knew that. She was a tramp. Had to be. A designing tramp who'd used sex to get her hands on what didn't belong to her. Now it was Dallas's job to persuade her to give it back—and move herself and the kid far enough away to make sure he was never likely to lay eyes on them again.

That would cost.

Dallas could afford to pay.

He shrugged away from the pine and walked slowly down the slope where he'd taken up a position from which to watch. Nice place. Expensive. She wouldn't want to go, but he'd make sure she didn't want to stay in the end.

Rae Maddy of the watchful, dark green eyes was about to get a big surprise. She wouldn't like it.

The house was brick, with a veranda that wrapped around as much as he could see of the building, and brick pillars. Fragrant shrubs lined beds on either side of a pathway from the drive to the front door.

Dallas stepped softly, a skill learned from having to leave a place or two late at night—or any other time—in a hurry, and without making a sound.

Oh, yeah. Flashy, provocative women with agendas were something he understood. He'd soon learn his way around one understated, but sultry woman who also had an agenda.

Light shone through etched glass around the front door. More light showed through drawn drapes to the right. Mrs. Maddy hadn't gone to bed.

Dallas chewed down hard on his stalk of grass.

Hell, the thought of that slim body between cool sheets turned him on. Must have been too long since he had a woman. *Hell.* She wasn't his type anyway, but if necessary he was going to have to force himself to pretend she was. He already knew she could be bought, but if money wasn't enough—less money than she'd expected to make over the lifetime of the cozy deal she'd been working—then he'd just have to find some other inducement to get back what was his. Surely Dallas Calhoun could sweet-talk—or sweet move—one little woman into seeing things his way.

There wasn't a doorbell.

He tipped his hat lower over his eyes, and knocked.

Rae dropped her glass on the kitchen floor.

She watched as it seemed to shatter in slow motion. Iced

tea blossomed across the cream tiles, and rose to splatter the fronts of cabinets in the cooking island.

Whoever was at the door knocked again.

No one came at night. Not without calling first. People around here were considerate. They looked after each other, but they didn't presume on friendship in inappropriate ways—like knocking on a woman's door at night when she was alone with her child.

Everyone hereabouts knew Rae was mostly alone. She knew she could call on any of them if she needed help.

She was alone now.

She was always going to be alone.

No.

Another knock.

Rae walked around the broken glass and into the short hallway with its stuccoed walls. She approached the front door slowly. A shadow showed through one of the long panels of etched glass.

She cleared her throat and said, "Who is it?" as firmly as she could.

"Mrs. Loder told me where to find you. She said it'd be okay to come by."

Rae felt all the breath escape her body. It was him. But then, she'd known it would be.

"Who is it?" she repeated, and sucked her top lip between her teeth. Somehow this man was tied up with what was happening to her. He had to be. The timing couldn't be pure coincidence. She must be very cautious, but she also had to find out if there was a way to use him to find John.

"It's Dallas Calhoun, ma'am. We met in the post office."

After he'd followed her around town all day. "I remember, Mr. Calhoun. What can I do for you?"

He didn't answer immediately. "I'd like to talk to you, ma'am."

She pushed a hand inside the collar of her blouse. Her skin flamed, but she felt cold. "Well—" She must weigh every word. "I'm sure you understand this isn't an appropriate time. It's late."

"It's late, and you're alone. Yes, I know."

Rae sat down with a loud thump on a polished oak bench by a wall.

The man laughed. "Hey. You okay in there? I don't want to frighten you, ma'am. I just don't have much option but to come by now. The sooner we talk, the better." The voice was too confident, too cultured. Not the voice of a simple man.

Why couldn't John be here? John was calm and had a way of making things around him seem calm.

John had never spent much time in Decline. Only a day or so every couple of weeks—until now. Their marriage was a convenience, a convenience for both of them, but Rae was fond of her husband.

John wasn't coming home again. How could that be?

Rae rubbed her temples. Buelah would get in her old Cadillac and roar over here in a minute if Rae asked. And what would Buelah do, threaten to throw Mr. Dallas Calhoun out?

At least Ginny slept so soundly she didn't tend to wake up at any noise except Rae insisting she get up in the morning.

This time Calhoun tapped the door steadily, insistently, but softly, and said, "Come on, Mrs. Maddy."

"You must think I'm mad," Rae said, standing up again. "I'm going to let a strange man into my house at night? I don't think so. I'm going to call the sheriff right now."

Ernie Sage had been Decline's sheriff as long as Rae had lived there. He was accustomed to dealing with the occasional drunk at Skeeter's. But it wasn't a common occurrence because Skeeter was almost seven feet tall and dealt with his own problems. Ernie wouldn't cotton to being called out of his comfortable home unless it was for a really good reason.

Calhoun had fallen silent, but his shadow remained.

"I'm making that call right now," Rae said.

"Do you think that's what *John* would want you to do?"

Utter stillness overtook Rae. Feeling went out of her limbs, and she couldn't make a thought stick around long enough to mean anything.

"I'm not here to hurt you," Dallas Calhoun said in his hot-night, dark-places voice. "I want to help you."

What would she say to Ernie Sage?

"You're going to have to talk about you and John eventually. The sooner, the better. The better the chance you won't end up in trouble, ma'am. Big trouble."

Rae sat down again and buried her face in her hands.

"I'm sure we can sort things out and be on our way with no problems."

Be on our way?

"Look, ma'am, I don't want to threaten you, but I do know what you've been doing. Do you want the law to know? Do you think John would want the law brought into this?"

"Who are you?" she whispered.

"Excuse me? I didn't quite hear that."

Rae raised her face. "I said, who are you? And what do you want from me?"

"I want to make things easy on you. I want to help you clear up your troubles and start fresh."

Tightening in her scalp sickened Rae. Could he know . . . surely he didn't know something about Glad Times.

"You already know my name," Dallas Calhoun reminded her.

"But I don't know *who* you are," she told him through her teeth. Anger came slowly to Rae, but it made its presence felt now. "Go away. Leave me alone."

"Or you'll call the sheriff? What will you tell him? If I mention certain things, how will you explain your little arrangement with John Maddy? The money, and everything? If you don't care for yourself, you might want to think about that cute little girl of yours."

He knew about the money. "Wait there. I'll let you in. I've got to deal with the alarm." Rae got up. She hadn't set the alarm yet. A few hurried steps took her into John's little study where she felt on top of a bookcase for the key that opened the lower right drawer in his desk.

John had taken her down by the river, as far from the house as possible, and taught her how to use his Sauer. She took it from the drawer now, checked the clip, and returned to the hall.

She threw open the door and pointed the weapon at Dallas Calhoun's solid chest. "Speak up," she told him. "And speak fast. You've scared me, Mr. Calhoun. If that's what you intended, congratulations. Let's get this over with so we can both get on with our lives."

"Well, ma'am, I've gotta tell you I'm relieved."

"Relieved?"

"You had me almost fooled for a while. I thought maybe I'd found the wrong woman."

"You're going to have to explain that."

He took a step toward her.

Rae braced her arm and assumed a ready stance.

Calhoun held up both hands. His hat put his face in deep shadow, but she saw his smile. The bastard smiled at a woman with a Sauer aimed at his heart. He didn't think she'd pull the trigger.

"Maybe you should call that sheriff," he said. "If you don't mind us having our little discussion in front of an audience, I surely don't. After all, you'll never be able to say I didn't try to save you from landing in jail."

She didn't answer him, but she tightened her grip on the gun.

Calhoun smiled. He was too handsome in a dangerous way—and he knew it. Rae wasn't a gambling woman, but she'd bet money Dallas Calhoun was accustomed to using his considerably physical charm to get his way. He sure wouldn't make much headway using his personality.

"You thought you could bleed the Calhouns, didn't you?" The smile disappeared as if it had never existed. "You thought you and John could make fools of us, and we'd never find out. Well, lady, you thought wrong. The Calhouns have been part of what counts in this state for as long as this state has counted for anything. We don't lie down and let trash walk over us."

Confusion broke Rae's concentration. "I don't know what you're talking about."

"Oh, sure you don't. You don't know how this expensive little house was bought, do you? You don't know what paid for it?"

"I'm a writer. I earn good money. And John—"

"You don't earn enough to buy this kind of property, Mrs. Maddy. And John? Where does John get his money?"

"He's in refrigeration sales." Her voice rose, but she couldn't do anything about it. "He's a fantastic salesman. He travels all over."

The man laughed, tipped back his head and gave a barking laugh that showed off fine, strong teeth.

Arrogant.

Arrogant, and wrong-headed.

"You've got nerve," he said. "I'll give you that. The kind of audacity I don't recall seeing the like of before."

His laughter died; then he took the gun from her before she even registered his hand had moved. Just as swiftly, he spun her around, held her in one arm, and covered her mouth with his free hand.

Rae kicked at his shins with her heels, lost her footing, and squirmed. The entry lights made blinding patterns before her eyes.

Calhoun used the butt of John's gun to grind the breath out of her, and jerked her upright at the same time. "Give it up," he said into her ear. "You can't win anymore. Got that?"

Her brain roared. Nothing she did would make a difference.

Once he'd walked her inside the door and closed it, he steered her straight ahead and into the kitchen, where he closed the door again.

He brought his mouth to her ear. "There's no need for any noise, or fuss. You wouldn't want to frighten the little girl. Neither would I. We can do what has to be done and I'll be on my way. For now. Okay?"

For now? The muscles in her thighs felt like jelly. She nodded.

The instant he relaxed the hand over her mouth, she screamed.

Started to scream.

No more than a squeak made it past her lips before he clamped the sound off.

"Okay, you want it rough, you can have it rough." With that he turned her to face him and backed her to the wall, keeping her mouth covered so hard her teeth hurt. He loomed over her, a much bigger man than John, John who had never raised a hand against her.

Rae willed the tears from her eyes and stared directly into his.

"What made you think you could get away with it forever?" Calhoun put his face close to hers. "If I tell the law what I know, you'll spend the rest of your good years behind bars."

The tears burned. She spoke into his fingers.

"What?" His ice gray eyes narrowed even more. "Are you going to behave?"

She nodded.

He shook her again. "Don't take me for a fool, lady. It's you and me, and one little girl. I wish the child wasn't involved, but that's not my fault. Am I making myself clear?"

Rae nodded again and prayed John would walk through the door. Then she felt the gun digging into her belly and prayed he wouldn't.

"I am bigger, ma'am. And I am stronger. And I have the

gun. That all means you don't have a hope in hell of doing anything but losing around here. Got it?"

Before Rae could nod again, he removed his hand.

She passed her tongue over her dry lips and watched his face.

"Do you need some water?"

She shook her head.

"Okay. Start talking."

Her blouse stuck to her back. She needed to hang on to something; but Calhoun was the only possibility, and that *wasn't* a possibility.

He leaned close enough to brace his thighs against her. "Talk."

It all shattered. All the composure she'd honed and drawn around her like armor. "Willie hurt me," she whispered. Apart from telling an edited version of the story to John, she'd never mentioned that name since she left Glad Times. "Willie hurt Mama. And Ginny. He hated Ginny."

Calhoun blinked slowly. "Who's Willie?"

Bewildered, Rae worked to find enough saliva to swallow.

"I asked you a question," he said.

Willie. Pain gathered behind her eyes, and pictures that moved like frames on a reel of film. Old pictures. She closed her eyes, but the pictures wouldn't go away. After she left Glad Times she'd watched the papers and listened to the news, waiting for some mention of a man and woman found dead in a cabin in Glad Times, Georgia. She never heard a thing.

A couple of years later she made a call to the broiler plant where Mama had worked, only to be told Mrs. Skeggs had left a long time ago. No mention of anyone dying.

But Willie had been dead; Rae was sure of that.

She focused on the man's gray eyes again. He watched her steadily, but she couldn't read a thing from his expression, unless it was patience. He wasn't in a hurry. He believed he'd get what he wanted eventually.

Calhoun hadn't been talking about Willie Skeggs.

"Okay," he said. "Good diversion, but it's bought you all the time you're going to get. You're something, Mrs. Maddy. Amazing. What you've pulled off shouldn't be possible. And you've pulled it off for years."

"I don't know what you mean," she told him honestly.

"Of course you don't." He turned the corners of his mouth down. "I've made some inquiries about you and John. Here in Decline. People around here don't know John too much, do they?"

"He's a quiet man."

"There are those who say they don't recall ever seeing him. Not up close. That's what that nice Mrs. Loder said. And she'd have described him knuckle and knee if she could have."

They understood each other, John and Rae. Privacy was everything to them. "We aren't real fond of company."

Calhoun eased away a little, but only so he could take a good look at her from head to foot, and back again. "Well, I think that was very selfish of John. He deprived the world of something good for any man's eyes."

She grew hot. "He's due home."

"No, he isn't."

Before she could stop herself, Rae caught at the front of his denim shirt and held on.

"Feeling poorly, are you?"

"Could I have that water?"

"Surely." He gathered her wrists into one of his large hands and took her to the sink. There he set the gun on the counter and looked around.

"In there," she told him, indicating a cupboard. "Please let me go. I won't run."

"You wouldn't get anywhere if you tried," he said, and turned on the faucet. He tested the water, then filled a glass.

Faintness frightened her. She had never passed out, and she couldn't do so now of all times.

"I only need one hand to drink," she said.

He raised the glass to her lips and tipped slightly until she was forced to take a sip. "You only need one hand to throw this in my face," he said, tipping again.

The water cooled her aching throat. Her lips were so dry they felt cracked.

Calhoun inclined the glass for her to drink some more. "I don't have anything against you," he said. "I don't know you, and you don't know me. I'm just an inconvenience, but I'm an inconvenience you're going to have to deal with."

"Tell me what this is all about."

"Oh, I think you know. What you don't know . . . well, you're going to find out what you don't know. How would a man manage to live in a little town like Decline for years and have some people still not know what he looks like? Most people?"

Rae stared at the water, and he gave her some more.

"You didn't marry him here, did you?"

"No. We went to Las Vegas."

"Romantic."

She sent him a defensive glare. "Not everyone's life can be neat and tidy. Hearts and flowers. John's a good man. He's good to Ginny and me."

"Touching. You married, set up house, and John came and went without being seen. And he didn't come here too often from what I gather."

Rae swallowed. "It isn't like that."

"Isn't it? How is it, then?"

"I wish you would go away," she whispered, and added, "you're frightening me." Wrong thing to say to a man bent on doing just that, frightening her.

He pressed the glass to her lips and said, "Drink," and sounded angry. "How come people around here don't know John?"

"I told you," she said, and coughed. "He's quiet."

"Not too quiet to take one look at you and know he wanted you. Not too quiet to hook up with you."

"That was—" She didn't owe him explanations. "It's not your business, but I was working at the library. The one you followed me to."

He smiled faintly.

"John came in—"

"To the library?" His short laugh shook Rae. "Like hell. Why? To ask where the nearest church was?"

Rae set her teeth. "He saw me go in there. He followed *me* in there, John's a—"

"Quiet man," Calhoun finished for her. "Yes, I know."

"He came back again and again. He'd wait for me outside in his car. He's gentle and kind. He cares for me—and for Ginny. He loves Ginny."

"You're in shock," Calhoun said suddenly. "Sit down." He pulled out a chair from the kitchen table and pushed her into it.

She was relieved to have some space between them. "Please go away."

"Can't do that. Yet. John cares for you? He loves Ginny?"

Rae understood the distinction. She chose to ignore it. "John and I have things in common."

"I bet."

She hated the inference. "We were both alone in the world," she told him, sickened that she felt forced to defend what she and John had together. "I had Ginny. But she was just a child. John took care of us. Takes care of us."

"Sweet." He glanced around the airy kitchen, and down at the tea-spattered tiles. "Did you do that when I knocked?"

"Yes."

"Are you always so jumpy?"

"Look, I don't have any idea why you're here, or—"

"Don't you?" She got the full force of his attention. "I understand John's late back from . . ." He let the sentence trail away.

"He's often late. He gets tied up with jobs and can't leave until they're finished."

He chuckled, actually chuckled. "Cute line. Mrs. Loder says she thinks she saw John once. How can that be? And I talked to the schoolteacher. Nice lady. She didn't seem to know much about your husband, either."

Rae couldn't think for an instant.

"Private, that's what the teacher said about him. But don't you think it's strange for a man to live in a town for years without anyone coming to know him."

"John isn't like that." She didn't want to talk anymore. "He doesn't need people. He didn't want to need me, but he did. He couldn't stop himself from coming back and finding me. He'd wait till I left the library and wait for a chance to talk to me alone. Then we decided we could help each other. We both needed a place to feel safe. A person to feel safe with. Even if it was just for a little while now and again."

Calhoun pulled out another chair and dropped to sit down. He stretched out his long legs, one on either side of Rae's, and put the gun on the table. He rested his hand loosely on top.

"John will be home anytime now." She couldn't meet the man's eyes.

"So you keep saying. But we both know that's a lie, don't we?"

"No!"

He leaned forward to work his wallet from a back pocket in his jeans. With one hand, he flipped it open, set it on a thigh, and worked a photograph out. He closed the wallet again and tossed it on the table.

Holding the picture between middle and index fingers, the back to Rae, he wiggled it. "Do you like photographs?"

Rae stared at his fingers.

"You're going to love this one." He turned it around. "Good, huh?"

The shot was of a man and woman sitting in white rattan

chairs on a veranda. Each held a glass and smiled for the camera.

The man was John.

Rae moved to get up. Calhoun used his legs like a vice to keep her where she was. She tried to pry herself free. Hopeless.

"I see you know who this is."

"I never saw those people before."

"Lies? Oh, you disappoint me. This is quite recent, you know. Maybe a few months ago."

"It can't be." She met his eyes again. What did she see there? Pity? Damn him. "So what if it is. John gets around a lot."

"You said it, ma'am. This was taken on the veranda at my home. Looks like a happy, relaxed man, doesn't he?"

She made herself look again at John Maddy, her husband, the quiet, refined man she'd married four years earlier. Blond, blue-eyed, tanned, handsome, he smiled out at her. "Where is your home?"

"Finally accepting that I know the truth? We're making headway. Now, if you'll agree to cooperate with me, help me set straight the havoc you and John managed to pull off in my family's affairs, I think we can come to a mutually acceptable solution."

His legs were an insistent pressure against hers. Rae was acutely aware of her own legs being bare beneath the old shorts she'd put on when she got home. Calhoun followed her gaze, and his ghostly little smile appeared again. "Nice," he said. "He's got good taste."

Rae's cheeks burned.

Calhoun leaned forward and ran the photograph down her thigh.

She would not let him see any reaction at all.

He stroked her skin again. "Very nice. How old *are* you?"

"Where do you live?" she asked.

"In a town called Glory." With the next sweep he made sure his fingertips met her skin. "Heard of it?"

Her skin tingled. She hated him. "No, I can't say I have. Where is it?"

"Far enough evidently. About a hundred and fifty miles from here. North. My family settled there—Never mind that. It wouldn't interest you. Not that John hasn't already told you all about Glory, and Sweet Bay. I expect the two of you talked about what it might be worth. How much you could hope to get out of it."

"Sweet Bay?"

"Don't tell me John never mentioned the house, either."

Hell might be like this. Confusion and fear and a stranger who didn't believe a word you said. "No," she said simply. "He never did."

"How old are you?"

"None of your damn business."

"Twenty-seven."

"How—" Rae bowed her head. "How do you know?"

"Buelah—the schoolteacher—told me."

"Buelah wouldn't talk to you about me."

"She'd talk to your long-lost brother. I told her I'd been looking for you for years."

Rae pushed her hair away from her face. She had to get rid of Calhoun and think about what to do next.

He watched her eyes, then, slowly, every other part of her before saying, "Nice age in a woman, twenty-seven. Old enough to know how to do things the way they're meant to be done."

"What things?"

Abruptly he leaned forward and used the corner of the photograph to outline her bottom lip.

Rae jerked her face away.

"Come on, now, Rae. You know what things. *Things.* I expect to come to an agreement. We'll work out something agreeable to both of us. Very agreeable."

He was referring to something sexual, but she couldn't figure why. "You want to have sex with me?" she blurted out. "Why? What does that have to do with John having a drink on your veranda?"

"Damn, but you're direct. It may have everything to do with it. Maybe sex is part of the bargain for you. I'm sure John kept you happy. He certainly had plenty of practice. But—"

"Don't. Don't you dare say things like that about John."

Calhoun drew the corner of the photo along her jaw.

Rae slapped it away.

Calhoun made a line from her chin, down her neck, to the vee where her blouse came together between her breasts.

She slapped him away again.

"At first I couldn't figure what he saw in you. Now I can. You're very—*southern*. Hah. Never told a woman that before. Never thought of it before. You're sultry. I'd like to swim with you. Naked."

She began to panic again.

"If sex is something you want as part of the bargain, just say the word, ma'am. I think I can humbly say that I'll at least manage to equal good old John's efforts."

"You are disgusting."

"I know. And you love it."

Without warning, he clasped her arms to her sides and kissed her. A purely sexual kiss. Hard, invasive. He used his lips and tongue in a way that left no doubt about the message he was sending. And while his tongue told her what he'd like to put where, he contrived to stretch his big hands wide enough to play his thumbs over her nipples.

And she responded.

She opened her mouth wider, and closed her eyes. She leaned into him.

"No!" The instant he paused for air, she flung his hands away and crossed her arms. "Don't you touch me. Don't you ever touch me. Say whatever you've got to say and get out."

"Because you just gave yourself away?" He wasn't smiling. His eyes were so dark they were more black than gray. The skin over his high cheekbones shone paler in his lean, tanned face. "Okay, I think we're getting somewhere. But we're going to have to set down the ground rules, little lady."

"Don't you call me that. I hate that condescending—"

"Ground rules," he repeated. "You give me what I want. And I'll give you what you want. All the security and comfort you want. All the sex you need."

She slapped his face, and flinched, waiting for him to strike back.

"I like spirited women," he said. "But don't try that move too often.

"I think I've got a better idea than the first one I had. You look after me. I look after you. You can stay right here in your cozy nest, and I'll come to visit from time to time. Often, if it suits both of us."

"I don't believe this. Why—"

"Be quiet. I've got a lot to do yet. Before we get our little arrangement going, you'll have to give me what I need, of course. You know what I mean."

She could only stare at him. He was a mad man.

"I'll want to know where everything is. And I'll want your word that our agreement is strictly private. Strictly between the two of us. And you'll never try to contact me."

"You don't have a thing to worry about," she told him. "And I don't have a thing that you could want. And you don't get to say where I can or can't live, or what I can and can't do. And as for wanting your . . . *company,* you'd better be long gone before John gets back or he'll make you wish you'd never put a hand on me."

"He won't do that."

"He most certainly will."

Calhoun picked up the wallet and flipped it open again. Rae looked at the gun.

He settled his hand on it once more, and smiled at her.

"Somehow I don't think you're a killer, but I don't believe I want to find out." Leaning aside, he tucked the weapon into the low-slung waist of his jeans. "Now, take a look at this." He gave her a folded piece of news print.

She opened a clipping from the *Glory Speaker* and read the headline:

Plane Crash Kills Warren Niel: Early this morning, in a fiery explosion the authorities are referring to as "a tragic accident." Glory society figure, Warren Niel, was killed. Mr. Niel's Stinson Biplane, apparently on a flight back to Glory from the Macon area, crashed and burned. Wreckage was said to be scattered over a wide area of wilderness. Expert sources confirm that the biplane's fuel, situated in wing tanks, would have exploded on impact. Authorities report that there is no chance of Mr. Niel's having survived the blast. He did make radio contact with Glory Field shortly before the accident, but at this point no details of that conversation have been released.

Rae took in a breath. "Horrible. You must have known him."

"Very well. This happened last week."

"I'm sorry."

"You shouldn't be."

She didn't know what else to say.

"I wouldn't be if he hadn't been my brother-in-law." He showed her the photograph again. "That's my sister, Fancy."

Rae looked at the couple in the picture, and for the second time in one night, she felt faint. "How sad for her." It couldn't be. What this man was going to suggest couldn't be true.

"Sad for you, too. End of a great setup for you."

She let the news clipping fall through her fingers.

Calhoun dipped into a breast pocket in his denim shirt

and slipped out an envelope. From this he took another photograph. "I found this in a box under a bed," he said. "An acquaintance of mine owned the bed—and the box. Look familiar?"

Rae glanced at a shot of herself and Ginny—one she'd given John—and couldn't smother the grinding sob that broke from her throat. "Stop it!" This man wanted her to lose control. Well, he had what he wanted. "What's happened? Where's John?"

Calhoun smoothed open a second news clipping that had been in the envelope with the snapshot. It was from the same paper as the first, and on the same topic. This time there was a photograph of Warren Niel, husband of Fancy Calhoun Niel.

"Oh, no," Rae murmured.

"Oh, yes. Nowhere else to hide, Rae Maddy, or whatever your name is. Of course, I won't hold it against you in our negotiations. But if you and Niel went through a wedding ceremony, you married a bigamist."

She couldn't feel anything anymore. Calhoun pushed the piece from the paper at Rae, but she dropped it, and whispered, "No. It's a mistake."

"No, ma'am," he said, patting her hand on top of her thigh. "No mistake. But look on the bright side. That was the bad news."

Nothing he said made sense. "Bad news?"

He took her hand in both of his and chafed. "Sure. Of course, you could say the bad news doesn't matter. But on the flip side, there's good news. If you hadn't married a bigamist, you'd be a widow."

Three

Fancy Calhoun Niel rang the silver bell her daddy had given her for her sixteenth birthday. "My little princess is gonna have whatever she wants, whenever she wants it," Daddy had said, and he'd told her to ring the bell and ask for what she wanted the most on her birthday.

She'd kissed him first—the way he liked, with her sitting on his knee and hugging him. Then she'd lowered her lashes—the way he liked—rung the bell, and said, "You know what I want before I do, Daddy."

And he did.

A powder-blue convertible Cadillac, a matching satin bow covering the steering wheel, waited in the driveway in front of Sweet Bay.

That had been a few years ago. Not too many, but a few. Stretched out in a white cane chaise on the veranda, Fancy looked at that driveway now. Daddy had died of a heart attack last Thanksgiving Day, and no gleaming new Cadillac stood there to surprise his little princess today.

And no scuttling feet rushed to answer the summons of the princess's bell. That was going to change. Everything around here was going to change. "Where's that skinny-assed Tully?" Fancy asked her mother. Ava Calhoun sat in a cane chair with her ankles crossed and tucked to one side. "Really, Ava, she should have been sent packing years ago. She's deaf. She's past it."

Fretful in the late afternoon heat, Ava flapped a painted

ivory fan before her perfectly made-up and unlined face. "Fancy Lee," she said, flapping even harder, moving the smooth blond hair that curved to frame her rounded features. "Oh, Fancy Lee, you do provoke me. You are not the lady you were brought up to be. Why, your mouth ought to be scrubbed."

"Sure," Fancy said. She shook the bell wildly. "What does it take to get fresh drinks around here these days?"

"Where's Dallas?" Ava asked. "I don't know what things are coming to. All this commotion over Warren getting blown up like that. So much talk and fuss. So upsetting. Where's Dallas? He didn't say a word to his mother. Just left that silly message with Tully. Can you credit that? My own son leaves town when he knows how much I need and rely on him, and I have to hear about it from a servant."

Damn Dallas anyway, Fancy thought. Where was that brother of hers? She shifted in the chaise and brushed a stray rose petal from the snug skirt of her white linen dress. Tyson LaRose would feel the whipping edge of her tongue for this, too. He should have shown up hours ago. After all, he was her lawyer, and a lot of other things. Mostly he was supposed to make sure she didn't waste energy agitating, energy better used in more diverting ways.

She needed to see Tyson and find out if he knew why Dallas had taken off when he was supposed to be dealing with Warren's business—and Fancy's. Of course Tyson knew. He made it his business to know everything about the Calhouns, because their fortunes were his fortunes. He sank or swam with Fancy, who was finally about to get the respect she deserved from her family. She was going to be a princess again; *the* princess. Cozy, if you liked knowing you could bring a man running whenever you felt like it. Where Tyson was concerned, Fancy liked knowing just that. For now.

All of Glory would pay attention at last.

Smiling at the thought, Fancy rested her head against a pink-and-white-striped cushion. Ava's friends who ignored

Fancy because they were jealous of her would start simpering
and looking for ways to entice her into their circle. But, best
of all, Joella LaRose would find out who was really the win-
ner in the biggest game in town—the game of wealth and
power. Tyson's fatuous wife might think the competition had
ended during their senior year of high school. That was when
Joella got voted Miss Glory to Fancy's first runner-up. Joella
was wrong. The competition wasn't over. For Fancy the
stakes had grown bigger from year to year.

"Fancy Lee?"

She gathered her heavy red hair and pulled it on top of
her head. "What is it, Ava? Ring for Tully, will you? I swear
she can tell if it's me who wants something, and if it is, why,
she doesn't come. Contrary, that's what she is."

"You do fuss," her mother said.

"Don't I deserve a little consideration? My husband killed
in a horrible accident. Left alone in the world. I'm mourning
my loss, Ava."

Ava Calhoun took the bell from Fancy's lap and swung it
as if the effort cost her dearly.

Tyson had made Fancy swear she'd never tell Joella about
them. Fancy smiled again, and wiggled a little in her seat.
As soon as she could persuade Ava she was tired and ought
to take a nap, Fancy would brighten up Tyson's day for him.

"All over the papers," Ava remarked, sounding pettish.
"Warren never should have been allowed to play around with
that expensive stunt plane, or whatever it was. Who ever
heard of a grown man flying such a thing? He was probably
drunk. I'm so embarrassed for you, Fancy Lee. Such noto-
riety. All those comments about you and Warren not getting
along. What your poor, dear daddy would have said, I don't
know."

The same comments had been made a dozen, dozen times
in the two weeks since the event. Answering was a waste of
words.

When Fancy came into what she was owed, she'd pay

Joella LaRose a little visit and tell her all about the good
times Tyson and Fancy had. She'd make sure Joella understood there wasn't a thing she could do about it if she wanted
to hold her head up in this town.

Joella still pranced and stuck out her tits like a common
street walker. When they were in school, Joella had made a
lot of how she was bigger than Fancy.

"Poor, poor Biff," Ava murmured. "He would have suffered so to know your husband came to such a *tawdry* end."

"I don't see how being splattered all over some horrible
mountain in a horrible accident can be a tawdry end, Ava,"
Fancy said, glancing down at her very satisfying cleavage.
With a teensy bit of help from a surgeon in Atlanta, Fancy
had made sure of the blue ribbon in that contest, too. "Daddy
hated Warren. So did you—when you weren't enjoying him."

"Fancy Lee!"

"Now, hush. I didn't mean that the way it sounded." Oh,
yes, she most certainly did. "I was only referring to the sinful
way Warren used to flatter you when he wanted to turn you
against me." She was referring to the fact that she was certain
her supposedly ice-blooded mother had slept with her daughter's husband.

Scuffing of wide, black tennis shoes, and a whistled ren-
dition of "Rock of Ages," announced the arrival of Tully,
who had worked for the Calhouns since before Fancy was
born.

Thin, tall, and dressed in shiny black, Tully didn't halt the
serenade as she set down a fresh gin over ice with a twist
for Fancy and a glass of champagne for Ava.

Ava picked up the champagne and raised it to the light.
"Are you sure this is—"

"D.P.? Yes, ma'am, Mrs. Calhoun." Tully shuffled away,
her sparse white hair glinting in the low, afternoon sun.

"Past it," Fancy told her mother. "I told you that woman's
past it. You look tired, Ava."

"Something's going on," Ava said. She sipped her champagne, then rolled the cold glass against her brow. "I know we haven't heard the last of all that nasty business. Dallas is off dealing with something about it right now. Why else would he go away without telling me?"

"Dallas goes away all the time," Fancy pointed out, more mildly than she felt. "That darling boy of yours goes away and screws women all over the county."

"Fancy Lee."

"Well, he does. You've probably got an army of bastard grandchildren out there."

"Fancy Lee." Ava guzzled the entire contents of her glass and set it on a table. She closed her eyes, wafted her fan, and took short, loud breaths. "You will be the death of me. You'd like that, wouldn't you?"

"Don't be ridiculous." That would be just dandy, Fancy thought. One woman was all it took to run Sweet Bay, and she intended to become that woman. Dallas would probably never marry. If he did, he'd never allow another woman to take her place in her own home.

"Well, it isn't going to happen," Ava said, so sharply that Fancy jumped. Ava turned in her seat to look her daughter straight in the eye. "Don't think I'm getting ready to move over for you. I may be your mother, and may think I'm past carin' about such things, but I'm still a young woman. A very desirable young woman, I might add. There's a lot of life in me yet."

"And I'm glad of it," Fancy said. Her stomach tilted. The direct attack wasn't Ava's usual style.

"This is my house, Fancy Lee. Don't you forget that."

Fancy wondered what could have prompted this outburst. "I am glad it's yours, Ava. Daddy wanted you to live the life you were born to, and this is it. He was dedicated to making sure you enjoyed the fruits of what you brought to your marriage." Fancy had always been certain Daddy would have left Sweet Bay to her if he hadn't been afraid Ava and Dallas would find ways to punish her for it.

The sharp flash didn't fade from Ava's bright blue eyes. Fancy smiled and studied the lilac silk jumpsuit that hugged every one of her mother's lush curves. Her father had married a rich girl twenty years his junior. Ava had only been eighteen when Dallas was born; nineteen when Fancy arrived. "You were everything Daddy wanted." When Daddy wasn't finding something he wanted somewhere else. "I used to creep into the dressing room from the other side and sit on the floor. You didn't know that, did you?"

Ava rested the fan over her breasts. "I can't think what you're talking about."

"When you and Daddy were in bed," Fancy said, recalling the excitement those forbidden expeditions had brought, while she relished shocking Ava. "On so many of those afternoons when you said you needed a nap. He would follow after a few minutes. Discreet. And I followed a few minutes after that. It was best when the dressing room door wasn't closed on your side."

A rosy glow bloomed on Ava's creamy pale face and neck. "How could you, Fancy?" she murmured.

"A girl ought to get the best education she can. The most useful. You taught me how to please a man the way he dreams of being pleased. And I haven't forgotten a thing you taught me."

This time it was Ava who rang the bell with vigor.

"You shouldn't feel awkward," Fancy said, offering her own gin to her mother. "If I'm asked, I'll say I learned everything I know from my mother."

"Fancy Lee, I forbid you to say another word on this subject," Ava said.

It was working. Fancy hadn't planned this line of approach, but it worked beautifully. She'd have to remember to use it again when she wanted her way.

"I've got a few things to say to you," Ava announced. "And I want your full attention because I'm going to need your help convincing Dallas we have to do something about it. People around here aren't as respectful as they used to be, and it won't do."

"Ava—"

"You hush," her mother said, closing her fan with a click and pointing it at Fancy. "Do you know Jean Nunn actually asked if we were having money trouble? The idea."

Fancy knew. The only surprise was that it had taken so long for one of her mother's cronies to take pleasure in mentioning the question that was being aired behind every closed door in the town.

"That woman suggested there were rumors that we've been losing money for years and covering it up. I tried to talk to Dallas about it, but he wouldn't listen. Laughed at me just like he always does."

"I know," Fancy said quietly. "And I don't like it any more than you do."

Ava leaned toward Fancy. "Do you think that's where Dallas is now? Dealing with something he doesn't want us to worry about? Something about money? You know how he likes to protect us from unpleasant little details."

"I think Dallas is taking a break from business."

"With Warren hardly cold in his grave? And exactly when there are people in this town who are spreading ugly rumors about us? When they're saying Calhoun has lost enough money to make it prudent to think twice before doing business with us?"

"They're saying that?" Fancy hadn't guessed talk had gone that far.

Ava looked over her shoulder and through the row of French doors that opened onto the veranda. From inside came the muted click of wicker-bladed fans suspended from high, pale yellow ceilings in the living room.

"There's no one to hear us," Fancy said, following the direction of her mother's glance.

"You've got to be discreet."

"Oh, I will be." If it suited her.

"I even heard some whispers about how an investigation might be a good idea. Something along the lines of suspicions that funds—clients' funds—have been diverted. Why, Fancy, nothing like that could be true, could it?"

"Of course not." Tyson had found out about Warren's excesses, about how he'd invested in several wildly speculative land deals that failed. "Don't you give any of that another thought. It isn't true."

"No," Ava said, shaking her head. "No, I knew it couldn't be. I do think Dallas must be attending to something important to all of us, though. When he gets back, we're going to have to insist he confides in us. All this not knowing is so exhausting."

"What you don't know isn't exhausting to Dallas," Fancy said, speculating on Dallas's sexual adventures. Then her thoughts returned to more pressing matters. Her brother must be stopped from poking too deeply into Warren's affairs. Honesty was Dallas's weakness. If he discovered the land fiascoes—and learned the money lost had been acquired by inflating renovation bills to residential property buyers—he could decide to confess all and insist on making restitution.

Thanks to dear departed Warren, Fancy would come into a fortune very soon. Damned if Dallas was going to insist that one cent of all that insurance money—or everything else Warren must have stashed away in his private account—belonged to anyone but Fancy.

Warren had told her he'd taken care of them in a big way and she wasn't to worry. Keeping the accounts in his name was safer, he'd insisted. That way he could move faster to maximize their potential. He'd refused to tell her exactly what they had. She'd find out when and if she needed to, that's what he'd assured her. Warren was no fool. He was the kind of man who took care of details. By the time his affairs were dealt with, she'd get what was hers.

"Darling," Ava said, allowing her eyes to fill with easy

tears. "You do think Dallas will make sure everything's all right for us, don't you?"

"You're fixating, Ava. Asking the same questions over, and over. I think you're overwrought. I think you should take a nice, long nap."

"You're avoiding the issue," Ava said, her voice trembling. "If I went to bed, I wouldn't close my eyes for an instant. I want Dallas. I want to know exactly what he's doing."

Fancy was growing bored—and she felt sexy. "You don't really want to know exactly what he's doing," she said. "I'm worried about you. You look peaked, and it doesn't suit you. Sleep is what you need."

She needed to find Tyson. He'd promised to come by around two. Fancy had looked forward to that, looked forward to showing him some new things she'd bought to wear just for him. He'd broken his promise. She'd have to make sure he made that up to her—quickly.

"Dallas—"

"Will you stop talking about Dallas?" Fancy said sharply. "I told you, you don't want to know exactly what he's doing. But you will insist on pushing."

Ava moved to the front of her chair. "So he *is* up to something. And you know what it is. You're keeping it from me."

Fancy sighed loudly. "Don't say I didn't try to save you. He's with a woman."

"I don't want to hear about—"

"He's with a woman, and he's screwing her brains out. I'm not sure of her name, but she's married. So are the other two he's been with in the past two days."

"Fancy, you're disgusting."

"Just truthful. I wasn't the only one who spent afternoons in your dressing room when you were with Daddy. Dallas and I inherited our appetites for some things. And I don't know if Dallas is lying, but he tells everyone how he used to go along with Daddy and wait in the car while he visited his friends. Only Dallas didn't always wait in the car. Sometimes he found ways to watch what Daddy did." She patted her mother's hand. "He told me none of Daddy's whores satisfied him the way you did."

Standing up so quickly she knocked the table and tipped over her glass, Ava walked past Fancy without another glance. "I believe I'm getting a headache," she said. "I'm going to take a little nap. Tell Tully not to call me for dinner."

"I will," Fancy said, grinning into her gin.

Free at last. Time to hunt down Tyson.

Joella stood behind Tyson in the steamed-up bathroom and rubbed his damp back. "I love taking showers with you, baby." She cupped his hard butt. "You feel so good."

He grunted, and she felt how he'd already moved away from her in that busy brain of his.

"You're quiet," she told him. "You weren't so quiet a few minutes ago."

"You know I've got things on my mind," he said, toweling his thick, blond hair in front of the hazy mirror over white marble sinks.

"Doesn't make a girl feel great when she's told she's served her purpose and now she's a nuisance."

He dried beneath his arms. "Let it be, Joella."

"Okay, okay. But why don't you tell me about it, darlin'? You're all tight. I can feel how tight you are." And if she felt him in another place, she'd find that was already tight again, too. One thing she could count on with her husband was that no matter if his mouth said otherwise, he was always ready to ride.

Joella appreciated a man of action.

She kissed his naked shoulder. "Are you ignoring me?"

"I've got an appointment. I'm late. I was late hours ago."

"You complaining?" She reached between his legs and found what she expected. "Oh, baby, maybe I should take care of this before you do yourself an injury."

"Not now," he said sharply. "I told you I've got an appointment."

He had an appointment with that bitch Fancy Lee.

"Honey"—she let the word hang for just long enough—"honey, don't leave me tonight, huh?" She wrapped her arms around him, nuzzled her lips on his spine, and made sure he felt how stiff her nipples were.

"I won't be long."

Just long enough to screw that bitch every which way from Sunday. "When I'm alone I think about Warren." That was no lie. "I don't want to be alone."

Tyson turned to face her. "I'm sorry your brother died. You know that."

"Yeah." She swallowed and made a line with her forefinger from Tyson's neck, down his very nice chest, over his very nice belly, to the dense hair at the base of his more than nice cock. "Yeah, I know you're sorry. Take me to bed, baby." She surrounded him and stood on tiptoe to guide the tip of his penis between her thighs.

Muscles worked in his tanned face. His lips parted and he gritted his teeth. "Let's make it fast," he said, tweaking her nipples, then bending to nibble at one of them.

Joella didn't want to make it fast. She wanted it slow, and hot, and dark, and again, and again, in a few ways Fancy Lee Niel never even guessed at.

Sometimes you had to drag a man in too deep for him to want to get out—slowly drag him in.

She dropped to her knees and drew him into her mouth. The result was predictable, and instant. The breath went noisily out of his lungs, and he made a small, keening sound. Next he could turn rough. That was a side of Tyson LaRose only a woman who had slept with him ever got to know.

He caught at her hair and helped him work him.

And Joella allowed him to do it just long enough to feel him come close to the edge. Then she let him slip from her mouth and rested her face against the slick, wet skin. She supported him, and massaged.

"Finish," he panted. "C'mon, Joella, finish it."

"Oh, I will. I'm just priming the pump. And, baby, what a pump you do have."

He pulled her head back and looked down into her face with glittering brown eyes. "I don't have time for games now."

Anger swelled, turned her hot. Damned if she was going to be nothing more than a convenience. She could have any man in town. Tyson was going to come to heel. Right now he was under Fancy Lee's thumb because he wanted a piece of the Calhoun pie—a big piece. Joella wanted to share that pie, too. She'd earned it. But she'd get what she had coming from that quarter without playing the opening act to Fancy Lee Niel's star performance—unless it helped move things along faster.

"Why don't you take what you want, baby? C'mon, take it." She brought her lips together and dropped her hands to her sides.

"I—" He clicked his jaw in a way she'd come to recognize. Appointment or no appointment, he still needed what she could give him. And he still looked at her naked and almost came without doing another thing.

"Yes?" she said softly.

Silently, he swept her up into his arms. He held her high enough to play his tongue over her breasts while he pushed a thumb between her legs and far enough inside her to make her hips jerk.

Joella let her head hang back. "Tyson, you are the best."

"How would you know?" he mumbled. He laughed. "Scratch that question."

She smacked the top of his head and parted her knees to make his task easier. "Let's go to bed, you bad boy."

"Let me show you how bad I can be," he told her.

When she looked at his flushed face she throbbed with

excitement. "I already know," she murmured, deliberately coy.

"Sure **you** do. I think I want to go for a record." With that he swung her to stand on the counter between the sinks.

"Let me down!"

"Uh uh."

Tyson had a very long tongue. A very strong tongue. There were more than a few little pricks out there who would pay big bucks for the transplant of Tyson LaRose's tongue. He used it now, held her thighs apart and darted hard strokes over that lovely zone they both appreciated so much.

Joella's knees threatened to give out. "Honey." She moaned. "I'm gonna break something up here."

"Hang on for the ride, baby," he said when he came up for air.

She climaxed, and started to fall.

Tyson clamped his big hands around her ribs, under her breasts, and held her right where she was while the throbbing slowly faded.

"Now I want you." She panted, and reached for his shoulders.

"Not so fast. I'm going for a record, remember. When I'm done I figure you'll be unconscious. That should keep you quiet long enough for me to get a little business done."

"Damn you!" She struggled, but couldn't break free. "Let me go."

"When I'm ready." He buried his face in her crotch again, and the darting pressure worked the same magic.

The bastard was going to carry out his threat. Damn his eyes, she'd get him for this.

He knew her too well. Most women took longer with each climax. Joella came faster and faster the more she got. In seconds she was bucking and urging herself against his mouth.

"Stop it this minute," she said when she could. "I'm not joking, Tyson. You stop it this minute."

He laughed and used her breasts as handles to keep her in place this time. Heat and pleasure washed through her. "If you think you can get by this way, you're mistaken, sir," she told him, growing too weak to even want to stand. "I want to go to bed. Now. We've got things to talk about."

Laughing, Tyson tumbled her to sit on the edge of the counter. He kissed her—hard—and brought her to ecstasy with his fingers this time.

Joella was getting tired, and sore. "Stop it," she told him as he started rubbing her again. "I mean it, Tyson. Stop it, now. I'm not having fun anymore."

His response was to pull her closer and tease her with his distended penis. But when she tried to get him inside her, he drew back.

She'd already waited too long for him to take her into his confidence about the whole Calhoun situation. The truth angered her; but the truth was that he didn't think she knew what he was up to, and he never intended to tell her.

"You gonna do this with Fancy Lee when you get there?"

Tyson stood still. At first his expression was smooth, empty. Then he bared his teeth in a way Joella recognized too well. He gripped her arms so tightly she cried out.

"You are a fool, Joella. Don't say stupid things. Saying them to me is bad enough, but if you open your damn mouth that way anywhere else, you could ruin everything. Y'hear me?"

"Don't tell me what I should or shouldn't say," she told him. "Did you think I didn't know what was going on between the two of you? All she's ever wanted was to try to take away what's mine. Always the same. Even when we were kids."

"Shut up."

He didn't scare her. The thought exhilarated Joella. "What are you going to do if I won't? Slap me around? You've thought about it times enough before. And you know what'll happen if you do, don't you?"

Their eyes met, and his hold on her arms slackened. His chest rose and fell with the power of his emotion.

"Thank you," she said, chafing her stinging skin. "If you didn't push me, I'd never make threats like that. You know I'd never go to your daddy, not—"

"Shut your goddamn mouth," he told her. "I'm leaving."

"Not until I've said what I need to."

He turned away from her, and turned back, pointing his right forefinger at her. "I'm not afraid of that old buzzard."

"Sure you're not.

"I'm not," he shouted. Tyson only shouted when he was close to losing control completely. "I could take him any time."

Joella lowered her eyes and nodded. What Tyson wouldn't say was that he was afraid of Carter LaRose, had been afraid of him all his life. Joella knew all about the complicated web strung between Tyson and his mother and father. That web had the power to bring Tyson to his knees, but she wouldn't use it unless he ever threatened to leave her.

"We've got to talk," she said calmly.

He poked the air in the region of her face one more time, but she saw the fight go out of him. He let his hand fall to his side.

Joella hopped to the floor. She opened the bathroom door and went into the bedroom with its lush deep greens and soft beiges. Long, sheer drapes billowed in the cool evening breeze.

"Come here," she said, stretching out on the bed and folding her hands behind her head. "You and I are partners. We always have been. You just forgot for a while, but I'm going to forgive you, baby. Joella always forgives her baby when he has his little slips."

Still naked, and as comfortable as he'd always been in his solid body, he came to stand beside her. "I don't like being told what to do," he said.

"I know. You had a lifetime of that before we hooked up together, didn't you, baby?"

"Say your piece. I'm going out."

She would deal with her anger later, when she was alone. "Sure you are. I want you to. And I want you to be thinking about a few things while you're with Fancy Lee."

He tilted his face up to the ceiling and closed his eyes. "I am going to Sweet Bay. I told you that. I'm Fancy's lawyer, and she's got things that need tending to."

"Warren's will? Oh, she surely does need to deal with that. Just the two of you—in the evening."

"Not the will, Joella. Other things. It's complicated.

She sat up and braced her arms beside her. The flicker of his eyes to her breasts still pleased her. He knew he had what every man in town dreamed of having. "Quit treating me like an idiot," she told him. "You're going to screw Fancy."

"Damn—"

"No. *No.* Damn you. Damn you both, but you've got my blessing."

Tyson stared at her.

She smiled. "Shocked you? Never sell me short, lover boy. I'm going to lay things out for you, so listen carefully. I didn't intend to do it this soon, but it's probably just as well. The sooner we deal with what has to be done, the better."

He gave her his full attention.

"My brother's death was the answer to your prayers."

"No, I—"

"Yes. You know it. I know it. With Warren gone you can see your way to moving in on Fancy. You're going to find a way to get a piece of Calhoun for yourself."

He frowned and worked his jaw before saying, "How in hell would I do that?"

"You testing me, Tyson LaRose? You think I'm bluffing, that I don't know what you're up to?"

"I don't know where you're heading with this."

"Listen up. Listen good, and you will. It's time to show your daddy you're twice the man he ever was, right?"

The instant wash of red over his face gave Joella her answer, not that she needed it.

"Your mama was second best to Ava, wasn't she? If your daddy could have got his hands on Ava's money, he wouldn't have spent his life trying to make a fourth rate newspaper pay. But Ava married Biff Calhoun and took her money with her. And your daddy ended up with your mama because what she had was better than nothing. Your mama may have up and left your daddy, but she didn't go to Chicago without giving me all the ammunition I'm ever going to need."

The red in Tyson's face turned darker. Veins stood out at his temples. "You don't know what you're talking about."

"Oh, but I surely do."

He took a threatening step toward her, but checked himself. "Tell me exactly what Mama told you."

"Oh, I couldn't tell you that, now could I? Why, that'd be breaking a confidence, and a lady doesn't break a confidence."

He managed an unconvincing shrug. "Doesn't mean a damn now, anyway."

"Doesn't it? I think it does. I *know* it does. All I'm doing is making you face up to what you're doing. And I'm making you understand that I know what you're doing. You and I are partners. You're going to get what you want from Fancy, and we're going to share, just like we always have."

"You're threatening me," he said, softly enough to make her heart beat faster. "You think you can control me."

"I can."

Tyson shook his head slowly. His boyishly handsome face took on a sinister cast. "Get in my way and I'll make you regret it."

"Keep me very safe, or I'll make you regret it."

His nostrils flared. "Aren't you afraid you could go too far with me?"

It was Joella's turn to shake her head. "Go to Fancy. Tell her you're going to leave me for her."

"For God's sake!"

She smirked. The shock in his eyes thrilled her. "Tell her you're going to make me look a fool in front of the whole town. No speedy divorce because that would look suspicious, like the two of you had been planning to get together. So you'll take your time."

He was so still she knew a shiver of fear.

There could be no stopping now. "Warren was smart. He made sure he looked after his own interests. That meant that if Fancy had tried to divorce him, she'd have said goodbye to too much of that lovely money she worships."

"I don't think I understand you."

She swung her shoulders back and forth and wiggled her toes. "I'm just thinking out loud, really. Seems to me that if Fancy got tired of Warren and wanted you instead, it might have been real convenient for Warren to have an accident. That way everything they had would be hers."

"His plane crashed. You're out of your mind."

"Am I?" She looked at him. "Maybe you're right. But if a little bird was to give your friend the sheriff an idea along certain lines, he could make your life real difficult, Tyson."

"You wouldn't do a thing like that."

"I don't plan to. After all, I know I don't have to worry about staying healthy. Two accidents would raise too many eyebrows—even in this one-horse town."

Tyson bent over and brought his face close to hers. "Are you really suggesting I managed to get Warren's plane to crash? What a crazy idea."

She widened her eyes. "What would make you think up a thing like that, darlin'? All I'm telling you is that when I said, 'till death do us part,' I meant it. And it wasn't my death I had in mind."

Four

Dallas didn't feel "brotherly" toward Rae Maddy.

She must have heard him coming down the driveway to her house. The door was open, and she stood on the veranda with her back to him, gesturing to someone inside.

No, he didn't feel at all brotherly.

He wondered if she'd slept as little as he had. Oh, he'd been out once he was out, but that had taken some hours. Staring at passing truck lights through sagging slats at the window in a musty motel room, he'd had plenty to keep him conscious.

Ms. Maddy turned around and stepped forward holding a small, blond girl by the hand.

Shit! This was messy. He did not want to victimize children—or helpless females of any variety.

Rae Maddy wasn't helpless. Everything his family had built was at stake. He mustn't allow an interesting face, and the mind that went with it, to push him even an inch off track.

She stood still. He saw the way she froze in place at the sight of him—not that she could actually see him with the early morning sun on the windshield. Obviously she'd heard his engine and expected someone else to arrive. The child looked from her mother toward the Land Rover, but from his perspective she showed curiosity, rather than alarm.

Dallas took his hat from the passenger seat, settled it over his eyes, and slid from the Rover. He slammed the door and walked toward the duo on the veranda. Gravel crunched beneath his boots. The night's snap was still in the air. On any other morning he might just send up a whoop because it felt so good; not today.

The green-eyed lady, who had rested her hands on her daughter's shoulders, wasn't whooping either. She looked like she might be thinking about that Sauer again.

"Mornin'," he said when he got closer. Keeping his pace leisurely, he smiled at the girl. "You must be Ginny. Hi, Ginny."

Blond, blue-eyed and freckled, Ginny didn't look much like her mama, but she was pretty in a fine-boned way. Dallas guessed that was something the two had in common; they were both on the skinny side.

"Hi," Ginny said after taking her time sizing him up.

Dallas arrived at the front step, rested his weight on one leg, and hooked his thumbs into his jeans pockets. And he smiled. "Glad I got here before you left." A cold front was in those green eyes of Rae's. "I forgot to get your phone number." He was a liar on that, but it was a small lie. The Maddys were in the phone book.

The sound of another engine diverted Rae's attention, but only for an instant before she concentrated on him again. Dallas glanced over his shoulder in time to see a '54 turquoise Cadillac, complete with rusted silver fins, grind and float its way down the driveway. The driver parked beside the Land Rover.

This interview was already going so badly, he was glad for the diversion.

With a mighty creak, the driver's door on the Cadillac opened, and a tiny, bespectacled woman climbed nimbly out. Buelah Wilks waved, including Dallas in that wave. And he waved back.

"Hi there, Rae," Buelah said in the cracked voice that had amused him yesterday. "You ready to roll, Ginny? We don't want to be late for school. Good morning to you, too, Dallas.

Guess you two have been talking all night, huh? Catching up?"

He didn't dare look at Rae.

"We met last night," Rae said. He heard the strain she felt. "He just arrived back. Buelah, what?—"

"That's right," Dallas said heartily. He met Rae's eyes and narrowed his own slightly. "We talked for hours, but I went to the motel up on the highway for the night. I wanted to make sure I met Ginny as soon as I could, though." This would be as tough or as easy as Rae wanted to make it; that was the message he wanted her to get without his having to voice it.

"I'm just so happy for all of you," Buelah said, her grin sending ripples of wrinkles across her cheeks. "You never said much about your family, Rae. I'm glad your brother found you." She wore her thick, gray hair cropped straight at ear-level. Dallas guessed her age at around sixty.

The child stared at him, and the confusion on her pixyish face bothered him. "Hi, Ginny," he said, "pleased to meet you. Your mama and I have a history." That probably wasn't the right way to win a kid's confidence, but it was the best he could do without outright lying. Dallas didn't like lies.

"Uh huh," Ginny said, her frown growing deeper, her blue eyes more frightened.

"Hey," he said, "I'm not the boogie man. Friends, huh?"

"I guess," the child said doubtfully.

"You'd better get going," Rae said, walking Ginny from the veranda.

When she drew level, the girl looked up at him. If she'd been a year or so younger, she'd have asked pointed questions. As it was, she wanted to ask, but knew better.

He smiled at her again, and bowed slightly.

Ginny didn't smile back.

"What do you think of your uncle, Ginny?" Buelah said, and Dallas braced himself for what would follow. "Isn't he a handsome man? I should have known he was your mama's brother. You can see it in the eyes. Not the color, but the expression. They're both cautious." She coughed awkwardly, and colored up.

"My uncle?" Ginny said, turning to her mother. "Mama?"

"His name is Dallas," Rae said. "We never knew each other well. We never knew each other at all. But he decided to look me up on his way through. He's just passing through."

With that piece of mostly fiction, Ms. Rae Maddy helped Dallas's cause more than her own. He felt the triumph of a small advantage gained. Maybe they could get their business over fast because she'd want to keep him away from Ginny.

"I'm a good bit older than your mama," he said, the grin starting to make his face ache. "I moved on before she was all grown up. We never did get a chance to really know each other, so I thought I'd do something about that. I didn't even know I was getting a niece thrown into the bargain."

"Off you go, Ginny," Rae said, suddenly bursting into motion. "We'll talk about all this after school." She hurried her puzzled chick to the Cadillac and shut her in while Buelah got back behind the wheel. Buelah looked through, not over, that wheel.

A rough roar, the spew of gravel, the honk of a cranky old horn, and the turquoise monster went up the driveway, bouncing majestically on shocks overdue for replacement.

"Okay, that's it," Rae said. She walked toward the house, but stopped some feet from him. "That's all I'm taking from you, whoever you are. Wait until they're out of sight, then get yourself back in that vehicle and blow. D'you understand me?"

Spirit. The lady had lots of spirit. Dallas abandoned the smile and said, "I understand you wish I'd get lost. It isn't going to happen. Not until I get what I came for."

"I don't have anything that belongs to you."

"Oh, yes you do. Why don't we talk some more about that?"

Today she wore baggy cotton sweats that had probably been green a long time ago. Her canvas tennis shoes were white from washing, but had holes in the toes, and no laces. No fashion plate, this one.

When he looked at her face again, she looked back defiantly. "I didn't think you'd be stupid enough to come again after last night," she said.

"Oh, I'm not stupid, Ms. Maddy. What you mean is you convinced yourself I wouldn't come back because you know you're in trouble, and you want it to go away. It isn't going away. I only left when I did to give you time to decide to do the smart thing and give me what I want. What I've got coming."

She raised her chin, and her scrubbed skin glowed, even if there were dark marks beneath her eyes. She said, "I don't believe a word of that line you fed me last night. I spent hours thinking about—"

"So did I. I thought about what happened until the trucks on that highway finally hypnotized me into a coma. I'm not sorry for being here, or for confronting you. But I came on strong. Too strong. I apologize for that."

"Don't bother. Your apology isn't accepted. What made you think you had the right to push your way in here and get physical? Physical, and sexual?" She raised both palms and shook her head violently enough to whip her dark ponytail from side to side. "Don't answer that. Just get out."

Color rose in her pale cheeks. Her eyes glittered. She interested him. "You've got guts," he told her.

"What does that mean?"

"You aren't scared of anything. Even a man with a hundred pounds on you. You just wade right in."

"The stuff you showed me from the paper. That man looked like John, but he isn't. Wasn't. You've made a mistake. John doesn't know anything about planes, or flying. That man was a stunt flyer. John's quiet, very private. He doesn't have any exhibitionist tendencies."

He studied her. "What about the photo of you and your little girl?"

"Maybe you followed a trail the wrong way and got here because John looks like your brother-in-law. And someone gave you the photo of Ginny and me."

She was searching for ways not to believe good old Warren was dead. No doubt about that.

One small woman with a kid. So far he hadn't found any trace of more family—and from what Buelah Wilks said, he wouldn't. *Shee-it*. He wasn't about to feel sorry for Rae Maddy when she very probably had a fortune in Calhoun money stashed away.

"The only trail I've followed led right to this door," Dallas said. It was time to get tougher again. "Right to a place Warren thought no one else knew about, to you. You haven't asked for the details of what happened. He sent out an SOS to say he was in trouble. Garbled, but they got it that he had a fuel leak, big time. The authorities surmised fuel sprayed everywhere and caught fire. When he hit, the plane was in about ten million pieces."

She crossed her arms, and he saw her shudder.

"They say he was drunk at the time. A smart man doesn't fly drunk."

"No!"

"There wasn't a whole lot left. Seems they may never figure the whole thing out."

She flew at him, but stopped when she was close enough for him to see a vein pulse beneath the fine skin at her temple.

Dallas signaled for her to keep on coming. "Do it," he told her. "Hit me—again. Or try to. For a woman who doesn't like things to get physical, or *sexual,* you sure have a way of making sure they do."

"Get out." Her splayed hands suggested she was working hard not to make fists. "Get out before I call the sheriff."

"Yeah, the sheriff. How come you never got around to calling the guy by now?"

"I don't like trouble," she mumbled.

"I believe you. That's why you don't want the law anywhere near this."

"If I didn't want to be sure Ginny and Buelah were out of harm's way, I'd have asked Buelah to stay until we could get rid of you. I'd have said what a liar you are right out."

"But you didn't. And you didn't because you wouldn't risk having me talk about you and good old *John* in front of the little girl and her teacher. Or do they already know?"

"No, damn it." She swallowed. "What I told you last night is true. And I'm not going to believe what you're saying about John. I think you're some kind of a grifter. This is a scam you work. I bet you've got those clippings made up with pictures of a dozen different men. All men who travel away from home a lot."

"Grifter? Funny term for a nice, innocent country girl to slide off her tongue so easily."

Her chin rose up again. "I came from nothing. Nothing except the bottom of the barrel and all the sludge that collects there. I've left that behind, but I haven't forgotten the smell. It gave me a real respect for clean air. Right now, something rotten is messing that up for me. *You."*

"Nice try," he said. "Nice theory, even. Another nice theory. But it isn't so, ma'am. If you don't believe me, just go to that cute little library of yours and request a copy of the *Glory Speaker* for the right day."

Silence greeted that.

"You don't know me," Dallas said. "If you did, you wouldn't question how serious I am. I've come to get what belongs to my family. We Calhouns don't give up on what's ours."

"You don't know me, either," she said quietly. "I don't take things from other people. But I'm not telling you anything else about me, or my family. I do believe you've got some sort of problem you're trying to deal with. You've come to the wrong place. But if you'd leave a card, or something, I'll do what you suggest. I'll go to the library. Then I'll get in touch with you."

Her change of heart didn't make him relax a muscle. "I'll drive you there."

"You won't take me anywhere. John doesn't like strangers, and neither do I. Do you think I'd actually get into a car with you?"

"I thought you might. After all, I've been seen all over town. Buelah and Ginny both saw me with you this morning. And Mrs. Loder knows she gave me your address. And they've got my license number at the motel. If I planned to rape and murder you, I'd probably keep a lower profile."

She took a step away from him, and he didn't feel particularly good about it. "You're horrible," she told him.

"I'm not going to hurt you," he said. "Hurting women isn't my style."

Her arms fell to her sides. "Would you please go away? Look, this is all crazy. It has to be. Please stop it. Please go away."

"If you were completely sure I'm some sort of a con artist, you wouldn't be standing here talking to me. But you're not sure, are you? In fact, you know damn well I'm telling the truth about you and Warren. The two of you worked together to bleed funds from Calhoun. You were part of his cover."

She rubbed her eyes, and put a hand over her mouth.

"Look," he said, taking off his hat and sweeping wide his arm. "I don't want a lot of talk to get around any more than you do. Work with me and we can come to some sort of arrangement."

"Leave me alone." Her voice shook.

"I can't do that."

"Even if I tell you I won't leave town? And I'll look into what you've told me?"

"Uh uh. Can't do it."

"I'm tired."

He saw the second when the fight went out of her. It was a sight that ought to make him feel good. It didn't.

With her gaze on the ground, she walked past him and sat on the bottom step.

Nothing looked as clear cut as it had when he'd driven in here last night. "Maybe we could continue this discussion over breakfast?"

She shook her head.

"What's the name of that place in town? There's a diner there, isn't there? I smelled breakfast."

"It always smells like breakfast," she said, dead flat. "Why don't you go and eat?"

He needed a next move. "I don't feel hungry anymore. D'you suppose I could talk you out of a cup of coffee?"

Rae didn't respond.

Hell, he didn't want to make her life a misery. What she'd done must have been Warren's idea. Going along with him was wrong, but who knew what had driven her to agree? And there hadn't been anything personal in what she'd done, not where Dallas was concerned.

"Okay, I'm taking charge here." Action was his strong suit. "Up you get."

Rather than do as he asked, she folded her forearms on her knees and rested her cheek on top.

"We've got a problem," he said, standing over her. "But it could be worse. I could be the kind of guy who goes for the jugular and the hell with what else happens."

Nothing.

Dallas touched her shoulder. "Hey, let's go inside and *I'll* make the coffee."

Still nothing.

"I don't blame you for wanting to keep your distance from me. Last night . . . Could we just say the kiss was a reaction to anger? And forget it?" He hadn't forgotten it.

She closed her eyes.

"Okay, play possum. I'm going inside to make that coffee."

"You're treading all over my life."

He'd climbed the steps and taken two strides toward the door. "Not my fault, lady. Coffee?"

"I haven't done anything to you."

Here they went again. "Yes, you have," he said slowly. "I'm sure you didn't set out to do it to me, personally. We've already figured out we don't know each other. But when you entered into Warren Niel's scheme, you did things to me and my family. I can't let that pass. I can't afford to let it pass."

"Why?"

He braced his hands on either side of the doorjamb and let his head hang forward. This had to be the most bizarre exchange of all time. "Are you finally admitting you've got a fortune stashed away? A fortune that doesn't belong to you?"

"No."

It was Dallas's turn to close his eyes. "There's a way out of this. You've got to make your way—for you, and for Ginny." Now the kid was becoming a person to him. Great. "You need money for that. Make a deal with me. Cut your losses and move on. Far on."

"This is our home. Ginny's home. She's more important. Anyway, John's going to come home."

"John doesn't even exist." He dropped his arms and walked into the house, into the kitchen.

The coffee was already made. A half-full pot sat on its burner. Dallas glanced around and saw a used mug on the cooking island. She must have been up real early.

He found two clean mugs and filled them. Something told him it would be a cold day in hell before Rae Maddy willingly entered this kitchen with him again, so he carried the coffee out to her.

Lowering himself to sit beside her, he held one mug in front of her knees until she lifted her head and accepted the offering.

"You know it's all true, don't you?" he asked, taking a mouthful of strong coffee and squinting through rising steam. "If you didn't, you'd have had me run off by now. Or at least got help. You had the opportunity once I left last night."

She had long, thick lashes. They flickered slightly as if she'd flinched, and made moving black shadows in her eyes.

Dallas had a wild desire to put an arm around her, to rest his chin on top of her mussed head and tell her everything was going to be okay.

He averted his face. He'd never had time to find out if he liked the tender side of being with a woman. Now wasn't a good occasion to even think about filling the gap in his education.

This was a new experience, a woman as an enemy. The situation had confused him. There couldn't be another explanation for him giving a damn about her.

"If John existed, and—"

"He *does* exist." She tugged on his sleeve until he looked at her again. "He's my husband. John Maddy. That's my name, too. And Ginny's."

And you are desperate to believe that. "Where is he?" Dallas asked. "If I'm wrong, contact him. Tell him about me. Tell him to come running home to save you."

Her eyes gradually lost focus. She stared at him, but he knew she wasn't seeing him.

"You can't, can you? You can't and that scares the hell out of you. Rae, you don't know what to do. Give it up. I won't leave you with nothing." He wasn't making any progress. "Heck, if you want to, you can stay here. At least until you figure out somewhere else to go."

Her grip on his sleeve tightened. "This is Ginny's home. This is where she's staying."

He covered her hand on his arm. "That's what this is all about, isn't it? You're hanging on to your story because you think you've got to for Ginny's sake."

"This is my house."

Whatever she was thinking was frightening her. Dallas would give a good deal to climb inside her brain. "Surely it's John's house."

"It's mine." Her eyes cleared. "In my name. John insisted."

"Did he now?" The house didn't matter. A small potatoes item on the long invoice Dallas intended to present. "But you can't call him, can you?"

One more time she stopped seeing him.

"You married a traveling man. Refrigeration sales. But you don't know how to get in touch with him. You never have."

"He doesn't stay in one place for long."

"Bastard," Dallas said under his breath.

She didn't notice he'd spoken. "I'm self-sufficient. I can look after myself."

"As long as John comes home from time to time? To bring home the lovely additions to those bank accounts?" Gently, he raised her chin. "To give Ginny an illusion of family? And to remind you you're a woman?"

"You don't know what you're talking about." The violence with which she stood sent coffee sloshing from her mug.

Dallas set his own drink down and stood up beside her. "There's a way we can both come out of this as winners," he said. His heart beat a little harder. "We can strike a deal that'll make you and me really happy."

The step he was about to make could turn out to be the craziest he'd ever taken, but why not? Why not come up with a compromise? He wasn't in a position to turn her over to the authorities, not when he knew the publicity that followed could possibly sound the death knell on Calhoun—and put his mother into a sanitarium.

Rae brushed absently at the coffee she'd spilled on the front of her sweatshirt. Her breasts weren't big, but from where he stood, they were nice. No bra. Hell, he ought to be a detective. And if she looked at his jeans she wouldn't need to be a detective.

"You've got to have someone to make sure you get what you need," he said. Taking chances wasn't a new concept to him. And this wasn't even a chance because he held all the cards. "That's all John was to you. A provider of sorts. If it had been more, you wouldn't have been happy to see him only once in a while, and have no way to even get hold of him if you wanted to."

Her breasts rose with her indrawn breath. She held that breath.

Dallas shifted his stance. "So this is what we'll do. We'll work out how to put back what you and Warren stole. We'll pull it off really quietly. Then I'll do what he did for you."

Her head whipped around, and her eyes narrowed.

"I won't ask for any more from you than he did. Less. You won't have to be a criminal for me. But I'll drop by now and then just to make sure you and Ginny are okay."

Understanding exactly what he meant came easily to the sharp-eyed Rae. "You've got to be kidding."

"No way. I don't expect you to jump right into bed with me." Although he'd sure like her to, and this would be a great moment to do just that. "We can take our time with that. You can let me know when you're ready, if you ever are."

"This is unbelievable," she whispered.

She was right, but he wasn't a man to chicken out—of anything. "No one's going to wonder why your long lost brother comes by now and then. It won't be any different than what you had with John. You'll never know where I am—or care. But when I show up, I'll look after you. You'll look after me. As soon as you think it's time, Ginny will find out her so-called daddy had an accident. She'll get over it. She'll get used to the change and never know the truth. And I'll make sure she never goes without anything she needs—or wants. Seems fair. More than fair."

Her laughter caught him off guard. Her laughter, and the way she threw the mug at him.

He ducked, but not fast enough. The thick china broke against his forehead, just above his right eyebrow. "For God's sake! You cut me."

"But I didn't kill you. Too bad. Get back behind the wheel and head home. I'm not for sale."

"Rae—"

"Don't speak to me. I've got a lot to do. I've got to find out if there's any truth to the line you've fed me."

"Good idea." Blood ran into his eye. "You do that and while you do, think over my offer. I guarantee it'll sound better all the time. I'll be on my way, but I'll be in touch."

"You bet we'll be in touch," Rae said. She turned and went back toward the house. In the doorway, she stopped and said, "You're going to wish you'd never come here. One day you'll apologize for trying to treat a woman you don't even know like a—like she could be bought."

"I don't think so."

"I do. See you in Glory."

Five

The theory of the "helpless little woman" was full of holes. Too bad men like Dallas Calhoun hadn't figured that out. Too bad for him.

The way Rae's life was heading, the pleasure she took in anticipating showing the Big Man she was no fool could only be grim. She'd started thinking of him as the Big Man since she'd arrived in Glory and begun hearing or reading his name everywhere she went.

Not that she went far.

People intent on hiding out until they were entrenched enough to feel a little secure didn't advertise their presence.

Dallas had walked away from her that morning two weeks earlier with a warning on his lips—and in his eyes. In the eye that wasn't fighting a losing battle with a stream of blood. She wasn't to *dare* to go near Glory. She was to stay in Decline, and right where he could find her. "Or?" she'd asked. And he'd said, "If you don't want to be a whole lot more scared than you already are, do as you're told."

He didn't know he was talking to the woman who had been the girl who felled Willie Skeggs with a rusty flashlight.

He didn't know what it would take to make her that scared again.

Rae had left Decline almost on Dallas's heels, left Ginny with Buelah, who would keep her safe and care for her as if she were her own grandchild.

Glory was like a dozen towns Rae had seen in Georgia, the

kind of towns she'd grown up passing through. Folks who settled in Glad Times saw a place like Glory as a big city.

Downtown was small, but neat, prosperous-looking. Magnolia trees lined wide streets and reflected in the shiny windows of well-kept and inviting stores. The business district gave way first to precise rows of modest homes, then to the graciously spaced houses of the people who either called a lot of the shots in Glory or commuted elsewhere to jobs that paid plenty.

The usual scraggle of rundown shacks and sad-eyed houses lined the road into town from the south, but that road skirted west and bypassed the sumptuous acres to the north and northeast.

This was the land of the rich, or those who refused to live as if they weren't.

This was the land of the people who really called the Glory shots.

This was the land of Sweet Bay, and the Calhouns.

Rae stood on the porch in front of the cabin she'd rented on the outer reaches of a large property due north of Glory. The place was for sale by absentee owners named Parker. A wide, dense stand of oak and pine shut the cabin into a marshy bowl fronted by a slow-moving river.

She rubbed her arms and stared across the river at more oaks, and pines—and hickory. She missed Ginny so much, but bringing her here had been out of the question. She needed to be in school, and Rae would never consider exposing a gentle child to the kind of hatred that might flare in this town at any time.

Rain fell. Heavy, driven by wind, it slashed sideways past the porch overhang. Warm rain. She could see how it whipped up the surface of the clay-red river. A steamy mist rose from the ground and melded with the encroaching gray of evening.

This was how lonely felt.

For the first time in her life she was completely alone.

Even as a kid, there had been Mama, or Cassie, and then Ginny. Sweet Ginny who had become her reason to fight.

And Rae was going to fight on. Dallas Calhoun had drawn the line in his personal sand, and Rae Maddy would meet him, toe-to-toe, on that line. He was going to be spitting mad when he found out where she was, but, if her luck held, she'd have at least a while longer to gather intelligence on the wonderful Calhouns.

The Calhouns were gangsters in gentlemen's clothing. Oh, they had been wearing that clothing a fair amount of time, but it didn't take a woman who knew her way around research long to dig out the glossed-over truth. The first Calhoun in these parts had been a carpetbagger with a talent for bargain hunting. He'd ended up with most of the best land in the area.

Rae had learned that Dallas had started looking for her two days after he'd left Decline with blood on his face. He'd gone back and found an empty house. Then he'd gone to Buelah's. Ginny and Buelah had no trouble saying they didn't know where Rae had gone. They didn't. Each evening, as soon as it was dark enough to give her hope of remaining anonymous, Rae drove out to a phone booth at a gas station on the main highway and called Buelah and Ginny. She continued her story to Ginny that she was away on business, and Ginny accepted this, especially since she loved being with Buelah. Buelah knew only that Rae was searching for information about John, and that she wasn't to confide in Dallas anymore. Rae had also determined not to divulge her exact location to her dear friend. And Buelah, feisty Buelah, had backed up Rae's decisions and told her not to worry about things in Decline.

After the telephone calls, and picking up what few necessities she needed from a rundown convenience store Dallas was unlikely to know existed, Rae drove back to the cabin in the second-hand brown Jeep she'd bought for the trip to Glory.

John Maddy had never existed.

Ignoring the rain that instantly soaked her, Rae walked down two weathered steps to a path fashioned only by feet. The Parker estate had been unoccupied for several years, and undergrowth had reduced the path to little more than a line through tall grass.

A trip to the public records office had yielded the kind of instant information she should have been grateful for. A myopic clerk, more interested in her telephone conversation with a friend than with Rae's request, had handed over a key and waved her toward a corridor.

On her way to the records rooms, Rae had only to look at photographs lining the walls to start her journey into the life of the man she'd married.

Married?

Rae squelched toward the riverbank. With each step, her tennis shoes sank into red mud. The rain bore scents of that mud, and of pine, and the verbena that grew, weedlike, in the unkempt grasses.

She wasn't married, had never been married. And Ginny, who had no mother, didn't even have an adoptive daddy—not legally. That was an issue Rae would have to confront. Not now. Ginny was too young to cope with it all now. When she'd left Glad Times, Rae had been too immature and too frightened to think things through as well as she might. Claiming Ginny as her own child had seemed the simplest thing to do, and she'd carefully managed to establish the legal necessities.

An upturned aluminum rowboat rested a few feet from the water. Rae had found oars in a shed behind the carport and intended to get out on the river when she could. She'd never rowed a boat, but it couldn't be that hard.

Rae had formed a plan, a goal. Sooner or later—she hoped it would be later—she'd have to confront Dallas Calhoun again.

She'd easily convinced Lucy Gordon, keeper of the town's

public records for fifteen years, that she was researching for a project. Lucy never asked what the project was and seemed thrilled to have someone come by who wanted nothing more than to listen to all the inside stories she could tell about the rich, and locally famous.

If Lucy was to be believed, and Rae thought she did believe her, the deepest mud in Glory wasn't on the banks of the river.

Lucy had been only too happy to talk about Dallas Calhoun. The mildest, most offhand comment on Rae's part had brought a dreamy look into the other woman's pretty, spectacle-magnified eyes. That Dallas was quite the boy. So handsome. Real quiet, but deep, if Rae knew what Lucy meant. And the stories about him? Well, if Lucy was one to gossip, those stories would curl Rae's hair.

Rae intended to visit Lucy again very soon, but she had some thinking to do first. Taking a step without looking first could be real dangerous.

John, or Warren as Rae now knew he'd really been, had never meant to hurt her. She blinked rapidly. Rain? Tears? What difference did it make what wetted her face? She did not want to cry for what couldn't be changed, that was all.

He'd wanted the peace they made together. He'd told her as much, and she hadn't minded, not wanting more from him than he had given. Their times together had been infrequent, but Rae couldn't remember a moment when he'd been less than good to her. And then when he'd known he couldn't return to her and to Ginny, he'd made provision for them. Good provision.

And that was why she couldn't leave this place until she'd done what must be done.

When John—Warren—had sent that note and money, he'd known something was going to happen to him.

As she'd done so many times in recent days, Rae fought against a tide of sickness, and the thud of her heart. Warren Niel had known something was going to stop him from get-

ting back to Decline, and then he had died in a plane crash.
Rae didn't want to think what she was thinking, but there
was no choice. She had no idea how such a thing as deliberately bringing a plane out of the sky could be accom-
plished. How did you start putting together the pieces of
something like that?

John had been a pilot! Quiet John who sat at home in Decline and watched television, and never wanted to go anywhere, had flown stunt planes for *fun*. She shook her head.

Her job was to deal with Dallas Calhoun's accusations, to
get him off her back permanently, and to find out if Warren's
death had really been an accident. And to try to work out what
had driven him to pretend to be someone else.

Who would want Warren dead, want it badly enough to . . .
to kill him?

She wasn't a detective. Maybe she should pack up the
Jeep, go pick up Ginny, and move on.

All she had so far was a list of names. Names of people
she didn't know, people with some connection to John in his
life as Warren Niel.

She was in a mess, a terrible mess. She'd worked hard for
some of what she had, and she could keep herself and Ginny
nicely, right where they were, as long as no big, ominously
quiet man came to victimize them.

Darn it all anyway, she had as much right to her home as
he did to his. And she didn't want his, or anything else that
belonged to him.

On the other side of the river lay Sweet Bay, the Calhouns'
big, beautiful estate. With each day, Rae became more curious about the place. She wanted to see the house, and get a
look at Fancy Niel, and her mother, Dallas's mother. Ava
Calhoun was the daughter of an old timber family. Rich?
Rich didn't come close to describing the financial condition
that had existed in Ava Davenport's family at the time of her
marriage to Biff Calhoun.

Rae wondered what it would be like to be with Dallas if he

didn't think she'd stolen a fortune from his family. How would he treat a woman he wanted to be with—as a woman?

She shouldn't care.

Rae considered the little boat. She slopped her way to it, slipped her fingers under its side and heaved. Heavy, but not impossibly so, she raised it until she could get a knee underneath. Next she hefted it to her shoulder, took a breath, pushed and ran backward at the same time to avoid getting hurt when it landed right side up.

Easy. She wiped her hands on her denim shorts. Mud smeared her thighs. Well, she'd just row across that sluggish little river, make her way through the trees, and take a look at what it was the Calhouns thought was so all-fired spectacular about their precious house.

No one would ever dare to blackmail Dallas Calhoun, not unless they wanted to find out they had made the worst mistake of their life.

Part of him was mad as hell that Rae—and he still didn't know what her other name really was—that she'd decided there must be a way to squeeze even more out of the stunt she and Warren had pulled off. Another part of him was fascinated by her audacity.

Too bad for her that she hadn't gotten the message that he was in the driver's seat now. Too bad she didn't understand enough about a town like Glory to know she couldn't sneak in and keep hidden from him—not for long. She plain didn't get it that in Glory the Calhouns, and anyone who was anyone, stuck together when it came to intruders, especially intruders who asked questions about any members of the establishment.

"The lady doesn't know she's playing with fire," he told Wolf. The mostly black Lab leaned from his customary spot on the passenger seat to snuffle at Dallas's ear. "Teeth, you mutt. I want lots of teeth on show. No grinning, either. Snarling. You hate women, remember?"

Wolf rested his oversized head on Dallas's shoulder and sighed. The dog sighed a lot, grinned a lot, and definitely hated females. Fancy had threatened to have him shot if he came near her again. The last time he had approached her, she'd ended up backed into a corner where she'd been trapped for fifteen minutes before Dallas showed up.

The Parker place. He hadn't even known the river cabin was up for rent. Evidently it hadn't been until recently.

This had been a day worth striking. Fancy was pushing him for money. His mother was pushing him for money. Together, they had pushed him to clean up the mess left by Warren's death. Fancy was angry because of a holdup in releasing insurance money and dealing with Warren's will. Ava thought they should give a splashy party to show everyone that any talk of the Calhouns being in financial trouble was a joke.

Dallas had come close to telling them both that there was nothing funny about the battle he was fighting for the survival of Calhoun Properties.

In the gloom of dusk, steam rose from the road to make the way ahead hard to see. He turned on his headlights. Rain reflected in the beams. The landscape dripped. This was a road he knew well. He ought to, he'd driven it enough times.

The Parkers weren't Old Glory. They had come, bought the old Werther family home, stayed a few years, then moved to California. Word had it they wanted so much for the property, it was never likely to sell. Since they were selling privately, he couldn't find out the asking price through his family's real estate agency.

Rather than use the main entrance to the estate, he took a narrow track he knew that led to the river cabin. The Land Rover bucked into deep ruts. Branches scraped the sides of the vehicle.

He went as far as a wide spot half a mile from the river and parked. This was a time when he needed every advantage he could gain. Surprise would be useful, should establish the right order of things. Then, when she found out he knew she was here, knew she was snooping around asking questions, and that if she stayed it would be with a new second skin—Dallas Calhoun—she'd do as she was told.

She could not, must not, remain in Glory.

With Wolf at his heel, he made his way downhill to the cabin.

"You're trained," Dallas muttered. "Don't you forget those damn classes I took you through. Saved your sorry ass from the sausage factory with those classes. My sister was tuning up for your wake, boy. Backslide, and you're gone. I'm not saving you again. When I tell you to sit, you sit. Stay and you stay. Down and you're flat, boy. Got it?"

Wolf lolloped along, his tongue hanging from the side of his mouth. "I should have let her shoot you. You don't give me any respect, you no-good hound."

Dallas paused, took Wolf's head in his hands and ruffled the animal's ears. "I nag because I care," he said, and bestowed a kiss between great, soft brown eyes. "You're the best. I've just gotta keep you on the edge so you don't get complacent."

What kind of a life did a man have when the only thing he knew for sure he could trust was his dog? Not so bad, Dallas decided, and set off again. At least he didn't have to be afraid of betrayal from the inside.

The cabin was in darkness.

"Shit," Dallas muttered under his breath. Then he saw the tail of a vehicle sticking out of the carport. So she was here.

The rain intensified. He raised the collar on his oilskin coat and ducked his head until he reached the porch. "Sit," he said, real low. Wolf sat and assumed his most ferocious expression—teeth together, lips apart, but curled, not smiling. "Good boy. Stay."

Dallas approached the door and groaned. It stood wide open, and instinct suggested the cabin could be empty.

He stuck his head inside and called, "Rae? Are you there?"

When there was no response, he stepped into the main room. In the all but darkness, he could make out shapes of furniture, but little else. "Rae," he said loudly.

Stillness blanketed the space.

She wasn't there.

Back on the porch again, he looked around. With her car there, where could she be? Walking in the rain? Uh uh, not that one. She was the kind who didn't do stupid things—at least, not that kind of stupid things.

Wolf barked.

"Hush," Dallas ordered.

Ignoring him, the dog shot by, barking madly, and headed for the river. Dallas took off after him, cursing roundly. Probably smelled a raccoon. Wolf had a thing for raccoons. He loved the chase, but tended to give up if he saw the whites of the other animal's eyes.

The last vestiges of light were failing. Great. So much for his tidy plan to shoehorn Rae out of Glory before nightfall.

Wolf arrived at the riverbank and rushed back and forth, howling. *Howling.* For God's sake, the mutt never howled.

Dallas opened his mouth to yell, but closed it again. He stepped off the mushy pathway and took cover behind the thick trunk of an old beech tree.

Something on the water glinted. On the water, not in the water. He narrowed his eyes and peered, watched carefully.

Wolf kept right on howling, but Dallas heard another noise between the howls.

A voice.

That was a boat out there, and unless his eyes were playing tricks, the thing was going in circles. Dipping, and spinning in slow revolutions. Some fool had taken a boat out in the dark, and the rain, and whoever it was didn't have a clue how to row.

He started for the bank, but stopped. The voice was clear when it shouted, "Don't you come near me."

Dallas pulled behind his tree again. The fool in question was Rae, of Decline fame.

"Get away! Go on. Go. *Now.*"

The big animal on the bank howled again, then subsided into low growling. It prowled back and forth.

"I'm not afraid of you, you horrible beast," Rae said with the next breath she managed to gather. "Git, before I hit you with my oar."

She'd lost the other oar.

Another howl split the fuzzy air. Oh, she shouldn't have done this without thinking first. No flashlight, nothing to help her see where she was, or how far downriver she'd drifted since starting out. She squinted, and swiped water from her eyes. At first she'd done okay. Sure, her right arm was stronger than her left and she'd curved in the wrong direction, but when she'd taken that oar out of the water and just used the left one, she'd sort of gone back on course again. The biggest trouble was that she hadn't seemed to make any headway for a long time. But then, right when she was in the middle, and feeling pretty good because she was going to get across, she'd lost her grip on the left oar, and it had slipped away.

Now she was who knew where, and there was a wild animal between her and safety—if safety indeed existed on the closest bank of the river.

She took a swipe at the water with her remaining oar. And the boat took another swirling, wobbling revolution.

Something hard banged the end of the oar.

Cautiously, keeping a low profile, Rae held the oar in both hands and drove it downward. She lifted and thrust it back down several times. The bottom. Her breath rushed out in a great, relieved gust. She must have managed to draw closer to shore than she'd realized. It was a shame about the bobcat, or whatever. But animals like that were more afraid of you than you were of them.

First she'd use the oar the way she'd seen punt poles used; then she'd use it to frighten the big critter off.

Rae dug the oar into the riverbed and pushed. She got to her knees in the bottom of the boat and pushed harder. The boat didn't move. It had even stopped swinging around.

Very carefully, she rose to a crouch and put all of her weight into the task.

Not an inch did she gain.

Loud panting made her look over her shoulder. She sat down with a thud and yanked at the oar. It was stuck. And a large, black head rested on the side of the boat. She could see glinting eyes, and bared teeth.

"Go away!" Her voice died in a squeak. Frantic, she tugged, and tugged.

With a sucking plop, the oar shot free. Rae staggered, but didn't fall. "Now you've had it," she warned the beast, raising her weapon over her head. "Come on. Come on. Get me now. I'm going to knock your nasty brains out. Come on."

"You need to do something about all that hostility," a familiar voice said. "First you smash a mug on my face. Now it's my dog you're after—with an oar."

Slowly, Rae lowered that oar.

She couldn't see his face, but she knew the man who held the bow of the boat was Dallas Calhoun.

Six

A lot of men within fifty miles, men with a mind to scratch an itch in obliging company, knew about Blue's Bar and Eats. A lot of men—and the women who tried to keep tabs on them.

The kind of itch Blue's catered to varied according to the man. For some it was just a hankering to get drunk with like-minded patrons. Others came for the music Blue's provided or the down-home food. Fights were accommodated—man-to-man, or an assortment of more exotic tournaments. And there was always a room available—for a price. No questions asked about the latter.

Pasted along the banks of a small feeder into the Ogeechee River, Blue's was little more than a straggling line of three or so big shacks, joined by sheets of corrugated iron resting between roofs, and filled in at the sides with plywood painted blue. The bridal suites, as the regulars called them, were individual cubicles in the woods beyond.

When it worked, a neon sign out front announced, "Blue's." And any night of the week, blues was the music that wailed from within. If a bridal suite was what you wanted, you found your way in the dark, and the only music out there you made for yourself.

Fancy figured she'd find Tyson at Blue's tonight.

She nosed her champagne-colored convertible Mercedes between a beat-up pickup and a Harley parked beneath the spreading branches of an ancient oak.

Rain pounded the convertible's soft roof. The instant she turned off the wipers, she couldn't see anything but the wavering neon "Blue's," "Coors," "Budweiser," and a flashing neon woman perpetually removing her green bikini and putting it back on.

She was pissed at Tyson. Again.

With the hood of her black silk raincoat pulled over her head, she pushed open the car's heavy door and delicately sought a firm spot to place one of her red patent Ferragamos.

An ocean of mud didn't make allowances for expensive shoes.

Fancy got out, locked the car and squelched toward the whining guitars, and the "we're so lost and lonely?" lyrics. Why did Tyson have to gravitate to the bottom?

Two beautiful men, both blond and muscular and without shirts despite the downpour, sat on the top step leading to the main doors.

Fancy looked at their chests first, then their faces. She smiled, and wiggled her fingers. They smiled, and wiggled their fingers, and draped their arms around each other.

"Damn," she muttered. "Waste of good material." She pushed her way inside the crowded bar and winced at the blare of shouts and laughter that fought with the music.

Heat muddled the scents of beer, perfume, cigarette smoke, and sweat into a noxious aroma that stung the eyes as well as the nose.

Tyson had been making himself scarce for days. There were a lot of ways out of Blue's. If he saw her first . . .

Fancy saw him.

Bastard.

Seated in front of a heaped platter of the Mississippi catfish that Blue—and there really was a Blue—bought from a crazy crop duster who took lucrative side trips, Tyson was too involved to notice Fancy's approach.

The catfish weren't holding his attention either.

Tyson had an occasional taste for nubile meat. Willing,

nubile meat. If the brunette he was with had seen her twentieth birthday, Fancy's talent for guessing age was failing. The girl wore a lot of green eyeshadow, and her eyes should have closed under the weight of her mascara.

She no longer wore any lipstick.

Tyson did.

A stretchy, cropped white top showed a lot of cleavage, pointed out sharp nipples, and gave coy peeks at the lush undersides of pale breasts.

Tyson nibbled his companion's lips until she wound her arms around his neck. Good old Tyson slid his hands from a smooth back and pushed inside white cotton shorts to cup the girl's fanny.

All the winding and grinding together of bodies took the white top high enough to take the coy out of those peeks.

Fancy had seen more than enough. She rapped the knuckles of her right hand on top of Tyson's skull.

He yelled, and jerked away from the girl. Rubbing his head, he looked up at Fancy. "What the fuck did you do that for?"

She pulled up a chair and sat down beside him. "I did it to get your attention, *lover.* Tell your little buddy to get lost."

Up close, Tyson's buddy didn't look quite so young. Blinking unfocused eyes, she smiled foolishly at Fancy. "Is it ready, Ty?" she asked, her voice high and light. "Let's go now."

Tyson wiped at his mouth with the back of a hand, then took up a paper napkin to finish the job. "This isn't a good time, Fancy."

"Something's come up. We've got to talk about it. Now."

"You are a jealous bitch," he said ferociously. "You'll do anything to make sure you keep your claws into me."

Fancy opened her purse and took a large bill from her wallet. This she handed to the girl. "I need to talk to Tyson. Business. Go into Savannah tomorrow. Buy yourself something nice, okay?"

A little girlish "Okay," and Fancy was alone with Tyson.

"Shit," he said. Sweat stood out on his face.

Fancy put a hand into his crotch, found what had him so worked up, and helped keep it that way. When he caught her wrist, she tightened her grip and kissed him.

"*Fuck,*" he said, after she'd sunk her teeth into his bottom lip.

"Exactly what I had in mind. Come on. I'll drive."

"I drove myself."

"Then neither of us will drive. It won't be the first time we spent the night in a backseat."

"We're too old for that."

"Speak for yourself."

"Number Three, Ty." A brass key clattered on the table, thrown down by Blue, who didn't even glance at Fancy. "How long?" Short and muscular, Blue's greased black ponytail glistened at his nape. His flat, pock-marked face also glistened. He'd been an institution in these parts for as long as Fancy remembered, yet he appeared perpetually frozen somewhere in his forties.

"How long?" he repeated, finally looking at Fancy with disinterested blue eyes.

She picked up the key and said, "All night."

He grunted and left.

She'd never been to one of the bridal suites, but the prospect held some appeal.

"You shouldn't have come here," Tyson said.

"That makes two of us, baby. Lead on to Number Three. I'm sure you know the way."

Seven

Dallas had hauled the boat up the bank—with Rae inside. His "You're already aground. You could walk away anytime," hadn't helped her pride. Nor had the way he'd lifted her out, dumped her on her feet in the mud, and strode away toward the cabin without another word.

Then, to complete her humiliation, when she'd lost a shoe and cried out, he'd come back, taken her by the hand, and all but dragged her along behind him.

But strong women didn't do shame.

The bobcat was a dog, a huge, black dog that wasn't quite one thing or another. Short hair, sort of, and long legs, a cropped tail, big ears that didn't belong, big dark eyes that glittered, and the biggest head Rae had ever seen on a dog.

And so many teeth.

When they reached the porch Dallas released her hand.

Rae climbed the two steps, conscious for the first time of how uneven a person's gait became when wearing one tennis shoe and only a layer of slippery mud on the other foot.

"I told you not to come here," he said.

How like a man. You stood there with proverbial egg on your face, mud over almost every other part, probably about to go into shock from exposure and fright, and all he could think about was getting his own way.

"Did you hear what I said, Rae?"

She kicked off the other shoe.

The dog promptly retrieved it.

"I —"

"I heard you." She sat on the edge of a hickory rocking chair and considered how to get inside the cabin without him. "Maybe we could talk tomorrow. I'm expecting company."

"No you're not. Not unless I'm it."

Rain ran from the brim of his hat. He wore a heavy oilskin duster. Rain ran from the cape on that, too. An avenging maverick in town to clean out the bad guy—or gal. The man looked huge, and mad. Mad in a way that suggested ice at his center.

"You don't have any right to tell me what to do," Rae said.

"Yes, I do."

"No—"

"Yes, I do. I have the right because whether or not you get thrown in jail for a very long time depends on me."

Rae truly wished she weren't dressed in a sopping T-shirt and shorts, and that her feet weren't bare. She'd never realized how vulnerable a person could feel with bare feet.

"I want you to pack up and get out of Glory."

She tossed back her hair. Heavy, wet hair didn't toss real well. "You're a misogynist, aren't you?"

He crossed his arms. "That's one of the most stupid things you've said so far. And you've said some pretty stupid things. I didn't come for conversation. I'm delivering a message, and I intend to be around to make sure you understand."

The dog deposited the disgusting tennis shoe in Rae's lap and rested his head on her knee.

Dallas said, *"Down."*

The dog contrived to lower the back half of its body to the deck without removing its head from Rae's leg. Gingerly, she picked up the shoe.

"Be careful," Dallas said gruffly. "If you'd said Wolf was a misogynist, you'd have been right. He really does hate women."

Her stomach clenched, but she made herself throw the shoe.

The dog took off.

Rae stood up. "I'm not inviting you in, so you might as well leave. We'll talk at a mutually agreed time."

"We'll talk now. I'm going to tell you the way things are going to be."

"You're making a mistake," she told him. "I'm not guilty of doing anything I could get into trouble for." An errant thought flew back to Glad Times. Rae closed her mind to it.

"This isn't getting you anywhere. Don't you get that? I'm not a man you can push around."

She went to the door and reached inside to flip on the porch light. "You've made a tactical error, Dallas. Is it okay with you if I call you Dallas?"

"You can call me anything you like."

"Good. Please call me Rae. Can I phone you tomorrow, Dallas? Or call on you, maybe? I could come over to Sweet Bay, and—"

"No. On both counts. And if you come anywhere near my home, I will have you arrested."

An odd sensation, an awareness, caught her off guard. She pulled her hair over her shoulder and wrung it out.

"D'you hear me?"

"I hear that you're scared of me." The instant she'd said the words she wished she could suck them back. She added, "Or scared of something," but knew she hadn't saved a thing.

A large, strong hand gripped her elbow. Dallas moved her ahead of him into the cabin, slammed the door behind him and spun her to face him so fast she stumbled and caught herself against a wall paneled with rough pine.

"You're trouble," he told her, and turned on the yellow overhead light. "But I'm making sure you take your trouble somewhere else."

He reached for her elbow again, but this time Rae was ready. She darted backward and put a big easy chair between them. "If you touch me again, you're going to be the one in jail."

Dallas swept off his hat. "You're unbelievable. I have proof—absolute proof—that you and Warren Niel fabricated identities for the purpose of diverting funds Warren embezzled from Calhoun Properties."

Rae said, "John Maddy was Warren Niel."

"I've already told you he—"

"I'm not asking, I'm telling. John was Warren. I know that now."

Dallas's eyes narrowed, not a comforting sight.

Rae cleared her throat. "How's your head?" she asked, looking at the scar above his eye where she had hit him with the coffee cup.

"It was better before I met you."

"I didn't mean to hurt you."

"Geez." He slapped the heel of a hand against the brow in question and let out a growl of pain. "Damn. Quit tryin' to divert me. I'm not discussing this with you here. Let's get started."

He really thought he could force her to pack up and get out. "Even if you put me and my things into my Jeep, you can't make me drive. Dallas, I am not leaving. I've got work to do here. The sooner you let me get on with it, the sooner I will leave."

"What work?"

"Finding out what made John—Warren—need a place to hide." The pounding of her heart made her swallow. If he killed her he'd get caught, but she'd still be dead.

"Expand on that, please."

There were times when terminal southern politeness grated. "Warren was a very unhappy man. At least, he was when I met him. And afterward, too, each time he had to leave Decline." She mustn't show her hand by talking too much.

"Touching," Dallas said. He threw his hat on a carved

chest by the single large window in the room. Pushing back his heavy oilskins, he settled his fists on his hips and bowed his head. "Isn't that what married men say to women they want to sleep with? I'm so sad and lonely. My wife doesn't understand me."

"You sound as if you know the lines personally."

He looked up at her. "I'm not married. I never have been."

"I know. I already checked."

"Damn, you're a gutsy female. Aren't you just a little bit afraid of pushing me too far?"

"I'm a lot afraid."

His head snapped all the way up. "I never hurt a woman in my life."

Now his gentlemanly honor was wounded. Rae sighed. "You've been rough with me."

"I . . ." He puffed up his cheeks and peeled off the coat. It went the way of the hat. "Maybe I've been forceful. You drove me to it. But I apologized for that in Decline."

"That was before you bruised my elbow."

"Bruised your elbow?"

Scratching noises at the door gave Rae an instant to think while Dallas ordered the dog to "Sit, Wolf! Down, Wolf! Stay, Wolf!"

"What can you do if I refuse to leave Glory?"

"Huh?" He turned back and approached. "What can I do? I've already told you what I can do."

"And I've told you I'm not going. So what's stopping you from doing it?"

"I'm a peace-loving man."

"Garbage."

"Will you do as I ask? Please? It'll be easier on both of us."

He was desperate, and she'd begun to get a strong notion she knew why—at least partly. "You're in trouble, aren't you?"

His short, sharp laugh didn't fool her.

"You're in trouble, and you're trying to bluff your way out of some of it. You think I've got something that belongs to you, and you need it so badly you'll do anything to get it."

His gray eyes lost all expression.

"How did you find me here?"

One more step was all it took to bring him too close for comfort. "You were born in Georgia."

"Tennessee." Actually, she wasn't sure.

"You've lived in Georgia long enough, lived in small Georgia towns long enough to know how they work. You can't blow into a place like Glory in the morning and not have the whole town know the color of your eyes by noon."

He had a point. "You exaggerate. By nightfall, maybe." It couldn't hurt to try lightening up a bit.

It didn't help. "You've been going through records down at Lucy's."

"I didn't realize they were her records."

"Don't smart mouth me. You've got to stop. D'you hear me?"

"I hear you. I'm not stopping."

"God, you've got balls."

"No, I don't. Not one."

Without actually shifting his feet, he loomed over her.

Rae stood her ground and raised her chin to meet his gaze. "John was a good man. I wouldn't have married him if he wasn't."

"*Warren* was already married. When he married you he became a bigamist, remember?"

"If I ever managed to forget, you'd make sure it came back to me." She would not let him see how much the knowledge hurt. "He was a good man looking for some peace. Something drove him to that. Or someone. I'm going to find out the truth."

His finger and thumb, lifting her chin even higher, made the next swallow an accomplishment. "Warren's dead now," he said. "Give me back what's mine and leave well enough alone."

"I don't have anything that belongs to you. But I do intend to ask questions about how he died." She glanced at her laptop computer on the table she'd claimed as a desk. "And I can take as long as I like to do that. I can write anywhere, and I'm already finding plenty to write about here."

Dallas flattened his lips to his teeth. The way his attention shifted to Rae's mouth caused her stomach to flip over.

"You and your family are so accustomed to calling all the shots around here, you can't believe someone would stand up to you."

He didn't take his eyes off her mouth. She heard his breathing change. She'd heard it said a threat could drive some men to want sex. . . .

She tried to jerk her chin from his hand. He looked fleetingly at her eyes, then slowly, deliberately, settled his fingers loosely at the base of her neck.

He rubbed his thumb back and forth along her collarbone.

"You want me gone because you don't want me to talk about John. Warren. You don't want it to get out that your sister's husband had another life somewhere else—with someone else."

"Damn you," he said softly. "What do you want?"

When she attempted to put space between them, he sunk his splayed fingertips into her shoulder and shook her just enough to remind her he was so much bigger.

"Haven't you victimized us enough?" he demanded. "Victimized strangers?"

"I've never done anything to anyone who didn't do something to me first," she said. "I never even knew you were alive until you turned up in Decline and started messing up my life—and my little girl's life.

"You're doing all this to protect your sister. You don't want her to know her husband was unfaithful."

His slow grin confused her.

"I think that's admirable. Family should look out for family. But I can't sacrifice Ginny's future for your sister."

The grin became a chuckle.

"What's so all-fired funny?"

"Nothing." He sobered. "Look, it's getting late. I'll let you spend the night here. But you'd better be gone before I come back in the morning."

Unfamiliar rage heated Rae's blood. "You aren't listening to me. Or, if you are, you aren't hearing what I'm saying. I'm in Glory on a fact-finding mission. If I discover I'm wrong, I'll leave. But I've got a month-to-month lease on this place, and I don't intend to go anywhere until I'm ready. In fact, I'll be starting a project in the morning, so I hope you won't try interrupting me again." She indicated the table against the wall, the computer, and stacks of papers.

"What kind of project?"

Something, anything would do. "An exposé." Anything but that.

Another gentle, but ominously rhythmic shaking commenced. "To expose what?"

She avoided his eyes. "Oh, I'm not exactly sure."

"I thought you were a ghost writer. Isn't that what Mrs. Loder said? You write other people's stories?"

"I write novelizations of movies. Not quite the same as ghosting. But I've decided it's time for a little faction."

His eyes narrowed again, and she found she couldn't make herself avoid them anymore. "Faction?" he asked.

"Fiction based on fact," she told him, and wetted her dry lips. "Kind of like Capote's *In Cold Blood.*" Some might say she had a death wish. Rae would argue she'd lost control of her mouth.

"Real murder fictionalized," he said slowly. "Did you have a particular murder in mind?"

"A potential murder."

"Anyone I know?"

Breath became a scarce commodity. "Maybe." She bared

her teeth in what she hoped looked like a smile. "Probably not, of course. I'll let you know."

"I'm going to drive you out of Glory."

"That's not a good idea. Not unless you want your sister—"

"Don't threaten me."

"Then don't threaten me." She caught at his fingers and worked to pry them loose.

"You can't win," he told her, holding her even tighter.

"Neither can you. Unless you work with me."

Rae gave up on his fingers and pushed on his chest instead. "Let me go. You said you never hurt a woman. This is the third time—"

"Did you enjoy Warren in bed?"

Her face flamed instantly. She didn't answer.

"Oh, come on. You're a tough lady. You can tell me."

"Go away."

"You're always telling me to go away."

"It's the only thing we have in common. We want to get rid of each other."

He took hold of a fistful of the front of her T-shirt. "Maybe I've changed my mind about that."

"No you haven't. This is just your latest way of trying to frighten me off."

He used the shirt to pull her even closer. "You came here to blackmail me. You've been sneaking all over town on a fact-finding mission, and you found something you think you can use to get what you want."

Having him think so was a start. The next step was to actually get the details he thought she had. "I'm not the blackmailing type. Just a working writer with a nose for a story. If John had dropped out of my life and you'd never come sniffing around, I wouldn't be here. This is your fault, not mine, but I'm grateful. Books about sin, sex, and corruption in the South fascinate the whole country. Take a look at the bestseller lists. Could you let go of my shirt, please?"

Lines around his eyes, and beside his mouth, suggested he'd laughed a lot. The set of his features at this moment made a lie of that suggestion. "What would it take to get you to give up on this idea of yours?"

"You'd be a lot happier, a lot sooner, if you'd allow me to get what I came for. Once I do, I'll be on my way. That's a promise."

He looked down, and she wished the old T-shirt wasn't wet, and that she'd put on a bra for once.

"It is Fancy you're worried about, isn't it? And Ava?"

"Don't talk about my family like you had a right to be on a first name basis."

The words stung. "I'm not interested in your family." That was a lie. His family fascinated her horribly. "Answer my question."

"I don't have to answer anything you ask. You're not in the driver's seat."

"I'm really tired. Could we talk again tomorrow?"

"I made you an offer in Decline."

Her stomach took another flip. "You insulted me in Decline."

"You're the first woman who was ever insulted at the chance of sleeping with me."

Rae curled her lip and said, "Arrogance isn't pretty." She struggled, and immediately knew her mistake. Dallas turned her opposition into a chance to jerk her against him. He didn't release her shirt. He did use his free hand to anchor her head while he kissed her.

Rae fought. With her bare feet, she kicked his shins, but only succeeded in hurting her toes. Winding his fingers into her hair, Dallas Calhoun showed her what a kiss could be when delivered by a master.

He played with her lips, her tongue. Deeper, and deeper, he reached into her mouth, only to pull back and use a feathery touch that pulled an ache into her belly, and a sexy sting into her breasts, and damp evidence of arousal between her legs.

With his mouth he played her body the way it had never been played. The reaction he caused was the stuff of dreams she'd awakened from, ashamed at her own longings.

"I can give you what you want," he whispered into her ear while he walked her backward against the wall. "We can both win. You give me back what's mine. I give you plenty to keep you happy. And I give you what you welcomed Warren home for. And you give me what you gave him. We're both happy. What do you say, Rae?"

She turned cold. She throbbed in hidden places, but her brain began to separate from desire. "I say I'm not the kind of woman you've decided I am. And I'm not interested in starting something with a man who thinks he can keep me quiet by servicing me."

"Ugly words, lovely Rae." His voice was thick with arousal. In one smooth move, he pulled up her shirt and bent to nuzzle a breast. "Mmm. Lovely, lovely Rae. Small and so sweet."

She made to grab his hair, but spread her arms wide instead. He flipped the tip of his tongue over a nipple, flipped back and forth, and moved to the other breast. Her breath came in gasps.

"No." She caught ineffectually at his shoulder. "Stop. No."

Dallas responded by hiking the shirt over her head. He pushed his thigh between hers, grinding against her until she tossed her head. He used his leg to hold her in place while he tore his own shirt undone and pulled it free of his jeans.

His chest was lean, muscular, his belly flat. Dark hair flared wide over his nipples and arrowed to a line that disappeared into his jeans.

He took her mouth again, and Rae kissed him back. This time she was the one who opened for him, and drew him in.

And she wrapped her arms around his neck to press her seared nipples to the maddening rough hardness of his chest.

"Still say we can't make each other happy?"

Panting, her lips swollen, she gazed up into his face. With light behind him, he was all shadow and stark bone. His features were flamboyant, drawn for drama, not subtlety.

He covered her breasts and pushed them together. Slowly drawing his eyes from her face, he bent his dark head to suck her flesh.

"This is crazy," she told him. "I know what you're trying to do."

"And you're not stopping me," he said, licking circles around the rim of a nipple. "Not really. Protesting, sure. But not because you want me to stop."

His thigh came up between hers again.

"I'm going to take you to bed, Rae."

"No."

"Oh, but I am. I'm going to make sure you decide I'm offering you a great deal."

She pushed on his shoulders. "That's it. All. Let me go."

"Soon," he said. "Just go with me a little longer. Then, maybe, a little longer again. Or not, if that's what you decide. I want you to be sure is all."

For a big man he moved with frightening speed and grace. He lifted her from her feet so smoothly she settled against him without as much as a bump. His only hesitation was when he looked at the two bedroom doors.

Heat was under Rae's skin, and in her blood, and seeping through her bones. She'd lost her mind. She wanted him, or wanted the sex, and she wasn't sure which, or if she cared.

He chose the right bedroom.

The metal-framed bed all but filled the tiny space. Dallas didn't bother with a light. He dropped her on the mattress and fell on top of her, fell to kissing her bruised mouth, her grazed nipples, the straining, tingling skin on her breasts.

She tossed.

He struggled out of his shirt, unsnapped his jeans, took her hand and pushed it down until she felt the hair where the base of his penis sprang rigid.

His breath became silent sobs.

Her sobs became moans.

Their sweat mingled on each other's skin.

The hot air cooled nothing. It didn't move. It didn't enter Rae's lungs. Her chest expanded and drew in life, but only to give her strength to be with him now. Nothing else mattered.

She raised her hips and wriggled to work her shorts and panties down.

Before she got them as far as her knees, Dallas slid his fingers over her clitoris and used her own moisture to stimulate her to mindlessness.

Their voices made incoherent sounds.

Rae felt her climax shudder on the edge. She moaned in the darkness. He delved inside her, then found her swollen center again.

And she went over the edge and dived. A dark, hot, writhing place. Sensation pumped through her, sensation that deadened the mind to everything but feeling.

With her heels, she tried to rid him of the jeans that kept her from him, kept him from her.

"Wait," he breathed. "For God's sake, wait."

She heard the rustle, felt air between them as he lifted away just enough to take care of protection.

The seconds he gave her to think didn't cool her need.

Then he was easing himself inside her. The only gentle thrust he made was that first thrust.

Against her neck he murmured, "If you don't want this, tell me now."

She didn't tell him anything.

"I sure want it, Rae." He began to move. "I want it. I *want* it."

His breathing kept time with each penetration. And his

breathing quickened, and quickened. "I wanted you the first time I saw you outside the school. I wanted you in the library." *Faster.* "I wanted to lay you down between the stacks and get inside you."

Her head throbbed.

"When you walked away from me in Loder's, I wanted to see the way your ass moved naked."

Sweat burned Rae's eyes. "Do it," she cried. "Just do it."

"Tell me you want me."

"Finish."

"Tell me." He forced her against the head of the bed. It banged the wall, and banged it again. *Tell* me."

She gripped the bars with both hands and hung on.

He came. She felt the warm swell of his ejaculation, then her own answering waves.

Panting, Dallas collapsed on her, buried his face in her neck. "You're really something," he said. "Something. I knew you would be."

She couldn't find the energy to ask him what he meant.

"We're great together, Rae. Everything's going to be just fine."

Exhaustion made her eyelids heavy.

"I'll be back first thing in the morning. Then we'll work out an arrangement."

"What do you mean by that?"

"The money. And how we'll work the other." He tweaked one of her nipples, and she flinched. "This. Damn, I'd like to spend the night. I wish I didn't have to get back."

Rae grew cool, then cold. She turned her face away and wished she could be the one to get up and leave.

He slid from the bed and turned on the lamp while he pulled up his jeans and zipped them. He paused in the act of putting on his shirt to look at her. With his head tipped to one side, he studied her from head to toe. "Good things come in small packages. Isn't that what they say? They're right. You're the best, sweetheart. Absolutely the best. But I should have expected as much."

Rae ran her tongue over the dry roof of her mouth. He was the most gorgeous man she'd ever seen. That was a fact and it horrified as much as thrilled her. Handsome men were trouble, she'd always known that. John had been handsome, but in an American boy way, not in the almost saturnine manner of Dallas Calhoun.

Suddenly her nakedness embarrassed her. She slipped from the bed and found a robe. By the time she'd tied the belt, he was on his way into the other room to swing the oilskins around his shoulders.

One foot on top of the other, Rae stood in the doorway to the bedroom. She'd messed everything up.

He put on his hat, worked it low over his eyes and tipped the brim to her. "Yes, ma'am, I should have known you'd be good. Warren always knew how to pick his women."

Eight

"What if someone tells Joella we were here?" Tyson said.

Fancy pulled a pink, rubberized curtain around a tiny shower stall in the corner of what passed for a bathroom, and looked at Tyson over her shoulder. "Rather than telling her you were here with the junior whore?"

His face turned red. "Goddamn it. She isn't—"

"Do we care? No. We all know the beauty of this dump. No one tells, because everyone's got something to hide—even if it's only the fact that they were here at all." She contemplated whether or not to take off her white lace teddy before getting into the shower. "If we hang around long enough, we'll probably run into Joella. And she won't tell, either."

"Joella wouldn't come here," Tyson said through his teeth.

For all the great advance advertising, he'd gone soft on her by the time they arrived at Number Three, and couldn't get it up again. She knew he was smarting from the failure.

He'd put his shorts back on and leaned against the doorjamb looking tense enough to twang if she touched him.

"Did you hear what I said?" he asked. "Joella wouldn't come to a place like this."

"Of course not. She stays at home like a good little girl and waits for her big daddy, Tyson, to drop by." She started the water running, and decided to keep the teddy on. "Come on. The hot water will loosen you up." Fancy giggled, and reached for his hand.

"What's so damn funny?"

"The hot water will loosen you up. That's what I said. Only you're already too loose, darlin'. Maybe I should make the water cold."

He tore his hand away and made to leave the bathroom.

Fancy grabbed for his shorts and held on to the elastic at his waist.

Rather than respond, he stood where he was.

"Come on, Tyson. Don't sulk. It's so boring. You had too much booze. It happens. Come wash my back—and anything else that catches your fancy."

"I'm not in the mood."

No kidding. "Come anyway. Hot water helps me think, and we've got a lot of thinking to do. I told you something happened. It could be nothing, but I don't think so. We need to talk about it."

"You weren't in any hurry to talk when I got you out here."

"Darlin'?" When he turned toward her she said, "I was the one who got *you* out here. Then I forgot about wanting to talk. I'm just an animal, aren't I? A teasing little animal, because you make me that way. Come in the lovely water with Fancy and I'll make sure you're clean all over."

He scowled at her for so long she thought he wasn't going to cooperate. "Okay," he said at last. "But talking's what this is really about, Fancy. Hear me?"

"I hear you, Tyson. Ooh, I just love it when you're forceful."

"Can you be serious? If the answer's no, tell me, and I'll see you around when you wise up."

Other than sex, what Tyson wanted and what she wanted were so far apart they couldn't even wave at each other. But he didn't know that. Fancy's job was to keep him thinking they had a common vision—until she was sure she could cut him off without any fear of reprisal.

She pulled him closer and said, "I can be very, very serious. That's why I came looking for you, darlin', because we've got serious things to deal with." That was the truth.

"I'm ready," he said.

Fancy looked at his shorts. "I do believe you may be," she told him, but without cracking as much as a smile. "You taking those off?"

He was erect, and his cocky smile advertised that he was a relieved man ready to be masterful again. "You bet I'm taking them off," he said, and stripped naked.

Anticipation caused Fancy an involuntary wiggle of her hips, a pressing together of her thighs. "Oh, Tyson, you are something else," she said, pulling him into the metal base of the shower and closing them under the water.

Self-absorbed, as only Tyson could be, he held his penis against her belly, against the soaked, white teddy.

"Feel good?" she asked. He was so easy to manipulate.

"You know it does. That's why you kept that thing on—because you know I like the way it feels."

She knew she liked the way it felt. "Shall we talk first?" With her palms, she made circles over her nipples and sucked air through her teeth at the instant response elsewhere.

"Did you talk to Dallas?" With total concentration, Tyson pushed himself inside the high-cut leg of her teddy. "There's never going to be a better time. He's off balance right now. Did you ask him?"

Careful. "He's preoccupied. It hasn't felt right. You know I trust my instincts in these things."

He looked at her. "You're playing me for a fool, Fancy." A swift move, and he pinned her to the shower wall by her shoulders. "This is why you've been avoiding me for days, isn't it? If I get what I want—and I will get what I want—you think I'll have more power than you."

He was so right. "Not at all, lover. You and I are like this"—she held up two crossed fingers—"together, forever. You and me against the world. We're going to make the rest of them know we're in charge. We've worked for that and it's finally starting to happen. And none of it would be worth a damn to me without you at my side." The wide-eyed, adoring act came easily enough.

"None of it's going to happen if I'm not at your side." He layered himself against her. "Make sure you don't forget that. I know too much about you, and about Warren, baby. I can blow everything up in your face. One word from me, and even your loving brother won't keep you out of the cold."

Anger festered in Fancy's gut. Just a little longer. Just long enough to get what she had to have, and she'd let Tyson LaRose know who was in the cold. "You've got to be patient for just a little while longer," she told him, reaching down to unsnap the crotch of the teddy and guiding him between her legs. "First things first."

"In-house counsel for Calhoun," Tyson said, his eyelids all but shut. "That's what's going to come first."

She nodded sympathetically and started moving her hips. "I know how badly you want it, darlin'. And I want it for you. But we've got to be smart. If Dallas gets even a hint that we're—well, you know. If he thought we'd been plannin' something, he'd get suspicious, and we can't afford that."

"With me as in-house counsel I'll be able to control things for both of us."

He'd control his own plans to pull down a big, fat salary, plus finally be a really big man in Glory. And everyone would see him as someone Dallas respected. Above all, Tyson wanted to feel equal to Fancy's brother.

She sank to her knees and took Tyson's penis in her mouth. The instant jerk of his thighs made her smile. She could make him do whatever she wanted.

"I went through all those papers you brought me." He panted, and threaded his fingers through her hair. "That's why I tried to get hold of you yesterday."

She'd been otherwise engaged yesterday. "I couldn't get away."

"And you couldn't even call?"

She made noises to let him know she had more important things to think about right now.

Tyson grunted and backed against the other wall. Fancy held his hips.

Seconds, and it was all over.

Kissing her way up his body, she stood up and rested against him, wrapped her arms around him. "The papers didn't show anything, did they? Just old stuff."

"Oh, baby." With his head tipped back, he let the water stream into his face. "That's why you need me. You don't know much, do you? Are you sure you're the only one who knew about all that stuff?"

"Sure. He kept it in the basement. Behind a piece of loose Sheetrock. He didn't know I'd seen him put it there."

"It's only the tip of the iceberg, but it proves we're on the right track. That husband of yours was robbing Calhoun blind. Did you give me everything you found?"

"Every last thing." Her heart speeded up. "Those papers showed what Warren was doing?"

"Not in the amounts I'm going to find elsewhere—when I've got access to everything—but enough, yes. Big bucks. This was just one of his scams. Simple enough scam. He paid the real contractor bills. The customer paid Warren's bills. Warren's bills were usually twice the sum of the real bills. The question is, what happened to the money?"

"We're going to find it," she told him, without feeling the confidence she wanted to feel. "We're going to go to those customers and ask how they paid." She'd use him to do what she couldn't risk being involved in.

Tyson was silent.

"They'll have the canceled checks, and we can see where he banked. The bank he used that I never knew about."

He sighed. "No, we're not doing that. The one thing we can't do is add to the idea that Calhoun's in trouble. How long do you think it would take for a few of those clients to get together and start asking their own questions? Then how long would it be before they started asking for their money back?"

"I've already thought of that." And those people weren't getting anything she had coming. "But we don't have to tell them why we want to see the canceled checks, do we?"

Tyson played with her breasts, and Fancy quit concentrating. She bit his shoulder. Business could wait.

"Save that mind of yours for important things, things you can handle, like games to play with me," Tyson said, lifting her and wrapping her legs around his hips. "When it comes to business, you won't take a step without clearing it with me. You understand?"

She nodded and rubbed against him.

"Dallas has been all over this town for days. There's no reason why you can't get him alone and persuade him it's time to give me the job he promised me."

She breathed shallowly. "He didn't promise. You asked. He said he'd think about it."

"If Dallas finds out what Warren was up to, and if he finds out you knew, or suspected, what he was up to, he'll make sure you have to beg for every penny from here on. It's only going to be a matter of time, baby. There's already trouble, and he's going to track it down."

"Touch me there," she panted. "He's never going to know."

"He will if I tell him."

Fancy opened her mouth to tell him he'd never do that, when Tyson shoved himself inside her and used her hips as if she was a jockey.

It never took long enough for Fancy.

When the clamor was over, Tyson kept her where she was and braced her on the wall again. "What I'm telling you is that I, not you, will call the shots. For the two of us." He kissed her to silence. "Shut up, Fancy. We're a team. But first you've got to give me a show of faith. There's only one show of faith I want. An inside job at Calhoun. I've kept a lot of things quiet for you, put a lot on the line for you—"

"You did it for you," she told him, fighting post-coital lethargy. "You want this with me. The sex. And you want to use me to get everything else you want. But Tyson's always going to be first with Tyson."

"I love you, Fancy, you know that."

He'd never said it before. The words made her glow inside. "Divorce Joella." Sooner or later she'd make him do it, and she'd enjoy every second.

"That would be suicide. We don't need anything official between you and me now. There's plenty of time for that."

"Why would it be suicide?"

"Whatever happens, we've got to put some time between when I come on board at Calhoun and when we go public with the two of us."

"I want it now."

"Just to get back at Joella because fifteen years ago she was Miss Glory and you were only the first runner-up?"

"It wasn't that long." She tried to slap his face, but he caught her wrist.

"Knock it off," he told her. "We're playing a bigger game than that—much bigger. And you're going to do what I tell you."

At last she managed to free a hand and hit the side of his head.

Tyson pulled his lips back from his teeth. "That was really stupid, Fancy. I'm going to make you suffer for it, and you know I mean what I say."

She lowered her lashes and pretended to look nervous. "Of course you are, darlin'. You'll just have to do that because I don't learn otherwise, do I?"

"You surely don't." He pulled her from the shower without bothering to turn off the water, or even grab towels. "I'm going to punish you, Fancy. I'm going to have to hurt you just to make you remember not to make me angry again."

She kept her face down to hide her smile. This was a game they both liked to play, and never grew tired of.

Tyson sat on the edge of the round, tousled bed with its heart-shaped, plastic headboard. Little shiny specks sparkled in the plastic. The room smelled of heavy floral air freshener, and the mold it didn't quite hide.

"Here," Tyson said to Fancy, yanking her to stand beside him. "I want you to tell me you'll speak to Dallas first thing tomorrow."

She must stay focused, concentrate. "I will if I can find him."

"What does that mean?"

"Maybe nothing."

Tyson cupped one of her buttocks and squeezed. "Wouldn't you like to finish with the business talk and carry on with the fun?"

He had a point. "Honey, we may have trouble. Real big trouble. On the other hand, it could be that something useful just blew into town. The last I saw of my darlin' brother he was heading away from a chat with Lucy Gordon down at Public Records."

Tyson's face tightened. He watched her face intently and squeezed her butt like he was milking it. He said, "Go on," and she knew she'd better not fool around anymore.

"Lucy called me right after she called Dallas. I got there when he was driving away. According to Lucy, a woman came around asking questions. She talked about doing some sort of research project, and wanting to look through the files. Well, you know how Lucy is. She wouldn't think of saying no to anyone. From what I've heard, Lucy never did know how to say no. That's how come she's got three kids and was never—"

"I don't give a shit about Lucy Gordon's love life. What files? What's this to do with us?"

Fancy wound a piece of her hair around a finger. "Lucy said it was files about us. About the Calhouns."

He chewed his lip. "Maybe she's some high school kid doing a paper on the city fathers or something."

"According to Lucy, she's somewhere in her twenties or so. Pretty, if you like little brunettes with big green eyes that make them look hungry. And when Lucy went back to see what she'd been looking at, it was all stuff about births and marriages in the family. Who's related to who. But she took a few things away with her."

"With all the dusty old crap in that place, how would Lucy Gordon know?"

"She knows where everything is." Fancy considered. "Actually, she doesn't, only the stuff she's interested in herself. Seems she'd been checking out Warren because of all the fuss. Left the folder on top. She decided she'd better go back and tidy up, only the folder had been put back in the cabinet and some things were missing—all about Warren and me. Our marriage. His death. That kind of thing."

Tyson grew very still. "So why is this supposed to worry us?"

"Because it worries Dallas. Lucy called me because she's such a gossip. You know that. And she's always doted on Dallas, so she thought she'd make points by telling him about this woman. But she got more than she bargained for from him. She said she thought I ought to know that when she got through telling him, he got real mad. He called your dad over at the *Glory Speaker*, and Carter said he'd check to see if this Rae Maddy had been by there asking questions."

"Rae Maddy?" Tyson frowned. "That's her name?"

"Seems. Anyway, this is what Lucy heard Dallas say. He said, 'I told her to stay away. Goddamn Warren, and his goddamn woman.' Then he left. That was early this evening."

"So you think—"

"I think it's the woman I was sure he had somewhere," Fancy said, cutting him off. "I told you it didn't make sense how he stopped catting around some years back, and started going out of town. And staying gone several days. Bein' more peaceful, and treating me like he didn't care what I thought one way or the other anymore. Like I couldn't get to him anymore."

"You think he had someone somewhere else? Long-term? Permanent type?"

"I think we'd better find out if this woman was someone he knew."

"What kind of project is she supposed to be working on?"

"I told you," Fancy said, beginning to want what he'd promised her. "Lucy doesn't know."

"And you think Dallas went to find her?"

"That's what Lucy thought. She knew where she was—in the river cabin at the old Werther place. I guess it's the Parker place now. Renting it. Lucy heard that from Linsay May. Can you believe that? Linsay May in Calhouns' own rental department. Apparently the cabin was always for rent, but no one wanted it till this Rae person."

Still with a faraway but angry look in his eyes, Tyson suddenly tipped Fancy, face-first, across his knees. She wailed, the way she knew how to wail when they played this game.

Fancy wailed, and pretended to struggle.

Tyson held her head down and swung one leg over both of hers, anchoring her with her rear exposed in the air.

"I'm going to have to talk to Linsay May," he said, slapping Fancy hard enough to make her shriek. "Maybe I'll have to notice how sexy she really is and take her out. She's been trying to get my attention long enough."

"Don't you do that." Blood pumped in her temples, and her bottom stung. "I'll ask her questions."

"You'll stay away. I've got ways of getting what I want. I don't need directions to the Werther cabin. What I want is information about this Rae Maddy. She'd have to give a fair amount of background to get the rental. Linsay May's a stickler for that kind of stuff. Everyone in town knows she is."

He dealt Fancy another slap, and another.

"Stop it, Tyson," she whined. "You're really hurting me."

"Then I may have to go pay Ms. Maddy a visit. Just to take a look."

"Tyson!"

"If she was Warren's piece, she could be planning to cause some trouble. We can't let that happen."

The knee beneath her ground into her stomach. The spanking wasn't fun this time, not when he hit her so hard. "That's a good idea," she told him. "It's probably nothing. If she did know him, she'll just need talking to. She'll get lost quick enough."

He changed tactics. Rather than strike her, he stroked her sore skin and ran his fingers along the cleft in her bottom. "If she knew Warren, and she's here because she thinks that's good for something, she's making a big mistake. I'll make sure she begs to leave town."

Fancy tried to get up. He had no trouble keeping her where she was, or using a finger where he knew it would count the most.

"If this Rae Maddy's got any information that could hurt us," Tyson said, his voice sounding funny, disconnected. "Well, if she does, begging won't help even if she does want to leave."

Even while Fancy bucked, she felt scared by what Tyson said. "Darlin'," she said, breathing hard. "We've got to be real careful."

"I've worked too hard to get what's coming to me. No fool woman's getting in my way now."

She felt sick. "Tyson, you wouldn't do anything . . . nasty?"

A second of his fingers joined the first. "Nasty?" He laughed, then laughed louder when Fancy helped make things easier for him. "Nothing nasty. I'd simply escort her out of town, and make sure she never had a mind to come back."

Nine

The sun came up as if the previous night's storm had been a mirage.

Apart from an hour or so with his head on his desk, Dallas hadn't slept. With Wolf collapsed, and snoring, on a rock behind him, he sat on the Sweet Bay side of the river looking across at the Parker place, and the cabin. He could see Rae's Jeep in the detached carport, exactly where it had been the night before.

He hadn't been down here in years, not since he'd been a teenager and still into exploring the outer reaches of the estate.

The thought of Rae in the grounded boat made him smile. At this time of year, and with a little care, you could walk from one side of the river to the other. The deep red color of the water fooled strangers into thinking there was some depth, but it often wasn't more than a couple of feet.

Rae had been doing wheelies virtually on the keel.

Sunlight hit the window in the main room of the cabin.

He felt lousy.

His brain wanted to make excuses for his behavior with Rae, to remind him that she hadn't fought to the death to avoid having sex with him. If she had held out, it would never have happened. But she hadn't held out. In the end she'd been as eager as he was.

He still felt lousy about it.

He also felt great about it. Oh, shit, this was a mess. She

was really something, and not just in bed. She got to him in a way he'd never experienced—made him like the idea that she was within reach.

Wolf snuffled, and chomped, and dragged groggily to his feet.

"You sit, Wolf," Dallas said. "Down, Wolf. Stay, Wolf. I'm going for a morning paddle." He didn't intend to apologize exactly, but trying to put things on a slightly less impossible basis couldn't hurt anything.

And he wanted to see her again, to talk to her again—now.

He pulled off his boots and socks, and rolled up his jeans.

His first steps into the silty water brought yelps to his lips. "Damn cold! Wahoo, I forgot how damn cold."

Ironic that she'd rented the river cabin when she couldn't have any idea about Warren's connection to the Parker place. At least, he doubted she did. Linsay May told him she'd been the one to suggest it.

Willows reached far out over the water, and he walked through their reflections. Splashing sounds behind him let him know just how short Wolf's memory was. Dallas ignored the dog and waded on.

He knew that funds belonging to Calhoun had been diverted to Maddy and Associates, at a PO Box address in Savannah. When Dallas had visited the post office in question and tried to use the key he'd found among Warren's possessions, he'd been told the box was closed.

Figured.

The trick was to delve deep enough for real facts and figures, without delving so deep he spread the damage already done. Warren had been smarter than Dallas had credited. A big mistake on Dallas's part.

He saw Rae before she saw him.

Wolf was a second behind Dallas and took off, showering red water all over his boss. "Heel, Wolf!" Dallas yelled, to no avail. "Wolf! Heel, you useless mutt. Get back here."

The dog bounded on, bounded up the slope to the cabin and accosted Rae as she came down the steps.

Dallas noted with approval that rather than scream, or wave her arms, or do any of the things she might be expected to do, she stood still with her arms at her sides and stared straight into the dog's face.

Dallas ran, cursing each time a foot slipped into a little deeper water. By the time he hit the opposite bank he was wet to his thighs.

"Don't move," he shouted, dashing toward Rae. "He rarely bites. Just keep absolutely still. Sit, Wolf! Down, Wolf! Stay, Wolf!"

He arrived beside Wolf in time to watch Rae scratch the pesky animal between his ears and admire the dog's offering: Rae's muddy shoe of the previous night.

Rae took the shoe.

Wolf raised a paw and waited until she took it in her hand for a friendly shake.

Dallas crossed his arms and let out a tuneless whistle.

"Nice dog," Rae said, still scratching. "Hates women, huh?"

"He's sneaky. One wrong move and he'll show his mean side. He's well-trained, though. I took him through obedience school. Twice."

"Uh huh." Rae shook Wolf's huge paw. "Well, boy, I'd like to stay and play, but I've got work to do."

"What work?" Dallas asked.

She glanced at him, and immediately away, and swung a purse from her shoulder.

Wolf retrieved the shoe Rae had dropped again and sat at her feet, looking up with adoration in his brown eyes.

"What work, Rae?" Dallas prompted.

Her cheeks had turned pink. She didn't respond, but made as if she intended to walk away.

"I wish I wasn't attracted to you." He set his teeth together. Of all the damn fool things to blurt out.

The pink in her face took on a brighter hue. Today she wore a soft green dress the same dark color as her eyes, and sandals. Her hair was wound up and pinned into a style that made her look a little older. Almost the twenty-seven she really was.

"Hey"—he shoved his hands into the pockets of his jeans—"what I really meant to say was I wish I hadn't allowed sexual attraction to get out of hand." Nice going.

She pulled the purse open and dug around inside. Her cheeks had reached the glowing stage.

"Are you going to talk to me?"

Rae produced car keys.

"I'm trying to have a conversation here."

She looked toward her Jeep.

"So, what kind of work? More poking around in my family's business?"

"Not today." At last she met his eyes directly. "At least not this morning. Later in the day, maybe."

"You're baiting me."

"I'm answering your question—although there's no reason I have to."

"There's every reason you have to."

She swung the bag back over her shoulder. "I'm not starting that with you again. If you've got hard evidence of wrongdoing to put in front of me, do it. Otherwise stop threatening me. I'm not afraid of you, Dallas Calhoun."

Once again her eyelids flickered down.

"What happened last night"—he touched her shoulder and hated that she flinched—"it wasn't planned. I intended to talk to you. Make you understand."

"You intended to force me to do what you wanted me to do. To go away. To give you something I don't have, then go away."

"Did you think any more about what I suggested?"

The thick lashes rose sharply, and her eyes narrowed. "I'm probably misunderstanding you. You aren't talking about . . .

Yes, you are. But I guess I can't blame you, can I? After what we did, I can't expect you to think I'm not an easy lay."

"Don't. Don't say that." It shouldn't matter, but it did.

The last thing he expected her to do was run back into the cabin, which was what she did.

Wolf followed, scratched the door, and whined. He carried the old shoe in his mouth.

With a sensation that he shared the dog's feelings, Dallas went to the door and stood with his head bowed, trying to decide what to do next.

"Rae?" He gave the door a gentle push and it swung open.

She was seated in the saggy, chintz armchair that faced the door, with her feet pulled up beneath her. "We have to deal with this," she said. "Then you have to let me get on with my life."

"Yeah."

"I'm embarrassed."

He nodded. "Sex can do that, I guess. It makes a person feel vulnerable."

"I haven't—" She shook her head. "It shouldn't have happened."

"Nope."

"I should have stopped you."

"Wouldn't have been easy."

"You would have stopped if I'd been firm about it."

He thought he would.

"Wouldn't you?"

It wasn't gentlemanly to tell a lady it was all her doing that they had made love.

"Wouldn't you?" she insisted.

Dallas crossed the room and sank into the matching chair beside hers. He stretched out his legs and looked straight ahead—at the computer he'd seen last night, and a stack of papers.

"Dallas—"

"I was awful pushy."

"Yes, you were."

So much for the gentlemanly approach. "But I'd probably have stopped if you'd made it real clear you wanted me to."

"You think I'm easy."

"No." He didn't think she had many scruples about using sex to get what she wanted.

"Yes, you do. We . . . it wasn't, well, it wasn't, was it?"

"Wasn't what?"

From the corner of his eye, Dallas saw her swing her legs around to sit on them in the opposite direction.

He repeated, "Wasn't what?"

"Heck. It wasn't . . . wishy-washy?"

Wishy-washy? "As in, half-hearted?"

"Sort of. Not just . . . cool, maybe?"

"Not kind of a wham-bam-thank-you-ma'am effort, you mean?"

"That's a guy thing."

"What's a guy thing?"

"That kind of disgusting expression."

He whistled and said, "You're the one who started the discussion. You were having trouble coming up with a description for the way we made love. I was trying to help you out."

"With wham-bam-thank-you-ma'am?"

"Hey, I never pretended to have a way with words."

"You don't."

This was going nowhere. "You were great."

She moaned, and when he turned to her, she covered her face.

"What did I say? That was a compliment. I was complimenting you on what a great . . . on how great you are in the . . . I've never had a better piece of . . . Ah, hell, I'm making a hash of this. I'll make love to you anytime you feel like it."

"That's awful," she whispered. "I'm not that kind of woman."

He laughed, regretted it, but knew when he was whipped. "We're a couple of walking—sitting—cliches."

"I'm embarrassed."

"You already said that."

"I'm not the kind of woman who goes to bed with strangers."

He laughed again. "Well, we're not strangers anymore."

Her head jerked around. "What does that mean?"

A little heat crept over his own face. He shrugged. "Whatever."

"No." She put her feet firmly on the floor. "No. You meant something by that."

"Okay. I meant that since we're not strangers anymore, and since we were so good together, if you wanted to make sure it wasn't just a fluke the first time, we could try again."

"You are really disgusting."

"I think you said that before, too."

Sun through the window shone on her hair, lighting blue sparks, and into her eyes, turning them clear green. "You're used to getting your way with women, aren't you?" she said.

"Yep." He couldn't seem to stop himself from saying the first thing that came into his head. "I'm not into chasing around with a lot of women."

"Just a few?"

"Yeah. I mean, no. I wish we'd met under different circumstances." About now, if he didn't know he'd take her apart to get what he had to have, he'd expect to see his heart bleeding all over his sleeve. "But we didn't. Last night was the result of a lot of stress on both sides."

She sat straighter. "Exactly. Just one of those silly things."

"I didn't think it was so silly," Dallas protested. "I thought it was damn good."

"Good for something that didn't mean anything. Something we used to get a little stress out." Wolf had positioned himself at her knee, and she rubbed his head absently. "There was passion in it."

"A lot of passion." Hell, he was getting hard. "You're a passionate woman, Rae."

"You're a passionate man."

"We're both passionate."

"Together," she said.

But for the sound of Wolf rhythmically licking Rae's hand, there was silence.

"Doesn't come along often, y'know."

Rae used a foot to scratch Wolf's belly. "What doesn't come along often?"

"Two people who make the kind of music we made last night."

She sighed loudly.

"A thing like that is precious. It ought to be treated with respect. With reverence. It's kind of the result of fate. Fate brings two people together who just—fit. We fit, Rae. Your parts, and my parts. They fit. Hell, I don't mean parts. That's a lousy word for . . . Hell, yes, I guess I do mean parts. But there has to be a better word for the way my—it just, well—"

"Quit while you're not ahead."

"I want to make love to you again." He closed his mouth, appalled at the baldness of what he'd just said, and waited for her to leap up and hit him. She was good at hitting him.

Silence settled again.

Dust motes swirled in amber beams through gold-toned brow panes at the top of the window. The same soft beams warmed the old, rough pine paneling on the wall.

River rock faced the floor-to-ceiling fireplace. A hodge-podge of mostly paperback books crowded shelves on either side. Dallas peered around, noting for the first time that the Parkers must have left the place pretty much as it was.

"Why are you called Dallas?"

"Why are you called Rae?"

"I asked first."

"I was conceived when my folks were on a trip to Dallas."

"You're kidding."

He considered. "Yeah. Probably. Maybe not, though. That's what my daddy always told me."

"And your mother."

"Ava doesn't talk about things like that."

Once more, the silence.

"This is very strange," Rae said. "You know that, don't you?"

"It's called stalemate. We don't know where to go from here. But we do know we want to go back to bed."

"You've got a one-track mind."

She was right about that, he thought. "It's your fault. If you weren't the sexiest woman on two feet—and off two feet—I wouldn't have stayed awake thinking about it all night. Ma'am, I just want back inside you." *Hell,* he must be tired.

"You can't talk like that."

"I just did."

"You'd think the only thing on your mind was sex."

"Right now, it is."

"I'm not that—"

"Kind of girl. I know. I'm sorry, I think." He'd rehearsed what he'd say the next time he met her. So far he hadn't used a word of the prepared text. "I wish you hadn't been involved with Warren Niel." That hadn't been part of the text either.

"He was my husband."

"No, he—"

"I thought he was." Her voice grew softer. "You see only whatever problems you've got. I'm going to ask you to think about mine. Just for a while."

He looked at her and waited.

"You can believe me, or not. You probably won't. I met a man who said his name was John Maddy. A man much older than me, much more sophisticated. In retrospect I should have wondered more about how little I knew about him. Almost nothing, really. And the fact that he avoided everybody in Decline. Now it's become clear he didn't want to run the risk of being recognized, but how could I ever have imagined a fantastic situation like this?

"We didn't fall in love," she continued. "We liked each other, though, and we both needed someone to rely on. Someone we knew would be true to us. I was true to John because he was kind to me."

He prepared to say that Warren hadn't been true to her, but changed his mind. Hell, he didn't know who Warren had slept with in the past few years. From the stories circulating about Fancy, she'd apparently been finding at least some of her entertainment elsewhere.

"Most of all, John—Warren—was important to me because he loved Ginny. And he did love her. The last thing . . ."

Dallas swiveled toward her. "Go on. The last thing?"

"Nothing. I don't care about myself. I do care about Ginny. For her I'll go through whatever I have to go through to protect a good future."

"Including using good sex as a weapon."

"Damn you." She was on her feet and coming for him. "Damn you, Dallas Calhoun."

He lunged, caught her by the waist, and held her far enough away to make her flailing arms harmless. "Calm down. That was a low blow."

"You are wrong. *Wrong.*"

"In other words, you're as attracted to me as I am to you?"

"Yes. No. Yes, maybe I am. You're a handsome man. Very handsome. But I should know better. Handsome men are always trouble."

"Warren wasn't ugly."

"No. But he wasn't in your league." Rae blushed and scowled.

Dallas smiled widely and said, "Why, thank you, ma'am. You're pretty interesting yourself."

"Thanks."

"That's a compliment. You aren't one of those pretty little things, but—"

"Quit while you're ahead this time."

"Yes, ma'am. But you are interesting. Fay. I think that's the word. And you have a great little body. Man, what you can do with that body."

"I can't believe I'm having this conversation."

He grinned even more broadly. "Good for you. Dirty talk broadens—"

"I do not talk dirty. You've got a great body, too. And you use it real well," she said, hating to admit it.

He considered that. "Like I said, we fit well. Where you dip, I jut. And the proportions are perfect."

"You're so poetic."

"I'm blunt."

"And strange. You say strange, inappropriate things. Juts and dips. Awful."

"I don't think I've ever tried to put these things into words before, so I'm feeling my way. But it strikes me that since you admit that you and Warren conspired to defraud Calhoun, we might as well get all this over with quickly."

She worked the muscles in her jaw before saying, "I've never conspired with anyone to do anything. I've admitted I'm now sure John was Warren Niel and that he's dead. For the rest, I'm going to have to do a lot of investigating to find out what's behind your accusations against him—and me."

One way or another—and it might be nasty—but he had to get her on his side. The thought was revolutionary. Get her on his side. Then she'd be more likely to give something away, or to actually agree to give up. "We got off to a bad start, Rae. And then things went from bad to worse. In a way. Not in all ways."

Her muscles relaxed, and gingerly, he let her go. "I accept your apology," she said.

"For what?" He frowned at her. "I didn't apologize."

"Yes you did. Sort of. If you hadn't come here last night—

pushing me around—it never would have happened. Now I keep wondering if you're thinking about it. And thinking about me being naked."

"I am."

She blushed so well. "I am, too. It's not dignified."

Dallas let that pass, trying to pull his thoughts back to his original purpose. "You were involved with Warren for financial gain."

She flung away, and back again. "You're unbelievable. You don't quit. I didn't get involved with Warren for financial gain. I didn't know what he did or didn't have. And he didn't have much at all when we first met. It wasn't until later that he did so well with his business."

"Oh, how true," Dallas said softly. His salvation or his ruin were wrapped up in this woman. "What if I promised not to prosecute? If I did what I've already told you I'd do and made provisions for you—and Ginny, of course."

"Not good enough."

"Naturally I'll sacrifice my body, too."

She met his eyes and smiled slowly. "You're incorrigible."

"And I'm glad you've got a sense of humor." When she smiled, she was almost beautiful. She was irresistible either way. "But I'm not joking. For a second there I thought I was, but I was lying to myself. I want you."

"You don't know me."

"I don't care." God help him, but it was true. "What I should say is that I'd like to know you a whole lot better, and I think we can come to a compromise that would work for both of us. Why not? The only people who know about Warren's other life are you and me."

Rae kicked off her sandals and pulled the pins from her hair. A rubber band on her left wrist soon secured a tail at her nape.

Dallas watched her with interest, but not with patience. "Are you comfortable now?"

She began to pace. "I've got to make sure we understand

each other. No—" pointing at him, she paused. *"You've* got to understand me. I will not be intimidated. What's mine is mine and I'm not giving it up. I can't. I've got a child, and she means everything to me."

"Oh, come on, Rae. Don't try to make me believe this is all entirely selfless." Despite her protestations of innocence, he could not bring himself to believe she had been ignorant of all Warren's schemes.

"I don't really care what you think of me." She turned up her palms. "But I'm giving you notice. I will be in Glory for the foreseeable future. I intend to find out more about John's life—and his death."

"His plane—"

"I know the story. What I don't know are the details. And I'm going to discover what it is I'm supposed to have that doesn't belong to me."

"You already know."

"No, Dallas, I don't know. Why don't you tell me? In detail?"

Hair on his neck prickled. The only time that ever happened was when instinct told him he was in danger. "When Warren sidetracked listings from Calhoun Properties, terminated the agreements with us, and then sold those properties privately, that wasn't legal. He was an employee of Calhoun Properties, but he arranged to pocket huge sales commissions that belonged to the company."

Her pacing ceased. "I don't have any idea what you're talking about."

Any backing off could only weaken his position. "If you don't have the money, prove it."

"I'd like you to leave now."

"I just bet you would." He glanced out the window and toward Sweet Bay. Fancy was unpredictable and dangerous, but his mother was unstable. She'd never cope with the kind of embarrassment Rae threatened to become. He gathered his considerable talent for persuasion and said, "Could we be reasonable about all this? I'm going to be absolutely honest with you. I've got a lot to deal with right now, but I'm not interested in making things difficult for you. If you'd go back to your place in Decline, I swear I'll keep everything as straightforward as possible."

"I was right. You are afraid of me."

He stared at her, but she didn't look away.

"You're afraid of gossip. It would humiliate your family if people found out Warren married me when he was already married to your sister. That's what all this is about, isn't it? You learned about me. Then you decided you'd better make sure I never showed up here, only what you did backfired on you because I don't frighten easily."

She didn't frighten easily, and she intended to take him for everything she could get. "It won't work," he told her. "You aren't going to blackmail me."

"No, I'm not. But I'm going to get to the bottom of whatever it is that smells so bad about all this."

"Rae—"

"Please, I know you're angry. You're used to having your way. Not this time. Trust me to think before I act. And you do the same. In the meantime, this is going to be a great place to write the novel I've been putting off for years."

Write a novel? This was becoming more bizarre by the second—if that was possible. "You're going to write a novel? Here? At this particular time?"

"I thought I already mentioned I thought I would."

"Faction. Right." There was not going to be any easy way to get rid of her. In fact, she wasn't going to leave at all as long as he tried to insist she did. "I can see how this might be a good place to do a thing like that. Peaceful. What about your daughter?"

"Decline isn't as far away as you said it was. I can be there in under two hours. And I've decided I'll bring Ginny here for weekends."

Damn, she was planning the rest of her life here. He nodded seriously. "Kids don't mind isolation for short periods."

"I'm glad you're getting used to the idea."

"Why not? Hey, Wolf, we'd better get out of here and go home for breakfast." Nonchalance cost him dearly. "I'm the only one who knows anything about you. Oh, sure, Linsay May at the rental office knows you're here—and Lucy Gordon at Public Records. But they don't have any idea that you and Warren—well, that you were together."

The sound of a roaring engine caught his attention. A vehicle drew up beside the cabin. He and Rae looked at each other. "Are you expecting someone?" he asked, and when she didn't answer, he said, "anyway, like I just said, no one else knows about you and Warren, right?"

"That's true. And it's really important to you that they don't."

It wasn't easy to ignore the implied threat. "I won't deny that." The sight of Tyson LaRose approaching the cabin panicked him. "We'll finish this later. For now we'll leave it that as long as no one else gets wind of your association with Warren, I'm prepared to reach a compromise."

Tyson knocked on the door.

When Rae made no attempt to respond, Dallas let the other man in. "Good morning." Later he'd have questions about what Tyson thought he was doing here. For now, the less said in front of Rae, the better.

"Mornin'," Tyson said. He was his usual smoothly handsome, well-dressed self. "Didn't see your truck."

"I walked," Dallas said without looking down at his bare feet or damp jeans.

Tyson looked, but made no comment. Instead he turned the full wattage of his sharp brown eyes on Rae. "I understand you've been asking questions all over town."

She sat down again and crossed her ankles.

"We don't take kindly to that sort of thing here. I'm not

giving you any kind of official warning. Not at this point. But—"

"Tyson," Dallas said. "Can we talk privately?"

"Surely. I won't be a moment with this. Ms. Maddy, I'm a lawyer. I represent Mrs. Fancy Calhoun Niel. Now, we may all discover we understand each other and can go on our way. Peacefully. On the other hand, if you should want to talk about Mrs. Niel's deceased husband, Warren, well that would be another matter."

Dallas closed his eyes.

"Well," Rae said softly. "So much for compromise."

Ten

"Remember me, Ms. Maddy?"

Rae glanced up from her notebook and iced tea, into the sharp, but pleasant features of Linsay May Dale from the rental office where she'd signed a lease for the Parker river cabin.

"Of course I remember you," Rae said, smiling despite the knowledge that it was from Linsay May telling Lucy that Dallas found out her own whereabouts in Glory. "How are you?"

"The question is, how are you?" Linsay May asked seriously, keeping her voice low, and looking furtively around the small, cozy café that was part of Buzzley's Fine Foods on the corner of Hickory and Main. "We heard—that is, Lucy and I heard about how the Calhouns are all over you like kudzu on a magnolia tree. May I sit down? Or would that be an imposition?"

Rae smelled a potential ally and widened her smile. "I insist you do sit down. What'll you have? Some tea?" Lunch time had already passed. She signaled to the balding man who by now had surely worn holes in the counter he'd repeatedly wiped while he watched her. "Another tea, please, sir."

"And a plate of those darlin' little cakes, too, Buzz. And maybe a fried egg sandwich, if it wouldn't be too much to ask."

Buzz grunted, served the tea and a huge plate of delicately

sized confections in record time, and returned to the grill behind the counter.

Linsay May instantly popped a pink-iced morsel into her mouth and rolled her eyes with apparent bliss. "These are the best. I get peckish about now," she said around the food. Then she dropped her voice again. "You've got to learn who your friends are in this town. And who to watch out for. The Calhouns own the place, although there's some talk going around about them. Chat that they may have money troubles. Never heard that happen before. Carter LaRose is important because of the paper, but there's no real money there. Melvira—his wife—she walked out on him a couple of years back. Tyson LaRose is their son. Only kid, but he doesn't get along well with his daddy, or so they say. He's a dish, but you've got to watch that one. His wife, that's Joella, isn't all bad; but I guess you'd say she's disappointed, and that can make her mean, too. Everyone knows everyone else in Glory. And everything about them. What they don't know, they make up."

Rae had already categorized Tyson as a pompous ass, and a nuisance. Apart from Dallas, the others were only names and the occasional photograph to her. Fascinated by Linsay May's litany, she wiggled her pen. She didn't know whether or not to take notes.

"Write down anything you like," Linsay May said as if she'd heard Rae's thoughts. "I guess I'm rushing in where angels, and so forth, but Lucy and I have decided you're a kindred spirit. Are you? Or are we wrong?" A chocolate ball covered with chocolate sprinkles disappeared through Linsay May's small, bright red lips.

"Kindred to what?" Rae asked, praying she wouldn't turn off this faucet dripping with information.

"Well." A gulp disposed of the chocolate before a lemon bar followed. "Would you like a cake?"

When Rae shook her head, Linsay May moved aside her dessert plate and put the serving plate squarely in front of her. If she weighed more than a hundred and ten pounds, Rae would be surprised, and the woman wasn't short.

"The way Lucy and I have it figured, since we've suffered at the hands of men, men in this town in particular, and since you seem like a very smart woman who may have suffered, too, maybe we should band together to help each other."

"With what?"

"Oh, support. Justice. *Revenge*. Anythin' we could accomplish would be an improvement."

"If you feel so strongly, why haven't you done anything about it before now?"

"The truth?"

Buzz's approach silenced Linsay May, who thanked him for the slab of a fried sandwich with egg whites spilling from all sides. Her compliments sent him away glowing.

"The truth is that until you came into town Lucy and I never talked about what we've been through. Each of us thought we were alone in all this. Then there was you coming in and renting the river cabin. And you went to Public Records to look stuff up on the Calhouns, and so on. And Lucy did what she's got to do, which is let Dallas know if anyone wants to know about the family." A deep frown drew Linsay May's fine, black brows together. "I'm not sure she would have done that if we'd talked first. But with Dallas callin' Carter at the *Speaker,* and someone telling Tyson—he's a lawyer in town and thinks he's God's gift to women—well, with all that goin' on, Lucy and I got to talkin' and one thing led to another and we opened our hearts to each other."

"I see," Rae said. She didn't.

"Lucy saw you here and called me. She's going to come over just as soon as she can."

Rae nodded politely.

"We figure you're here in Glory to get back for whatever Warren Niel did to you, and Dallas is going to try to shut you up."

Close. "How do you know I was acquainted with Warren?"

"Everybody knows," Linsay May said, all sunny confidence. "That's the way it is in Glory. Everybody but Ava and Fancy—that's Dallas's mama and sister. I doubt they know." She lowered her eyes. "I guess I shouldn't mention Fancy, her being Warren's wife. Used to be, that is."

Rae waved a hand to indicate an indifference she didn't feel.

"Anyway," Linsay May continued. "If Dallas has his way, he'll keep them wrapped up in that house of theirs and try to deal with you before they find out a thing."

"They're bound to find out eventually."

"Oh, they'll find out. Jean Nunn and Clara Bolling, and the rest of the club group, will make sure of that, and enjoy every minute. But we know Dallas will try anything to make sure that happens after the fact. When you're gone."

"Only I'm not going," Rae said.

"You're not?" Linsay May hailed Lucy Gordon as she walked through the door. "Over here, Lucy."

Plump, with frosted hair and hazel eyes that would undoubtedly be lovely without her glasses, Lucy came hesitantly to the table and slid into a chair. "Maybe we've acted hastily, Linsay May," she said.

The real estate clerk wrinkled her nose at Rae. "See what I mean. We've been cowed for so long, it's hard to stand up for ourselves, but we're going to now. Don't you worry about a thing, Lucy. Now we've found out about each other, and we have Rae, we're going to be unstoppable. We're too young to throw in the towel on a meaningful life yet. Lucy's thirty-eight," she announced. "And I'm thirty-six. And we've both got a few good miles left in us. Trouble is, we're emotionally wounded. Isn't that what I told you, Lucy? Emotionally wounded by powerful men who took advantage of us. Now we're fighting back and makin' this town sit up and take notice. We're goin' to show we're worth having, and some

good men are goin' to want us. You wait and see if they
don't.

"Lucy could shake up that prissy Jean Nunn, I can tell
you. That husband of hers wasn't always in a wheelchair.
And even that didn't slow down more'n his legs for a long
time. Didn't mean other parts weren't still wigglin'."

Lucy tried to shrink in her chair. "Don't shout, Linsay
May."

"The main thing is we got to get behind Rae, here, Lucy,"
Linsay May whispered hoarsely. "Even if we don't do a
whole lot for ourselves, we can't let her try to take on the
muscle in this town on her own. She's going to find it hard
to get any information. You know that. Unless we give it to
her."

Even while Rae shied away from forming a bond with the
two women, she was excited at the prospect of gaining some
useful insights. Then there was always the other approach to
take. "I'm a writer," she told them, praying they wouldn't
clam up. "What I'm interested in doing is writing a story
about the way society really operates in a town like Glory."

Lucy raised her round shoulders to her ears, and her eyes
grew even larger behind her glasses.

Linsay May grinned, and glowed, and giggled. "It's wonderful. It's the best. The dirt on Glory. That's what Rae
means. Whooee. And let me tell you it's the kind of dirt you
don't want under your fingernails. Lucy, can you imagine?"

"Yes," Lucy said. "I'll lose my job."

"No, you won't," Linsay May insisted. "You won't because they won't dare do anything to you for fear it'll make
them look even worse than they already will in Rae's book.
Right, Rae?"

"Possibly." A woman peered around the end of a grocery
lane. The same woman had already peered twice before, and
stared at the trio in the cafe. "I think we'd better arrange a
meeting somewhere else. At another time. We're being
watched."

"Ooh." Lucy clapped her hands to flaming cheeks. "Who is it?"

"That was Joella LaRose," her companion said shortly. "Like I said, she's okay. I expect she'd just like to meet you because Warren was her brother. The other two women work at Calhoun. In accounting. The bald man's Guthrie, the funeral director. He's Glory's coroner, too. The dark one's from the *Speaker*. He's Carter LaRose's right-hand man. Another mean one."

Aghast, Rae stared around and saw what she hadn't noticed before, a procession of customers with empty carts, trailing around the store at measured distances from each other. A display of toilet rolls gave a particularly advantageous view of the café, and each shopper seemed repeatedly drawn to admire the artful, pink pyramid.

Rae's stomach rose, and made a sharp turn. Then she got mad. "My daughter's coming to spend the weekend. She'll be going back early on Sunday afternoon. Why don't the two of you come down for a visit after she's gone."

"You've got a daughter?" Linsay May's piercing eyes sought out Lucy's. "How old is she?"

"She's ten," Rae said, smiling a little. "She isn't Warren—wasn't Warren's child."

Linsay May pointed at her. "No, but you just admitted there was something more than pinochle games between you and Warren Niel." She got up and Lucy followed. "We'll be down on Sunday. I'll bring whatever I think might be useful for your book."

"There's plenty that'll be useful," Lucy said. "And you were right, Linsay May, they can't do a thing about it if we want to talk to Rae."

"Sunday, then," Rae said, uncertain she wasn't making a terrible mistake.

Linsay May gobbled what remained of her fried egg sandwich and put money on the table. "Sunday. It'll be like old times going to the river cabin."

Before Rae could question the comment, the two women hurried from the shop.

She got up, paid her bill, and took a grocery cart. So far she'd bought only what she could get at the convenience store near the gas station. The idea of buying real food in decent quantities seemed almost exotic. With Ginny coming, and Buelah, who would drive her up, a bag of stale bagels, graham crackers, and peanut butter couldn't continue to be the only items in the pantry.

Rae always enjoyed grocery shopping, especially in a store like Buzzley's where the variety was wide, and of best quality.

She also wanted a closer look at all the interested parties currently present.

Evidently Buzz was the son of the elderly owners, both of whom presided over the rest of the store. The senior Buzzleys, both squat and red-faced, stood shoulder-to-shoulder behind the cash register. They eyed Rae, then looked pointedly away. Evidently they weren't into courting fresh custom.

Rae took careful note of the people Linsay May had pointed out. Joella LaRose classified as gorgeous. Tall, with thick, honey blond hair curling about her shoulders, she had wide blue eyes and soft, regular features. She was that unusual phenomenon, a cheerleader type improved by age. She had a show-stopper figure.

The rest of the curious were unremarkable.

The entire group displayed common behavior when each changed his or her mind about needing to shop, and replaced empty carts before leaving.

If Rae were feeling more charitable, she'd pity their shallow obviousness.

Rae wasn't feeling at all charitable.

Eventually she took her purchases to the cash register and unloaded them before the silent Buzzleys. Each time she glanced at them, they glanced at each other. "How do I go about setting up an account?" she asked pleasantly.

After a lengthy pause Mrs. Buzzley said, "We don't do much of that. Only for longtime customers."

"I see," Rae said, keeping her voice, and her smile, even. "I had it in mind to become a longtime customer."

That brought no comment at all.

When everything she'd selected was heaped on the counter, she busied herself with her purse, found her checkbook and pen, and looked to the Buzzleys again. Neither had made any move to start ringing.

"I am in a bit of a hurry," Rae said at last.

"We don't take out-of-town checks," Mr. Buzzley announced.

Rae regarded his small eyes steadily and said, "Do you have any problem with cash? Legal tender?"

With excruciating slowness, Mrs. Buzzley rang the items through, while her husband put them in bags. At some sign Rae didn't see, Buzz from the café appeared, to put the bags in the cart. She glanced at him and was more pleased than she should have been to catch a faint, but friendly smile aimed at her.

The silence was broken by the reappearance of Joella LaRose, who blustered back into the store and went directly to Rae. "I'm Joella LaRose," she said, and Rae thought she detected a little wobble in the woman's voice. "Warren Niel was my brother."

The facts were presented like two parts of a challenge. "I'm pleased to meet you," Rae said quietly, and offered her hand.

Joella definitely considered options, but she shook hands with Rae. "I just wanted you to know that I know who you are."

Rae's palms grew moist. This was the first head-on confrontation with anyone but Dallas—and Tyson, of course, although his formal approach had been of a different variety. There had been no emotion in Tyson's manner.

"I'll load these up for you, if you like," Buzz said to Rae. "The brown Jeep, right?"

"Right," Rae said, thinking, but not saying that people hereabouts were paying minute attention to everything about her. "The back isn't locked."

Buzz trundled off with the cart. Rae couldn't ignore the way his parents all but leaned over the counter in anticipation of what might be about to happen between her and Joella.

"There's no point," Joella said. "No point in you coming here to Glory."

Rae swung her purse over her shoulder and started for the door.

Joella gripped her elbow. "Don't walk away from me."

Rather than aggression, Rae heard an appeal in the other woman's voice. She glanced back past Joella and into the avid faces of the Buzzleys. She said, "Let's go outside, shall we?"

Joella dropped her hand and did as Rae suggested. The instant they were on the sidewalk, beneath the magnolia trees, with the heated afternoon breeze whipping at Rae's skirts and Joella's hair, Joella crossed her arms tightly, scrunched up her features, and said, "You've got to go away. Say you will."

"No," Rae told her simply. "I can't do that."

"Why? What makes you think you have a right to come here and stir things up? Don't you think we've suffered enough?"

"I'm really sorry you've suffered," Rae said, and meant it.

Joella pushed her tossed hair away from her face. "You're digging into things that don't concern you. Making trouble. This is a small town. My husband and I have to live here, and we'd like to be able to hold our heads up. Do you think it helps to have you here? You want to be paid off, don't you? You aren't a real writer. You just made that up to see how many people you could scare into paying you to back off."

"Extortion?" Rae said. "D'you think there's a lot of money in that?" She was too angry to feel ashamed of baiting the woman.

"What kind of person are you?" Joella asked. "Apart from someone who doesn't think anything of sleeping with other women's husbands."

"How many other women's husbands am I supposed to have slept with?"

Joella's face pinched. "You're a hard bitch. You don't care who you hurt, do you? Warren had better taste than to pick you. You aren't his type. You aren't like any of his other—" She pressed her lips together while a woman in red denim passed pushing twin toddler boys in a side-by-side stroller.

A hard bitch didn't flinch when she was told the man she'd thought was her husband had other women, in addition to his legal wife. Rae settled the hint of a tough smile on her lips and stared into Joella's eyes. "I am Warren's last . . . I was his last woman." She swallowed with difficulty. "And I liked him. I hope that counts for something with you." Later she would allow herself the tears she felt like crying.

"I loved him," Joella said, and didn't stop tears from filling her eyes. "Next to my husband, he was my best friend. He was a good man."

"You don't have to tell me that," Rae said quietly. The one thing she must not do was reveal that she'd considered herself married to Warren. "He was very good to me." If she made her so-called marriage public in Glory, Dallas would have no reason to tread lightly around her.

Tread lightly? She almost laughed. If he'd been treading lightly to this point, she'd better run for cover if he ever decided to put his feet down hard.

Joella frowned at her, and Rae could see the woman was trying to decide what to say next. What, Rae wondered, would Joella say if she knew the accusations Dallas had made about his brother-in-law? And what would she think if she knew Rae had made love with Dallas? Made love?

Rae felt herself redden. Was that what it had been, that hot, wild, intense, incredible thing that had happened between them?

She thought she knew the answer, and the warmth in her skin increased. She definitely knew she'd thought about being with Dallas, thought about it too many times to count.

Buzz finished packing the groceries in the back of the Jeep and trundled the cart back toward the store. He nodded to Rae, and gave Joella a long look. Any man would give Joella LaRose long looks, Rae thought. She said, "Thank you," to Buzz, without expecting any answer.

"You're surely welcome, Ms. Maddy," he said, shocking her. "You come back. I'll see to that account for you. River cabin, right? At the old Werther place."

When she collected herself, she said, "Yes. Thank you. And I'm Rae."

He smiled a little shyly and said, "Buzz. Welcome to Glory," before turning to back into the store, pulling the cart with him.

"Why the Werther place?" Joella asked. "Because you found out we used to live there?"

Rae blanked.

"That's it, isn't it?" Joella said, casting furtive glances in all directions, and lowering her voice. "You're making another point. You know Warren and I grew up there before my daddy had his troubles, and the Calhouns managed to get their sticky fingers on what had been in our family for generations."

"I don't have any idea what you're talking about."

"Sure you do. Why else would you take the river cabin? You're making yourself as obvious as possible. Warren Niel's woman's in town, living at the place Warren never stopped loving, the place he always planned to get back one day."

"I tell you, I don't—"

"And I don't believe you. He must have broken down and told you all about it. You must be something in the sack, babe, because Warren never talked to anyone about that. Not anyone but me."

Rae came close to snapping that she wasn't "babe" to anyone, but she knew real pain when she saw it. Joella was suffering, and Rae had felt enough of that kind of hurt not to want to make it worse for someone else.

"Maybe our daddy was wild when he was young. Maybe he did drive Granddaddy into debt. But he wasn't a bad man. No, ma'am, he was a good man, and you aren't goin' to write anythin' to the contrary. Do I make myself clear?"

The writer in Rae began to feel familiar excitement. She might have started the rumor about her book as a cover, but it could just become an interesting project.

Now she was practicing diversionary tactics. "I didn't know John ever lived at the cabin."

"John?"

Rae made herself shake her head. "I meant Warren." The less attempt at explanation, the better. "I went to the real estate office and the cabin was listed there. Coincidence, pure and simple."

"I don't believe you."

"That's up to you. I have errands to finish. So, if you'll excuse me."

Joella cut off Rae's path to the Jeep. "Why would you come here unless you intend to make trouble?"

For an instant Rae was tempted to say she was in Glory to stop other people from making trouble for her, to make sure no trouble spoiled what peace she and Ginny could have in Decline. "I don't want trouble, Joella. Not for you, or for anyone. I'm sorry your brother died, more sorry than I can tell you. He was a dear man, very dear to me."

Joella's mouth worked, and she squeezed her eyes shut. "Go away and leave us alone," she whispered. "We've suffered enough. We're still suffering."

"Your mother and father—"

"Are dead," Joella said flatly. "Thanks to the Calhouns, Daddy didn't want to keep on living, and Mama couldn't live without him."

Standing on a hot, windy sidewalk, beneath magnolia branches, in a town where she was a stranger, with a woman who was a stranger to her, Rae felt separated from reality. Parts of John's life flowed on the irrepressible tide of his sister's sadness and anger.

So much hate in paradise.

She squinted at the lowering sun. A pretty, pristine town called Glory. On the surface the name was perfect. Under the surface, the glory was more than tarnished.

"I'd like it if you'd talk to me about Warren," Rae said, surprising herself. But she had a need to know more about the man, and not just to help her prove she hadn't had any part in defrauding the Calhouns, if indeed John had done what Dallas suggested. "We're both raw, Joella. I'm not here to do any harm. I know you don't believe me now, but maybe you will."

"I just want you to . . ." Joella faltered. There were no tears in her eyes now, nothing soft about the brilliant blue. Cold determination shone there. "I believe you. I believe you had some feeling for Warren. He never mentioned you— why would he? You were one of many. Men have certain weaknesses. Women were his.

"He never meant to hurt people, but he couldn't help himself. Put it behind you. He's gone now and there's nothing here for you. Go home."

A rush of sickness made Rae draw a breath through her mouth. "Thanks," she said, turning away. "I plan to do just that." As soon as she had what she'd come to Glory to get.

Half an hour after Rae left Joella LaRose outside Buzzley's, she drove the Jeep north out of town. The sun had slid out of sight behind the high pines that lined the road, but air through the rolled-down windows still smelled of fresh-roasted dust and melted tar.

She'd picked up a copy of the *Glory Speaker* for that day and planned to spend the evening reading every word, and then studying several small, locally printed books on the history of the town, its founding fathers, and "Families of Note." The last had been hurriedly pressed into her hands by Linsay May Dale, who had rushed breathlessly to the side of the Jeep just as Rae was preparing to drive away from the bookshop.

Rae was glad to know there was Lucy, and Linsay May. It helped to think she could reach a friendly voice if she had to.

No other traffic followed or approached her on the winding road. Only large estates lay in this direction, and there were few of those.

The Bolling acres were the first she reached. Fronted by a white stone wall that must be ten feet high, the property was heavily wooded, and no glimpse of the house could be seen.

Next on both sides of the road came the tree-studded parklands belonging to the Calhouns. As on each previous drive past the estate, Rae longed to go in search of even a glimpse of the house called Sweet Bay. Before she left these parts, she'd do at least that.

One day—after Ginny knew all about John and she'd healed from the sadness she was bound to feel—Rae would try to make her see that the man he'd been when he was with them had loved his little, stolen daughter. Then she'd show Ginny the place he'd called home.

Once past the Bollings', and Sweet Bay, the road narrowed, and Rae didn't know who owned the property on either side for the next fifteen miles. In these parts, if you didn't know what a house was called, there was no painted sign or carved stone to tell you.

She ducked to look skyward. The narrow strip between towering pines had turned to the intense blue of almost sundown, and when she set her eyes ahead once more the faded white center line was less distinct.

Joella had told her to go home.

Had she ever really had a home? Rae didn't like the answer, and liked the threat of self-pity even less.

A critter darted from the trees and across the road.

Rae braked, and registered gray fur and a black stripe down a long back. Raccoon. Ginny loved raccoons and had to be dissuaded from feeding Rae's eggs to them.

Tomorrow, after school, Buelah would drive Ginny here. It was time to take Buelah into her confidence a little more, and enlist her help in deciding what to tell Ginny, and when.

Ahead, on the right and between the crowded tree trunks, a flash caught Rae's eye. She saw it, and it was gone again. Sun on broken glass or a scrap of old metal.

A small bridge with white railings, the ones on the left broken, lay ahead. The bridge spanned a more southerly bend in the same river that ran in front of the cabin.

Another flash.

Same spot.

No. Only just ahead of the Jeep now. Rae tapped the brake. It couldn't be in the same spot anyway because she'd traveled several hundred yards.

Again, a flash.

She almost hit the brakes hard, but stopped herself. Sun? What was she thinking of? The sun was already down.

Maybe she only thought she'd seen something.

The crack she heard wasn't imaginary.

Rather than brake, Rae put her foot on the gas and drove it to the floor. Sweat broke out on her brow, and her throat burned.

The next flash came from a spot parallel to the front passenger door. She cowered, and gripped the wheel hard.

The nose of the Jeep was already on the bridge when

something exploded. The impact jarred Rae. A bucking motion slammed her brow down on her knuckles.

Spinning. Slipping away. With a screaming sound the rear slid sideways. Not fast, but she couldn't stop it.

Bags of groceries in the back flew forward. Glass broke. *Steer into a skid. Don't touch the brakes.*

She turned the steering wheel to the right. Too much speed. She'd given gas when she should have been slowing down.

A blowout, that's all. Rae swallowed, and swallowed again. She'd got spooked by her own imagination and blown out a tire—one of the brand-new tires she'd had put on the Jeep when she bought it.

Still the rear swung around, shrieking and grinding.

Then it floated free.

Quiet.

The back of the vehicle fell several inches, and there was the sound of snapping wood.

Rae flipped off the engine.

More snapping, then silence.

She covered her eyes. There was no need to look to know what had happened. The two rear wheels had slid off the bridge, and the weight of the already slowing Jeep had brought it to rest on its underside, but far enough forward for her to be sure she wouldn't slide from the low bridge to the riverbed.

The thudding of her heart nauseated Rae. She remained hunched over the steering wheel, almost unconsciously trying to balance the tipsy angle of the vehicle. Bile rose in her throat, and she grimaced when she swallowed.

Finally her pulse began to slow down. The sweat that stung her eyes and filmed her body grew cold. She undid her seat belt, opened her door, and climbed down onto the frayed and bleached bridge decking.

On legs that quaked and wobbled with each step, she walked back to survey the damage. Just as she'd assumed, one tire had blown. Rather than hanging over the trickle of water below, the rim, surrounded by sagging rubber, rested on a concrete span underpinning the wooden beam. It was the good tire that had swung free.

"Thank you, God," Rae said aloud. This, she could handle.

The next time she drove this road she'd take it much slower. For a moment back there she'd been imagining maniacs firing from the trees. But everywhere she looked there was evidence that she was much more likely to have been the victim of a broken bottle, or an old nail—and a lead foot on the gas.

Within minutes she'd assembled the jack and spare tire. If things went well, she would change the tire and manage to drive forward, very slowly, and ease to safety. If things went badly? . . . She smiled wryly and put the jack together. If things went badly, she'd start walking.

Dusk turned the light a gritty mauve. With a faint hiss, shallow water sneaked around river rock.

Rae cranked the jack once, and paused, waiting to see if she was about to take a long walk.

Everything held and she cranked again. Gradually the rim cleared the ground. The process was taking too long. If she couldn't get the job done by dark, and if no one came along, she'd have an unpleasant time ahead.

On her hands and knees, trying not to notice pebbles digging into her skin, she worked harder, sweated again, and prayed a lot.

Blessedly the lug bolts moved easily enough, and she heaved off the destroyed tire.

She was going to make it.

Also new, the spare slid into place, and Rae paused to catch her breath. Her hands trembled, so did the muscles in her arms. She should have eaten some of Linsay May's cakes, and maybe another meal sometime during the day. Her last meal had been breakfast, and that had been only half a bagel because thinking about the night before. . . . She bent to the tire again. Having sex with Dallas Calhoun had taken her appetite away. Except for wanting to be with him again, dammit.

A slap, like wet rope against glass, jolted her to her feet. She swung around and flattened her back to the Jeep.

Huddled over, someone ran toward the trees on the Glory side of the bridge. Huddled over and draped in some dark clothing. A coat, or cape. It shone in the gathering darkness. A sheet of dark plastic?

"Hey!" Rae shouted. "Hey. Stop. Please stop."

The figure disappeared between the trees.

Who was it? Why didn't they stop?

She crossed her arms and willed herself not to cry. For God's sake, she wasn't a scared little kid.

But what if it was a crazy person?

It was getting dark. The tire was almost finished, but if she couldn't drive the other wheel onto the bridge, she'd be faced with having to decide what was best to do. Unfortunately, with Sweet Bay and the Bolling place behind her, no one would drive this far unless they were going to the Parker place.

Like Ginny's favorite egg trick, the one where she tapped a knuckle on top of Rae's head and spread her fingers lightly as if breaking an egg there, something moved Rae's hair.

She made to brush it away, but stopped.

The light touch became heavier. A dark thing slithered before her eyes, and down the side of her face.

She screamed so hard her throat closed.

Past her cheek.

Cold. Wrapped around her neck. Sliding across her back.

Rae's knees locked. She stared ahead. Twin pricks of light pierced the distant darkness.

A rattlesnake glided beneath the neck of her dress, between her breasts.

Eleven

Fool woman. She stared into the headlights of the Land Rover as if she couldn't move. *Damn.*

When he'd set out from Glory to catch up with Rae, he'd been angry, savagely angry. Now he saw her and anger got mixed up with wanting her.

Dallas slammed the palms of both hands against the wheel. Of all the crazy things. This female was poison to his life, yet he only had to think about her to get excited at the idea of overdosing on that poison.

Seeing her just about guaranteed a lethal dose.

Cool Dallas Calhoun wanted the woman his dead brother-in-law had bigamously married, the woman who had become his accomplice in throwing Calhoun Properties into the threat of financial disaster.

"I am going to tear you apart, baby," he murmured. "Today you went too far." Tear her apart, and gobble her up again if he could figure out a way to pull off both.

With her back to her Jeep, she stood with her arms bent at the elbows and pressed against the vehicle.

As if she was terrified.

Dallas applied his breaks, stopped, and leaped out. Leaving his headlights on, he strode toward her. "What in God's name do you think you're doing? No lights. Parked across the damn bridge. Anyone going too fast, or too drunk, would spread you all over the road."

She shook her head and stared at him.

"Why the terrified victim act?" he asked. "You've been doing your homework. You know I'm no killer. Your life is safe—probably. Or it will be if you finally do as you're told."

When she still didn't respond, or move, Dallas stopped walking toward her. The Jeep was parked crosswise on the bridge. Tools scattered the planks. "Flat tire?"

Not a word.

"Scared because it's getting dark?"

Big, horrified eyes. Parted lips drawn back from gritted teeth. Shit, women were more trouble than they were worth.

"Okay. So you didn't know who I might be, but now you do know. You're in safe hands." Uh huh, real safe hands, real appreciative hands. "Let's finish up that tire and move out."

"Help," she whispered, so softly he wasn't sure he'd heard correctly.

Dallas looked from side to side, and behind him, not that he'd be able to see much out here with his headlights walling off the darkness outside their beams.

"Did you say help, honey?" he asked her quietly. No point in coming on too strong until they were past whatever was bugging her right now. "Hey, it's me, Dallas."

"Get it away." Again she whispered.

Then he saw it—and turned cold.

Hanging from the front of her dress was a large rattler. Its head and part of its body were inside her bodice. "Oh, my . . . Don't move."

"Snake," she said.

"Yeah. Keep still." He went slowly toward her. "It's okay. Just let me take care of it."

"I'm . . . I can't." He heard that she breathed from the tops of her lungs. Her eyelids flickered. "Snake."

Oh, great. Now she was going to pass out on him. "Hold on, Rae. Did it bite you?"

She moaned.

He got within a couple of feet of her. "Tell me. Have you been bitten?"

Suddenly, with a flurry of motion, stamping her feet and shaking her head, she grasped the reptile and pulled it from her. Instantly she dropped it, and cowered back, her hands crossed in front of her face.

Dallas moved in, ready to kick the thing out of the way.

Rae bent forward, shaken by her own harsh sobs.

"I'll be." Dallas stopped in the act of applying the toe of a boot to the rattler. "The thing's dead. Rae, listen up. It's dead. Where did it come from?"

She cried more brokenly, and began to slide down the side of the Jeep.

Slipping an arm around her was the most natural thing he ever remembered doing. Too natural. "Lean on me, honey. And concentrate. Was that snake moving when it . . . Was it moving?"

"Don't know."

He looked at her dress. "We'd better take a look."

She blinked rapidly and muttered. "If they strike you feel it."

"So I've always heard."

"It didn't strike." She crossed her arms over her chest.

And she probably thought it would be preferable to die, than to have him take off any of her clothes again. "Okay. Good."

A shudder racked her. "It slipped around my neck. Down my dress." Revulsion contorted her features.

"Horrible," he said. "But stick with me. Please. Help me get us through this. Where did it come from?"

"It fell on me."

He looked up and saw nothing but midnight blue sky. "I don't think so. Not unless it's a new kind of rain."

She filled a hand with his shirt and struggled for composure. "I had a flat tire." She sounded almost sensible. "I was changing it. Something hit the Jeep, I think."

"That?" He pointed to the unmoving snake.

"I guess. There was someone out there. Running away. I saw him."

"Who?"

"How would I know?" She jerked upright and glared at him. "You tell me who it was. You're the one who's in such a hurry to get me out of this town."

He regarded her with narrowed eyes. "You think I'd send someone to throw dead rattlers at you?"

"I think you'd do anything to make me leave."

"If I was going to throw rattlers, they sure as hell wouldn't be dead ones."

Her face crumpled again.

And Dallas looked at the sky again. Tearful women were beyond him. "I didn't mean that. You make me say things no other woman ever made me say."

"You never hated any other woman the way you hate me."

"I don't hate you, goddammit."

"Yes, you do."

"I *don't.* I'd like to wring your scrawny neck, but I don't hate you. I could be crazy about you . . . Hell." He ran a hand over his face. "You are the most infuriating woman."

She'd heard what he said, every word, damn his careless mouth. Confusion showed in her eyes, confusion and curiosity. *I could be crazy about you.* Why—why would he let a statement like that slip?

"Your battery's going to be dead," she told him. When she put her lips together, they trembled. "You can go back now. I'm going to be okay."

He laughed, he couldn't help himself. "Sure you are. Some crazy just threw a snake at you, then ran away. Your Jeep's got a flat tire—"

"I fixed it already."

Taking her with him, he went to look at the tire in question, and saw that the other rear wheel hung over the river. "Were you planning to put the lugs back on? And hoping you wouldn't lose the back end when you try to drive away?"

"Yes."

The old defiance returned, and he knew he shouldn't feel so glad about it.

"You can put yourself back behind your wheel and run along, Dallas. Thanks for shocking me into getting rid of that thing."

"Put myself back behind my wheel and run along? Is that what you just said to me?"

"Exactly."

"Well, ma'am, I'm not accustomed to upstarty females making that kind of suggestion."

She sniggered, a snigger that held just a trace of hysteria. "There's always a first time—for everything."

He decided to let it pass. "In case you didn't notice, I was coming out your way. Did you notice that?"

There was no comprehension in her stare.

"I'll take that as a no." He hooked a thumb over his shoulder. "I live back that way. At Sweet Bay. The place you made sure you're within spitting distance of each time you snuggle into that lovely, rented bed of yours. If I was going home, I'd be there by now, not here."

"You were following me."

The girl was quick. "Uh huh. But we're not having this discussion out here where it might start raining snakes again at any moment."

She gasped, and covered her head. And Dallas wasn't sure whether to smile, or apologize. He said, "Sorry. That wasn't funny. Let's get you running, and I'll follow you home."

Awkwardly she straightened up. "All my groceries are messed up."

"That's too bad. I'll put the lugs back."

"I can do it myself."

"Sure you can." He went to one knee and picked up a bolt. "Go get the flashlight out of the box in the back of my rig. Then turn off the headlights. Please."

"I'd almost finished when—"

"When it started hailing rattlers. Yeah, I know."

"I've got a phobia about them. I've always had it. About all snakes. I hate them."

"No. Geez, you could have fooled me. The flashlight?"

She continued to hover, until he looked up at her. She swayed and didn't meet his eyes.

"You're still afraid, aren't you?"

Rae shook her head, and chafed her bare arms.

"Yes, you are. You're afraid whoever threw that snake is still out there." And come to think of it, he didn't like the idea much himself. "We'll get the flashlight together."

On his feet again, he took a firm hold on her hand and pulled her behind him to the Land Rover, found the light, switched off the headlights, and returned to the Jeep.

She didn't slacken her grip on him.

Dallas screwed up his eyes and dug around in his feelings for what he wanted to do about holding Rae Maddy's hand longer than necessity dictated.

He felt good about it.

The flashlight beam picked out the damaged tire. "Shit," he muttered, bending over. Gently removing his hand from Rae's grasp, he examined the rent in the rubber, both at entry and exit point.

"Did someone shoot a hole in it?" Rae asked.

He shot to his feet and rounded on her. "Why would you ask a question like that if you didn't suspect that's what happened?"

"I did. But then I thought I must have driven over some glass. There's junk all over the place."

"That's it," he said, and took her hand again. "I don't want another word out of you. You're a menace to your own safety. Just do as you're told. Your keys are in the ignition?"

"Yes, but—"

"You've got a purse or something?"

"On the front seat, but—"

"You don't learn real fast, do you." He leaned into the

Jeep and retrieved the keys and her purse. "You had your tire shot out from underneath you. Then, when you were changing it, the sky started dropping snakes. Only we both know someone threw it at you and ran away. What does all this suggest?"

Her face shone pale in the darkness. "Someone's trying to frighten me."

"Got it in one! Damn, you're swift. Someone's trying to frighten you to death. And couldn't you have had the kind of accident that would have made sure you never got frightened again?"

"What do you mean?"

"As in, the type of accident that left you *dead?* Oh, I agree it wasn't likely, but it could have happened. That joker must have weighed the odds and decided to take the chance. That's reckless, Rae. That's a guy who made peace with the possibility of killing you. You're not safe in that cabin anymore. If you ever were."

"You're overreacting."

He laughed, and clamped a hand at her waist to hustle her to the Land Rover. "In you go. We'll discuss my reputation for overreacting if you want to. It doesn't exist."

He put her in from the driver's seat and locked the doors before she could think about hopping out on the passenger side.

"I can't leave the Jeep," she said when he gunned the engine, reversed, and set off in the direction from which he'd come.

"Want to bet?"

"My milk."

"What about it."

"It'll go bad."

He slapped his brow and slid through the gears until the Rover roared along the narrow road.

"My milk!"

"You're hysterical. Forget the goddamn milk. Where we're going there's plenty of milk. At least, I think there is."

She struggled into her seat belt, but promptly braced herself with both hands on the dashboard.

"Relax," he told her. "I'm a damn good driver."

"I've got to get ready for tomorrow. Buelah's bringing Ginny."

"Another lousy idea. It's not going to happen." With every passing mile he watched each side of the road for gunshots. "You make sure that child stays where she's safe."

Rae put the back of a hand over her mouth. "Don't you think I want to keep her safe? I'm going to call the sheriff."

"You bet your sweet ass we're calling the sheriff."

"Don't talk like that."

He grinned and said, "Sorry, ma'am. Didn't mean to offend your delicate sensibilities. I should know any woman of Warren's would be a lady."

By the light of the dash he saw her glare at him, and he didn't feel proud of insulting her. But he had to make up for the stupid slip he'd made. "The sheriff's going to say you got in the way of a hunter."

"A hunter aiming for my tires?"

"Yup. Only the sheriff won't believe that's what the guy was doing."

"What about the snake?"

"A dead snake on the road. And you want to tell the sheriff it fell out of the sky? You go right ahead if that's what you want to do."

She pounded the dash with a fist. "You don't want to help me."

"That's right. I sure don't. I want you to help me, and I'm going to make sure you stay alive and kicking until you've done just that."

"Stop this thing and let me out."

He pressed the accelerator closer to the floor.

"How do I know it wasn't you who shot at me?"

"That's one of your more stupid suggestions."

"My car." Her voice rose. "I can't leave my car like that."

What he needed was time, time to think, time to plan. "Would you be very quiet, please."

"Quiet? You're taking me away in this thing against my will and asking me to be quiet? You're mad. The whole world's mad." Her hands rose, and fell with a thump into her lap. "No. It's just my world that's mad. I'm ordinary now. Do you understand? I live an ordinary life. I live in an ordinary house, and look after Ginny, and wait for John . . ."

With grim concentration, he watched the road in the headlights.

"I used to wait for him," she finished quietly. "And I write and make money for my writing. I've never done anything to hurt anyone—not anyone—not anyone who didn't hurt me."

He didn't miss the hesitations. There was a lot about the lady that he might have to look into, but not right at this moment. At this moment he was about to take a bold step. He was going to gamble on pride, and the oldest instinct of all, the instinct to survive and hold on to what was yours.

"If you didn't do that back there, or arrange for someone else to do it for you, who did?" Her tone was cool, but it didn't mask the fear.

"Point one, it would be impossible for me to be firing at your tires from the angle that shot must have come from. I was driving in the same direction as you, on the same road."

"You could have parked somewhere. Then shot at me and run back to drive around behind me."

"Sherlock Holmes eat your heart out," he said. "But there could be a hole or two in that theory. I didn't shoot at you. Or arrange for snake rain."

"You know I meant it was thrown."

"And I didn't throw it, did I?"

"No."

"I also didn't arrange for someone else to do either of those things. Know why you can believe that?"

"I . . . No. You're the only—"

"I'm obviously not the only one who doesn't like having you around. And the reason you ought to know I wouldn't send someone else after you is because I surely do not want anyone else to know I've got a great big reason to want you as far from Glory as I can get you."

Seconds passed before she said, "Oh," very quietly, with hollow acceptance. "Are you planning to drive me back to Decline?"

"Not without making sure we understand each other completely."

"Where are we going, then?"

"To Sweet Bay."

Twelve

Ava Calhoun was a price Tyson had decided to pay. Not that the price didn't reward him with both a weapon he intended to use against Dallas if necessary, and a sense of forbidden thrill. But despite her intriguing appetite, her tireless pursuit of his pleasure, and her willingness to learn, the girlish petulance that had served her well all her life exasperated him.

And although she had a lush body, she was only four years younger than his mother.

The first time he'd chosen to understand that all the sidelong glances meant she wanted him, he'd thought flirting and the occasional furtive pawing would be enough for her. He'd been wrong. Ava never stopped short of the whole enchilada.

He glanced at the gold-framed clock on his desk. The door to the outer office had opened and closed—right on time—and Ava's high heels clicked on the dark oak floors in the suite he couldn't afford.

Her shadow showed through frosted glass panels in his door. Just as always, she paused to take a compact from her purse and hold it high to check her makeup, and pat her hair.

The tiny tap was her idea of a coy signal that bliss was imminent. His cock stirred, and he flared his nostrils. Forbidden thrills shouldn't be underrated. They turned him on every time. "Come on in, sugar," he said, holding his pen between both hands and resting his elbows on the desk.

She opened the door a few inches and peeped in at him.

"Hi, handsome." Her makeup was just right. Soft and carefully light. Peachy lipstick on pouty lips, and a hint of shadow applied to accentuate the upward tilt of her eyes. "I'm not interruptin' anything, am I?"

As if she cared. And as if she didn't come by at the same time every Thursday. Tyson crooked a finger, beckoning her into the office. "Close the door. And lock it. And get your pretty rear over here. I'm tired of waiting for you." The talk usually went about the same. Tonight there would be modifications, but not until he'd made certain he had her full attention.

Ava shut the door and turned the key in the lock. Then she put her hands behind her and pressed against the jamb with her chin raised, her lips parted, her breasts thrust out.

Ava watched too many B movies.

"I told you to get over here," he said softly.

She pushed away from the door and approached with measured, hip-swaying steps, the full skirt of her blue silk dress floating about beautiful legs. When Ava reached the other side of his desk, she rested the heels of her hands on the edge and leaned toward him, still swaying. "Have you missed me, Tyson?"

"You know I have." Anyone who mistook Ava for a fool made a dangerous mistake. Total self-absorption disguised sly intelligence. So far Tyson had played the game just right with her, and he didn't intend to put a foot wrong now. "I've had a difficult week, sugar. I need you to make me feel better."

The flicker in her eyes let him know she'd noted the slight switch in tone from the expected script. Any asking was supposed to come from Ava, any show of affected weakness. Tyson's part was to do the telling.

"What is it, baby?" Ava said. A small crease formed between her fine brows. "You know I like to give you whatever you need."

He needed to fuck her, scare the shit out of her, and get

her out of his office. Fast. Joella expected him home, and he'd be ready for her by the time he got there.

"Sugar," Ava said, wheedling. "Don't hold back. You don't have to be tough for me."

"Drink?" he asked suddenly.

The frown deepened. "I thought you didn't like kissing me with liquor on my breath."

What he didn't like was remembering the time she'd arrived drunk and fallen asleep on his couch. Fancy had called and told him she was coming by later. He'd had a hard time getting rid of Ava before her daughter showed. That had been too close.

Ava sashayed around the desk and went to the mahogany credenza behind him. "Brandy?" Without waiting for a response, she splashed generous measures into two glasses and came to his side. She handed one glass to him and set her own down while she slid her round bottom onto the desk and crossed her legs. A practiced flip twitched her skirt up.

"Nice," Tyson said on cue, pushing back his chair and inclining his head to study the place where ivory lace at the tops of her stockings rested on smooth thighs. He drank, and breathed deeply when the liquor fired his throat and seared his veins.

"Better?" Ava asked, pointing her toes and kicking off beige pumps. "Drink up. You need relaxing, and satisfying. The brandy's the appetizer. I'm the meal."

Tyson upended his glass and almost choked when Ava slid her toes between his thighs. She nudged him, said, "Ooh," and made owl eyes. "What a beautiful thing you've got there."

"Glad you like it," he told her, coughing. "With a little help from you, it's getting more beautiful all the time."

As she sometimes did, Ava had come minus panties. He could imagine the pleasure she'd taken in anticipating his reaction. From her wide smile, and the way she held her tongue between her teeth, he could tell she was congratulating herself on tonight's response.

She sipped her brandy and reached to take off his tie. "There's something I want to ask you." Already her focus had shifted back to herself. "I've heard certain rumors. Now, there's always jealousy, we both know that. People are *so* envious of people with so much more than they have. But I'm not used to it, and I don't like it."

The buttons on his shirt received her full attention.

"What kind of rumors?" he asked, already knowing exactly what she was talking about.

Concentrating, she curled the tip of her tongue upward. Satisfied with having finished unbuttoning his shirt, she hiked her skirts higher around her hips, but crossed her legs again, and scooted until she sat directly in front of him.

Tyson's attention wandered. He liked a little challenge, and from where he sat there wasn't any in sight. "Rumors," he reminded her, taking both of her feet into his lap and pressing them against him. He sucked air in through his teeth. "What rumors? And who's asking?"

"Not really asking"—the insides of her feet gripped him—"just tellin' stories. How Calhoun Properties is in trouble. Losing money. Maybe trying to cover up certain things we don't want other people to know. That sort of thing."

Smiling wouldn't be the thing. If Warren was around, he'd kiss him. When Fancy's husband had set out to line his pockets with Calhoun money, he'd presented Tyson with the chance he'd hoped for since his teens, the chance to get Calhoun eating out of his hand.

Tyson realized he was staring fixedly at Ava's pride and joy, her large, round breasts with their dark, saucer-sized nipples. He hadn't even noticed when she parted the draped front of her dress to show him that the dress and the ivory stockings were all she wore.

"Mmm," he murmured, holding her ankles, and easing

closer. "More beautiful things." Care had to be taken with Ava. He'd tried getting rough once and she'd gone into hysterics. Not a pretty sight.

She held her arms out to him.

Ignoring the gesture, he went for her breasts instead, weighing the heavy flesh, and offering thanks to the surgeon who had taken care of gravity's effects.

Tutting, Ava slapped his hands away. "No, you don't, naughty boy. You're in entirely too much of a hurry for me."

How close to being right she was, Tyson thought. He was in a hurry, but not for her precisely.

"I told you you don't like kissing me with liquor on my breath." Her pout drove a web of lines into the skin around her mouth. "And you don't. Well, I'm just going to have to teach you to like it."

She pushed her fingers into her glass and wiped brandy over her nipples. "Now, we both know you can't stay away from some things, don't we?" When she made a move to put her hand between her legs, he stopped her. "You let me go, you big bully," she said.

He ought to let her go ahead. "If you do that, you'll wish I'd stopped you, honey. I don't want you to hurt yourself is all."

By the time she'd considered what he said, Tyson darted to bite one of her nipples. Instantly she burst into high-pitched giggles and waved her arms as if to fend him off. Only while she waved her arms, she wriggled her dress from her shoulders and lay flat on the desk.

Covering boredom got tougher every time, but Tyson pushed her tits together and made a meal of them—and pretended she was a stranger he'd just met at a party. A girl not out of her teens whose pointed pink nipples showed when she bent over. Every man in the room had made a play for her. But she'd found a way to isolate him and bring him here. This was her parents' place, and he'd never been here before. She was in a hurry because she was afraid her folks would come back. But she was crazy for him, wet for him, writhing for him the way she'd never been for any man before.

"You're hurting me."

"Trust me, baby," Tyson said, sweating. She'd soon learn to beg him to hurt her every time. "You've got beautiful breasts. Big, beautiful young breasts." Spreading his legs, he trapped her thighs between them and ripped the dress at the shoulder seams. You had to teach the young ones to respect mastery.

"My dress!" She slapped his face. "You've ruined my lovely dress."

"I'll buy you a new one."

Sucking her nipples brought the cries of ecstasy he'd known would come. He sucked, and pushed his hands under her soft bottom to the cleft, and squeezed.

"What's the matter with you? Stop it. Stop it right now, Tyson LaRose."

"Do as you're told"—rather than squeeze, he pinched, and her cry excited him more—"just stay open for me, honey, and we'll get along fine."

Her violent bucking caught him off guard. So did the blow she landed on his mouth. He tasted blood.

The rest of the dress parted in his tearing hands, and he tossed it aside. Naked but for the stockings he liked right where they were, she pushed up from the desk, pushed her breasts into his face.

Tyson caught her hair and bit her lips until she wailed and beat at him. He kept his mouth on hers and managed to free one hand to undo his belt and pants. Then he released her just long enough to free himself and sit down.

One jerk and she was on his lap.

And he was inside her with his hips pumping up and down while she clung to his shoulders and cried.

"They all cry the first time," he panted.

He barely felt the next slap, but vaguely registered that she'd hit his ear.

"You're going to pay for this." She sounded hysterical. "I'm going to punish you. You're going to owe me forever, and I'm going to collect."

"What are you going to collect, baby?" He laughed aloud and gripped her waist while he surged into her. His breath stung his lungs and throat. "More of the same? Is that what you're going to collect? Try this." As carefully as he could, he closed his hands around her throat and squeezed, and felt a rush of air escape her lips.

"Don't. You're . . . Oh, Tyson."

"Yeah. Oh, Tyson." He squeezed a little harder. She contracted around him, contracted tighter, and tighter. "Oh, yes, baby. You're a quick study, baby. Come on, come on, come on." Reason pierced sensation and he took his hands from her neck.

"Just you wait, Tyson. I'm going to get you. You'll owe me forever. Aah. Dammit, Tyson. Aah, yes. Damn you."

With his arms wrapped about her, and his teeth sunk into her shoulder, he went over the top, and kept on going. Longer than he had, maybe ever.

His chest heaved, and energy rushed from him.

With her toes on the floor, she kept right on riding him and begging him to "Come on, Tyson. Oh, come on," before she did her own coming on and fell in a sweating heap on top of him.

Their hoarse breathing filled the room.

She pushed her face into his neck and nuzzled there, crooning.

The hot, whirling place in his mind gradually cleared. The woman astride him, with his shriveling cock still inside her, was no nubile teenager. She was Mrs. Ava Calhoun, mother of Dallas and Fancy Calhoun, and he had her right where he wanted her.

He held her close and kissed her temple, and said, "Lovely, honey. Now it's chat time," nice and loud.

A click, and the door to the bathroom off his office

opened. Tyson hated the man who walked quietly toward him, but he didn't let the hate show in his face.

Ava didn't hear the newcomer. "Let's lie on the couch," she said, rubbing her breasts against the hair on his chest. "We can stay longer tonight, can't we? I want to do it again, sugar. You are fantastic."

Tyson ran a hand the length of her spine and traced the rounded curves of her hips, and watched the man.

Never taking his eyes from Ava, Tyson's daddy picked up the glass she'd left on the desk and downed the dregs of her brandy.

"Ava, honey, it's talk-time now," Tyson said, meeting Carter LaRose's bloodshot eyes. Still tall and distinguished in a dissolute way, Carter's thick gray hair was brushed straight back from a high forehead.

Stroking the sides of Tyson's face, Ava rocked her hips and said, "Not yet. I'm not ready to talk."

"Not even about those rumors?"

"You find out why they think they can say those things. Dallas won't talk about it, but I think it's something to do with Warren. It all started when he made all that terrible fuss they're still talking about."

"When his plane crashed and he was scattered around in about a million pieces, you mean?"

"Such a mess."

The inscrutable expression his daddy had perfected made Tyson long to ask the other man what he was thinking; but Carter had set the ground rules for this event, and questions, other than any he might have, weren't on the program.

This was, Tyson reflected, the first time he and his daddy had ever joined forces to achieve anything. For his whole life, Tyson had existed virtually outside his father's notice. He didn't want to think about the reason; he just wanted Carter to do what he'd promised to do, and help Tyson get what he must have if there was any hope of holding on to what he had—and getting a whole lot more.

"I want to make love again," Ava murmured, finally sitting up. She bowed to kiss his chest, and curled her fingers into their mingled hair between her legs. "Come on, Tyson."

He sat very still, held very still, stared at Carter LaRose.

Ava raised her head slowly until she could see Tyson's face; then she swiveled to look over her shoulder.

Rather than scream, as he'd anticipated, she said, "Carter," almost under her breath, and placed a hand over each of her breasts. The effect was ridiculous. Her small hands, the fingers splayed, only drew more attention to the swell of voluptuous flesh.

"Nice to see you, Ava," Carter said formally, without cracking even a hint of a smile while he put himself in the way of seeing everything there was to see of Ava Calhoun. "It's been a long time."

Her throat made a sound as she swallowed. "This is disgusting."

"Anything but disgusting," he said, drawing closer. "You were always something. You still are."

"Go away. Tyson, make him go away. He's looking at me."

"Would you prefer it if I didn't want to look at you? Never used to be the case. I remember when you couldn't get enough of being naked with me. You used to prefer beds in those days. Or the backseats of cars."

"Stop it." Scarlet suffused her face. "Why are you doing this to me?"

"Tyson invited me. He seemed to think I could be of some help to him. And to myself. Life hasn't been very kind to me, Ava. I blame you for that."

"Give me your shirt," Ava said to Tyson. "I can't stand this."

There could be no going back, but Tyson had lost his appetite for humiliating this woman. "Be quiet," he told her, deliberately abrupt. "Listen. And do as you're told. Then it'll be all over and we'll be fine. You'll be fine."

"I like you better with more padding on your bones." In

a motion that surprised Tyson, Carter brushed Ava's hair behind her shoulder. "When we were kids, I liked you the way you were then, too. But Biff had more money."

Ava's chin rose again, but Tyson saw how her eyes glistened. "Biff had a great deal more money. You hardly had any, and what you did have, you were never going to keep. Bad habits. My daddy warned me you had bad habits, and he was right."

"So you took the money your daddy gave you, and married it to Biff's money, and lived happily every after. Almost. But you went back on your word to me. We were going to be married, remember?"

"No," she said, flinching as she must have felt Tyson slip out of her. "We were just kids making kid promises. Those things don't count."

"Not to you. They did to me."

"You married Melvira fast enough."

This time Tyson flinched. He didn't want to think about his mother, not here in this room, with this woman naked and sitting on him. Traitorous, that's how it made him feel. Melvira LaRose had suffered enough at the hands of the Calhouns.

"Well, you did, Carter," Ava said when he didn't answer her.

Studying her face, then her breasts, where his eyes lingered, Carter said, "Let's leave Melvira out of this. You wouldn't want anyone else to know what you did in this office tonight."

Ava covered her mouth.

"Or what you've been doing in this office every Thursday night for a long time?"

The tears she could so readily summon were real this time. They welled and ran down her cheeks and over her hand. She shook her head.

"That's good because Tyson and I surely don't want it talked about all over Glory, either."

A choked noise erupted from Ava. She whispered, "You wouldn't. You'd be destroyed in this town."

Carter laughed and said, "I'd probably be better off than I've ever been. The sales of the paper would skyrocket. In, and out of Glory. I wouldn't be surprised if we'd get subscriptions in Atlanta and Savannah and everywhere in between."

"Why would you do this?"

Tyson wanted to put distance between himself and Ava, but couldn't make himself move her. "Let's finish this," he told Carter.

"Great idea. This isn't about you, Ava, not really. You're just a convenience to us. You've got trouble. Calhoun Properties, that is. Dallas promised Tyson he'd take him into the business, make him in-house counsel. He hasn't done that. Now he's going to."

"I can make Dallas do anything I want him to," she said, pushing back her hair, "but I've got to be real careful he doesn't get suspicious—about Tyson and me. So I can't ask for—"

"Yes, you can." Carter LaRose could be colder than any man Tyson had ever known. "You can because the stakes are too high for you to do anything else. Tyson deserves it. I deserve it. Tyson knows Warren was milking Calhoun Properties, and he'll do what Dallas hasn't managed to do—he'll find out how Warren did it, and where the money is. And he'll help take things back where they were. And higher. Success, that's what Tyson can give Calhoun, if only Dallas will quit being too jealous to let him inside."

"I want to go home," Ava said.

Bending, Carter swept up the destroyed dress, turned it over in his hands, and threw it on the couch. "Dumb move, Tyson. It's time you could control your little fantasies."

Tyson throbbed with embarrassment. "Ava's got a change of clothes in the closet," he said. "I'll get them."

Ava clung to him.

"Wait till I leave," Carter said. "All I want from you, Ava, is a promise. And this time you'll keep it."

"Because if I don't you'll talk about Tyson making love to me? What if I say it was rape? He raped me to try to subdue me and make me do what he wants. If Biff was alive he'd kill both of you."

Pity ebbed from Tyson.

Carter shook his head. "Biff's not alive. And nothing you say will alter the sensation value of what's been happening in this room—between you two. They'll never stop talking about the widow who took up with her dead husband's son."

Ava's mouth fell open.

"Don't tell me you didn't know." Very gently, Carter smoothed a hand from her white cheek, to her neck, to her breasts. He covered and lifted one of them. The expression in his eyes was of rapt absorption. "When Biff was engaged to you, he was sleeping with Melvira. She loved him then, and she loved him till he died. I just filled the gap when he turned his back on her. As much as she ever let me. And she did her best to help me stop thinking about you. It didn't work. For either of us."

Tyson lowered his eyes.

"Maybe I raised Biff Calhoun's son. We'll never be sure, but now it's time for the payback."

Ava recoiled from Carter's touch and stood up. "You'd never talk about it."

"Can you afford to take the risk?" Carter asked. "Could you still hold garden club meetings if Clara Bolling and Jean Nunn thought you'd been sleeping with Biff's boy by Melvira?"

"Dad," Tyson said, desperate for this to be over. "I'm sure Ava gets the idea."

Turning his back on them, Carter went toward the door. "If she doesn't, ask her if we should start by discussing things with Fancy."

Ava made a dash for the cupboard where she kept an overnight bag.

As Carter let himself out, he said, "After all, a stepmother and stepson sleeping together is titillatin'. But if you're banging Fancy, well, Tyson . . . Need I say more?"

Thirteen

Dallas drove around a circular drive in front of his white-columned, wisteria-draped mansion and parked at the foot of a great, curving flight of stone steps.

"You've lost your mind," Rae said, finding her voice for the first time in the fifteen minutes it had taken to get there. "You don't want me here any more than I want to be here."

"I want you here."

Why? "I don't think so." Unless he'd set up some trap, and she was going to walk through the front doors of Sweet Bay, never to be seen or heard of again. "No, I definitely don't think so."

His big, black dog erupted from the side of the house and bounded toward the Rover. Dallas opened his door and got out to come around to Rae's side.

She held her purse on her lap and, when he opened her door, didn't move.

"C'mon, Rae," he said, touching her arm. "You started something, and now we're going to have to keep rolling with it to the end."

"The end?" she said, not liking the sound of that. "If it's all the same to you, I think I'd as soon postpone this part. You go on in. I'll head back out to the highway."

"You know I won't let you do that. Snake man's out there somewhere. Next time the snake may not be dead, either."

She shuddered and hugged her purse to her chest. "I've got to get back to the cabin."

"Why?"

"My things are there. And it's where I live at the moment—in case you've forgotten. Tomorrow's a work day for me. And I've got things to get ready before Ginny and Buelah come tomorrow night."

"Yeah, well, we're going to talk about that, too."

"Too?"

"Don't play dumb with me, Rae. You and I know each other too well for that."

Rae didn't want to discuss, or even to think about, how well they knew each other. The situation was awkward, but not beyond mending. "I'm very grateful to you for coming along the way you did. That was a horrible experience."

"I didn't just *come along*. The reason I was there was to find you. You've been a busy girl. Too busy. That's also on the agenda. Rae's mischief making."

The dog pushed past his boss and planted his front paws on the floor beside Rae's seat. Two rows of large, white teeth were very much in evidence.

Something told Rae that Dallas Calhoun wasn't the kind of man who responded to appeals, but she had nothing to lose by trying. "You're right," she told him. "It probably wouldn't be such a good idea for me to go out there on my own. And I really appreciate you wanting to help me out. But if you'd just drive me back to my car, I know I can take it from there."

He rubbed his dog's head. "I'm not big on instincts, but I've decided to follow mine. At least for tonight. You need a safe place to be, and I can't think of any place safer than keeping you with me."

"If that's true, I'm in deep trouble."

His smile was faint, but it did such nice things for his mouth, and eyes. "Dangerous dude, huh? That's what you think I am. Good. That's a good start. Maybe if you figure out I could be dangerous to your health, you'll stop messing with me."

The threats might be subtle, but they weren't that subtle. "I really think you're too honorable a man to take advantage of my being in a difficult position."

"You overestimate my honor. Please get out and come into the house."

"The Jeep can't be left where it is." She'd simply snow him with how reasonable she was. "I've got to go back and move it. I've got to go back to the cabin—simple as that, Dallas. I know you want to discuss some things with me, but it doesn't have to happen now."

"It certainly does."

In other words, the only way she'd walk away would be with his blessing. "I'm sure you think it must be now. I'm like that, too. Always in a hurry to get things done."

"How nice to know we've got so much in common."

"Most human beings do if they ever get the chance to learn about each other."

"Well"—he leaned into the Rover and rested his forearm on the back of her seat—"we have managed to learn a great deal about each other in quite a short space of time, Ms. Maddy. Kind of boggles the mind just thinking about how much more we may learn if you insist on hanging around Glory."

She could not go into that house. "Your mother and sister live here."

"Yes."

"They aren't going to want to have me using the same air with them."

He propped his brow on a fist, so near the side of her face she felt his breath on her skin.

Wolf had wedged himself between Dallas and Rae. He moved his doleful, dark eyes from his boss to Rae and settled his muzzle on her knee as if mimicking Dallas.

Dallas sighed.

Wolf sighed.

Rae hugged her big purse even tighter. And sighed.

"I can't let you go out there on your own, Rae."

"I've been on my own most of my—" Stressful situations could loosen the tongue. "I'm used to being on my own. And I'm not your responsibility."

"I'm making you my responsibility."

She frowned and turned her face from him. Being in the same space, so close, made clear thought a struggle. And she was starting to read things into little comments he made, little comments that couldn't possibly have any hidden meaning.

"This is the pits," he muttered.

He was so right. "I know."

"I didn't handle you well in the first place."

"Handle?" She swung toward him again and discovered just how near he was—almost nose-to-nose with her. "I suppose you mean you misjudged me? That you'd expected *handling* me to be a no-brainer, only it wasn't."

"No, it wasn't."

"Well—"

"My brain has been engaged with you ever since."

Rae grew a little warmer. "I'd apologize, only it isn't my fault you decided to ride into Decline the way you did. You assumed too much."

"Uh huh. I surely did. And I assumed too little. I didn't expect you."

She wasn't about to ask him what he meant by that.

"Do you think I'm the kind of man who leaps into bed with any willing female?"

Wolf sighed again.

"I wasn't that willing," she said softly.

Dallas rested his chin on his forearm and ran the tip of his right forefinger along her jaw. "Know what I think, Ms. Maddy?"

She lowered her lashes.

"I think you'd like to believe you didn't want to make love

with me. But you know it isn't true. You wanted it. You want it again now, just like I do."

"Stop it." Jerking her face, she tried to elude his caressing hand. "There's more to a man and woman being together than sex. Even if it really works. And it really did work, Dallas. Oh, yes, I'm not denying that. But it won't happen again."

"It won't?"

"No, I—"

His lips, softly settling at the corner of her mouth, stole her breath.

She closed her eyes. "You know I respond to you, and you're using that. Don't you feel ashamed?"

"I feel"—the end of his tongue touched her lower lip—"I feel that we're going to have to work things out between us. Don't misunderstand me. You are a problem, Rae Maddy. You're the biggest damn problem who ever came my way. But I'm going to make sure I know how to find you from now on."

She let her head fall back against the head rest. "It's a sex thing. Nothing else."

"Familiar with that, are you? Sex things?"

"No." An explanation wasn't owed, but she'd give it to him anyway. "I'm probably going to regret telling you, but this is new to me. I've never felt as if the only place I wanted to be was close enough to a man to forget where I start and he ends. You have to be the most . . . Just the most, Dallas Calhoun. But I'll get over it. I'll just chalk it up to lack of experience, followed by sudden overdose of opportunity."

"I wish you wouldn't."

She felt him incline his head and turned to look at him.

"Don't toss this off," he said. "I don't know how we're going to figure it out, but we've got to make sure we find a way."

Lights in rose beds lining the veranda threw soft arcs over the venerable, two-story facade of the house. The same lights turned Dallas's eyes to pewter, and cast a wedge of shadow beneath his cheekbone, and deepened the dimple at the corner of his mouth.

Rae didn't miss the smallest detail, but she'd learned the wisdom of clinging to reality. "You do understand that I can't go into that house, don't you?"

Rather than answer, he kissed her. Possibly the sweetest kiss she'd ever known. Gentle, caressing, devoid of demand. She saw his eyes close, heard his breathing quicken, felt the light touch of his fingertips on her face and neck.

A kiss of love.

Rae's eyes filled with tears. Still a fool after all these years.

Dallas raised his face, kissed her once more, quickly, and looked at her. He said, "Damn," really quietly, then, "do you understand that I can't let you go to that cabin tonight?"

She shook her head.

"Well, I can't. I don't know what I'm going to do about this, but I've got some very complicated feelings going on here. I'll deal with them, but for now I'm struggling."

He wasn't the only one struggling—not that she ought to believe a word he said. "If you could see me inside the cabin, I'd lock the door."

"Nothing doing." He kissed the skin between her brows. "Stick with me, kid. It isn't going to be easy, but I'll steer us through the storm. And there's going to be a storm. But I've made up my mind how we're handling this mess. It's the best answer I can come up with."

Suspicion finally made itself felt. "You're very persuasive. I think being kissed by you is just about the most exciting thing that ever happened to me."

"What's the most exciting?"

"I don't think I'm going to tell you." How easily he brought her to the brink of dropping her guard entirely. "I just wanted to tell you I appreciate incredible sensuality when it comes my way. Possibly because it never came my way before."

"Not even with . . ." He pressed his lips together.

Rae said, "Thank you for stopping yourself. I wouldn't have answered, anyway."

"You still think I'm only interested in getting back what Warren stole, don't you?"

"What you think he stole. Aren't you?"

"I wish I was. But, no, sweetheart. No, once this is settled, I'm going to have a hard time trying not to chase after you if you try to get away."

Her heart performed what should be impossible antics. "This is ridiculous."

"You think I don't know that." Swiftly, he slid his hand around her neck, used his thumb to tilt up her chin, and kissed her deeply.

When he pulled back and stood up, Rae wasn't too clear-headed. But that was what he wanted, to muddle her, to use what he knew he did so well to get his way.

"I'm not letting you go out there. Not under any circumstances. You may be the most dangerous thing to come my way—ever—but if you are, I'm just going to have to reform you somehow. I don't know if I'm being punished for every sin I ever committed, but somehow I care about you."

He sounded so believable. To cover what she felt, Rae bowed over Wolf and buried her face between his ears.

"That's a problem, Rae—caring about you—but I'll have to live with it. Come on. First things first. I'm going to be doing some talking you won't like. Keep your mouth shut. Do I make myself clear?"

There was nothing for it but to try to go along. She slid to the ground. "I'd appreciate it if you didn't speak to me like that. I don't respond well to rudeness."

"You're unbelievable," he said, taking her elbow. "Absolutely bottom of the heap when it comes to leverage, but you still keep dishing out orders."

Knowing when you were beaten was as important as knowing when you were winning. Buelah had warned Rae never to forget that. At Dallas's side, she went up the stone steps and crossed a wide veranda to double front doors flanked by jewel-toned leaded glass panels. Light from inside glowed through a red and green sunburst in a fanlight above the door.

Dallas opened one of the doors and ushered Rae ahead of him.

She stood still on beautiful black-and-white tesselated tile in a gracious foyer and wished herself far away.

"Tully!" Dallas said behind her. "You okay?"

Rae had been too distracted to notice a thin, white-haired woman seated on the staircase that curved upward from the center of the entrance hall.

"Just waitin' for one of you no-goods to decide to give up your ramblin' ways," the woman said. Dressed in shiny black, with huge black tennis shoes laced loosely around skinny ankles, she held her knees together and her feet far apart. She pointed a long, arthritic forefinger at Dallas. "About time you showed your face, boy. I've got a few things to say to you."

Dallas's hand was firm at Rae's back. He urged her forward. "Not now, Tully, there's a dear. Is Ava home? Fancy?"

Tully shook her head extremely slowly from side to side. Her hair, pulled tightly into a bun atop her head, showed streaks of scalp. "Uh, uh, uh," she said. "Gallivantin'. Not that it's my place to talk about the way a woman of your mama's age chases around the countryside, doin' who knows what, with who knows who. No, siree, not my place."

"They aren't home?" Dallas said, and Rae heard amused tolerance in his tone and, for the first time, felt a true softening toward him. "Never mind. I'm sure they won't be much longer. I expect my mother's got her garden club."

A bony, but elegant hand flapped from a loose wrist. "Garden club? Is that what they call it now? Well, my-oh-my, I'll just have to watch my mouth in future. Garden club. Mm, mm, mm. And I suppose Ms. Fancy Lee's garden clubbing, too. Mm, mm, mm. I got to get me some of that garden clubbing."

"Tully's been with us a long time," Dallas said, his voice conversational. "I'm afraid she sometimes gets carried away wanting to look after us all."

"Who is that?" Tully asked, her impressive pointer aimed at Rae.

"A friend of mine," Dallas said. "We'll be in the conservatory. No need to worry about us."

Tully waggled her head. "No need to worry, huh? Scrawny little thing, ain't she?"

The pressure on Rae's back increased, and she was propelled past dark wood benches that lined the walls.

"Pretty enough," Tully said, obviously unbowed. "I can see how she'd be the one."

"Now, Tully—"

"Uh, uh, uh," Tully said, stopping him from continuing. "You know what I'm saying to you, boy. When did you ever bring a woman home? I'll tell you when. Never. You never brought a woman home because you never met one you cared about. Exceptin' that silly thing you thought you were going to marry when you still had pimples on that devil face of yours."

In other circumstances Rae might have felt sorry for Dallas. As it was, she enjoyed hearing him treated with absolutely no respect by someone who evidently worked for him.

"You'll do, girl," Tully said. "I do believe this boy's been hiding good taste all these years. Why, I'm a happy woman tonight. About time we had something good to look forward to around here."

Dallas cleared his throat and put an arm around Rae's shoulders to rush her into an airy living room with pale yellow walls and very high ceilings. The furnishings were also yellow, and softly feminine.

"Don't you take no nonsense from him, mind," Tully called after them. "Make sure he keeps his hands where they ought to be. Nowhere on your body, girl. Let 'em have what they want, and it's all over. Keep up the mystery. Keep your top buttoned up, and your skirts down. Keep 'em guessing. Why—"

The rest of what Tully said was lost when Dallas closed the doors to the foyer. His face faintly red, he avoided Rae's eyes and strode to one of two sets of doors, one each side of a white, marble fireplace, and pushed them open.

With no choice but to follow, Rae entered a hexagonal conservatory built onto the side of the house. Palms, gardenias, orchids, fragrant vines with sprays of tiny flowers, the care lavished there was evident.

"My favorite place to be," Dallas said, still without looking at her. "Sorry about that out there. Tully's been with the family since before I was born. In my book that buys her the right to say just about anything she wants to say, but she can unnerve strangers."

"She's wonderful," Rae said, and allowed herself some enjoyment at the discomfort she sensed in Dallas. Her humor was short-lived. She could only think that she was about to be ambushed by the Calhouns, collectively. "What have you decided to do?"

He did look at her then. "Tully's right. You're pretty. Not really pretty. Just too damned appealing for my good."

"Don't change the subject." Before his mother and sister got back she'd like to know what she was about to face.

"I intend to introduce you to my family."

Humidity hung in the conservatory. Usually Rae enjoyed moist warmth, and the exotic scents of hothouse flowers. Tonight they seemed cloying and did nothing to lessen her uneasiness. "I thought you didn't want them to know about me." If he'd really changed his mind, she was about to lose the best leverage she'd thought she had.

"Are you hungry?" Dallas asked.

"What are you going to tell them?"

"I can call Tully. She'll bring us something."

In other words, he intended to let her sweat. "I'm not hungry."

"Sometimes you have to be able to adapt fast. Things have changed. It's time for damage control."

"Meaning?"

"You shouldn't have gone all over Glory asking questions. Poking in our affairs."

She felt slightly sick. "Was that why you were following me to the cabin?"

"You bet your goddamn . . . Yes. I warned you I'd never allow you to interfere. You've already done enough damage." The dangerous edge to Dallas's voice didn't cool the temperature in the room, just the blood in Rae's veins. She felt wobbly.

"Don't blame me for trying to find a way to defend myself. You stormed in and called me a criminal and a liar. You threatened me. And you brought the happy news that—"

"Keep your voice down."

Aha, Rae thought, so he still wanted to keep that part quiet. Relief relaxed a muscle or two in her back. "You brought bad news. Then you threw orders around as if you owned me."

"I will own you." Cold didn't come close to describing the set of his features, or the tone he used. "I already do. You just haven't accepted it yet. You will. But it won't be tough, not if you play the game—my game. I always win, Rae."

She wanted to say, *not this time,* but decided she'd save it for when she'd done what she now knew she had every intention of doing. Rae Maddy would take the lid off this town, and this family—and others like them who thought they could victimize people just because they were poor by Calhoun standards.

"No snappy comeback?"

She regarded him, and tried to inject nonchalance into her saunter as she set off over the brick floor of the conservatory. "I'm writing that book I told you about. I've already started."

A fib, but it wouldn't be tomorrow. "This is a free country, Dallas. If I want to write and publish a book about the rot behind the pretty glass in front doors like yours, I have a right to do it. And lots of people will want to read it."

"That type of thing's old hat."

She pulled a spray of waxy white flowers beneath her nose. "Not the way I'm going to write it. What exactly did Tully mean out there? About *garden clubbing?* Surely not that your mama might be out seeking entertainment of some other variety."

"Damn you," he said, and she heard the smack of his approaching boots. "Would you let me get away with making lewd suggestions about your mother?"

She shrugged. "You can if you like. I don't even know who she was. Never met her—that I remember. And I didn't make lewd suggestions. I asked questions, is all. That's one of the things I do best."

"You sure do. At the records office. In my own real estate offices. Even Nick Serb at the bookstore. He couldn't wait to let me know the kind of questions you've been asking. Doing me a favor, he said he was. He said he was concerned. 'Surely there couldn't be anything worth writing one of those smutty exposés about in Glory.' His words, not mine. And the bastard rubbed his hands all the time he was talking. Probably planning a launch party for the book."

"I met Joella LaRose," Rae said casually, aware that she was playing a dangerous game. "I hadn't known Warren had a sister. Interesting."

"Damn you," Dallas said, taking her by the shoulders and spinning her to face him. "Let well enough alone, will you. It's not going to stop me from taking back what's mine, so don't meddle. The post office box in Savannah. It's closed. What did Warren pick up there? Mail from the clients he took from Calhoun? It was in the name of Maddy and Associates."

She blinked, confused by the sudden switch in topics.

"Maddy and Associates was the name of our company," she said, distracted.

"*Our* company? Who were the associates?"

Defensiveness was something she shouldn't feel. She felt it anyway. "There's no reason I have to answer personal questions."

"Personal questions about how you and my brother-in-law defrauded me? I found the keys with his stuff. When I went to see what was in the box, they said it had been closed and wouldn't tell me exactly when."

A post office box? In Savannah? "We, um, found we never used it, so John—Warren decided to let it go."

"The two banks you got correspondence from in Decline. First Travellers, and Federal Union. They were addressed just to you."

"You looked at my mail?"

"Sure I did. You saw me."

"I'm not answering any more of your questions. I'd like to use a phone."

"Why?"

"To call a taxi."

He laughed at her. "Buzz is the only taxi in town. He and his folks run—"

"The grocery store," she finished for him. "So what. I'll call him."

"He won't take you."

Rae parted her lips to ask the next question, but already knew the answer. "You people—and people like you, cronies—you run things here, don't you. You can stop me from getting a taxi. What if I call the sheriff?"

"Do it. Nick Serb would love an excuse to drive the fancy car we provide. Loves to set those lights whirling, and the siren wailing. I expect he'll bring Buzz with him, too."

"The man at the bookstore is the sheriff?"

"Surely is. Mostly his wife does the book selling, he just stands in when she's over at the church. Buzz is a deputy.

We don't have a lot of trouble around here. Not trouble we don't know how to take care of quietly, and quickly."

While he propped himself against a green-painted cabinet, Rae wrapped her brain around the idea that she was in what sounded like a town out of the old wild west. "You people are your own law?" She would not allow him to demolish every shred of her confidence. "This gets better and better. This is the stuff of a truly scuzzy piece of almost-fiction."

The crash of a door slamming shut diverted Dallas. He straightened, and frowned toward the sitting room.

A woman's voice, raised to shrieking pitch, came closer. "Don't you argue with me, you deaf old fool. Gin. Tall. Over ice. No vermouth. And *now.*"

Rae shrank back between two potted palms. What sounded like the same door slamming again made her flinch.

"Ava?" the woman shouted. "Is that you?"

Dallas looked from Rae to the open doors, and back. There was little light in the conservatory. They must be invisible to whoever was in the living room.

"Ava?"

"You hush, Fancy Lee," a new female voice ordered. "I've got a headache. Ring for Tully. I need a drink; then I'm going to rest. After I talk to Dallas."

Rae saw how Dallas hesitated, trying to decide whether or not to walk in on his family.

"Go on up," Fancy Niel said. "I need to talk to Dallas first. I'll have him come up to you later."

"You'll do no such thing," the older woman said. "In case you've forgotten, you aren't in charge around here. I am. This is my house. I decide who does what."

"How can you be so mean, Ava? It's my home, too."

"Not now," Ava Calhoun said. "We're not talking about this now. I've had a most difficult evenin'. You can't imagine how difficult."

"Joella accosted me at the club." Fancy delivered the announcement as if she'd been physically attacked. "To tell me how *sorry* she is for me. Can you imagine that? That piece of no-good trash saying she's sorry for me?"

"Don't pay her any mind. Where's Dallas?"

"I've got to talk to him first, Ava, I tell you."

As if he'd forgotten Rae was there, Dallas walked into the living room, and she inched far enough forward to see a slice of the scene beyond the doors.

"Can we keep it down?" Dallas said as he approached a blond woman dressed in pink, a pink blouse and pink wraparound skirt. She wore light-colored shoes with very high heels. Dallas stood in front of her and said, "Ava, we've got to talk."

"I should think so," the woman said. She looked rumpled and angry. "Every time I need you, you're nowhere to be found."

"Everyone's talking about us, Dallas." Into Rae's line of vision moved a second woman, this one younger, with heavy red hair wound into a loose knot on top of her head. A beautiful woman. Even at a distance, Rae could see that Warren's wife had a spectacular face and figure.

Warren's wife. John's wife.

Rae wondered why she didn't feel something more than interest. Her life had changed so completely, so fast, all she could concentrate on was survival and proving to Dallas that she was innocent of any wrong. An image of Ginny hovered in her brain. She didn't want her anywhere near the sordidness—the promise of danger—that coated this town.

"I want the two of you to sit down and be quiet," Dallas told his mother and sister. "We've got something to deal with. You aren't going to like it, but we don't have any choice."

Something to deal with that they weren't going to like. And the name of that something was Rae Faith Maddy.

"You're going to listen to me first," Fancy said. "Before anything you think is important. You always think whatever matters to you is more important than what matters to me.

Tyson LaRose has been very good to this family. He's discreet."

Dallas said, "Tyson is a swaggering ass with a big opinion of himself. I know he's been working on you to get him into Calhoun. It's not going to happen."

Ava sat down and burst into tears.

"Oh, do control yourself," Fancy said. "You know Dallas and I see right through those tears of yours. You just use them to get attention."

"That's *it*," Dallas said, holding up his hands. "Enough. You're both going to listen to what I've got to say."

"I'm so upset." Ava sobbed. "I've been through so much. When I picked up that pretty little pair of earrings from Godwins, they actually asked me to pay cash money. Can you credit that? Cash money! From Ava Davenport Calhoun. Like I was some common person. You've got to take care of this talk about us, Dallas."

"Tyson's earned our thanks," Fancy said as if her mother didn't exist. "You said you would ask him to join Calhoun, Dallas. You promised he'd be offered the job as in-house counsel."

"We don't need in-house counsel—not the kind he's talking about—and I never said we did. We've got all the legal help I want."

"Oh, but we surely do need him," Fancy insisted. "With everything I hear, we most certainly do need in-house counsel. We need someone who cares about our interests, to look *after* our interests. Tyson's the only possible candidate. I want you to go to him first thing in the morning and beg him to join us. You hear me, Dallas. *Beg* him."

"I don't think it's your—"

"Fancy's right," Ava said. "Tyson certainly is a faithful friend to this family. And I've made up my mind it's time for me to take some part in the business. Clearly you need the occasional helping hand. If you didn't, we wouldn't be hearing all these dreadful rumors."

"Helping hand?" Anger loaded Dallas's voice. He paused a long time before continuing. "You know I respect your opinions, Ava. We'll talk about that later. But I don't need help from you, Fancy. Other than to be sure you're not getting in my way."

"Ava," Fancy said, "tell him he's to hire Tyson."

"I will, I surely will. You call that boy first thing in the morning, Dallas. And do what we're asking. I'd hate to have to force something unpleasant, like drawing attention to the fact that you don't own Calhoun all on your own, but I will if I have to."

"I don't get this," Dallas said. "Why are you suddenly so interested in dragging Tyson into the business?"

"I just am," Ava and Fancy said in unison. Ava continued, "Your daddy hasn't been gone a year, but everything he built—everything his daddy built, and his daddy before him—is shaking on its foundations. He adored and respected me. He gave me everything I wanted, or he thought I wanted. Biff made me the center of his life. I owe it to him to make sure we look after what he loved so much."

Fancy crossed her arms. "That's absolutely right."

"Tyson's a good man," Ava said.

"He surely is," Fancy said. "It's time we brought some good, fresh blood in to help us take Calhoun into the next century. We can't keep on running a business like we were still in the dark ages. We need some daring moves, some *vision.*"

"I get it," Dallas said, more softly. "Tyson's been feeding you a line, hasn't he?"

"He has not," Fancy argued. "Ava and I have been talking, is all. We're not so involved as you, so we can be more objective."

"You're not involved at all. I own seventy percent of Calhoun Properties. We all know what that means. Now drop the subject. I've got someone I want you to meet."

"Meet?" Another chorus.

Dallas turned back toward the conservatory. "Yes." He held out a hand, and Rae had no choice but to emerge from the gloom, into the bright light of the living room.

Avoiding Dallas's hand, she stood beside him while Tully entered with a tray of drinks. "Gin for Miss Fancy Lee," she said. "D.P. for Ms. Ava. Bourbon for Mr. Dallas. I brought you a lemonade," she told Rae, giving her a giant wink.

"Thank you," Rae said, noting that only she and Dallas acknowledged the old lady.

"About time there was cause for a toast around here again," Tully said on her way from the room. "Mr. Dallas brought his woman home. *Finally.*"

In the short silence that followed, Rae kept her eyes on Dallas's face. His mother and sister had frozen, with their drinks in midair.

"I brought someone for you to meet," Dallas said. His gaze didn't waver from hers. "I want you all to sit down. We've got a lot to discuss."

"Who is that?" Ava Calhoun's voice lost some of its strident confidence. "And why was she out there in the conservatory, listening to family business?"

"We were both in the conservatory," Dallas said. "We weren't listening. We couldn't help hearing the two of you shout. Not that you said anything. She's a friend. We're going to get to know each other very well."

With one hand spread over the cleavage revealed at the low neck of her cream dress, Fancy raised her glass to drink, assessing Rae over the rim at the same time.

"We're all going to be very calm," Dallas told his mother and sister. "If we can do that, we'll survive and get past difficult times. If we can't, well . . . there isn't a choice."

An enameled clock chimed on the mantel of the white marble fireplace. Everyone present glanced in the direction of the sound until it faded again.

"What is he saying, Fancy?" A querulous note entered Ava's voice. She put a hand behind her and felt her way to sit on a white couch piped with yellow satin. "Fancy! Make Dallas explain himself right now."

"Nothing to explain." He waved Rae toward a love seat and said, "Sit down, please. I'll try to keep this as short as possible. Then we'll talk to Tully about fixing you up with a room."

Rae's instant reaction was to tell him she'd rather sleep with the dead rattler she'd left behind on the road than stay under this roof.

"We've got private business here," Fancy told Dallas, frowning. "This isn't a good time for socializing."

"I don't think I'd call what I have in mind socializing." Dallas swallowed some of his bourbon. "I decided it was best if everyone knew everyone else. Ava, meet Rae. Fancy, meet Rae. Rae Maddy. She was a very good friend of Warren's."

Fourteen

Sometimes you had to give up on waiting for some luck.

Sometimes the only way to get any luck at all was to grab it.

Even with the tip-off about where he'd find her, the past few weeks had been hell. Weeks of hell after years of hell. Hanging on with the prize somewhere out there, just out of reach. It had been a killer. But luck time had just about rolled around.

His turn, and no one would take it away again.

She was the answer to his prayers. So was the kid. Who could have dreamed she'd bring the kid to Glory, too? That threw him at first—the move from Decline just when he'd been ready to close in—but it was good in Glory. She didn't have friends watching out for her there. Now he wanted to be real sure she didn't change her mind about the little re-union with the girl.

Timing would be everything. And patience. Hell, he hated hanging around.

He ran into the trees above the Parker place. The property sloped downhill from the road. It was important to get every-thing just right before he made his move. When the time came he'd have to get in fast, get it done, and get out fast. After-ward they would never find out it was him. They'd never think of putting him together with a thing like that; why would they?

The undergrowth by the pines was thick enough to hide

in. He crouched against a trunk to catch his breath. Too long since he'd had any reason to run. He sniggered at the thought, and got up to carry on.

A deep layer of sodden leaves slowed him down. The shit sucked him in. He had to run, had to practice how it would be. It would be dark, just the way it was now. He wouldn't have to worry about noise. He'd make sure of that. No one would shout—or scream.

Geez, he'd panicked when she first left for Glory. Then he'd figured out how to make everything work for him. Oh, yeah. Rae Maddy was going to make all his dreams come true after all.

It felt good to smile. He'd earned it. And she owed it to him for everything he'd gone through. They all did.

The leaves made the going heavy. With the weight he'd be carrying, that could make it real tough.

He ran into a tree, cursed, and staggered on. Too little light from the moon. When he came for her, that moon could be a good news/bad news deal.

His lungs sounded like a rusty saw. In and out, in and out. Sawing, sawing. Ticker was loud, too. Dark shapes. More tree trunks. Felt like they were watching him. More and more of them. The forest got bigger. No, smaller. It got bigger and smaller with all the noises in his head. His legs shook. He was out of shape, but not too out of shape for what he intended to do.

His turn.

No woman was going to stop him now.

The trees ended at a bunch of scraggly shrubs. He bent low and crept forward until he brushed through grass that reached above his knees. So this was the Parker mansion. It looked dead. The outline showed pointed rooflines. There wasn't a light anywhere.

Separate garage. Covered drive-through. That would lead to the grounds at the back.

He slipped along behind the shrubs until he reached the

drive-through. If something went wrong at the cabin and he needed a place to hide out with her, he'd use the empty house till things quieted down.

Tonight he just wanted to be sure he'd made the right decision about the way to approach the cabin. Going in by the side road they all used would be too obvious. This way took longer, but it would throw them off.

He needed a drink.

Soon. First he'd make it to the cabin and back. Then a drive to that dump, Decline. And afterward, well, afterward there would be plenty of time to do whatever made him happy—real happy—until he decided to take her out.

Fifteen

"Rae's decided to base a novel on life in Glory," Dallas said. There was a slim chance that diversion might work. "She agreed to visit with us this evening to discuss what she has in mind."

Ava stood up, slopping champagne on her skirt. She stared, slack-mouthed, at Rae.

Any advantage he gained from a bald approach wouldn't last long. He managed a chuckle and said, "You know what they say. If you can't beat 'em?"

"How dare you bring her here?" Fancy spoke to Dallas, but looked at Rae, who hadn't accepted his invitation to sit down. "It's her, isn't it? One of Warren's whores? The one they're all talking about? Get rid of her, Dallas."

He saw all color drain from Rae's already fair-skinned face. She clutched her purse before her, and met Fancy's glare without flinching.

"You hear me, Dallas?" Fancy cried, shaking with rage. "Get her out of here before I faint from horror. The idea. Bringing one of his women into this house."

"The idea," Ava echoed. "What your daddy would have said, I can't imagine."

Ava lived in a dream world where her late husband was remembered as adoring, faithful, and respectful. In truth, in this situation Dallas's daddy would have said all the self-righteous things expected of him, even while he calculated how long it would take him to get back to his current woman.

"Tully," Fancy yelled suddenly. "Tully, you get in here now."

"Why?" Dallas asked, clinging to the thinning end of his temper. "What is Tully supposed to do?"

Fancy pointed a shaking finger at Rae. "Escort *that* to the front door."

"Disgusting," Rae said clearly. She swung the strap of her purse over her shoulder and looked around for somewhere to set down the glass Tully had given her. "Thank you for answering a lot of my questions in such a short time."

Her demeanor, her control, impressed Dallas. "My mother and sister are shocked," he told her. "We can't really blame them, can we?"

"We can always blame people for spitting out words before they've made brain contact," Rae said. She put the lemonade on a Limoges tray Ava kept on the grand piano. "I regret your loss, Mrs. Niel. A terrible, terrible thing."

"Don't you presume to commiserate with me," Fancy said. She had finished her gin and jiggled the glass, cracking ice cubes together.

Ava shook herself visibly. "What's going on here? Is she going to make trouble, Dallas? Is that why you brought her into our home? Oh, dear. Please call Tyson, Fancy. We need his advice about this woman."

"Tyson, yes," Fancy said. "That's what we'll do. Call Tyson."

"You will not call Tyson." He'd expected the storm; now he had to weather it and bring them all through in one piece—more or less. "And I don't want to hear Tyson's name mentioned here again this evening."

Fancy threw herself into an armchair and let her head rest against the back. "We *need* Tyson. I need him. He's my lawyer, and he's going to be a member of the firm. That means he's as good as family, as well as being in a position to deal with whatever she intends to try."

"Would you be kind enough to drive me home?" Rae asked.

"Home?" Swinging the hand that held her glass, Ava splashed more champagne, this on the couch. She didn't notice. "Where is her home, Dallas? She doesn't live in Glory, does she?"

"She's renting the river cabin at the Parker place, Ava," Fancy said. "I thought of telling you, but I knew how upset you'd be."

Ava looked bemused. "You know her, Fancy? You knew she was in Glory?"

"No," Fancy said, rolling her head from side to side. "I don't know her. She wants to make us pay for Warren's indiscretions. She wants to embarrass us because he was a weak, careless man."

Dallas saw Rae look at the door. He went to her side and said, "Hang in with me, please," very quietly. "It'll be for the best—for all of us. Trust me."

"You ask too much," she said, equally quietly.

"I know."

Pacing, Ava said, "She rented the river cabin. Surely that's a Calhoun listing. Why would we rent her anythin', Dallas? Turn her out. Send her packing. Oh, my God, the *talk*. Haven't I suffered enough?"

"It went straight to Linsay May," Fancy said. "You're going to have to fire that woman, Dallas."

"For doing her job?"

Fancy ignored him. "The Parker place isn't our listing. Only the rental of the cabin, and that came on the books just recently."

"Linsay May didn't know who I was," Rae said.

"Shut your mouth," Fancy raged. "How could Warren take up with someone like you? How could he risk dying and having you turn our lives upside down?"

"Warren lived here? With you people?"

At Rae's question, there was silence.

Wolf chose that moment to enter the room, on his belly. He slunk over the blond wood floor to the daffodil-scattered English rug designed especially for Ava Calhoun.

Fancy was in the habit of shouting if she as much as caught a glimpse of the dog. Tonight she didn't seem to notice him— or the filthy tennis shoe he carried.

"Dallas?" his mother said, sounding weak. "What does she mean about Warren living here?"

Sitting straighter Fancy said, "Warren was my husband. Of course he lived here. He spent the happiest days of his life here with me. I'll never stop grieving for him."

"His happiest days were spent in a house with people who only care about what other people think? People who mourn him by being angry that he was in a horrible accident that took his life? And you wonder why he searched for peace somewhere else?"

"Oh!" Fancy rocked forward as if her stomach hurt.

Ava flopped to the couch once more.

"I've invited Rae to spend the night here." Things couldn't get worse. Sometimes the bold stroke was the only stroke. "She had some car trouble."

Ava moaned. "You've lost your mind, Dallas. Don't you care if you kill me? How much more do you think I can take? My entire life has fallen apart. Everywhere I turn there's gossip. Lies. Now this. If you love me, you won't let this go on a moment longer."

"You don't have anything to worry about, Mrs. Calhoun." Rae made to pass Dallas, but he stopped her. "I'm upsetting your family. That wasn't my aim in coming to Glory."

"My family is making me ashamed," Dallas said, preparing for the inevitable explosion. "They aren't thinking. If they were, they'd figure out there are two ways to get through this. We can be civilized and—"

"Or you can be uncivilized," Rae cut in. "The decision's already been made. We don't have any common ground."

"Don't we?" He waited until she met his eyes. "Believe me, we have common ground. A couple of weeks ago I'd have laughed at the idea; I'm not laughing now."

"She suggested Warren went to her because he wasn't happy with me."

Rae turned to Fancy, and Dallas held his breath. "If I did suggest that, I'm sorry. I'm sure the oldest line in the world is that a man turns to another woman because his wife doesn't understand him. Warren never said that."

Courage should be Rae's middle name. Dallas settled a hand on her shoulder and squeezed. "I'm sure Fancy appreciates your honesty."

"I appreciate nothing about this madness," his sister responded promptly. "Where are you from?"

"Tennessee," Rae said.

"Tennessee," Fancy repeated as if the word tasted bad. "Why would Warren go all the way to Tennessee just to find a way to scratch an itch."

"That is so coarse, Fancy Lee," Ava said. "Sometimes I wonder where you learn these things."

Dallas decided he didn't want to see his mother and sister through Rae Maddy's eyes. He said, "Rae's suffered, too, Fancy. She didn't know about you until after Warren died."

"She read about it in Tennessee?" Fancy exclaimed. "All the way in Tennessee. I don't believe that. I believe she expected Warren back and he didn't come because he insisted on playing with that silly plane and managed to get himself killed like that."

Rae looked at the floor, and Dallas felt her sag beneath his hand.

"She knew he came from Glory," Fancy continued. "She got worried she was losing her grip on the easy life he paid for, so she came looking for him. Isn't that the way it went?"

"I expect it must have been," Rae said.

Fancy slapped her thighs and stood up. "Of course it is. You came looking for Warren. When you found out he'd managed to die on us, you decided to take advantage of us. You want money. How much?"

Dallas groaned.

"How much are you offering?" Rae asked.

"See?" Pointing, making a triumphant circle around Dallas and Rae, Fancy's face turned red. "I told you. She's nothing but a tramp. An opportunist, and a tramp. Well, we can't afford much, but we'll come to an agreement. Tyson will have to draw up a paper and you'll sign it."

Fancy had never been long on brains. "Would you please sit down and be quiet?" Dallas said.

"And watch you let her suck you in because you're as much of a patsy for a pair of big eyes and a sob story as Warren was? I don't think so. How much do you want? Hurry up, before I change my mind."

"I want a lot," Rae told Fancy. She glanced at Ava. "I want everything I can get. Start at the beginning. Where did Warren come from? He never did tell me. And Joella LaRose. She's his sister, right? We already met. I'm going to interview her just as soon as we can find a convenient time."

Fancy pressed the back of a hand to her mouth and subsided into the chair again, moaning as she did so.

"Oh, do calm down," her mother said. "You are absolutely no help to me. I'm going to call Tyson this very minute."

"You are not going to call Tyson," Dallas said. "You're going to stop babbling and listen to what's going to happen. First, Rae will be our guest, at least for tonight."

"Under no circumstances—"

"*Yes,* she will be our guest. I'm not going into the reasons, but they're good. She doesn't want to stay any more than you want her here, but it's for the best. End of subject."

He waited for Rae to protest. She'd erased all expression, and he could only guess at her thoughts. They would be ugly, and mostly wrapped around making connections between the man she knew as John Maddy, and the quiet life they had lived in Decline, and what had been real about him as Warren Niel.

"Ava. Fancy. This is hard. I don't underestimate how hard. But I didn't make this decision lightly. Rae's a writer. That's how she earns her living."

Fancy snorted and averted her face.

"I've asked her to give up this notion of hers to write about Glory. And all of us."

"Us?" Ava's eyes and mouth made horrified ohs. "What do you mean, she intends to write about all of us? We're a dignified and distinguished family. She can't just decide to write about us."

"Not about us directly. She's going to fictionalize reality, use Glory as a pattern. And the kind of people who live here as patterns."

"I'm going to write an exposé," Rae announced.

Dallas tipped back his head and sighed.

"We'll all know it's an exposé," Rae continued. "The names will be different, and enough of the facts, and the situations, to keep me out of court. But we'll know—and so will all the people you're so afraid will talk about you."

"We'll sue," Fancy said. "I'm calling Tyson."

"He must be really something." Rae ducked away from Dallas's hand and sat on a love seat. "A warlock or something. Does he wear a black cape and bring a wand?"

"Don't you be flippant," Ava said.

"He's going to come in and make me disappear," Rae pointed out. "That's going to take powerful magic."

Dallas had reached the end of his patience some minutes earlier. "I'm going to give Rae all the help I can," he said. "I expect you and Fancy to do the same, Ava."

"Impossible."

"Essential. Either we make sure she learns about us from

our point of view, or she'll have no difficulty finding a whole line of folk aching to talk about us."

"Tyson—"

"Don't mention Tyson again tonight, please." If his control snapped, it would be ugly. Rae had already witnessed enough ammunition against the character of the Calhouns. "I think for some reason Rae's got the impression we're unreasonable people."

"How could that be?" Rae said, straight-faced.

He would not lose his temper. "All I can think is that we've got enemies in this town."

"Think of that," she said.

Fancy took a cigarette from a box on the table beside her and lit up. Breathing out a stream of smoke, she said, "It's hard to believe when everyone around here has done nothing but benefit from what our family has done for the area."

"True," Ava said. "All the jobs we've provided."

"Tully must feel so honored," Rae remarked.

"She does," Fancy said. "And you and I are always willing to volunteer our time, aren't we, Ava?"

"We sure are, honey. Just think of all the things we do for people."

"All that garden clubbing," Rae said.

Dallas barely contained his grin.

"Why, Ava, there isn't a soul hereabouts who doesn't know I get my hair done twice as often as I really need to just to give that little shop the extra business it needs."

Rae murmured, "Selfless."

"So do I," Ava said. "And my nails. If it was up to most around here, a shop like that wouldn't do half as well."

"Trickle down economics," Fancy remarked. "Isn't that what you call it, Dallas?"

"Gush down," was Rae's comment.

"So don't you think it would make sense for us to be-friend Rae?" If he were a superstitious man, he'd cross his fingers.

Ava fluffed her hair, and flapped a hand before her face. "How's that? Ring for Tully, would you? And get that no-good hound off my hand-loomed rug."

"It would make sense because if the town sees we've taken Rae into our home, and into our hearts, so to speak, then surely we make it harder for them to try to poison her against us."

"Aha," Fancy said. "But you do know she's ready and willing to be poisoned, don't you? Why, Dallas, only minutes ago she was waiting for us to make her an offer to keep quiet."

"You still didn't make the offer," Rae pointed out.

Dallas had to grin. He caught her eyes and narrowed his in warning. "I think Rae has a wicked sense of humor, Fancy. Dry. You know what I mean?"

"No, I most certainly don't know. I'm a very serious person myself. And considerate of other people's feelings. I'd never think of barging in on someone else's grief and making silly jokes. Not that I think she's joking at all."

"Fancy," Dallas said patiently. "What I'm suggesting is very simple. There are those who are holding their breath waiting for us to react to Rae. They're rubbing their hands and praying we make a big fuss. If we tried to throw her out of town—"

"You couldn't," Rae said helpfully.

"If we tried to make her want to leave, they'd line up to tell their stories about us."

Ava huffed loudly. "There aren't any stories."

"I'll bet," Rae said. "Nothing but a lot of garden clubbing."

Ava ignored Rae. "They'd only look foolish because we'd know they were showing how jealous they are. We've always been the most powerful family in these parts."

"Tyson should never have married Joella Niel," Fancy said, her tone distant.

"Not now," Dallas told her. "Don't start on that now, please. We're going to play this smart."

"If he'd kept his pants zipped with that one, she wouldn't feel near as important. I know she handed out *favors* to some of the judges in that contest, if you know what I mean. I know you know what I mean."

"What contest?"

Fancy glanced unseeingly at Rae. "Miss Glory, of course. She never got over winning, not that she really did win. A miscarriage of justice, that's what it was."

"Fifteen years ago, Fancy," Dallas said, growing edgier by the second. "Are we agreed about how to proceed with this thing?"

"And Melvira LaRose may have left her husband flat and run off to Chicago, but you know she's still so jealous of Ava she could just *spit*. Melvira wanted Daddy so bad she could taste it."

"You were there, were you?" Rae asked mildly.

Ava said, "She was not there. The idea. That's all in the past. Forgotten."

"The past is where we get the present from," Rae said. "The past is where I'm going to be getting a lot of my material, and you two are being so helpful."

Fancy and Ava were finally quiet.

"Rae has a little girl." Might as well deal with all possible roadblocks.

"How old is she?" Ava and Fancy chorused.

With a loud sigh, Rae said, "Ginny is ten. She isn't Warren's child."

"Of course she isn't," Fancy said. "Warren always detested children."

Rae let the comment pass, and Dallas sent up thanks. "Rae tells me her little girl will be coming to Glory to visit sometimes until the research is finished, so I expect we'll get to know her."

"Why would you decide to write a story about Glory?" Fancy said.

"Because it fascinates me more than any other place I've ever been. In fact, I get the feeling I'm going to tap into enough interesting details here to give me a book that'll make me a successful woman."

Dallas studied her. Every word she spoke had more than one meaning. She designed them that way.

"The only books that do that these days are the smutty kind that ought to be banned," Ava said. "Sex and violence. Lust, and dishonesty. Disgraceful. No self-respecting person would read them. And if they did, they'd deny it."

"Like I said"—Rae smiled around—"this place could make me."

Ava Calhoun and her daughter were stereotypes. Insular southern belles with little knives for tongues, and appointment books for brains. Appointments to boost their egos, preferably with people to whom they felt superior. When the two of them had left the room, Rae sank back on the love seat with a sense that she'd just traveled back to another time.

"They've never been far from Glory," Dallas said, pacing before the fireplace. "They never wanted to because they feel safe here. Sure of what's expected of them. That kind of life makes for a narrow outlook. They aren't bad people."

"You were reading my thoughts." Rae smiled a little and retrieved her warm lemonade. "I guess it's the circles I've moved in. Ordinary people. Some of them with enough money to be comfortable. None of them with enough to waste time worrying about it. If I'd thought your mother and sister could understand, I'd have tried to explain that I'm fighting here. Fighting to hang on to my simple little life."

"They'll go along with what you want to do."

He either hadn't or didn't want to hear what she was telling him.

"Go along with what you're trying to do, you mean," she said.

"It'll make your way easier."

Rae studied his face. "You're thinking about how much easier it may make your way, not mine." How far would he go to safeguard what was his?

"If we could both come out ahead, I'd be a happy man."

The little flip in her stomach was becoming too frequent, and entirely too familiar—and not entirely unpleasant. He tossed her a few vaguely intimate crumbs and she scuffled for them. Then she tucked them away for later and turned them over and over, looking for the meaning she hoped to find. She wanted him to care about her.

"Do you believe me, Rae?"

"It doesn't matter what I believe. That was a pretty tale you spun for them. The truth is I'm going to confront the accusations you've made against me and find a way to prove you wrong."

Softness fled his eyes. He went to a table behind the couch and lifted a decanter from a black lacquer tray. "Bourbon," he said. "This was what my daddy drank. Me, too. It's always been the only liquor kept readily available around the house."

"Paternalistic," she commented.

Dallas breathed slowly in through his nose. "I can't argue with that. But my mother doesn't want the tradition changed, so it stays. Will you join me?"

She shook her head. "You feel you've pulled off a brilliant move, don't you? You think you've neutralized me. It won't work, Dallas."

"You'll try to make sure it doesn't."

With a heavy crystal goblet in hand, he sat on the arm of the love seat. "This could all be so simple. Help me, Rae. I'll make it worth your while."

She was too tired to be really angry anymore, and she had

an increasingly pressing problem—Ginny. She had to figure out a way to stop her from coming to Glory without making her heartbroken with disappointment.

"Rae?" Dallas said.

"Why don't you explain exactly what it is you think I can help you with?"

"Sure. Warren established himself as John Maddy. Then the two of you set up business as John Maddy and Associates. That was nothing more than a clearing house for the proceeds of what he took away from Calhoun."

Tired, she might be. Beaten, she wasn't. "It's not true. So I can't help you."

"Yes, it is. But we'll come back to that. I want you to move in here."

She wrinkled her nose. "Move in? What do you think I am? A masochist? How long do you think it would be before I woke up dead?"

"I would never let anything happen to you."

Another of those little comments of his. "Not deliberately, maybe." Or maybe very deliberately. "Are you going to take me back to my Jeep?"

"Not tonight. And there's no other way for you to get there. Don't say you can walk, because even you wouldn't be dumb enough to do that."

She considered. "There's nothing dumb about me. Ever. Or mostly not ever. And you're right. I'm not going out on that road alone tonight." Was she really left with no alternative but to spend a night under the same roof as the Calhouns?

Tully came in without knocking. "I made up the room just like you said, Mr. Dallas. Real cozy. Mm, mm, mm. She's a good one. She's a keeper, Mr. Dallas. I always did say you'd probably have good taste if you ever—"

"Thanks, Tully. This is Rae Maddy. Would you show her to her room, please? She didn't bring anything with her. Would you make sure she's got what she needs, please?"

Tully leaned forward from the waist and pressed a big hand to her hip. "I'd like to do that, Mr. Dallas, but my old bones just won't climb them steps even one more time tonight. Besides, I've put her in the room next to yours. Seems like she won't need nothing else."

Sixteen

He really thought she would go up those stairs.

"After you," Dallas said, sweeping his arm toward the second story of the house.

Rae hadn't stayed alive as long as she had because she accepted defeat easily. "Are you nuts?"

He grinned. Rae wished he wouldn't do that. Distrusting Dallas Calhoun was so much easier when he didn't look like a dangerously appealing boy.

"Is this a standoff?" he asked, showing teeth now.

"If you were me, would you consider going to bed in this house?"

"Absolutely."

"You would not."

"I know when I'm in the way of a good thing, ma'am. I would not turn my back on the best offer I'm ever likely to get."

"The best offer?"

He puffed up his cheeks, hooked his thumbs into his pockets, and rolled onto his toes. "Well, far be it from me to brag, but not everyone gets the chance to sleep in the room next to mine."

She laughed. She had to. "Brag? You? Never. Look, we've been around and around about a lot of things. We're both tired of it. I'd really like to get some sleep."

"So would I."

A pause was inevitable. What was she supposed to ask

him to do? "I would appreciate it if you'd drive me home," was the only thing she could think of to say.

"Nope."

Rae glanced up the stairs.

"It makes sense," Dallas told her. "At least for tonight and until we can take a good look at the cabin to make sure it's secure."

"Your mother and sister don't want me here."

"I do."

Why did she long to think he might say that for some reason other than his believing she had something that belonged to him?

Dallas wasn't grinning anymore. He studied her face intently. "I'm not going to let anything happen to you. Nothing will hurt you because of me. Do you understand?"

She didn't.

"Rae?"

There wasn't a choice. "Thank you, I'll accept your kind offer." What kind of woman learned of her husband's death and found another man attractive so soon? "Point me in the right direction and I'll get out of your way."

"I'll take you there."

She looked at him with a raised eyebrow. He couldn't expect her to do other than wonder exactly what he expected of her.

"I said I'd take you there," he told her. "I'm not about to force myself on you."

A woman who hadn't been in love with her husband might fall in love with another man when she found herself alone.

In love.

Rae turned sharply from him and started up the stairs. His footsteps were heavy behind hers. Climbing the stairs together. How could something so mundane feel so intimate?

She was not in love with Dallas.

Falling in love was something she'd never experienced, never had a chance to experience.

As they reached the top he moved beside her and rested a hand at her waist.

If she wasn't in love with him, she was certainly more than mildly aware of him as a man.

Laughable. She had never, ever, allowed herself the luxury of not facing reality. Being in love was something she probably wouldn't recognize if it happened; but she was definitely feeling something for this man, and it wasn't ambivalence.

"My great-grandfather built this house," Dallas said. "I've lived here all my life, but I still admire its elegance. Great-granddaddy had taste and style."

"It's a beautiful house." Suspended from the domed ceiling of the second floor, a fabulous crystal chandelier hung over the semicircular foyer. A garland of carved oak leaves wound about the banisters. "Incredible. I've never been in a house as magnificent."

Dallas led her to the left and through a door leading to a corridor carpeted in dark red. He closed the door behind them and ushered her onward. "I'm the only one who uses this wing. Ava's in the wing that mirrors this, on the other side. Fancy's at the back of the house."

"There must be a lot of empty rooms," Rae said, absurdly conscious that she was alone with him, in his territory.

"A lot." He pressed ahead. "Years ago there used to be a great deal of entertaining. And I think there may have been some thought of a big family at one time."

There was nothing absurd about feeling edgy. "I'll make sure I'm gone before anyone else is up in the morning."

"Why?"

This was how it would be if they were . . . if they were a couple on their way to bed. On their way to the same bed.

He must be thinking about their being together at the cabin.

She was.

"Are you nervous, Rae?"

"No!"

"Sorry. You seem a bit tense. I thought you might feel anxious."

"Of course not."

"Of course not. You aren't the type to be wound up because she's in a strange house and heading for a bedroom with a man she already knows she fits like a really good glove."

Rae stood still. "I don't believe you said that."

"Yes, you do. I said it, but you thought it."

Of course she did. "I did not."

They passed several doors until they reached one that stood open with light spilling out. "This is your new home," Dallas said.

Rae leaned forward to see inside. "You're sure this is the one Tully got ready?"

"It's the one beside mine." He indicated that his was the next room. "You're probably still jumpy from what happened out there on the road."

"I'm not planning to go looking for snakes real soon."

"Didn't think so. Why not come and share my room. That way you won't be so jumpy."

Rae almost laughed. "A lot of responses come to mind. I don't think you'd like any of them. Good night."

"You're turning my offer down?"

"With regret."

With the grin right back, and just as wicked, he rested a shoulder against the wall. "Never do anything you'll regret. That's my motto. You might want to adopt it."

"Maybe I will. That means I should turn around and go back where I came from."

"Standing on the highway with a snake between your . . . with a snake around your neck."

Rae felt the blood in her face grow hot.

"Sorry about that," Dallas told her. "Kind of slipped out. Guess I was feeling jealous of the snake."

"The snake," Rae reminded him, "is dead."

"Oh, yeah. Forgot that."

"Good night, Dallas. And thanks."

He jerked upright and gave an exaggerated bow. "Good night, Rae. And, you're welcome."

She walked sideways past him and into the room.

He stayed right where he was.

Covered with a faded, blue chenille spread, a single bed stood against one wall. The spread had been turned down to reveal sheets scattered with musical notes—also faded. A set of drums occupied an alcove opposite the bed. Secured with thumbtacks, posters of vaguely familiar pop stars adorned the walls.

A teenager's room. Circa, some years ago.

"There's a bathroom over there," Dallas said, pointing.

Rae was grateful to note that it didn't adjoin his quarters. "Thank you."

"You're welcome."

She hovered.

He rested his opposite shoulder, against the doorjamb this time.

"I'll be fine."

"Want a T-shirt to sleep in?"

"Thanks, but no. That won't be necessary."

"Going to sleep nude?"

Her skin throbbed, actually throbbed. Every move she made felt as if she was pulling against a tight string. "Good night, Dallas."

"Uh huh. This room always got cold."

"It's August."

"September, now."

"September then. It's warm."

"If it gets too cold in the night, knock on the wall. My bed's on the other side."

"I won't get cold." Even if she might like to.

He pointed again, this time toward the windows. "If you get too warm, open those. Veranda outside. Same veranda is outside my room."

"I'll remember that."

"Make sure you do."

Either he was into torture or he was just trying to drag this out.

"Of course you are." Horrified, Rae couldn't believe she'd spoken aloud, but of course he was trying to make the encounter last.

"Of course, I am what?"

She was flustered. "Of course . . . I don't know. That men will be . . . well, they will, that's all."

The darned grin returned. "Men will be men? Is that what you were going to say?" He shook his head. "You don't have to answer that. But you're right. Men will be men, but this isn't about just any old guy thing, ma'am. Oh, no, it surely isn't."

It would be so easy to let this happen. "You said I'd be safe if I stayed here."

He bowed his head, then glanced up at her in the mannerism that he so often used. "How safe does safe have to be? I promise nothing's going to hurt you."

Sure. "I think you and I might have different ideas about what it takes to hurt a person."

"I'm not going to hurt you, Rae."

Her throat dried out. She put her purse on the bed and rubbed her arms. "This is a kid's room."

"My brother's."

"Why is it still the way it was?"

He looked around. "I kind of like it this way." Frowning, he added, "Jesse was my twin. I lost him when we were sixteen."

Rae let out a long, soft breath.

"I'm okay with it most of the time. I don't even know why I told you. I never mention it."

"I'm sorry." There was nothing else to be said, but she thought of Cassie and averted her face quickly. Her present dilemma was Ginny, the building horror that Ginny might be in danger through no fault of her own.

"Good night then, Rae."

"Night. And thanks, again."

"I don't want to leave you."

This wasn't real. He couldn't be interested in her as anything but a way to get to what he thought John had taken from him. Questions rolled in. They overwhelmed her. "I need to be alone. I've got thinking to do."

"Think aloud. Let me be part of what helps you find the answers to the questions."

"I'm not going to ask anything you could answer." Doing something became imperative. Rae went to the window and pulled back a blue cotton drape to reveal one side of a French door. Light from the rose beds illuminated the veranda Dallas had mentioned.

"Moon's gone," he said. "Feels like thunder."

She dropped the drape and walked to look into the bathroom. Wallpaper depicting musical scores covered the walls above white-tiled wainscots. "Your brother liked music."

"We were going to have our own band." Dallas clicked his tongue on the roof of his mouth. "Like a lot of kids. It was long ago and far away. Jesse was a hell of a musician."

"How about you?"

"Nothing special. He was a drummer."

"And you played the guitar?"

"Piano. Mostly a keyboard in those days. Let me get you that T-shirt. And a toothbrush."

"I'm okay. Tully's put toiletries out already."

Dallas started to speak, turned away, and back, and shrugged. "I can't go. Not yet. Lie down and go to sleep. I'll just sit in the chair." He entered the room and closed the door behind him.

Her stomach sucked in so tight it ached. And she ached in other places—and had a mad urge to run and fling her arms around him. And she was wrong, *wrong,* to be sparing even a thought on this now, let alone almost her entire waking and sleeping attention.

"Brush your teeth first, if you want to."

"Yes." This was so dangerous. If she threw her resolve aside, it could be all over; she could lose everything Ginny needed. "I mean, no. It's outrageous for me to be here. You know that. You must leave me alone, Dallas, or I can't stay."

He crossed his arms and squinted into the light from the lamp beside the bed. "Were you ever married?"

"Yes!" Whatever the legalities were, she'd been married. "John—Warren and I got married."

"I meant to someone else."

Rae shook her head slowly. "No, I wasn't. Why would you think about that?"

"You are so—I can't forget what it was like, Rae."

Pretending she didn't know what he meant would be pointless.

"You think about it, too," he said.

She ran her fingers through her hair, and the band at her nape broke. "I don't think people ever forget things like that. At least, I couldn't. Nothing like it—" Sometimes less was more. She'd said enough. "I haven't forgotten."

"No. I wondered about Ginny. You know."

Rae had picked up her purse. "Ginny? Oh, Ginny. I wasn't married to Ginny's daddy." The innocent skein of lies came so readily now. "All that's behind me. Warren helped me make sure it was." That was true.

"I'm glad he did."

With a brush already in her hair, Rae paused. "Are you? Yes, I think you are."

"We all make mistakes when we're kids."

"If you mean Ginny, don't even think it. Ginny was never a mistake."

"She's cute."

"She's beautiful. Inside and out. She's the center of everything that's important to me. I've got to keep her safe."

Mostly Rae managed to forget that Willie Skeggs had been Ginny's father. Suddenly she remembered his face looming over her on that frightful night. Sometimes she wished she'd found a way to stick around Glad Times and see him buried.

Rae felt Dallas waiting for her to continue and said, "I can hardly wait to see Ginny tomorrow."

"You've got lovely hair."

He confused her, tied her up in smaller and smaller knots. "Thanks." If she stopped brushing, she'd look foolish, so she didn't stop.

"Want me to do that for you?"

She dropped to sit on the side of the bed and brushed her thick hair forward, covering her face. "No thanks. Please go and get some rest."

He was silent, but she didn't have to hear him, or see him, to feel him. Or to know when he'd quietly come closer.

"You're tired." He removed the brush from her hand. "Relax and enjoy it."

Relax? Rae rested her forearms on her knees and tried not to react to his left hand anchored at the base of her neck. At first he caught bristles in snarled strands, but slowly he worked until the brush moved smoothly from her scalp to the ends of her hair.

She was never going to relax again.

"I haven't done this before," he said, and he stroked her nape. "There's red in it."

"No, there isn't."

"Yes, there is. Take it from me. When it flies after the brush, the light catches the red."

She was sitting on Dallas Calhoun's dead brother's bed with Dallas brushing her hair and talking about how the light turned her hair red.

"It's peaceful," he said. "I love touching you."

Rae's eyes closed. "Don't say those things."

"I love touching you. I loved making love to you."

If he'd just stop brushing, she could put distance between them. He continued in measured strokes.

"You said you were going to think. Think aloud."

"So I'll tell you the things you think I know."

He hesitated, then resumed brushing. "You are a cynic. A suspicious cynic."

"I'm a realist. And I'm also slightly deranged. If I wasn't, I wouldn't be here with the enemy."

"I'm not your enemy."

What had happened to her quiet life? "You say I've got something that belongs to you. A lot of something that belongs to you. I say I don't have it. That makes us enemies."

"It makes us opponents, not necessarily enemies."

"Semantics. I'm the woman your sister's husband married. Bigamously. Don't tell me you're not on your sister's side."

"Tonight I'm only on my side."

"A sex thing," she muttered.

She felt him move, and when he pressed his lips to her shoulder, just above the neckline of her dress, she knew he was on his knees. He held her shoulders lightly.

If she didn't stop him, they were only going one place. She mustn't go there again, not with him—and definitely not here.

And if not with him, then with no one else, ever.

Rae pressed her forehead into the hollow above his collarbone, and he wrapped his arms around her. He held her and rubbed her back, and murmured meaningless words against her ear.

"You shouldn't want anything to do with me," she told him. "I was married to a bigamist. And he was your brother-in-law."

"Did you know?"

"I told you I didn't."

"And I believe you."

But he was dangerous, and this was wrong. "You and I can't be anything but adversaries."

With one large hand, he moved her face to rest against his neck. He stroked her hair back.

"Warren lived in this house. I should be seeing him everywhere I look. Or at least trying to imagine him here."

"But you're not?"

She didn't want to answer him.

"Did you love him?"

"That's not a question you should ask."

His cheek, when he brushed it against her temple, was beard-roughened. "I think you just told me what I'd wondered about," he said. "You had a primarily business arrangement, didn't you?"

He was pushing her to tell him things she didn't know, but she wasn't a fool. It was entirely possible that Warren took funds from Calhoun. He hadn't been any refrigeration salesman, she knew now, but he'd steadily had more and more money.

Rae moved to pull away.

Using his thumbs, Dallas tilted her face up. "D'you think I don't know this is crazy? I can't believe you don't have a stack of Calhoun money hidden somewhere, but I'm having a hard time seeing you as deliberately stealing from us."

She tried to shake his hands loose, but failed. "I'm honest. Anyone who knows me would tell you I am."

"Who should I ask?"

Avoiding his eyes became impossible. "Buelah would tell you."

"Who else?" His voice grew fainter. He inclined his head, looked at her mouth. "Tell me the list."

The next breath Rae took didn't go far. "I get my assignments from an agent in New York. She suggests me for jobs and I do them well enough to be asked again."

He moved fractionally closer. "And these people know whether or not you're honest?"

"I know I'm honest," she told him, at a loss for more

names. "They'd tell you at the library in Decline. I worked there." She'd forgotten the library.

"I don't give a damn how honest you are." His lips met hers and grazed gently back and forth. "Not now. Maybe never."

She saw his eyes close, and her own drifted shut. He cared, she knew he did. It was this thing that was between them that closed out common sense.

"Rae," he murmured. "We've got to find a way out of this mess."

"Yes."

"I mean it. D'you believe in fate?"

"I don't know."

"I never used to. Then I met you." His brief kiss, his fingers slipping over her shoulders, his thumbs rubbing her collarbones . . . all these combined to destroy what was left of reason. "I'm going to have you, Rae. I've got to have you."

She kissed him back, held his face in her hands and parted his lips with her tongue, and heard him groan. "Kissing you is something," she said, when she could. "You said you wouldn't let this happen."

"Uh uh." He sat on the floor and pulled her into his lap. "I said I wouldn't force myself on you."

Once more they kissed.

"You should leave," Rae said.

"You don't want me to."

She didn't. "I ought to. This is no good, Dallas."

"No? I think it's great. We're just going to have to work things out."

"You wouldn't care if your mother and sister never spoke to you again?"

He studied her raptly. "Could we think about that another time?"

At another time—after they had made love again. She felt

how ready he was, and couldn't stop herself from moving against him. He clenched his teeth.

She wanted him, too. But afterward nothing would be different. He'd still be hunting her. She'd still be hunting for a way to save herself, and Ginny, from running again.

She'd checked the bank accounts in her name. There were plenty of funds, but not enough to account for what Dallas was suggesting. She had yet to make it to the safety-deposit box in Savannah.

He slid his hand upward from her waist and settled a thumb on the side of her breast. His gray eyes were the pewter color she'd come to recognize so quickly. Dallas had only one thing on his mind.

If Warren had stolen from Calhoun, what had he done with the money? She had to find out. And she had to find out what had happened the day he died, and whether or not it could possibly be coincidence that he had chosen to drop out of her life right before his death.

"Rae," Dallas said, "will you let me take you to bed?"

So polite. Yet, if she agreed, he'd become that hard, driving man with iron hands, and an iron body, the one she already knew existed. And then? Would he get up again and say he regretted having to get on with his life?

Could she tell herself the truth—that he would leave her again—and have the control to stop this?

The pad of his thumb found the center of her nipple; then his nail scratched lightly through the thin, green dress, and she shuddered.

"Come on, Rae," he said into her neck, kissing her there, gently nipping at the lobe of her ear, and blowing. "Come on. We need each other."

The door opened, and Rae jumped so hard she felt sickened.

Fancy Niel swept into the room and slammed the door behind her. She didn't glare. Her eyes showed little, but she smiled as she crossed the room and sat on the edge of the bed with her hands folded in her lap. She sat so close, her shoes touched Rae's.

"For God's sake, Fancy," Dallas said, holding Rae tighter. "What d'you think you're doing?"

"Protecting my interests."

Rae's heart beat hard. Her face glowed.

"Go back wherever you came from," Dallas said.

"And let you continue with this disgusting thing?" Fancy's voice rose abruptly, rang out in a dreadful, splitting shout. "Disgusting. Do you hear me, *brother?* That woman was sleeping with my husband. Is that what this is about? You want to see what kind of women Warren preferred to me?"

Rae shut her eyes.

"That's enough," Dallas said. He got to his feet and helped Rae to hers. When she started away, he put an arm around her shoulders and held her at his side. "You're making a fool of yourself, Fancy."

"Am I? What are you doing, then? Are you planning to sleep with her because you want to hurt me?"

"Stop it."

"Answer me, and I may. Is that it, or is it that you're the one who's been involved with her all along?"

"You're not making any sense."

"Oh, I think I am." She got on her feet and paced back and forth, flipping her skirts each time she turned. "I'm making so much sense I can't imagine why I didn't see it all before. You two already knew each other. And you came up with a plan to get what you need. Money."

Dallas didn't say anything to that.

"It's true, isn't it? Calhoun is in big trouble. It's been losing money and you're scared we're going under. Somehow you found out about the insurance money, and you want it. Well, you're not getting it. It's mine. It's all mine. I was married to that man and I earned it."

Dallas shifted slightly. "Go to bed, Fancy. You're making a fool of yourself. I don't know what you're talking about.

Even if Calhoun were in trouble. And if you've got insurance money coming—"

"I do." Fancy raised her chin and smiled with triumph. "A bundle. It was part of the agreement Warren and I made. He let me take out the insurance policies, and I didn't interfere with the way he lived his life."

"But—"

"No," Fancy said. "Don't try to shut me up. You two found out about the insurance and you want it. You want to split it between you."

"How would we do that?" Rae asked, unable to stop herself.

"Oh, you're so innocent, aren't you? By working it so I'd pay you off to keep quiet. Well, it's not going to happen. And if you open your mouth about Warren, I'll tell everyone it's a lie."

"And they won't believe you," Dallas said quietly.

Fancy raised a hand to hit him, but he caught her wrist.

"Don't," Rae said, horrified. "Please, don't. It's dangerous."

"Dangerous?" Fancy spat, struggling to free herself. "You bitch. You haven't seen dangerous yet. Let me go, Dallas."

"No." Sweat broke out on Rae's face. Violence between men and women led to more violence, and to violation. "Stop it, please."

Dallas released Fancy, but not without pushing her hard enough to land her back on the bed. "Just how much money are you getting, sister dear?"

When she tried to rise to her feet, he plunked her back down. "None of your business," she railed. "It's mine. All of it's mine. There's no way I'm going to give up what I suffered for just so you can give it away."

He grew still beside Rae. "You're afraid I'm going to give your money away?"

Fancy's mottled face cleared a little. Her eyes lost some of their feverish glitter. "It's not that much. I just don't like it that you've cooked up this fantastic plan to take it away from me."

"Fancy," Dallas said. "You're so far off base, it's pathetic."

"Prove it."

"I don't have to. What I said to you and Ava stands. Either we work with Rae, help her get her story, or someone else will. And if we leave it to others to tell our story, we are probably going to hate what she makes public about us."

Fancy started to laugh. She choked, and laughed some more, wrapped her arms around her middle and shrieked with laughter, sounding more hysterical by the second.

Snorting and coughing, she pointed at Dallas and said, "Help her? Is that what you call it? New term for what you're doing together." Wiping tears from her face, she made fists and pounded the mattress. *Help?* What's the matter, brother? Are you afraid the whore will write it in her little book that you're no good in bed?"

"You've lost it," Dallas said coldly.

At the sound of knocking on the door, he let out a low curse.

"Probably Ava," Fancy said, giggling. "I expect she's come to see how you're helping the bitch."

Tully, not Ava Calhoun, opened the door. Puffing, she scuffed in. "So much trouble," she said. "I knew as soon as it started again it would be like it was before, Mr. Dallas. Your daddy—"

"Tully," Dallas snapped. "That's enough."

"Yes, sir. But we got trouble. It's a message for you, on this contraption."

Rae hadn't noticed that Tully carried a cordless phone.

"Who is it?" Dallas said, reaching.

"Hospital," Tully said, rolling her eyes. "Trouble all over, I tell you. Get the LaRoses and the Calhouns mixed up in anything, and you've got trouble."

Fancy sprang to her feet and delivered a sharp blow to the woman's face.

"No," Rae cried, wrenching away from Dallas. She shot to stand between Fancy and Tully. "No violence. You mustn't do that."

Fancy had raised her hand again. And Dallas had grabbed her wrist. He spun her around, backed her across the room and shoved her into a chair. "Tell Tully you're sorry. *Now.*"

"You can rot. So can she."

Fancy's fingers had made red marks on the old woman's cheek, but she stood, unflinching, with her hands at her sides. "Don't mind her," she said. "She's got a devil in her. She was born that way. The hospital's on the phone, Mr. Dallas."

Keeping a grip on Fancy's wrist, Dallas raised the phone to his ear and barked, "Yes. This is Dallas Calhoun. Who is this?"

He listened, and his expression gradually changed. He said, "Yes." Then, "Where?" Then he looked at Rae, and away, and finally said, "We'll be there," before switching off the set.

Rae came close to utter panic. Hospital. Could it be Ginny? "Has something happened to Ginny?" she blurted out.

"No," Dallas said. "Nothing like that."

"I told you it was trouble," Tully said. "You better get goin'."

"I think you know Linsay May Dale," Dallas said to Rae.

Her stomach contracted. "We've met twice."

"Once when she rented you the cabin when she shouldn't have," Fancy said.

If Dallas heard his sister, he gave no sign. "She was on her way to see you."

"Me?" Rae said, overwhelmed by dread. "You mean at the cabin?"

"Evidently she wanted to talk to you about something."

Something about the Calhouns, or some other powerful people in Glory. "What's happened?"

Dallas looked at her steadily and gave a very faint shake

of the head. He was cautioning her about something. "Evidently she had some problem on the way. On that bridge right before you get to the Parker place."

"Oh, no! She had a collision with—"

"No. Not that. They aren't sure exactly what happened, but they found her on the riverbed."

of the bunk. He's confined to her about something." Evening air. See, you's promised you this wire fella had a big
night trouble with not leavin' Fish—[illegible]

The nM She had a solution with S[illegible]
of [illegible] this little, they won't cause crucifixial [illegible] [illegible]
nu. this forbidding for the pressure [illegible]

Seventeen

Nick Serb, thin, and thrilled in his starched khaki uniform,
struck an attitude in the sole patient room corridor of tiny
Glory Medical Center. With glittering black shoes regulation
inches apart, his silver-braided, navy Stetson beneath his
arm, and a notebook in hand, he watched the approach of
Dallas and Rae with toothpick-chomping anticipation.

"Fatuous ass," Dallas muttered.

Rae said, "Poor Linsay May. This is my fault."

He'd had no choice but to bring her with him. Leaving
her at Sweet Bay with Fancy was out of the question, and
she would have found her way here on her own anyway.

He took hold of her upper arm and said, "She can't be
too bad. They said we can go in and see her."

"One at a time, and don't stay long. That's what the nurse
said," Rae pointed out.

"Evenin', Dallas," Nick said as they reached him. "Sorry
you've been troubled with this little thing. I told them there
was no need to go botherin' you, but—"

"Not a bother," Dallas said quickly. Nick was likely to
say something it would be preferable for Rae not to hear.

"Are you standing guard, Mr. Serb?" Rae asked. "Has
there been trouble here at the hospital, too?"

Dallas glanced at her. Pale and big-eyed, she nevertheless
appeared calm.

"I was waiting for Mr. Calhoun, Ms. Maddy." Nick met
Dallas's eyes with knowing familiarity. "Nothing out of the

ordinary, wouldn't you say, Dallas? Just a case of neighborly concern. Glory's an old town, ma'am. Those of us with deep roots here stick together. Others move on, anyway."

Nice going. Leave it to Nick to wallow in subtlety, Dallas thought. "Linsay May was asking for me?"

"Do you mean *all* others move on?" Rae asked Nick Serb.

He spread his feet a little wider, tucked his notebook into a pocket, and ran his fingers around the brim of his hat. "Well." His frown, and the roll of the toothpick from one side of his mouth to the other, suggested deep consideration. "Let's just say this doesn't tend to be a good place for strangers. Especially trouble-making strangers."

"Do you suppose that kind of mentality caused someone to shoot out a tire on my Jeep?"

"Well, ma'am,"—Nick cleared his throat and widened his stance—"well, I wouldn't like to comment on a thing like that without studying the evidence, but you ought to remember that we've got a lot of hunters around—"

"Is that Linsay May's room?" Rae caught Dallas's eye, and walked to the door beside Nick. When Nick didn't answer, she said, "It is? Okay. Linsay May offered me her friendship and I accepted. She's a sweet woman. She was on her way to see me when this awful thing happened. So why don't you keep right on posturing while I see if there's anything I can do?"

She tapped on the door and opened it, whispering, "Linsay May?"

Dallas avoided making eye contact with Nick and entered the room behind Rae.

"Evenin', Dallas." Buzz, Nick Serb's clone minus some of the silver braid, bobbed up from the chair he'd occupied at the foot of one of two beds. The second bed was empty. "Evenin' to you, too, Ms. Maddy. Rae, that is." The man smiled at Rae, and Dallas didn't miss the signs of admiration in Buzz's eyes. It shouldn't irritate him, but it did.

"Oh, Dallas." Linsay May, pallid, bruised, and plaintive,

held both hands toward him. "Thank you for coming. I just knew you would."

Sure she did, Dallas thought. Thumbscrews were tightening all over. Thanks to Warren's indiscretions, days in Glory were becoming one long trek through a minefield.

He took Linsay May's hands and told her, "Everything's going to be fine," while he glanced at Rae. Warren had brought trouble cascading into town, and that trouble's name was Rae Maddy.

Thanks, Warren.

She was the only thing he was ever going to thank his sister's philandering husband for.

"Oh, Linsay May," Rae said. "I'm so sorry this happened to you. Where are you hurt?"

He was in love with Rae Maddy.

He'd thought there was no such animal as "being in love," but he'd been wrong.

"I guess I'm hurt all over," Linsay May said faintly. Her black hair stood out in all directions. "All those rocks down there. It was awful. I was so scared. He was a big thing, not that I could see him. He grabbed me from behind and just threw me off the bridge."

Could he be in love with Rae Maddy? Scary thought. In love with the woman who might very well have conspired with Warren to suck the life from Calhoun Properties.

"Now, Linsay May," Buzz said. "Don't you go talking too much. The doctor said you was all shocked up. You're supposed to be taking it easy."

"Listen to what Buzz says," Rae agreed.

"I was driving out to see you, Rae," Linsay May glanced at Dallas and lowered her eyes. "But we won't talk about that now."

In other words, Linsay May had decided to become the problem she'd promised Dallas she'd never be. She intended to find out if there was money in discussing what she knew about the Calhouns with Rae.

Rae said, "We don't have to talk about anything. I'll just sit with you, if you like."

Linsay May still clung to Dallas's hands. She cast him a beseeching look. "Rae and I met the other day. We're both alone. That gave us something in common, so I was going out to see if she wanted some company."

Linsay May, Dallas decided, was protesting more than necessary if she had nothing complicated on her mind.

"Your Jeep was on the bridge, Rae. I had to see what had happened. As soon as I was out of my car and walking around to the driver's side of the Jeep, he just jumped me." She turned her arms. "Look at my elbows. And my knees are just as bad. And my face. Oh, I feel so sick."

"It's lucky someone found you," Dallas said, desperate to stem the flow of what felt like rising hysteria.

"She drove herself in here," Buzz said. "Brave little woman. She got herself back up on that bridge and drove herself here. Doc called Nick and me right off."

Dallas noted that the story had already changed slightly.

A loud voice in the corridor said, "Scum rising to the top finally, Nick? Bound to happen. Time we did some pullin' together around here."

Nick Serb stuck his head into the room and said, "Excuse me, Dallas. I think you'd better get out here. Buzz—go to the car and get on the radio. See if you can round up some of the fellas. Tell 'em to stand by the phones till I get back to them."

Dallas followed Buzz into the corridor to be confronted by the unwelcome sight of Carter LaRose's hooded, bloodshot eyes.

"Time you boys were searching around that bridge," Carter said to Nick and Buzz. "Never mind standin' by. You get the rest together and fan out. Comb through the trees."

Exuding thwarted importance, Nick said, "Linsay May always was the panicky type. Probably fell off the bridge, then got embarrassed and made up a story."

"Rae's tire was shot out," Dallas said.

"Like I said," Nick said right on cue, "hunters and stuff all over these parts."

"Nevertheless," Carter told him, "you go do what we're all paying you to do, y'hear?"

Nick opened his mouth, saw Dallas's hard stare, and turned away. Buzz gave Carter a nervous glance and hurried after Nick toward the lobby.

"Quite a situation you've got on your hands here," Carter said to Dallas.

"I've got?"

"Sure. The shit's hit the fan, boy. We always knew it had to one day, but not this way."

Dallas inclined his head toward the partly open door to Linsay May's room.

Carter gave no sign of understanding. Rather he placed himself between Dallas and the room, and took a notebook from the pocket of his white linen jacket. "I'm here as a friend," he said. "I'm also here for the *Speaker.* Why not talk to me, Dallas? Your daddy and I were old friends."

"Old enemies," Dallas muttered. "You hated each other."

"No such thing. Nothing of that nature at all. I admired that man. If I could have had a brother, I'd have chosen Biff Calhoun."

Liar. "That's not the way I ever heard it."

"We're southern men. We're not likely to make our feelings obvious. You know that. Linsay May got in a little trouble and sent for you. Isn't that the way it went?"

Dallas made to close the door.

Carter propped his back against the jamb and scribbled on his pad.

"I expect Linsay May always calls you if she needs somethin', doesn't she?"

"Carter, could we—"

"Not so surprising, really. She's still a pretty thing in a way."

"I don't think there's anything more to be done here tonight," Dallas said. "There surely isn't any story for the *Speaker*."

"You were good to Linsay May when her mother was sick. Helping them out at the end like that. You're probably still her primary source of income, wouldn't you say? That job at the rental office can't be worth much."

"You're prying." Dallas's temper thinned. "You'd better go."

Carter snorted. "Once upon a time you people owned this town. The way I hear it, you're havin' trouble hanging on to clients these days. Lots of stories circulating. Don't tell me where I can and can't be."

"This isn't doing either of us any good," Dallas said.

"I'm kind of enjoyin' it myself," Carter said, smiling. "I expect Linsay May sent for you because you know what good care she took of your daddy."

Dallas grew cold. Chances were every word could be heard in the patient room behind Carter.

"Does our little writer know where Biff was when he died?"

"That's enough." Dallas stepped close to Carter. "Not another word. Understand?"

Carter doodled on his notebook. "I don't think it would be a good idea for you to hit me, boy. Do you? Might not read real well on the front page tomorrow."

"Go home, Carter."

"I intend to. Soon as I've said everythin' I came to say."

"Good night to you, then."

"I just wanted to be sure you don't get careless and forget anything really important. The way I heard it, Linsay May was on her way to see the little writer tonight."

"Get this over with."

"Seems to me Linsay May could have temporarily forgotten that she was the last one to see your daddy alive. Then, when she remembered, she decided she ought to run out and tell her new friend. Warren's lady friend."

"Damn you, Carter," Dallas said through his teeth. "What's your angle? Why bring this up now?"

"Oh, you worry too much. Just like your daddy. A niggler. I'm helping you out is all. Making sure you watch your back. You probably don't have a thing to worry about. I understand you've got the writer in your pocket." Carter sniggered. "Or should I say you've got her right where you get all your women, and it ain't in your pocket, boy, is it?"

Dallas scrubbed at his face. He could almost feel the two women listening on the other side of the door.

"Too bad this was one of Warren's pieces, though," Carter continued. "Could make things real awkward around Sweet Bay if things go wrong."

"Keep your voice down."

"I always did think Biff made a poor choice with Linsay May. He should have given her up after she tried to shoot him that time."

Dallas itched to grab Carter.

"Don't worry about the bridge thing. There's always been the odd wanderer in these parts. Any parts. He'll move on and we'll never hear from him again." He raised the hand holding the notebook and waved. "Hey there, Tyson."

Groaning, Dallas turned to watch Carter's smooth son approach. "What are you doing here?"

"Fancy called," Tyson said promptly.

He might have known his sister would go against his wishes—again. "You aren't needed here."

"That's not the way I hear it." Tyson nodded to his father. "Fancy thinks you'll want me on board now, you being in the way of having to deal with fighting for Calhouns' reputation—both the personal kind, and for the company. She thinks that since Linsay May was probably on her way to talk to your friend about things that shouldn't be talked about, you'll probably want the company lawyer to keep your hands clean for you."

"If you two aren't out of here in two minutes, I'll throw you out."

"Violence is so distasteful," Carter said, smoothing back his straight, gray hair. "And Tyson might have something to say about that."

"I know what you're trying to pull," Dallas told them. "It isn't going to work. You're not a team player, Tyson."

"It's going to work." Tucking his notebook back in his pocket, Carter brushed at his jacket. "It'll work because you won't have a choice. You're going to have to do what you should have done a long time ago and take Tyson into the firm. Just remember, the main thing right now is to make sure your dear mama never has to deal with the town finding out what Biff was doing when he died."

Dallas made fists.

Carter started walking.

Tyson followed, saying over his shoulder, "Last Thanksgiving Day. It must have been sad for you and your mama. But from what I hear your daddy was really sending up those thanks. Gave Linsay May his all, and died a happy man."

Eighteen

With hushed respect a dapper assistant manager ushered Rae into a small room with a security lock on the door, and a reinforced window.

Savannah's First Travellers Bank spoke of ancient wealth. Pink marble columns, mahogany panels, brass grills, discreetly placed, brass-studded, leather chairs, and a heavy scent of polish and old cigar smoke. And employees who never spoke above a whisper and who wore, to a man and woman, dark suits and impeccable, subdued shirts and blouses.

"Will you have tea, Mrs. Faith?" the assistant manager asked, regarding her seriously through his highly polished lenses.

Rae declined. How odd it felt to be addressed by her old name. Her only real name.

"Knock on the door if you require anything," he said while a young man carried two safety-deposit boxes in and set them on a table. "Mr. Bennett here will be right outside."

She thanked them both and waited for the door to close, and for the lock to click home.

More dark paneling covered the walls in what felt to Rae like a plush cell. Green and gold carpet added to a padded atmosphere. She sat on the single leather chair provided and pulled herself close to the round table that held the boxes.

If she had time, she'd be exhausted. Despite Dallas's anger, she'd refused to return to Sweet Bay for the night. She'd gone to a motel instead and immediately called Buelah to tell her she mustn't bring Ginny to Glory.

Rae propped her elbows and buried her face in her hands. She needed help, but where could she turn? Ginny had told Buelah about a man who watched from the fence around the school yard, a man who whispered her name on the one occasion when she got close enough to hear. When Buelah and some of the other teachers checked, there was no sign of a stranger, but then Ginny said she'd seen him again near Buelah's house, and that he'd slipped away when she looked at him.

And Ginny had stopped eating.

Children imagined things, but Ginny had always been sensible. They had learned to rely on each other, and help each other. Ginny wouldn't make up a story like that.

Buelah had lowered her voice when she begged Rae not to call off the visit. And Rae had agreed.

What man would be watching Ginny? Could it be a coincidence? If there really was someone, he didn't have to be a part of what was going on in Glory.

Rae dropped her hands to the table. It didn't matter who he was; she had to protect Ginny.

She must hurry.

Getting away from the motel quietly that morning had taken planning. This was one excursion Dallas must not know about. She'd been afraid he might have asked the motel manager to call him if she showed any sign of leaving, so she had walked through the predawn, and gone as far as the gas station on the highway where she hitched a ride with a trucker.

Rae grinned a little. She'd been lucky. The trucker had spent the trip exploring the condition of her soul and, when he dropped her off in Savannah, had given her a rusty smile and a Bible, before driving away with warnings about the dangers of putting trust in men.

Dangerous indeed.

She must deal with whatever Warren had left for her to find here.

The smaller safety-deposit box—she'd never seen the contents of either—was the one to which she'd always had a key. It yielded the papers for the Decline house, in the name of Rae Faith, which was the name she'd finally managed to establish before John—before Warren had come on the scene. If she'd had any other name, Betty Skeggs never told her. Her high school diploma gave her name as Rae Faith. Eventually, and with the expensive help of a gentleman who disappeared shortly afterward, she'd gathered other documents in the same name, and Ginny had become Ginny Faith. Until Warren.

Also in the box were stocks and bonds. Curious, and with her stomach reminding her she was scared, she examined each document. Again they were in the name of Rae Faith. Not Rae Maddy, but Rae Faith. Because Warren had known there was no Rae Maddy and that if she ever had to come here for them, he'd want her to be able to claim them simply by using her maiden name.

Rae already knew about many of the investments. She and Warren had discussed them. Some of the money she'd made had gone toward their purchase. They were hers, hers and Ginny's. Relief at the knowledge made her temples pound.

She replaced the papers in the smaller box and rubbed her smarting eyes. Warren had cared for her in his way. They could say what they liked about him, but he'd been grateful for the safe haven they had made together, just as she had.

Now there was Dallas Calhoun, and all the truth he'd brought tumbling down around her. There was Dallas, and there were her feelings for him—jumbled as they were.

They had made love.

How could that be? How could it be that a woman who had never known what she assumed was considered to be *passion,* found it so quickly after she discovered the man she'd thought of as her husband was dead?

Reaction to shock?

Lust? Lust she'd never known herself capable of feeling, of wanting to feel?

She might lust for him, but there were other more complicated feelings, more threatening feelings. She didn't want to think of days ahead when he'd be one more part of her past.

What was she going to do?

When she was finished here, she'd make her way back to Glory, get the Jeep attended to, and get ready for Buelah and Ginny to arrive. Despite her fear, the thought of seeing Ginny warmed her. She wanted to hold her, to feel the pressure of her small-boned, responsive arms.

The second box was bigger, heavier. She pulled it toward her and flipped the latch open. More plastic envelopes of stocks and bonds confronted her. She went methodically through them, using a pad of paper to jot down figures. Once more each investment was made out in the name of Rae Faith.

With every number she wrote, she grew more incredulous. Gradually she emptied the box until she found what made it so heavy. A shoulder holster and another Sauer, and spare clips. Her heart beating hard, and fast, she glanced at the high window in the door and put the gun and holster in her purse.

Next came a layer of banded wads of large bills. She counted one, then counted the wads, and made another note on the sheet beside her. Her head began to feel light.

In front of her, in diversified assets, was a fortune, more money than she'd ever considered as existing in the possession of one person.

Under the bills lay an envelope which simply bore the name Rae. She opened it with fingers that no longer wanted to work. On lined paper Warren had written:

Rae,

Confession time, my dear. I've lied to you. As far as you're concerned, everything about me has been a lie; but it was the only way to have you, and I don't regret doing whatever it took for that.

My name isn't John Maddy, it's Warren Niel. That's why I made sure everything was in your maiden name.

*I can't make myself write that we aren't married. In
all the ways that matter, we are. I have a wife who has
the right to call herself legally my wife, but she means
nothing to me. She hasn't since she made it clear I'd
never be sufficient to keep her satisfied. Forgive me
for pouring all this out, but I have to. I also have to
keep this much shorter than I'd like to. I have to keep
it clear.*

*Wait a few weeks, then retain a really good lawyer,
Rae. Be honest with him. Tell him you didn't know my
true history, but that everything in this box is in your
real name. It is your real name, so there can't be any
question.*

Rae set the letter down and wiped her hands on the skirt
of her wrinkled green dress. She trembled more and more
steadily. The last thing Warren had expected was that Dallas
would find her and reveal the truth before she came here to
read it from Warren's hand.

*You and Ginny have the only right to what's mine.
The lawyer will make sure no one tries to meddle. My
wife's name is Fancy Calhoun Niel and she lives in a
town called Glory, on an estate called Sweet Bay
where her family has lived for generations. She made
sure she was well-provided for, and I gave her my
blessing on that. She'll get enough to make her a very
wealthy woman.*

Rae had to stop, to think. Warren had definitely known
he was going to die. There could be no other explanation for
the preparations he'd made, or for the content of this letter.
She read on:

*Rae, I want you to stay away from the Calhouns.
STAY AWAY FROM THEM. Do not let them find out*

about our connection. Our marriage is something we must carry in our hearts. Carry it in your heart for me, Rae. I wish we'd met—well I wish a lot of things.

The gun is just in case you've got rid of the other one. You're such a gentle woman. But wear it, please. Don't be frightened because I'm asking you to do this. It's only a precaution. Now to the other. The rest of what I'm leaving you could make you some enemies if anyone ever finds out who you are. This is what I want you to do. Look over the papers in the packet beneath this letter. Then put them back in the box and return to Decline. Wait a few weeks, then make the move. It'll be good for you and Ginny. It's what you deserve.

Rae, honey, if the Calhouns do find out about us, stand firm—especially with Dallas Calhoun. He's my brother-in-law. That family has already got their share. No matter what he might tell you, remember what I've written here. We have a right to what you're looking at now. You and Ginny have a right to it. It's yours, so keep your mouth shut and don't let anyone take it away from you. The Calhouns are the greediest people in the world. Dallas wants everything. He'd like your share as well as his. And Tyson LaRose, my so-called wife's lawyer, is a louse, too.

Don't forget any of this.

Follow your star, Rae. Keep writing. Now you can work on all those stories you always said you had in your head. You can do whatever you want to do and be whatever you want to be.

Please, honey, never forget what I'm telling you now. The Calhouns are rotten news. They took advantage of a man's bad luck—he was my father. If they ever discovered about you and me, they'd never stop hounding you, and Fancy would try to destroy you.

Do what I'm telling you to do. Do it quietly. And

*remember, Ginny doesn't ever have to know that John
Maddy was Warren Niel. Just tell her I had an accident
on that last business trip.*

Go get 'em, Rae! John

On the bottom of the box lay a fat manila envelope. She
opened it and slid out the contents. A sheaf of heavy papers
triple-folded, and yet more keys. Two identical sets.

Ray wiped her hands again and flattened the papers.

She read a typewritten cover page. It was dated early that
same year.

An utter stillness settled, in the air, and in Rae. All feeling
left her limbs. She could not possibly be looking at what she
thought she was looking at.

Not possibly.

Yet she was. She held the keys in her hand and reread the
top of the first page, then riffled quickly through the rest,
skimming the information contained there.

Rae Faith had inherited the property known as the Werther
Place in Glory, Georgia. The said property was recently pur-
chased by Warren Niel from John and Marjorie Parker of
California.

"Find what you were looking for?" Dallas asked Rae,
shrugging away from a pillar directly outside the room where
she'd been closeted for more than two hours.

Her colorless face caused him a twinge, but he couldn't
afford to soften up on her too quickly.

She turned her back to him while a bank employee carried
two safety-deposit boxes toward the vault. Rae followed, and
Dallas gritted his teeth with the force of wanting to go after
them and demand to know what she'd been examining in
that little Fort Knox of a room.

After a few minutes, Rae hurried back to the lobby. "How
did you find me?" she said, and made to go around him.

Dallas cut her off. "Best not make a fuss. We wouldn't want to draw too much attention to ourselves, would we?"

"I think it would be a good idea if you and I didn't have anything else to do with each other."

"Good day to you, Arnold," Dallas said to the bank manager, waving, and slipping an arm around Rae's rigid waist.

Rae walked with him to the sidewalk before applying a fist to his chest and pushing herself away. "You bank here?" she asked, nodding to the impressive facade behind him.

"No."

She wore the same dress she'd worn yesterday, the dress that had been all she'd had to put back on when she got up at the motel early this morning and headed out.

"If you don't bank here, how come you know the manager?"

"I know all the bank managers in Savannah."

"How nice for you. You know them well enough for them to tell you whether or not one of their clients is in the branch? Incredible."

"He didn't. I knew you had something on your mind when I left you last night. The Land Rover's comfortable, but it's not a great place to sleep."

She started walking. "You mean you were outside the motel all night?"

"Yep." Keeping up with her was easy.

"And you followed me."

"Yes, ma'am."

"Why?"

"To see where you were going."

"It's none of your business."

He pulled her to a halt and swung her to face him. "Isn't it, Rae?"

"You and I are enemies, Dallas. We've got to be. You think I've stolen from you. You blame me for whatever trouble you've got. I'm going back to Glory—alone. Back to the cabin to get things ready for when Ginny and Buelah get there."

"You shouldn't bring that child there. You know damn well it may not be safe."

Tears stood in her eyes. "I think someone is trying to scare me away, but I'll never let anything happen to Ginny."

He didn't need a translation of what she was suggesting. "You think I'm trying to scare you away."

"What would you think in my place?"

"I don't have to defend myself. What did you find in the safety-deposit boxes, Rae Faith?"

Her lips parted and remained parted.

"Arnold's glad I've found someone I'm finally interested in settling down with. All I had to do was breeze in looking for Rae—he told me where you were. He'd never seen Ms. Faith before. Evidently the signature cards for the boxes were signed and sent in by mail."

She ran her tongue over her lips and glanced around as if searching for escape.

"Kind of raises the question about how whatever's hidden away got there, doesn't it? Who brought it?"

"He had no right to discuss my business."

"My fiancée's business."

"You lied." Her fingers tangled in her hair. "It's all the good ol' boy network. I ought to call the police and report you. And him."

"But you won't because you and I are both caught in the same mess. What's in the boxes?"

"Absolutely nothing that has anything to do with you."

Moving swiftly, he caught her hand and held it tightly. "I think it does. And I think you're going to tell me."

"I'm not," she protested, running to keep up with him when he strode a short distance along Montgomery, toward West Liberty and Orleans Square where he'd parked the Rover. She began to pant. "Stop it. Let me go. I'm not going anywhere with you."

"You're going where I say you're going. You're going with me today, and"—he almost said, *today, and every day*—"and you're going to take some advice, sweetheart. You may not see it, but I care a whole helluva lot about what happens to you."

"You've got a funny way of showing it." Each breath she took made a sobbing sound. "I haven't done anything to you, I tell you. Not knowingly. If I had, I'd find a way to put it right."

He stopped abruptly and tugged her against him. "I never wanted to give a damn about you, Rae. But I do, so help me. I really do care about you. That means I'm in deeper trouble than I've ever been in my whole, no-good life. I never cared about a woman before. Do you hear me? Never." And he'd lost his legendary self-control. "We've got to find a way to start. Do you understand? *Start,* Rae. Find a starting place for us. To do that we've got to put whatever lousy thing Warren created behind us. What was in those boxes?"

She seemed about to say something, but turned her head away instead.

Anger overtook him and he shook her. "So help me, I'll get a court order to see for myself."

"You can't," she whispered. "Not unless you want it made public that Warren was a bigamist."

Dallas loosened his grip on her, but didn't let go of her arms. "Maybe that's something we'll have to let happen." Could he do it? The thought turned him cold.

He felt the steadiness of Rae's gaze and met her very green eyes. "If you decide to do that," she told him quietly, while a breeze whipped her long, dark hair across her face, "it might be a good idea to discuss it with me one more time first."

It was Dallas's turn to feel cornered. "What do you mean by that?"

"Linsay May would probably hate people to know she was having sex with your father when he died. But it should make the kind of tidbit that'll sell a lot of copies of my book. At least in these parts. I'd rather not use it, but the call's yours."

Nineteen

Heat hung in a shimmering haze above the road. Even through a layer of dust, sunlight slicked the Rover's hood. Two boys on bicycles careened from a lane and pedaled, heads down, trying to outpace Dallas. He grinned, and waved as he drove past them.

The boys waved back.

"You know everyone around here, don't you?" Rae asked. "How does that feel?"

"Quit slobbering," Dallas told Wolf, who stood on the backseat, his nose against his boss's neck. "I'd guess most people who grow up in small towns know all about the way they work. Everyone knowing everyone. How about you?" He studied her profile.

"We moved around a lot," she told him.

In other words, she got to ask all the questions and expect answers. He wasn't getting any information out of her. "You don't want to talk about yourself, Rae. I wish you trusted me."

She laughed.

"Did I say something funny?"

"Not really. You mean it, don't you?"

"That I wish you trusted me? Surely I mean it. I think I've gone past being discreet about my feelings. It may be suicidal, but I think I've got what they call a case on you. In fact, I don't think, I know." And the only way he could deal with those feelings was to keep throwing the ball into her court.

"I'm the woman who threatened to tell the world your daddy was an unfaithful husband. By the time I've finished, he'll be painted as a sanctimonious phoney who paid for sex with women young enough to be his daughters. And I'll make sure I point out that he kept his lovers quiet by threatening them."

"You don't have proof of all that."

"I'll get it."

"You won't carry through. You're the least convincing tough lady I've ever met."

She sat a little straighter and tried to smooth her crumpled skirts. "You obviously don't know me. I've gathered a number of interesting tidbits about your family. Like the way your mother lives in a dream world where she believes her husband adored and revered her, and put her first in all things. And she believed he listened to her advice about his business—just the way she thinks you listen to it now."

How had she found out grubby, painful, inside details like that? He knew the answer, of course. Linsay May had talked, and Rae had put her journalistic spin on the words to sharpen them up.

"Your sister has a reputation for needing sex. *Needing,* Dallas. And getting it in a variety of places. Word has it that her husband was disassociated. Always. That he was considered unpredictable"—here she paused, and swallowed noisily—"unpredictable. He drove fast cars and performed stunts in antique planes. People . . . people say he lived in a world of his own."

Slanting a glance at her, he set his jaw. She was trying to convince him to give up on her, but it wasn't working. And what she'd just said about Warren showed her guts. It must cost her a lot to face up to the truth that she'd had no idea what kind of man she'd "married."

"It'll all make quite a story," she said.

"You're not changing my mind, Rae," Dallas told her. "Save your energy. You need me as much as I need you. I'm going to have you. Accept it."

Without warning, Rae jerked forward. She pulled her heels onto the seat, wrapped her dress around her shins, and hid her face against her knees.

Dallas waited.

Wolf sighed, and wedged himself between the two front seats until he could settle his big head on Rae's back.

She was crying.

"Rae?"

Softly, almost without any sound at all, she cried.

They approached Glory and set off on the road that skirted the town.

"Hey," Dallas said, "I don't want you to cry. You were made to laugh. You just haven't had enough practice." He sounded inane.

Wolf licked Rae's arm, and she reached to pat his head with her fingertips.

"Look at me, please," Dallas asked.

"I'm embarrassed," she mumbled. "This is stupid."

"I'm falling in love with you."

"Oh . . ." She covered her ears and scrunched into an even tighter ball.

"Don't pretend you can't hear me. I know you can. I'm not falling in love with you. I've fallen. You think I'm the big bad demon around here, but I'm not. You've got troubles. I've got troubles. We could probably throw our troubles together and work things out a whole lot quicker. But you don't trust me and I don't blame you. I'm going to make you trust me, Rae. I've got to."

"Don't, Dallas."

"I've got to. I can't help what I feel, and you aren't going to want to go any farther with me until I can make you believe I want to fix things for both of us."

Her hands curled over the back of her head.

Dallas veered from the road onto the grassy verge, beneath a ragged row of gray-barked cypress trees. He applied the brakes hard.

Scrambling to keep his balance, Wolf growled.

Dust rose from the sun-dried earth.

Cutting the engine, Dallas turned in his seat.

"Sit, Wolf! Down, Wolf! Stay, Wolf!" The dog withdrew a few inches.

Dallas didn't know what to say. Darn it all, he couldn't think of the right words. Or any words. Dallas Calhoun, the mouth of Calhoun Properties, was out of his depth here.

"Can I take you back to Sweet Bay?"

She shook her head.

"You'll be safe there. I'll tell Fancy and my mother you're with me, and they'll just ignore you."

Again, she shook her head.

"We can get in touch with Buelah and tell her to bring Ginny to my house."

"No."

"I'm not giving up, Rae. I want you. I think Warren dragged you into something without you having any idea what was happening. Even if that wasn't what happened, you didn't even know I existed. You never set out to do me any harm."

She turned her face toward the window.

Cautiously, he smoothed back damp strands of her hair. She felt hot, feverish. "You're trapped, aren't you, Rae? Or you think you are?"

"Please will you drive me to the cabin? I've got to make arrangements to have the Jeep fixed."

"It's already fixed. It's back at the cabin. I didn't want to send it there, but I don't have the right to take away your decisions."

"No, you don't. But thanks."

His chest expanded, and he realized he'd almost stopped

breathing. "When I found out you were at the river cabin it was a shock."

"Why?"

"Calhoun used to have the listing for the Parker place. Then we lost it, except for taking charge of its rental. We never knew why. At least, we didn't until I found out Warren had approached the Parkers and worked a deal with them to represent the property for a smaller commission. He did that with a lot of properties. Did you know?"

"He wouldn't do a thing like that."

There was something in her voice that didn't convince him she believed her own protest. "Never mind. It is true. Anyway, that property used to belong to Warren's grandparents. Until some years after his father married the only daughter and got into enough trouble to cost the family their home. The Werthers needed money in a hurry. My father bought the place and sold it to the Parkers. As far as Warren was concerned, that somehow translated into the whole thing being our fault."

"I've only got your word for that."

He couldn't argue with her. "Warren wasn't a bad guy."

"He was a good man," she said, raising her head and turning a tear-stained face toward him. "I don't care if everyone here thought he was strange. He was good to me, and to Ginny."

How he hated thinking of Warren with her. "And you loved him."

Her eyes cut away.

"You loved him?" Dallas pressed.

"We cared for each other a great deal."

The triumph he felt was out of proportion. "But? There is a 'but' isn't there?"

Tears welled again, and she pressed her lips together.

"I'm sorry. I'm pushing you because . . . Rae, I've fallen so hard. Maybe it's because it never happened to me before, but I feel disoriented. I can't concentrate."

"How did you find me in Decline?"

The switch in topics caught him off guard. "Warren used a room in one of the other properties he just happened to inherit from Calhoun as an agent. That is, he used a room there and I found out about it. Didn't matter to me one way or the other. I assumed he went there with"—*great going*—"when he wanted some peace. After he died I checked it out and found a box of personal things he stored under a bed. The bed was the only thing in the room. The photos I showed you were there. And some business cards in the name of John Maddy with a PO address in Decline. And one in Savannah. There were other papers that introduced me to Maddy and Associates. All I had to do was follow the trail of bread crumbs. They led me straight to you."

Wolf had sneaked forward again, and Rae scratched between his ears. A hint of a smile crossed her lips when he sighed.

"Open up with me," Dallas said, never more out of his depth than at this moment. "Tell me why you cried just now. Why you're close to tears again now when you aren't a woman who feels sorry for herself."

"I'm tired, that's all."

"Not good enough."

"I'm such a mess."

He chuckled. "Why do women always worry about the way they look at times like this?"

"I don't know. I've never been through a time like this before."

Petting Wolf gave Dallas an excuse to touch Rae's fingers. "Maybe we're not talking about the same thing. What would you say is going on here?"

"Something impossible." Her eyes met his. "We're together, and it's impossible. I promised myself I wouldn't allow myself to feel this. I definitely wasn't going to tell you I felt it. You are . . . If you've set out to make sure I'll never forget you, you've done a great job."

In a more perfect world, he'd take her in his arms. Right now his world stunk—except for the words Rae Faith had just spoken to him. Half expecting her to push him away, Dallas ran a forefinger down her straight nose.

"Please don't touch me," she said.

Dallas went on to trace the outline of her mouth.

Rae closed her eyes, and pain crossed her features. "It's never going to be possible."

"For you and me?" The question was rhetorical, but he wanted to keep her talking. "But you want it to be possible?"

"Someone's going to drive by and wonder—"

"Let them. Do you want me, Rae?"

"Yes."

If she'd wound herself about him, kissed him, made love to him right then and there, he could not have felt more aroused. And he couldn't have felt more raw, or more confused—or more jubilant.

He didn't dare try to kiss her. "It's enough, then. For now. We'll work it out."

Her small, secret smile twisted something inside him. She reached to rest the backs of her fingers against his unshaven jaw.

"I sure didn't want to fall for you, Rae."

Her fingers slid to the point of his chin and back, and down his neck. "You came to tell me the man I thought was my husband had died. And while you were telling me, I was trying not to feel you." She pressed her other hand to her middle. "In here. I felt you inside me. That never happened before. Even when I was afraid of you, I wanted you. That probably makes me depraved. Or at least immoral in some way. But it's true."

Hope and hopelessness made difficult partners. Dallas squinted ahead and considered what to say next.

"What happened between us," she said, her fingers in his hair now. "What happened never happened to me before. I mean, it wasn't . . . I didn't come from a happy family, Dallas. I saw a lot of ugliness. I'm not complaining. It made me strong. But it also taught me that what happens between men and women can be disgusting. If that makes any sense."

"I think I understand." Although he wished he didn't have to. "Did something happen to you? When you were growing up?"

The corners of her mouth jerked down. "Bad things happened to me, but I wasn't sexually abused, if that's what you mean. I did see someone I cared for sexually abused, and I couldn't help her. Being the one who could only stand by was almost worse. She was the gentlest girl I'll ever know."

His gut squeezed so hard he felt sick.

She withdrew her hand and put her feet on the floor. "I don't know why I'm telling you this. I never told anyone before."

"Not even Warren?"

Her glance held a rebuke.

"Sorry. I shouldn't have asked. Put it down to this possessive thing I'm starting to feel for you."

"Don't feel possessive. People don't own other people. They try, and it always destroys anything they might have had. I told Warren a lot of things, but we didn't deal in feelings, too much."

He started to say something, then forgot what it was.

"All I was trying to explain was that with you I felt what I've never felt before," Rae said. "I was overwhelmed with wanting you—physically at first. Then I wanted you in every other way. I'm never going to forget it."

Dallas held out a hand, palm up, until she placed hers on top. He threaded their fingers together. "I'm never going to allow you to forget it."

"There's too much pushing us apart," she told him. "It won't work between us, but I wanted you to know how I felt."

"Rae—"

"No, Dallas. I need to get back to the cabin. I'm not happy

at the thought of my Ginny being here when so much has happened, but she needs to see me. And I need to see her."

He was a patient man. He could wait—a little while longer. "I understand. Will you agree to try something?"

She looked questioningly at him.

"Will you agree to try to work through whatever you think is going to keep us apart?"

Her fingers tightened in his. "What I *think* is holding us apart? Aren't you the man who has accused me of conspiring with his deceased brother-in-law to ruin the family business? Didn't you tell me I'm living in a cabin on property belonging to ex-Calhoun Property clients Warren stole from the firm? Aren't you suggesting that I was a party to all this supposed wrongdoing?"

"I've suggested all those things."

Exhaustion etched darkness beneath her eyes. She slumped against the seat. "There's your answer."

"Good." The forced cheer wasn't fooling anyone, including Dallas. "We're in agreement. We've got a big job ahead of us."

"Dallas?"

He started the Rover, slipped it into gear, and steered back onto the highway. "We're going to figure out how to come through this mess together. We can do it. After all, we've got something great to shoot for."

Rae hauled her hair on top of her head and leaned toward him until he glanced at her. "When you say we've got something great to shoot for, what do you mean? That I'm supposed to be delighted because you intend to prove I'm a criminal? But you want me to believe you love me now, and you'll still love me when you've managed to haul me into court?"

They passed the Bolling place on the right.

"Dallas, is this supposed to be some sort of half-full, not half-empty, situation?"

"No." He gave the Rover enough gas to turn the trees

beside the road into a blur. "I told you we've got something great to shoot for. Together, forever, Rae Faith. I'm going to marry you."

Ginny sat, cross-legged, on the porch in front of the cabin. She sat and stared into the eyes of Wolf, who faced her and stared right back.

Dallas had driven Rae into the carport only minutes before Buelah arrived with Ginny. There had been no graceful way to ask him to leave, which meant there had been no opportunity for Rae to talk about the man Ginny insisted was watching her in Decline.

"You mustn't ever look away first, Mama," Ginny said. "You've got to make them look away first or they won't know you're the boss."

"Your eyes are going to cross," Rae said, controlling the urge to smile. "Then they'll get stuck there forever." She hadn't known just how badly she missed Ginny until Buelah's old Caddy rock 'n rolled down the track to the cabin. Rae had never been parted from Ginny for more than a couple of days until Dallas had roared into Decline.

"Parents aren't supposed to tell lies to their children about things like that," Ginny said. "You could give me nightmares and ruin my life forever."

Rae threw up her hands. "I'm going to take away your psychology books."

Ginny kept right on staring into Wolf's glazed eyes. "Mr. O'Lean told me it's dangerous to let a dog think he's getting the upper hand."

The dozing row of old men on the sagging porch in front of Minnie Loder's place seemed far away. "Fats O'Lean doesn't know Wolf," Rae said. "This dog's a misogynist."

She glanced at Dallas, and her next breath caught. He looked right back at her, just as he'd been looking at her almost unceasingly since they had arrived back at the cabin.

"No you're not, are you, Wolf?" Ginny said, rising to her knees and shuffling to put her arms around the dog's neck. "What does it mean, Mama?"

Buelah rocked in the wooden rocker and chuckled.

"A misogynist is someone who doesn't like women," Rae explained.

"He likes me," Ginny said, screwing up her face while she suffered Wolf's thorough licking. "It's fun here, Mama. If we lived here, Wolf would visit us all the time."

"Wolf belongs to Dallas," Rae said without thinking.

"Uncle Dallas would let him come."

Rae whistled silently and met Dallas's eyes fleetingly. He raised his brows. She shook her head. The only way to deal with the lies Ginny had been told about him was to put distance between them as soon as possible.

Wolf's next sigh was huge, and he rested his head on Ginny's shoulder.

"Pretty place, Rae," Buelah said. "Lush. And to think you had family here all this time and didn't know it."

Lies and more lies. Rae fidgeted. She didn't respond to Buelah, whose sharp eyes shifted behind her glasses, shifted from Rae to Dallas, and back again.

With Wolf at her heels, Ginny went to Dallas, who was weaving the frayed strands of a piece of rope together. She put her nose above his hands, and he smiled at Rae over the girl's head. Smiled and tried to reassure her with that smile. He wanted to marry her—or said he did.

Rae only felt herself descending the slippery slide toward disaster faster with every passing second.

In a bank in Savannah there was a fortune in her name. Some of it was hers, but not all of it could be. A huge portion probably belonged to Dallas and his family. She'd make sure they got it back, but she owed it to Warren to proceed with great caution where the Calhouns were concerned.

"You do some," Dallas said, giving the rope to Ginny.

"When my brother and I were growing up, our daddy didn't allow waste. We got used to mending and making do."

"You're kidding," Rae said before she could stop herself.

He shook his head. "We all have our childhood skeletons. My father just about owned Glory, but he worried about the small stuff with us kids—except Fancy. My dear sister was always spoiled. But Daddy sure as hell didn't censor himself on any front. He redefined excess in these parts."

"I can do this just fine," Ginny said, holding the rope aloft in her long, thin fingers. She was oblivious to the bitterness in Dallas's voice.

"You surely can," he said. "D'you like boats?"

"I love boats," she said.

Rae intervened. "When were you ever on a boat, Ginny?"

"With Daddy." Ginny turned pink beneath her freckles. "Once, anyway, I think."

Rae crossed her arms and thought there might be a lot of things Ginny had done with John in her dreams.

"Come on, then," Dallas said, taking the child's hand. "You can be my second in command. First mate. I've been messing around on that river since I was a little kid. We'll go look for monsters in the depths."

Rae hid a smile, but said, *"Depths?"*

"It rained the other night," Dallas responded, straight-faced. "It's probably *real* deep now."

Ginny pulled him down the steps to the path. Wolf bounded along, first behind them, then in the lead to the upended aluminum boat at the river's edge.

Rae watched them for a moment before saying, "She looks thin."

"She's always been thin," Buelah responded. "Her appetite will perk up now she's seen you."

"Did you call Ernie Sage about the man—the one Ginny saw?"

Buelah snorted. "Our intrepid sheriff? Sure I did. He got

a whole bunch of fellas together, and they went over the area. Nothing. Not a thing."

The news didn't make Rae feel any better. "Do you think he's watching Ginny in particular?"

"I'm not sure he's watching anyone."

Rae turned around. "What does that mean?"

"She's jumpy. She wants you, and John."

"You think she imagined the whole thing?" Rae dared to hope.

Rocking steadily Buelah winked, and said, "I reckon so. She hasn't said a word about any man since we set out to come here. And she ate a hamburger, and two orders of fries, and an ice cream on the way. Think about it, Rae. Wouldn't some stranger who was watching the children be easy to spot in a little place like Decline?"

Sure he would. "Yes," Rae said. She turned to lean on the railing again and watch Ginny with Dallas. "Yes, of course." Maybe she shouldn't be so quick to feel relief, but she felt it anyway.

"Love at first sight," Buelah said in her cracked voice. "Will you look at those two together?"

Rae glanced over her shoulder at her old friend. "Strong men and little girls make natural pairs."

"Little girls need father figures. Isn't that what you mean?"

"I guess it is." Pouring tea from the jug she'd set on the porch railing, Rae filled a glass for herself and topped off Buelah's. "Ginny certainly seems to like Dallas a lot, doesn't she?"

"That makes two of you."

Speechless, Rae stared at Buelah.

"Well, doesn't it?" Buelah frowned at Rae.

"Yes." There was a subtext here, Rae decided.

"Seems a nice enough boy."

"Mmm."

"Too bad about him, though."

Working for nonchalance, Rae dragged an ancient straight-backed chair forward and sat down facing Buelah. "Too bad about Dallas?"

"You know what I mean." The spectacle of Dallas turning the boat over held Buelah's attention. The man's deep laugh reached them, and the child's high giggles.

"I don't know what you mean," Rae said, suddenly agitated.

"Well, the wheel's spinning, but the hamster's dead. If you know what I mean."

Utterly incredulous, Rae choked on her tea.

Buelah rose to administer a crippling blow between Rae's shoulder blades before plopping back into the rocker. "Honesty's the best course so I always say. And I'd also say you and that boy don't have a live hamster between you."

Sputtering, Rae put her glass on the porch floor. "What on earth are you saying?"

"If you were thinking straight, you wouldn't make dumb mistakes. Maybe it's like him, but it isn't like you. Where did you get another brother? The one Dallas practiced being frugal with because their daddy was a miser? The miser daddy who spoiled Dallas's sister?"

Rae could only study her hands.

"He wasn't talking about you unless your name used to be Fancy. And he's been fooling around on this river since he was a little kid. Doesn't sound to me like he decided to take off from the bosom of your family to make his way in the world. Remember that story? How Dallas left home when you were quite young? From somewhere up north? Doesn't quite hang together, does it?"

"Buelah—"

"He's not your brother, is he?"

Dallas had placed Ginny in the bow of the boat and was pushing it away from the bank. Wolf splashed after him and jumped in.

"*Is* he, Rae?"

"No."

"Are you in some sort of trouble?"

"Yes."

"Big trouble?"

"The biggest. I'm fighting for our lives—Ginny's and mine. If I don't win, we could lose everything."

"It's something to do with John, isn't it?"

Rae hadn't expected that.

"Your face is too open," Buelah said. "You'd never be good at cards. I always knew there was something strange about John. I was right, wasn't I?"

When Rae had been seventeen and alone with a baby, Buelah had saved her. She owed her the truth. "Yes. I didn't know it until Dallas came to Decline, but yes. There was something very strange about John. I've got to find out more about him, and for that I've got to stay here."

"Are you going to tell me why?"

After thinking for a few moments, Rae said, "Yes."

By the time she'd finished her tale—omitting the part about Warren's marriage—the sun had begun to sink, and Buelah's weathered face was pale, her bony hands wound tightly together. "You've got to come back to Decline with me," she said finally. "Now. Tonight. I can't leave you here."

"Buelah," Rae said seriously, scooting her chair until she could take Buelah's dry hands in hers. "I can't go. I won't. John—Warren Niel knew he was going to die. You see that, don't you?" She hoped she'd never have to tell Buelah that Warren had been a bigamist.

"Just come home," Buelah said.

"You do see it?" Rae persisted. "He knew."

Buelah nodded.

"But it's entirely possible that a good deal of what Dallas has accused Warren of is true. There's no way he could have accumulated everything that's in that bank. So where did it come from if he didn't . . . ?" She couldn't bear to say aloud that Warren might have been a criminal.

"You don't know that for sure."

"I feel it in my heart that most of what's supposedly mine belongs to Dallas Calhoun, and I'm going to have to find a way to give it back without losing what really does belong to me."

Pulling her hands away, Buelah used her toes to rock the chair rapidly. "Just give back what you know doesn't belong to you. If you're sure."

"It's not going to be that easy."

"Sure it is. Just sign it over."

Rae looked away.

"It's not just that, is it?" Buelah said. "That's not even the most important thing to you."

"All I want is what's mine. But I've got to find out why Warren expected to die."

"That's a job for a sheriff."

"The law around here has him dead from a plane crash, and scattered to the winds. They aren't about to go looking for anything new."

"And you've already had warnings that you're not wanted here, but you intend to stay and poke around? Girl, you're sounding as if your receiver's off the hook."

She knew she would seem stubborn, but said, "I've got to stay."

"And, like I said, it's not just the money, or John, is it?"

"What else would it be?" Rae aimed an angry glare at Buelah.

"If I had to guess, I'd say it's tall, dark, and too handsome."

Rae blushed. "John's only been dead a few weeks."

"And you never loved him."

Protests would be useless. "I want to ask you something before they get back," Rae said. "I'm afraid for Ginny to be here. I want you to take her with you tonight. To Decline. I think she's better off there than here."

"Rae. She misses you. And you promised she'd get to stay the weekend."

"I know, I know. But I've changed my mind."

"Then you're coming, too. And don't you argue with me."

"Please do as I ask, Buelah. I don't think it's a good idea for me to be anywhere near her—or you. And I can't leave. I won't. Not until I do what I set out to do. I mean that."

"It's not safe for Ginny and me to be here, but it's safe for you?"

Rae stood up and looked toward the river. "I'll be okay."

"How can you say that?"

"What do you think of Dallas, Buelah? Really?"

"I don't know him."

"A snap judgment. You made one of those before, remember. When you met me."

Buelah got up and joined Rae at the railing. "Best decision I ever made. Taking you and Ginny in."

"You'd say you've got good taste in people, then?"

"I guess," Buelah said. "Yes, I'd say so. And I'd say that boy's got a good heart. And he's got a thing for you."

Rae's blush freshened up.

"Are you finding out about falling in love?"

"Buelah," Rae said softly.

"Good enough answer. If he hurts you, he'll have me to deal with. I can't leave you here, you know."

"Yes, you can. I'll tell Ginny I need her to be a good girl about this. And that she's to stick close to you and tell you if she sees the man again. I'll call Ernie myself and ask him to keep a special eye on things."

"That child is precious to me," Buelah said. "I'd never let anything happen to her."

Laughter continued to float toward them from the river. Rae could see Ginny dipping her fingers into the water and flicking drops at Dallas's face. His hands were busy with the oars, and he could only sputter and shake his head.

"You look after Ginny," she said, taking in a deep, bittersweet breath. "Dallas will look after me. He wouldn't let anything bad happen to me."

Twenty

He slammed a fist into a tree trunk and cursed the pain. "Damn bitch." His breath hurt his throat. And his lungs. He wasn't well. He didn't deserve this. "Damn you, you bitch. You're gonna pay for what you're doing to me."

The coughing started again. He coughed more and more these days.

Clouds had rolled in to mostly cover the moon. There was wind, and it moved the clouds along; so he had to be careful not to get caught in the open if the light got brighter.

The big car was still there. The old bat had brought the kid in that. Dallas Calhoun's truck was parked right behind the Jeep.

Shit!

Last night she hadn't come back with the kid the way he'd expected. He'd been sure she would, that she'd lock the two of them inside the shack she believed could keep people out, and then he'd get her. He'd get her and get what he had coming.

Then, when he'd thought his luck was finally turning and he'd cornered her, he'd almost made a mistake. Thinking she was Rae, he'd grabbed the woman on the bridge.

He needed a drink, and a smoke. If the woman on the bridge had seen him, he'd have had to kill her. Then he'd have been forced to wait till the dust settled before moving again.

The pain hit again. He turned cold. Sweat soaked his shirt,

*and he stumbled, holding his chest. Thanks to that bitch he
was a sick man. He felt like throwing up.*

*Sliding down a tree, he sat at its base and held his knees
to his chest.*

The pain eased slowly.

Tired.

*That was it. He'd been hiding out, waiting, and watching,
for too long. Women. It was always women who brought men
down. They used them while they wanted something, then
walked out when they thought something better had come
along. Rae hadn't had to walk out on Warren Niel. He'd up
and gotten himself smashed to pieces, and she'd jumped right
into Dallas Calhoun's pants—and his wallet.*

Only Dallas didn't know he was sleeping with the enemy.

*She was going to be the worst enemy the rich boy ever
had. She was going to take him down, cost him everything
he had. And, in the end, they might both have to die anyway.*

*He laughed, and coughed, and wiped his sleeve over his
mouth.*

*Flames rose from a barbecue kettle out front of the cabin.
He could see them moving around outside, and hear them
laughing. Calhoun was playing the tough woodsman, lighting fires and cooking.*

Next they'd break out the goddamn campfire songs.

"Uncle Dallas!"

*He held his forearm over his mouth and listened more
closely.*

"Wolf wants one, Uncle Dallas."

Sheeit.

Calhoun shouted, "Fetch, Wolf," *and something flew from
the flickering light around the fire, into the darkness. The
dog ran after it.*

The girl laughed. A high, giggly laugh. A girl-child laugh.

*Well, hell, what did a man know? Maybe he'd got some
of this all wrong. Maybe some things were different than*

he'd thought. He'd planned to threaten the kid so Rae would go with him quietly.

It could be Calhoun wouldn't be in too much of a hurry to come up with the price of a woman. He'd had plenty of women. But Uncle Dallas might feel real different.

He got to his feet. This called for a celebration. He'd make his way out to Blue's, get him a few stiff drinks and something good to smoke. And he'd find him a little woman with big tits. Forget for tonight. Think in the morning when everything felt better. Everything.

Tomorrow he'd be back.

Tomorrow he'd start watching and waiting again.

Tomorrow he'd be ready to make the move that would give him the insurance he needed.

All he'd need was a few seconds when no one was watching, and the kid was alone.

Twenty-one

TYSON LaROSE, ATTORNEY AT LAW.

The brass plate on the wall outside his office suite used to make him feel excited. Now he looked at it and wished he could tear it down and not give a damn. Hit the road going anywhere. Or nowhere.

He wouldn't care as long as he could have Joella with him, and know he was enough to keep her happy, with or without a fat bankroll. But he'd blown his dreams for that. They had blown them together.

When he'd taken out the loans to go to law school, he'd thought his father would be proud of him for making the decision to build an important future on his own.

How had he got from there to here?

When had the whole deal gone so stinking rotten?

Tyson stared at the sign and silently cursed every lousy decision he'd ever made. As many of them as he could remember without consulting his lousy-decision files.

"Hey," Joella said, arriving beside him. "C'mon, Tyson, let's move it. I've got things to do."

Things to do. "Yeah, sure." He unlocked the door. She had things to do; but they didn't involve him, and she didn't feel any need to discuss them with him. "Going out of town again?"

She walked into the reception area ahead of him. "I like it here on a Saturday afternoon. Feels kind of like being in a department store in the middle of the night."

He watched her, watched the way she moved.

Joella swung to face him. Her blue eyes were vivid, and her hair was the same honey blond it had been when they had started dating in junior high school.

She frowned and walked toward him. "What's the matter with you, baby? You sick or something?"

Or something. He shook his head. "Just checked out there for a while. I've got a lot on my mind. How much do you want?"

With her fingertips tucked inside the pockets of her tight, pale blue jeans, Joella opened the door from the reception area to his office and walked inside. "Come on," she called to him. "I always did believe in mixing pleasure with business."

Tyson battled his instant reaction to her. Even when he was at the bottom—and he was at the bottom now—even down there when everything he touched turned to shit, Joella could turn him on.

Nothing was working out. He'd done his best to win. At the start it had been for Joella, because he knew she needed to beat Fancy Calhoun in more than a hick town beauty pageant. And for the failed man he'd like to know was his father, the man who had treated Tyson with contempt all his life. And he'd wanted to win for himself, to feel what he'd once been so sure he knew, that he was as good as Dallas Calhoun.

Somewhere he had to find a reason to go on fighting.

"Tyson? What's keeping you?"

"Coming."

Dallas Calhoun who could just be Brother Dallas.

He had to keep on keeping on. The game wasn't over, not nearly over. From now on he had to forget pleasing anyone but himself, working to make success for anyone but himself.

If Joella hadn't let him know in a dozen subtle ways that she needed him to give her back what she'd lost when her daddy ruined her granddaddy—and for sex—and nothing else, he wouldn't be in so deep with Ava, and Fancy.

Would he ever get out, ever be free of them all?

"Tyson LaRose, get your butt in here *now.*"

He went into his office and shut the door out of habit. "How much?"

"Not so fast, lover. First I want a progress report. Things have been happening, but you haven't been talking to me. I'm your wife, remember? We're supposed to share everything."

She was baiting him. He wasn't biting. "I haven't been talking because there's nothing to say really." Not entirely true, but if he spun out what he did have to say, he could keep her here longer, and he didn't want to be alone today. "I guess I should say that I'm hesitant to tell you what I know. I don't like upsetting you, sugar."

Joella closed in on him, ran her forefingers from his collarbones, slowly downward over his nipples, his ribs, to the waist of his chinos, and underneath to tug lightly.

He opened his mouth and let out a long, long breath.

She smiled up at him. "Upset me? Thing's are so much more interestin' when there's an edge on them."

Impressions filled this room. Everywhere he glanced he saw Fancy. He couldn't sit in his chair without remembering the horror of being inside Ava with Carter's cold eyes regarding them.

"Come on," he said, walking around her and going to the wall safe. "How much do you need? And, by the way, where are you going?" He deliberately kept his tone offhand and avoided looking at her.

"Who said I was going anywhere? I heard Ava Calhoun's giving a party is all. Sooo, I need a new dress. You wouldn't want your wife being the worst dressed belle at the ball, would you?"

"I don't think Ava's going to be holding any parties real soon." He opened the liquor cabinet, swung a mirrored wall of bottles forward and rapidly worked the combination on the safe. "But there's nothing I like better than seeing you in a new dress."

"Nothing?"

He closed his eyes momentarily. "Not a thing, Joella." With a battered cardboard box and some money in one hand, he followed ritual and closed the safe again. "Enough?"

Automatically Joella took what he put in her hands and slid her purse from her shoulder before looking at the money. She glanced from the bills to his face. "What'd you do? Rob a bank?"

"Is that a 'thank you'?"

She fanned the money. When she looked at him again he couldn't read what he saw in her eyes. She said, "It's too much, and you know it. But, thank you." For an instant he thought she might give it back, but then she put it in the bag. "Where did you get so much?"

"We've been cleaning up a few delinquents," he lied. The money was what he'd asked for in cash retainers for cases he shouldn't even be entertaining.

"What's the box?"

The box was proof that he was still trying to make himself a big man in her eyes. "Evidence. All of it against Warren."

She threw the bag on a chair. "What kind of evidence?"

Evidence that would show her brother had been a criminal, just as surely as it would put Calhoun Properties in a hammerlock that could break its back. "It's complicated." If nothing more, by the time he'd finished she'd stop suggesting he'd conspired with Fancy against Warren.

"Try me," Joella said. "Show me what you've got."

He made as if to give her the box, but turned on his heel and rapidly reopened the safe to seal the box inside again. "It's too soon. Maybe I'm being fed a line. A bunch of lines."

"What kind of lines? Tyson, don't do this to me."

"I don't know."

She paced.

"Okay, okay. Several individuals have approached me with

complaints they want me to look into. Slow work performed by contractors they were told Calhoun had recommended. Failure to complete the work until the owners were faced with potential financial disaster. All big residential stuff. Condos. Top-end housing. Warren's territory. In each case they approached Warren, who apologized and did them the great favor of taking over as general contractor for them. Seems his margins were supposed to be narrower than Calhouns'. Only the type of labor he hired was cheap, real cheap. Result? Mega-kickbacks for good ol' Warren."

Joella stopped pacing. "How would anyone find out about something like that?"

"It was inevitable. Sooner or later someone didn't get paid by Warren and went looking for their money. Happened almost right after Warren died. Then one outfit talked to another outfit. And there were suggestions made that Warren paid someone to make sure key people working for the original contractors went slow. These people I'm dealing with can't afford to shout too loud until they're sure Calhoun's good for what they intend to get out of this."

"So you've taken their money to help them do that."

"Anything you don't like about that?"

"Not a thing. I think it's beautiful."

"Thanks." He considered before saying, "I'm going to get Dallas to take me on. He'll do it."

"You mean you'll make it impossible for him to refuse?"

"Not in exactly the way you think," Tyson said. "I hope I can do it without being a louse. Will that be okay with you?"

She looked thoughtful. "As long as you know what you're doing."

"Believe in me, Joella. Just this once."

She studied him before turning away and saying, "I need to go to the bathroom."

Of course, he'd asked too much. He quelled the urge to tell her he'd called her bluff and gone to Carter LaRose with information and a proposition: Tyson knew that Carter thought he might not be his father, and they could use the possibility to their mutual advantage. Waiting for Carter's reaction had been the most charged event in Tyson's life. Carter hadn't revealed anything about his real feelings, but he had held his legendary temper and agreed to do what Tyson suggested. They had set Ava up. So Joella no longer had a hold over him because he'd once been fool enough to tell her too much about himself. He'd told his father he knew the whole story from his mother, and invited him to join in pushing for a payback from the Calhouns. Carter wanted to punish Ava for jilting him, and snatching the promise of her inheritance from his grasp. Tyson? Tyson wanted to work with Dallas and never worry about proving himself again.

Minutes passed, and Tyson sat on the couch. He wanted a drink, but it could wait till Joella left.

The toilet flushed, and the bathroom door opened again.

She came out.

Naked.

"Now you don't need me? Well, now I don't need you." Joella had one of those achy singing voices that half broke, half laughed through a song.

Tyson raised his eyelids a fraction and saw her peering through the slats at the window. With a shoulder against the window frame, she sang softly, hummed a few bars, sang another line she remembered of a song he didn't remember at all.

She twisted him up. After so many years, she still took and turned him to mush. With her arms crossed beneath her breasts, she was completely comfortable nude. Her waist was small, her hips generously flared, and her legs pretty. The hair between her thighs showed dark gold in the subdued light. When she'd stripped him, he'd turned off everything but the green glass-shaded lamp on his desk.

She'd stripped him, and made him stand there while she

walked around him, touching here, touching there, moving far enough away for him to look at her. Piling her hair on top of her head, she'd revolved slowly, giving him every angle, ordering him not to reach for her until she gave him permission.

He got hard again at the thought—instantly.

Joella knew how to make him do as he was told. She made it worth his while.

"No second chances," she sang, very low, and hummed to herself some more, settling her thumbs on her nipples and rolling them back and forth until she dropped her head back and sucked air through her teeth.

If he went to her, she'd rebuff him. He'd bide his time until she was excited enough to turn to him again.

Just watching her was almost enough. Her breasts had the full-blown beauty of maturity. The nipples were large, and dark, and pointed straight out. He loved the way they pressed into his hands, or any other part of him she chose to favor. When she'd finally been ready to push him down on the couch and mount him, she'd taken his hands to her breasts first, covered and squeezed. Then she'd stared into his eyes while she reached between her legs and brought herself to panting readiness.

They had already made love twice. He was ready for number three.

Joella glanced toward him. She was breathing hard, but said, "Welcome back. You've been gone so long I'm just entertaining myself."

Slowly, he got up and beckoned to her. He pointed to himself. "No need to do that, sugar. Come here."

"Persuade me."

He went to the back of the couch and patted the cool leather. "I'm persuading you. Just bend over right here and present your lovely tush. And leave the rest to me."

The phone rang and they both exclaimed.

"On *Saturday afternoon?*" Joella said, plopping her hands on her hips. "Don't answer it."

"Okay, I won't. Over here."

She chewed a thumbnail and stared at the phone. "Answer it."

"Make up your mind, love," he told her and did as she asked. Fancy's voice said, "There you are, damn you. Where the hell have you been?"

"I'm working," he told her coldly.

Joella shook her head and trailed out into the reception area.

"Not now, okay?" Tyson said. "I've got a lot to do."

"You've got nothing to do but keep me happy, Tyson LaRose. And you haven't been keeping me nearly happy enough lately. I've been thinking we might take a little trip out to Blue's. Now *that* was really something."

He barely stopped himself from telling her to shut up. "What do you need?"

"You."

Lowering his voice he said, "Later."

"Make sure that's a promise. I'm going to send a man over to see you."

Tyson straightened.

"His name is Sam McIver. Such a nasty person. Not at all our type. I tried to get rid of him. But then I decided that might not be too wise. He came here looking for Warren."

He couldn't order his thoughts fast enough to respond.

"Tyson? Tyson, do you hear me? Just a minute. I'll be right back. You just hold the line."

"No"—the next sound he heard was the phone being rested on something at the other end.

He covered the mouthpiece. "Joella. I'll be off in a minute."

"Uh huh," her voice floated back.

At Sweet Bay the phone was picked up again. "Okay, I told him how to find you."

"Thanks," he said, furious that she had enough hold over him to make him jump whenever she wanted.

"Dallas isn't around or he could have dealt with that man. He's probably with that creature they say was one of Warren's women. Disgusting. Why hasn't she been run off by now? That's what I'd like to know."

"Whoa," Tyson said.

"Don't you tell me what to do. I think Dallas is . . . well, you know," she said delicately. "I think he's doing *it* with her just to spite me. And she's going to write some horrible story about Glory, mind you. About Glory and about all of us. Imagine what that could be like."

Tyson didn't want to think about it, not if there was any danger of Rae Maddy finding out about his connections to Fancy and Ava.

"Can I come over and see you after a bit?" Fancy asked, wheedling as only Fancy could wheedle. "Say in a couple of hours when I've had a chance to make myself real pretty for you, and you've had time to send that horrible man away?"

"No."

"Don't be unkind to Fancy. Oh, Tyson, I do love your office. We've done such *lovely* things there."

"No."

"You are being mean. I'm coming, and that's that. And after we do it there, we're going out to Blue's to do it some more. Now. Are you still saying no?"

Another voice on the line said, "Are you ready for me now, Mr. LaRose?"

Tyson wiped sweat from his brow. Joella was listening on the intercom. "Very soon, Ms. Evans. I'll call you."

Joella appeared in the doorway and sauntered into the office.

"Your secretary's there on a Saturday afternoon?" Fancy said.

"I told you I was busy."

Bending double over the back of the couch, Joella rested her hands on the seat and raised her face so that he looked at her cold eyes, and at a glorious view of her breasts.

"Tyson, I don't like it—"

"I don't care what you don't like. I've got something important to do and, thanks to you, not a whole lot of time to do it." He hung up.

"You said it," Joella told him. "Not a whole lot of time. But in this case, I've got faith in you."

He'd positioned himself behind her, his fingers curled around her hips, when she threw herself upright, whirled around, and hit him.

Tyson staggered backward.

She gathered her purse, ran into the bathroom, and locked the door.

By the time she emerged, he was also dressed—and smarting, from the blow to his face and ear, and from knowing they had slid even farther down the ravine toward hatred and contempt.

Joella unzipped her purse. She took out the money and tapped it to her lips before replacing it.

"Sugar. It's not the way you think. I'm only using her to get what we want."

"Did you do what I told you to do? Did you tell her you intend to marry her?"

"No."

"It would help get you closer to that job you want."

"Joella, please—"

"I hear a car. Gotta go. Time I paid Fancy a visit."

Panic all but choked Tyson. "Don't go near her."

"You don't have to worry. As long as you're really careful to remember I'm in the driver's seat. And you're not going to step out of line, so there's no problem."

"Don't do this," he told her. "You're angry. I don't blame you for that, but what I've done, I've done for us."

Joella zipped her purse shut and hooked the strap over her

shoulder. She said, "Oh, I know that, Tyson. It's okay. I'm only going to commiserate with her about the way men treat women. She might get careless and tell me something we could use against her. I'm going to make friends with her. Why not? We've got something in common. We're both getting screwed by the same man."

Twenty-two

Humor, Dallas decided, tacked to the element of total surprise, might catch her off guard. "I don't suppose you'd agree to just get it over with?"

Rae continued to stare through the window of the café at Buzzley's. Only moments earlier, Buelah and Ginny had driven away.

"Rae? What do you say?"

"About what?"

"Getting it over with. I know it's probably unconventional, but why not? We might as well. Who knows, it could solve all of our problems at the same time."

Finally he had Rae's complete attention. Or he thought he did. She lifted her coffee mug and held it in both hands, rolling it slowly back and forth between her palms.

Dallas smiled at her. Last night he'd hardly slept. He was tired, damn tired—maybe that was why he'd just made a gigantic leap in logic. He wanted something settled, anything settled.

"Ginny thinks you're something," Rae said, smiling faintly. "She's got a real case of hero worship."

"It's Wolf she's fallen for. That's the way it is with women; they never want you for yourself, only for what you've got."

Rae looked into her coffee.

Her mind was with her child. Last night, after Buelah had found a way to speak to him alone, he'd talked Rae into letting him sleep on the couch so she'd feel comfortable about allowing Ginny to spend the night. But with the morning she'd been adamant that Ginny and Buelah must leave.

"I'm still amazed that Buelah told you about our conversation," Rae said, giving him the uncanny sensation she'd seen inside his head.

"She's obviously a good judge of character. She knows I can be trusted."

"I've never understood how some people can joke when there's nothing to joke about."

Dallas winced and said, "Ouch. Did you ever think that someone might joke because they aren't sure what else to do?"

She considered that. "Yes, I have. What are we doing here? Together for everyone in this town to see?"

"I don't give a— I've never cared very much what people think of me."

"Really? It doesn't bother you that every person who has come into this store since we've been here—or passed the windows—has found us the most fascinating thing on the face of the earth?"

"Nope."

She turned sideways in her chair and crossed her legs. "Could it be you think that if you can win me over, I'll do whatever it is you want me to do?"

He might be going down here, but not without a fight. "You've figured me out. And I thought I was being so subtle. I want you to say you'll spend the rest of your life with me."

She almost missed the table with her mug. "Keep your voice down."

Dallas looked over his shoulder. "Is anyone listening?" Apart from three women at a distant table, the late lunch crowd had all left. "Doesn't look like it. I said I was making an unconventional proposition."

"An impossible proposition."

Sure it was impossible, but he wished it weren't. "Buelah

was very honest with me," he said. "She's worried about you being here alone."

"Buelah shouldn't have spoken out of turn. She wanted a way to have Ginny spend the night. Buelah would do anything for Ginny."

"Or for you," he said, then changed the subject. "They talk about green eyes, but I've never seen eyes as green as yours."

"You're sleep-deprived from spending the night on that saggy old couch. You're not making any sense."

"You didn't tell Buelah about Warren being married to my sister, did you? You left that part out."

He hated the blush that rose in her cheeks, and the way she lowered her eyelashes.

"Rae, I'm just putting everything out in the open between us. Trying to. Seems to me that if you told me everything about you and Warren—whatever the business arrangements were—I could attend to that side of things, and we could put it behind us."

"Do I look stupid?"

Dallas leaned across the table. "I don't blame you for thinking I could be trying to put something over on you. I'm not. All I want is what's mine. And you. I want you."

"A few weeks ago we were strangers."

"I've never been as close to a woman as I am to you."

She looked at him again, very directly. "Have you ever been close to a woman?"

He held one of her hands on the table. "I never wanted to be before. And I know it's outrageous. Dammit, Rae, I'm not sure I haven't lost my mind entirely. But I want you. Simple as that."

"Complicated as that," she whispered. "Those women are watching us. So is Buzz."

"Good. Let 'em watch."

"They all know I was . . . *involved* with Warren."

"They probably do. So they've really got something to talk about."

"I trust you, Dallas."

"You've got to stop worrying about—" He held her hand tighter. "What did you say?"

"I said, I trust you." When her lips came together, they trembled slightly. "Now do I get the prize for making the most outrageous comment of the day?"

"You mean it?"

"Yes. I probably need help, but I do."

Yelling would only horrify her, but he felt like whooping. "Okay. Okay, here's what we're going to do. No one ever has to know about the real situation between you and Warren. We'll move you into Sweet Bay and—"

"Stop. We may or may not be able to have something together, but I'm going to hope. Dallas, there are so many things to get through we can't even think about the future—not between us."

If he didn't push her for some sort of commitment, he could lose her. "Honey, you don't have to worry about providing for Ginny and you anymore. And you don't have to worry about how you're going to get out of the mess Warren got you into. We'll work things out."

She turned the corners of her mouth down and stroked the hairs on the back of his hand. "We'll work out that Ginny thinks you're her uncle? And find a way to tell her the man she thought was her daddy was never married to me—he was married to your sister? He's dead—from crashing his plane. We didn't know he could fly planes? Big deal. And somehow we'd be able to come through this and you'd carry on with your business here, and"—she paused and smiled wistfully at him—"and this doesn't seem like something we'll ever be able to make come true, does it?"

"Not easily." But he'd never been a quitter. "Just keep on trusting me."

Still smiling at him, she lifted his hand to her mouth and kissed it. "I'm going to make the next proposition."

"Anything." How could the touch of a woman's mouth on a man's hand make him hard, and hotter than he recalled being—since the last time she touched him of her own accord.

"I didn't come to Glory to annoy you."

Something in her tone had a cooling effect. "You came to let me know you wouldn't roll over and play dead just because I'd dealt you a blow that would cripple most people."

"That, yes, but it's only a scratch on the surface. I came to find a way to set Ginny and me free of any cloud, and to make sure we didn't lose what's rightfully ours."

He stopped himself from protesting that what she thought was hers was his.

Buzz strolled to the table. His nonchalance wouldn't fool a kid. "Anything else I can get you?" he asked, looking anywhere but at their joined hands. "Coffee must be cold." He refilled their mugs.

"Thanks," Dallas said.

"I guess Linsay May's her old self again."

"That's what I heard."

"Me too," Rae said. "Thank goodness."

Buzz rearranged packets of sugar and artificial sweetener in their stainless steel holder. "Nice little girl you had with you. Relation, is she?"

Rae raised her face. "My daughter. She is a nice girl. The best. The lady with her is an old friend. She's a schoolteacher, and she's looking after Ginny while I'm in Glory to look into writing a story about the town and the way society interacts in a small, inbred climate. I've decided there probably isn't a soul in this town without a grubby secret tucked away. It's my job to dig those secrets out."

Dallas realized his open mouth matched Buzz's and closed it.

"Now, you're an interesting character," Rae continued.

"Shopkeeper. Or restaurateur, I suppose. Deputy sheriff. What else are you, Buzz? I suppose you hear a lot of stories here—with so many people dropping in to eat. They all chat to you, don't they? I'll just bet you know a bunch of juicy stuff I'd find useful."

Buzz was backing away.

"If you think of anything, you get in touch with me," Rae said, more loudly. "At the cabin at the old Werther place. I'll leave my number for you."

When they were alone again, Dallas chuckled. "A new side of you, Rae. Mean streak. A torturer."

"He asked for it. I came to Glory because I think Warren knew he was going to die."

What she said took a while to make sense. "That's not possible."

"Yes, it is. At least it's possible he thought he might die soon."

"No. You don't understand. Warren died—"

"I know how he died. What I'm telling you is that he made provisions for his death. He warned me."

A magnolia tree in the verge outside took on a surreal caste. He felt his eyes lose focus. "That's impossible."

"Dallas"—pulling his wrist until he blinked and looked at her, she jabbed at the air in front of him—"it *is* possible. John wrote to me. I told you I trusted you, and now I'm proving it by telling you this. If I'm wrong about you, I could be putting myself in danger. Do you understand what I'm saying?"

He understood, but it didn't compute. "Go on."

"Twice—in two different ways—Warren left word for me. On each of those occasions, he spoke about not coming back, and being sorry, and not wanting me to talk to people about him. Or about our marriage. Dallas, he knew he would, or at least that he *might* die. As far as I'm concerned that can only mean he thought someone was going to kill him."

"He radioed the field and said he had engine trouble. Then he crashed. It was an accident."

"Maybe it was. But was the accident a coincidence?"

"Whoa, you're losing me, ma'am."

"Okay. I intend to find out who Warren was afraid of. He *was* afraid."

Dallas's shudder was involuntary. "He wrote to you? Show me his letters."

The shutter over her willingness to share closed almost visibly. Rae withdrew her hands from his and picked up the coffee. "I can't do that."

"You want me to believe a fantastic story like that without any proof?"

"Yes."

"Rae . . . for . . . Rae, give me a break."

"No." She pinned him with the intensity of her eyes. "No, you give me a break. You suggested we should get together. You said it would solve all our problems. Well, I'm asking you to help me. You've got problems at Calhoun Properties and you're looking for answers you think are tied up with Warren. I'm just trying to find out the truth about him. About what drove him to make a second life. And why he made sure he drafted letters for me prior to his death, *intimating* that he didn't expect to be around long. And, yes, I want to find out the truth about what you've accused him of doing."

Dallas got up and went around the table to sit in the chair beside her. "So you aren't staying with the story that Warren couldn't have been sticking it to Calhoun?"

"I'm asking you to go forward with me to find out what happened." She looked from his eyes, to his mouth, and stopped right there. "I haven't forgotten that someone tried to scare me off. And I haven't forgotten what happened to Linsay May either. I've got reason to be scared, but I'm darned if I'm going to give up and run away. It would be less scary if I knew I had a friend to count on."

Friend? "You've got a friend," he told her. He intended

to be far more than her friend. He couldn't get within feet of her without getting aroused. At a distance of only inches, he was in pain. "This may be bad timing, but I miss you, Rae. All the time, I miss you."

"You're with me." She leaned a little closer. "You've been with me a lot."

"With you, but not *with* you." Air was becoming a scarce commodity.

"I don't think we should discuss this right now. Not here."

"When? Where?"

Closer.

Her eyes almost closed, and she touched her mouth to his. Dallas held her face, forcing himself to be careful, not to go too far, too fast. They kissed softly, but with a restrained urgency that blotted out everything but her.

The sound of a throat being cleared only dimly punctured Dallas's brain.

"Sorry to interrupt, but Fancy's on the line for you."

Rae dropped her brow to his shoulder, and Dallas folded her close. "Buzz, you've got lousy timing."

"Yeah, I've been told that before. Fancy said she knows you're here. Says the whole goddamn—I mean, she said she's had several calls in as many minutes and she wants you to get your—she wants you to pick up the phone."

"Hang up on her."

"Aw, Dallas," the man moaned. "You know she'll only call back. And she'll be in here making my life a living hell. Shucks, Dallas, just talk to her, will you?"

Rae sat up and pushed at her hair. "Do what Buzz asks."

"I don't want to leave—okay, okay, I'm going." He stood up and pointed at her. "Promise you won't go anywhere till I get back."

"She won't, will you, Rae?"

Dallas glared at Buzz, and heard Rae laugh. She said, "I'll be here. Go talk to your sister."

Minutes later he returned and pulled money from his wallet. Tossing it on the table, he regarded Rae, making up his mind what to do about her next.

There wasn't a choice. "Come on. But remember, if you're taking me for a ride, you'd better be out of the country when I find out."

Tight-lipped, she got up and walked toward the door.

He followed her outside into a hot afternoon that held the threat of another thunderstorm.

"You don't need to threaten me again."

He held her arm and guided her along the sidewalk. "I'm not going to."

Their eyes met, and he knew she understood what he meant. He was giving her one chance to prove herself—one way or the other.

"Where are we going?"

"Tyson's. You remember Tyson?"

She sounded breathless when she said, "The lawyer. I didn't like him. His wife is—was Warren's sister."

"A man came by Sweet Bay looking for me. He told Fancy he wanted to talk to me about Warren."

Rae halted and twisted to face him. "Who is he?"

"I don't know. Evidently someone who thinks we owe him money. Damn Fancy for sending him to Tyson."

"Why would—"

"Because she's sleeping with him." That wasn't smart, spilling things that didn't need to be said. "Hell, don't listen to me. That's not important. He's her lawyer, and she turns to him for just about everything."

Rae still wasn't moving. "Fancy's sleeping with Tyson LaRose. He's married to Warren's sister; Warren, who was married to Fancy. Did this just start?"

He looked at the purple sky and kept his mouth shut for once.

"It didn't just start, did it?" she persisted.

"More stuff of a fascinating little exposé, huh? Rae, I've got to get over to Tyson's before he manages to force himself any deeper into Calhoun business. Maybe it isn't a good idea for you to come."

She started walking again, and when he didn't immediately fall in beside her, she stopped and waited for him to catch up. "We've both gone too far to pull back now," she told him.

Tyson's office was in a pretentious little square of professional suites built at the end of what had been a driveway to the back of some stores at the north end of Main. New "old" cobblestones, green grillwork gates with views of small fountains in atriums beyond, shiny black front doors with lots of equally shiny brass, the place was an ambitious, insecure man's dream. It was Tyson's dream.

Expecting the door with Tyson's name beside it to be locked, Dallas nevertheless tried the handle. He was wrong. Keeping Rae behind him he walked into the plush reception room and immediately heard a man's raised voice coming from the office beyond.

"Wait here," he told Rae. "And if I tell you to leave—don't stick around to argue."

Without announcing himself, he went into the office.

Rae was right behind him.

If Tyson was surprised to see him, he hid it well. No doubt Fancy had been thrilled to be able to track her brother down and make sure he witnessed her lover being indispensable to Calhoun Properties. At the same time, Dallas was certain, he was supposed to get the message that Tyson knew too much to be anywhere but on the company payroll.

"Hi there, Dallas," Tyson said from behind his desk, his heartiness decidedly hollow. "Come on in and meet—" He saw Rae and stopped talking. He frowned at Dallas.

"Afternoon," Dallas said, all sunny cheer. "Fancy asked me to come over. She said you had someone with you I ought to know."

The "someone" was a tall, broad-shouldered man whose flesh hung flaccid on his big bones. "Sam McIver," he said with a thick, slow drawl. "You Warren Niel's kin?"

"Maybe we should wait to have this discussion," Tyson said quickly, casting a significant glance at Rae, who hovered just inside the door. "Don't you think, Dallas?"

"No," he said, offering his hand to McIver. "Dallas Calhoun. Warren was my brother-in-law. This is Rae Maddy. She's a close friend of mine. You can trust her."

"Dallas," Tyson said. "What the—"

"You're too touchy, Tyson," Dallas told him, waving Rae into a chair before sitting on the edge of Tyson's desk and saying to McIver, "Tyson here is my sister's lawyer. He's an old family friend. We keep working on him to be more trusting, but you know how lawyers are."

McIver's small, dark eyes swiveled from Dallas, to Rae, to Tyson—and back to Rae. "Don't cotton to lawyers," he said, and coughed. "The woman sent me here."

"My sister," Dallas said in determinedly conversational tones. "Evidently you went to Sweet Bay looking for me. I'm glad Fancy managed to find me. What can I do for you?"

"We don't need him." The man indicated Tyson. "Don't—"

"Cotton to lawyers," Dallas finished for him. "No. But Tyson's different. He's like family." At this point, drawing Tyson in was preferable to pushing him out where he might get mean and become a real problem.

Sam McIver dug in the pockets of baggy jeans until he produced a pack of cigarettes and a Bic. Without asking if anyone minded, he lit up and dragged deeply.

"Maybe Mr. McIver would like a drink," Dallas said easily to Tyson. "I know I would. How about you, Rae?"

"Oh, yes," she said, sounding bemused enough to make Dallas want to laugh.

"A beer," McIver said.

Tyson got to his feet and opened the liquor cabinet. "No beer," he said, as if the idea amazed him.

"You got bourbon?"

"We'll all have bourbon," Dallas said, taking some pleasure in Tyson's discomfort over Rae's presence. "Think we're going to get more thunder, Sam?"

With a shrug McIver said, "Maybe," but watched Tyson pour and all but snatched the glass he was offered. "I got a brother. Les. He and Warren were real tight."

Dallas managed to squelch a groan. "Really? How was that?"

The bourbon in McIver's glass disappeared.

Without a word, Tyson refilled it.

Rae sniffed the contents of her glass, and took a sip—and wrinkled her nose.

"I do collections for Les," McIver said. "Les isn't real good at the business side of things. He leaves it to me to keep the money straight."

Dallas didn't think he'd be impressed by Les McIver. "Is that a fact? He's the brawn and you're the brain, huh?"

"Something like that." McIver downed his second bourbon. "But Les is no dummy."

"Absolutely not. Perhaps you'd like to tell me how I can help you."

The other man surveyed the offices of Tyson LaRose, then settled his tiny eyes on Dallas. "Nice place you got out there. The big house."

"Thank you."

"Warren lived there with your sister?"

"That's right." Dallas thought he knew where this was heading, and a glance at Tyson assured him he knew the same thing.

"Well"—McIver drew on his cigarette, closing one eye when he did so—"this is a friendly visit. Just to get us all past a little difficulty. Okay?"

"Maybe it's okay," Dallas said, letting the warmth fall from his voice. "We'll see."

A coughing bout doubled McIver over. He dropped the half-smoked cigarette into his glass where it fizzled and spat.

Rae's distress was something Dallas could feel, but he wanted her with him now. Now and throughout whatever it was going to take to clear up the mess they were in.

"We're sorry for your loss," McIver said at last. "But we got bills to pay. Les did work for you all, and now we need money to cover our costs."

Now they had come within reach of the man's destination. "What kind of work?"

"Construction."

"Why don't you let me take care of this," Tyson said, so loudly he surprised Dallas. "Since it's an issue between Warren and this man's brother, I'll make an advance on the settling of Warren's affairs. I am Fancy's lawyer. And I was Warren's."

Tyson offering to part with money—especially for someone else—was an exotic twist. "You said we're talking about an arrangement Warren made on behalf of Calhoun Properties, didn't you, Sam?"

"Well—"

"I thought you did. Where was this construction?"

"Here and there."

"Here and there, where?"

"Up Madison way. Condos and such."

"Is that home? Madison?"

McIver shifted. "Thereabouts."

"I want to make things right," Dallas told him. "I'd like to talk to Les, too. It's the least I can do."

"He sent me." Belligerence set the other man's soft jaw. He looked as if he rationed razors and combs. "He doesn't have time to go running around."

"But you do?" Dallas asked softly.

"Just pay something on the bill."

Rae surprised Dallas by saying, "I've been to Madison. Pretty place."

"Sherman didn't burn it," Tyson said, sounding inane.

Dallas took a pad and pen from the desk and offered them to McIver. "Write down your address and phone number. Unless you have a card?"

The expected shake of the head took several seconds to come. "A few thousand would do."

"I'd just like to talk to Les. I'm sure you understand that I need some corroboration of your story."

McIver frowned, then said, "Oh, yeah. No. Les sent me because he had to go out of town."

"Out of Madison?" Rae asked innocently.

"Macon," McIver said, and looked confused. "A thousand?"

"Where did you say Les was?"

"Los Cabos." Squirming a little, the man ignored the pad of paper. "He goes down there regular."

"I see." Dallas thought he saw a great deal, but needed to find out a great deal more. He could afford a small gamble to get closer. "Well, we can work something out until he gets back. Will a check do?"

McIver squirmed some more, and stared at Rae again. "Saturday," he said. "The banks are closed. Make it cash and we can go with a bit less for now."

Dallas didn't like the way McIver looked at Rae. "We've got a little problem here, Sam. I don't have the ready cash. We could get you a room at the motel till Monday and—"

"I've got cash," Tyson said, taking out his wallet.

"Tyson," Dallas interrupted. "I'll deal with my own business."

"I'm glad to help out. Just—"

"I wouldn't hear of it," Dallas said, skewering Tyson with a stare even a fool could interpret. Paying this man cash would be stupid, and could cut them off from a chance to find out more about Warren's activities prior to his death.

McIver pushed to his feet, and smacked his glass down on the desk. "I'll take what you got," he said to Tyson.

"Look," Dallas said, "I want to keep this in the business, Sam. A man like you understands these things."

Sam's head jutted belligerently. "I don't want to make no trouble here. We got money coming is all."

"And you'll get it," Dallas told him. "You go on down to the motel—only one around—and I'll call in and make sure your tab's paid." He took a couple of bills from his wallet. "This'll cover any expenses, and on Monday when the office is open I'll make sure you get everything you're owed. Okay?"

"Well—"

"I knew you'd understand how these things have to be done." Dallas eased the man toward the door and into the reception area. "You carry on to the motel and tell them I sent you. I'll give them a call shortly."

Disgruntled mumbling followed, but McIver left and Dallas returned to Tyson's office.

"What the hell did you think you were doing, Tyson?" he said. "First, if you thought you could get rid of that shit with a single payoff, you're wrong. He'd have been back for more, and more. Second, this may be our chance to get what we haven't been able to get—solid evidence of what Warren was doing to skim Calhoun Property funds."

Tyson drew himself up. His assurance didn't make Dallas feel easier. "It's not a good idea for her to be here," Tyson said of Rae.

"Rae's with me. And I know what I'm doing."

"Okay." Tyson spread his arms. "I don't get it, but I surely hope you do."

Dallas hoped so, too.

"Forget McIver, and Warren, for a moment," Tyson said. "For now I want a chance to talk to you."

"Talk then. Make it quick and simple. I don't like interference in my affairs."

"It may be time for your affairs to become my affairs."

"I don't think so."

Tyson came around the desk and stood facing him. "Because you don't want me. You've got something against my family, so you don't want me, even though I can do good things for Calhoun."

"I don't have a thing against your family," Dallas told him.

"It doesn't matter. I'm officially throwing my hat into the ring to become Calhoun Properties' in-house counsel. My main qualification is that you'd be very foolish not to hire me."

An uneasiness assailed Dallas. "I know you're going to expand on that."

"Not too much." Tyson's eyes went to Rae. "But we understand each other. You're vulnerable, Dallas. Not quite ready to go down if you make the right moves and make them fast, but getting close."

"Finish," Dallas said, beginning to have his own doubts about the wisdom of having Rae with him.

Tyson splayed the fingers of one hand on the desk. "There are more Sam McIvers out there. They're not the ones we have to worry too much about. Most of them have been paid. It's the people they did the work for who should scare the hell out of you. They're the people who got taken by Warren—in your name."

Twenty-three

Rae could smell a coming storm.

And she could feel Dallas.

She knew which was the greater threat to her peace and safety.

He watched her walk around the big, bare room that was his office in the building that housed Calhoun Properties. Her movements felt jerky, clumsy.

She'd asked to see where Warren had worked when he was in Glory.

In silence, Dallas had driven her to the parking lot behind the building. He had pointed out Warren's dark green Morgan—antique, of course—still parked in a slot that bore his name. When her eyes had filled with tears, Dallas looked away.

Inside the building he'd taken her to an office on the second floor. The room bore no trace of the man she'd known. An expensive rosewood desk and credenza, a deep red leather chair behind the desk, and two matching chairs facing across the highly polished, but bare top. Deep red carpet and drapes. Photographs of old planes and cars on the walls. Not a piece of paper in sight anywhere.

A room no one used anymore.

A dead man's room.

Rae had turned on her heel and walked out, and Dallas led her up a flight of stairs to his own office on the third floor.

Dallas had no photographs on his walls, or any photographs at all, no carpet on the linoleum-tiled floor, no leather chair behind his scarred maple desk. What he did have was plenty of evidence that he worked hard, and had plenty of work to do.

"You don't look impressed," he said, sounding vaguely amused.

"If I'd thought about it, I'd probably have expected you to work in a room like this."

He raised his big shoulders. "It'll never make it into *Southern Homes,* but it's functional."

"Exactly." The file cabinets were metal, the crammed bookshelves painted a similar tan to the color of the linoleum, and papers heaped the desk. "Are you a simple man, Dallas?"

He laughed at that. "I don't know. Am I?"

"Maybe. Maybe you're more simple in some ways than you'd like anyone to guess."

They regarded each other. The heavy, electricity-laden air pressed in on Rae. He'd told her she had the greenest eyes he'd ever seen. He had the grayest eyes she'd ever seen. They changed grays, it was true, but only from slate to charcoal, and shades in between—and always with penetrating results.

"My father's office was at the house. I like to be with my people."

"You like to keep your fingers in everything that's going on, you mean."

His smile lighted his too-serious face. "See? You already know me as well—or better—than I know myself. Some people don't take a long time to get close enough to read each other's minds."

"That's not even smooth," she told him. "We've got troubles. They're too big to allow us to even consider personal issues right now. I guess someone cleared everything out of Warren's office."

Dallas picked up a sheaf of papers that had slid from his

desk to the floor. "He was hardly ever there. There wasn't much to clean out."

"You mean it always looked . . . *sterile*."

"Warren was never into homey. He spent his life checking out for days, or weeks, at a time. And I'm not talking about the time he spent with you. Even as a kid he would disappear for a couple of days, then come back as if nothing had happened. I think it all started with the troubles in his family. I often wondered if he needed help. You know, therapy."

"I never saw that side of him," she said. "He was quiet, but so am I. It didn't seem strange."

"I guess it wouldn't." He pushed the papers onto the desk and turned his head sideways to read, frowning as he did so. She'd caused him to lose a lot of time at work. "Look, Dallas, I can find my own way home from here. You must have a lot to do, and I've taken up too much of your time."

"Nothing doing," he said, giving her his full attention again. "I didn't know how much I needed a friend until I realized you were available."

Despite herself, despite the seriousness of everything she confronted, Rae had to laugh. "Available, huh? You have quite a turn of phrase there."

"It wasn't anything," he said, grinning back. "I'm available, too."

Was he really? She really needed a friend, and she needed that friend to be Dallas. She didn't want anyone else. And she needed an end to the uncertainty and danger that had been thrust upon her.

Dallas was strong; she felt his strength. She also felt the outrageousness of their situation. Trouble had brought them together, and trouble didn't make an easy foundation for a relationship.

She shouldn't be allowing herself to fall in love with him.

"What are you thinking?" he asked.

She'd already fallen. "I'm thinking this is all fantastic."

"Yes," he agreed. "But some of the questions are being answered. We can work everything out between us."

He was a dreamer. For all his tough, world-worn exterior, Dallas Calhoun believed right could win out over wrong if you worked hard enough at it.

"We can," he insisted.

"There was a time when I'd have agreed with you, about the time I set off in the middle of the night with a baby and nothing but a few possessions in plastic bags. Oh, and my high school diploma and about seven dollars."

"Rae?"

Her smile was the kind intended to show she didn't really care about the past. "I was seventeen and I'd got away from hell. Things like that make you believe in justice."

"Honey, I didn't know." He reached for her, but she moved out of his range. "You never have to go back to anything like that. You've made your way. Rae, you're really something."

"You could find people like me in every city in the country. We're the survivors who were lucky enough to be born strong. It's our job to be strong for the ones who can't be."

"Like Ginny?" he asked.

She'd been thinking of Cassie, but said, "Yes, like Ginny when she was a baby. I hope I've done the right thing—sending her back to Decline like that."

"I think you have. Buelah's a tiger. No one's going to get past her."

"Uh huh." She'd managed a few minutes alone to call the sheriff in Decline. He'd told her he didn't think she had anything to worry about, but she was worried nevertheless.

A much-used coffeemaker occupied a floral tin tray on top of a filing cabinet. Rae eyed it and said, "Coffee would be good. Okay if I make some?"

"Sure you wouldn't like bourbon?" Dallas laughed. "You obviously have a taste for hard liquor."

Puckering at the memory of what she'd tried to drink at

Tyson's office, Rae said, "I'm sure." She filled the coffee-maker with water from a sink in one corner of the room and plugged in the cord. "I wish I could decide what to do next."

"It's easy. You've got to do the same as me. We're going to put all our cards on the table. Get rid of any surprises that could crop up between us. Then clear up this unpleasant business Warren left behind."

Rae wasn't ready to think of Warren as the cause, rather than the answer to her problems. "You make it all sound so simple. It isn't."

With his loose-limbed walk, Dallas went to a worn, gold brocade couch against a wall beneath the windows that reached from corner to corner. He sat down and stretched his arms along the back of the couch.

Hovering by the coffee, waiting for it to brew, Rae could not stop herself from looking at him repeatedly. Each time she did so, he looked back. He didn't smile.

Mostly he kept his eyes on her face, but there were flickering glances that took in the rest of her.

She wasn't practiced in the art of staying cool under exposure to undisguised desire. Too many sensations. Too strong a pull at the deepest parts of her.

"Not much of a view," she said of what lay outside, and remembered to breathe again.

"Views distract," he told her. "Anyway, I like a good brick wall. Something solid about a brick wall—especially when you're in real estate."

Rae laughed.

Dallas didn't.

Emotion rushed at her, so strong, so overwhelming, she gripped a handle on a file cabinet and clung on. For some insane reason tears filled her eyes. She parted her lips and looked at the ceiling, willing the tears back the way they had come.

Dallas sat forward and rested his forearms on his thighs. "Rae? You okay?"

"Of course I am."

"No you're not. What is it?"

For the first time since that night ten years ago, she wanted to tell someone the whole story of what had happened. "I never told Warren," she said, disoriented by the power of what she felt.

"Tell me."

"You don't know what I'm talking about."

"I will when you open up, Rae. And you want to."

Her heart made uncomfortable, jumpy moves. "Forget it. It's all been too much. That's the problem. I'm upset by other things. And confused."

"You're confused because you know things you want to tell me—about Warren—but you're too loyal. He was good to you. What man wouldn't be if he had the chance?"

The coffee stopped perking. She poured some into two mugs with discolored insides and faded green ducks on the outside, and took them to the couch. She gave Dallas one, but remained standing.

A rumble sounded in the distance. "The storm's coming closer," she mused.

"I like storms," Dallas said.

"So do I. As long as I'm somewhere safe."

"I kind of like it if I'm with someone, too," Dallas said. "Someone I'd like to keep safe."

Another pause stretched between them, another magnetized space.

She pulled his brown cloth-covered chair from the desk and sat down facing him. "You haven't lived the kind of life I've lived."

He cocked his head questioningly and hooked one very long, very muscular leg over an arm of the couch.

Rae said, "You were born into money. Right?"

"Uh huh."

"You always knew who your mother and father were, and that they'd take care of you?"

Raising the mug to his lips, he squinted at her through the steam and sipped the boiling brew carefully. "You don't know who your parents are?"

"I thought I more or less explained I didn't." Whatever was driving her to spill her history to him, she'd just follow it. Things couldn't get much worse than they were, and if there was even a small chance for something between them, it had better be based on complete openness. She'd had the other type of relationship. The results spoke for themselves.

"Forget the past, Rae. We can't go back."

"No kidding." She was making him uneasy. Men didn't do the deep, uncomfortable stuff well. "The man I thought was my stepfather tried to rape me."

In the awful silence that followed, Rae bowed her head.

Dallas's fingers, closing on hers around the mug, startled her. She hadn't heard him get up from the couch. He took the mug away and put it on the desk beside his own. "How many people have you told about that?" He leaned over her.

"Apart from Warren, only one," she said. "You."

"Thank you."

She looked at him sharply.

"Thank you for doing me an honor. Oh, Rae, you don't know what it means to me to hear you say you've trusted me with something you've all but hidden for years."

"I took Ginny and ran." Her chest felt tight. "I got lucky. Decent men picked us up. Truckers who had kids of their own and saw me as a kid with a baby."

"Thank God."

"I doubt if God's too pleased with me," she said quietly. Each breath cost more than the last. "They—those people I lived with—said I wasn't related to either of them. I thought Betty was my mother." That was a first. She'd never spoken the name aloud since she'd left. "That night she said she wasn't. She told me my father hooked up with her and brought my sister and me with him. Then he left us behind with her and never came back. I don't know why she kept us except—just maybe she kind of felt something for us when she wasn't drunk."

"Rae . . . Hell, what do I say?"

"Nothing. It's all grubby and cheap. And it means I'm nobody. I never was anybody."

"Don't." He hauled her to her feet, held her by the shoulders. "You know better than to talk like that. You know you're something special."

Rae regarded him steadily. "I'm not telling you all this because I want pity. It's because I don't believe you'll try to use it against me, but I also think it'll help you decide I could never be part of your world."

His eyes were slate again, and hard, and glittery. "I could never be other than very proud to have you at my side. And I'm insulted that you think I'm so shallow I'd be embarrassed by whatever pedigree you do or don't have."

"Don't have," she told him shortly. "Sometimes I have nightmares about that night. About Willie. Willie Skeggs was his name. He was a cruel, stupid man."

"What about your sister?"

She looked past him. "She died." The one secret that must live and die with Rae was the true identity of Ginny's parents.

"I'm sorry."

"She'd had a brain injury when she was young. She had a seizure and that was it. How about your brother?"

Muscles in his jaw worked before he smiled a little. "Car accident. Single car accident. Jesse wrapped my daddy's Cadillac around a big old tree. Daddy had just finished telling the two of us we'd never amount to anything. He did that regularly, but this was the time when we'd gone to him asking if we could go to a music college."

Rae felt the pain behind the nonchalance, the anger in the light tone. "Your daddy didn't like the idea?"

"Calhouns don't follow sissy careers. Calhouns make money in the Calhoun business, end of story."

"Only it's not the end, is it?" she suggested, looking up at him. "It's never completely over."

"It's behind us, though."

"Is it?" She pressed her flattened palms to his chest. His flesh was warm through coarse denim. "Sometimes I'm afraid I'll look up and see Willie. Then there are times I wish I would look up and see him."

Dallas raised her chin and frowned down at her. "Why would you want to see him?"

Rae squeezed her eyes shut. She couldn't believe what she'd said.

He chafed her cheek with the backs of his fingers. "Rae? Why?"

"Because," she said in barely more than a whisper, "because then I'd know I hadn't killed him."

His hand fell from her face.

From a great distance came a long, low rumble of thunder. A threat of things to come.

"How?" was all Dallas said when he spoke at last.

Rae shivered and rubbed her arms. "I hit his head with a flashlight. A big old rusty flashlight. He didn't move afterward. And I ran. I should have called for help somehow, but I ran."

"He tried to rape you, and you hit him."

"Yes."

"Then you took Ginny and ran."

"Yes."

"I wish he was still alive, too."

Her eyes shot open, and she took a step backward.

The lines beside his mouth might never have creased with laughter. They were deep now, deep, angry lines, as angry as his eyes. "I wish the bastard would walk through that door. Then I'd have the pleasure of killing him myself. Only it wouldn't be with one fast blow."

Rae felt the blood leave her head. She felt faint.

"You ran and found a place to hide. With Buelah, bless

her. A smart woman who knew a good thing when she saw it. And along came Warren—sophisticated, successful Warren—all ready to marry you and provide a home for you and Ginny. You'd have been a fool to turn him down."

The tan linoleum was a very long way away. Rae felt for the chair and sat down again. She bent forward and put her head between her knees.

"Ah, *shoot*," Dallas muttered, from somewhere almost as far away as the thunder that sounded again. "You poor kid. It's over. D'you hear me? It's all over, Rae."

"No." She covered her ears and waited for the swelling sensation in her head to fade. "It isn't over. I thought it was, but it isn't."

"Yes, it is." He went to his knees before her and guided her head onto his shoulder. He rocked her, murmured meaningless words into her ear, stroked her back, her arms.

"I should quit and go back to Decline, but I can't make myself do it. Warren did give me so much. He made me think I was worth something."

"Thank you for that, Warren," Dallas said with no trace of sarcasm. "You had some good in you, boy."

"Are you going to tell someone about Willie? What I did?"

"Are you going to write a book about Glory and my family—including the fact that my dear daddy was having sex with Linsay May Dale when he died?"

Rae raised her face, and he pushed back her hair, and said, "Are you?"

Summoning up a smile took more energy than she'd thought she still had. "Maybe."

"Okay. How about the fact that my sister's sleeping with her dead husband's brother-in-law."

"Don't think I could leave that out," Rae said, sniffing.

"Mmm. And how about the trouble my company's in? How my deceased brother-in-law sold us up the river. And how we're in deep trouble if we can't keep the dirt under the rug till we can sweep it away with the considerable amount of money it's going to take."

She swallowed, and said, "I'm definitely going to devote several chapters to that." But she couldn't smile. The money in the bank in Savannah, a lot of it, must belong to Dallas. She was tempted to tell him everything, to take him there and show him. And pray nothing led to questions about Ginny, and her own right to hold custody. If she allowed emotion to take over, she could turn her own life, and Ginny's, upside down.

Rae knew what she had to do. She had to move as fast as she could to set things right. First thing on Monday morning she'd return to Savannah, to the bank, and sort through everything. Then she'd find a reputable lawyer to help her return those assets to which she had no right.

Dallas smoothed the side of her face. "I wish I could remember what it was you think you did wrong; then maybe I'd be able to tell it to someone. But I surely can't remember. I did notice you had your computer ready at the cabin, and a mess of papers scattered around, though."

"Writers tend to have a mess of papers scattered around." He wasn't horrified by what she'd done. He was angry for her, and defensive of her. "Dallas, the timing's all wrong, but when I think of you I'm so full, I feel I could choke. Only it's with happiness, or something."

"Or something?" The twist of his lips was wry. "Can you elaborate on that?"

"I want to believe you mean what you say—about your feelings. About me, but—"

"I do mean it. Also"—he took her fingers to his mouth and kissed them—"also I wish it hadn't been the way it was. When you and I made love. I shouldn't have allowed that to happen. I took advantage, and I lost control."

In a tiny voice, Rae said, "And it was fantastic."

Dallas looked into her eyes, tipped his head back, and laughed. "You know how to ruin a man's abject apology.

Explaining things to Ginny won't be too hard, y'know. We'll ask Buelah to help. After all, she already knows."

Rae colored. "She dug it out of me."

"And she figured you and I have a thing for each other."

"I'm working on a novelization."

"Excuse me?" Blinking, Dallas frowned. "I don't follow."

"All the papers you saw at the cabin. They're for a project I've got under contract. A novelization of a movie. That's what I do mostly."

"You mean there's already a movie about my steamy life story?"

She batted his shoulder with a closed fist and shook her head. "Yes, of course, that's exactly it." With her hand still on his shoulder, she grew motionless. Lightning crackled, distant yet, with the quality of a thousand firecrackers.

Dallas looked back at her for a long time, then stood up and turned his back. The first drops of heavy rain hit the windows.

Rae took in his broad back, the way his denim shirt settled on his shoulders and clung to his big biceps. Tension etched every line of his body.

She got up and stood behind him. Very tentatively, she leaned, rested the side of her face between his shoulders, slipped her arms around his waist, and felt him sigh. Her sigh matched his.

The next burst of lightning was closer. It split the purplish sky and shot veins of white light earthward behind the opposite building.

Then came the thunder. The windows rattled, and Rae felt the earth had roared back.

Dallas pulled her in front of him and laced his hands around her neck. "I've spent my life working at something I never chose," he said. "I like it in a way. Looking back along a tunnel my daddy and my daddy's daddy—and his daddy before him—hacked out, pleases me. It wasn't all done with the sweat of their own backs, or without more than one man losing in the process, but I like to think I've paid back in a way. I am paying back. I'm ambitious, but I'm fair."

Rae heard every word he spoke, but any of his words would have fascinated her. She loved watching his mouth, and his eyes, and the way his face moved, and his throat, the hair at the open neck of his shirt.

The tips of his thumbs came together lightly beneath her chin. "Do you know what I'm saying?"

"I think so."

"If I have to scale down drastically because of what's happened, we'll still survive. I think we will. If we don't, I'll start something else. Hell, maybe it's time for me to get the old piano tuned and start practicing. I could play the bar scene. Can you sing?"

It was her turn to laugh. "Badly. We'd starve if I did."

He was serious again. "You're starting to think 'we,' Rae. Please think 'we.' And believe we can work things through and come out together. I'm going to search out these people Tyson's talking about and tell them we'll do right by them. God knows how much we owe, but if they close us down, they'll never get it. They might as well give us a chance."

He'd stopped talking about the money he thought Warren had stolen. She didn't know what to say or believe. Linsay May had probably believed Biff Calhoun loved her, that he would take care of her. She'd ended up in the rental office of Calhoun, working for very little and turning to Biff's son whenever she was in need of more money.

"What's behind those green eyes of yours now?" Dallas asked.

"Things I've got to think through on my own." Biff had already been married. And Linsay May knew as much. But who knew what influence he'd exerted to get what he wanted?

Lightning ripped behind Rae, and the ensuing thunder made her wince. She stood on tiptoe and brought her lips to

Dallas's. Softly, softly, with eyes closed and tears of emotion squeezing past her lashes, she kissed him. He took his time responding, but when he did the softness was quickly gone. Without his supporting arms, she would have fallen beneath the violence of that kiss. He bracketed her legs with his, ran a hand down to her bottom and pressed her hips against him.

Her thin cotton slacks and panties did nothing to shield her from the flagrant pressure on her belly.

Without warning he took hold of her arms and held her away. His nostrils flared, and he breathed through his mouth while he stared from her eyes to her breasts. She didn't need to look at herself to know he was seeing her nipples pressing against her T-shirt, and the rapid rise and fall of her breasts.

"If we don't stop. Now. It's going to happen again."

Rae nodded. She couldn't speak.

"Just the way it happened before."

She nodded again.

"No finesse. Just raw sex. I promised myself I wouldn't let myself do that to you again."

"We did it to each other," she murmured.

"Come back with me. To Sweet Bay. I want you in my bed. All night. I want you there in the morning."

The assault of rain on the windows made her raise her voice. "Not yet. I mean, no. I couldn't go there knowing they know about Warren and me. Some of it."

"They're going to accept you, Rae. As soon as I've told them we're together, and staying together, they'll know they have to, or we'll all have to go our separate ways."

"You'd leave Glory?" She shouldn't hope he'd say yes.

Dallas pulled her hips to his with one hand and covered her right breast with the other. He covered it and made circles with his palm. Her nipple tingled and pushed harder against his hand.

"I'd leave Sweet Bay."

"And go where?"

He bent to nibble her bottom lip. "Are we ever going to

be able to cuddle without wanting to tear each other's clothes off?"

"I hope not," she said, and buried her face in his neck, giggling. "I can't believe I said that."

"Please come home with me."

She wanted to be with him, but not there. "Come home with me," she said, and felt daring, and forward. "I'm going back to the cabin. I mean, would you come back and take a look around for me while I do a few things." She hadn't meant that, but with any luck he wouldn't know.

"You can't stay there."

"Yes, I can. I'm going to make sure it's secure. Then I'm going to call the sheriff and ask if they could make it known that they'll be driving by regularly. And I have a gun."

He sighed and rested his brow on hers. "Why doesn't that make me rest easy?"

She'd been reluctant to bring the gun back from the safety-deposit box in Savannah. Now she was glad she had. "I'm a good shot. I worked hard at it."

"Statistics show that people—"

"I know all about the statistics. They apply to people who haven't taken the time to make sure they know what they're doing."

"They apply to a lot of people who think they know what they're doing until they're confronted by some maniac who just broke in on them. You probably wouldn't remember where to find the trigger."

"Yes, I—"

"You didn't do a great job when you thought I was a maniac."

She grinned and it felt good. "I'll do a better job the next time you step out of line. Really, I want to go back and get settled again properly. I'm behind with my work, and I'd like to phone Buelah and talk to Ginny."

"Well"—slowly, unwillingly, he relented—"okay. But I'm not going to want to leave you there alone."

"Who said anything about you leaving me there?"

In the act of straightening away from her, Dallas stopped and narrowed his eyes. "What exactly are you saying, ma'am?"

With more audacity than she'd ever known she possessed, Rae tweaked him in a most sensitive spot and leaped away when he made a grab for her.

"Got your attention?" She made a run for the door. "Good. What I'm saying, exactly, is that you and I need a long, long talk. We probably need to talk all night. Maybe all day tomorrow."

"Talk?" he said, coming after her.

Rae fled down the stairs. "Among other things," she called back to him.

Twenty-four

The wipers swept wavering sheets of water across the windshield. Rain pounded the top of the Land Rover and enclosed it in a steamy tunnel of gray. The inside of the windshield sweated.

In the rearview mirror Dallas saw only Wolf, and the smeared mess he made of the back window.

Driving out of town, they made slow progress. Headlights on the few oncoming vehicles that passed cast brief, bleary glares.

Lightning continued to flash in the storm-darkened sky, but more distantly now, and they couldn't hear the thunder over the engine of the Land Rover.

With her hands clasped between her knees, Rae looked straight ahead, although Dallas knew she wasn't seeing anything but the thoughts and pictures inside her head.

He'd like to erase some of those thoughts.

He'd like to blot out the pictures that went with them.

He'd like, more than anything, to have been there to save her when she was seventeen and alone.

But he was with her now, and she liked it that way. He couldn't suppress a grin.

"Can you see where we're going?" Rae asked.

Dallas glanced at her. "No."

"Pull over, then."

The thought was tempting. "I could drive this road in a

blindfold. But I can see well enough. We're only making about ten miles an hour."

Once on the bypass road there were no more approaching headlights. With the nearing of Sweet Bay he briefly toyed with taking her there anyway. He must respect her wishes.

"What are you going to do about Sam and Les McIver?"

"Pray they don't turn into blood-sucking monsters. I checked the files when we first got to the office. No record of business with them. I'd have been surprised if there was."

"I knew John did business as Maddy & Associates."

They passed the entrance to Sweet Bay. Dallas made himself wait, and hope she'd say something helpful.

"But I didn't have any reason to question why, or what was involved. There's a study at home in Decline. John—Warren had a desk and file cabinets, but there's nothing much there."

"I know." He set his lips together and waited again.

"You *know?*"

More confessions. "When I went looking for you, and Buelah told me you'd left town, I . . . Well, John Maddy lived in that house. He made sure there'd never be any connection to Warren Niel."

"You broke into my house?"

"Uh huh." Now he wished he hadn't. "I'm sorry. I didn't have any idea where you'd gone or when you'd be back, but I shouldn't have done it. Nothing's broken or messed up."

"Watch it!"

Dallas slammed on the brakes in time to skid and miss a bounding white-tailed deer. Then, while Wolf growled his displeasure, the Land Rover came to a slithering halt on the wrong side of the road. "Thanks," he said, giving the vehicle some gas and setting off again. "Almost there. Have you changed your mind about wanting me around?"

Rae braced herself against the dashboard. "In your position I'd have done what you did."

He relaxed a little. Her power over him should scare him out of his mind. Maybe it did. "Does that mean no?"

"It means I haven't changed my mind. We're there."

"The Parkers ought to get this driveway cleared," he commented as he turned in between sopping shrubs and grass that brushed almost as high as the top of the hood.

Rae said, "I'll see to it," and he glanced at her curiously before saying, "why would you do that? Unless you're planning a long stay." He wanted her to say she was, but not at the cabin.

"Heck," she muttered, then, more loudly, "heck! I don't believe this. Darn it anyway, can't I ever trust anyone anymore?"

Bewildered, Dallas looked ahead. Then he saw what Rae had seen. To the right of the carport stood Buelah's '54 Cadillac. "Lighten up. They must have forgotten something."

"Hah. If I know anything about it, that's what Buelah will say happened, but I won't believe her."

"Rae—"

"She didn't want to leave me here. Hurry up. I don't want Ginny spending another night here."

Before the Land Rover came to a complete stop Rae opened the door. Wolf shot past her; then she jumped out and ducked as she ran for the house.

Dallas intended to check all doors and windows, to place screws where they would keep the windows permanently closed, and install drop-bars on the inside of the front and back doors which both opened inward. He had tools in the back, and screws. There were some two-by-fours in the carport.

Best give Rae and Buelah at least a few minutes alone.

He got out and retrieved the toolbox.

Rae met him on the porch. "I'm so *furious* with Buelah," she said. *"Furious."*

Dallas set down the green metal box. He didn't know what to say.

"She's brought all the stuff for dinner. Plain as you please. All set out. Something already in the oven and everything. I'd like to hear her try to pretend she only came back because she *forgot* something."

Dallas tried a grin and said, "What's she cooking?"

"Don't try distracting me. It won't work. Where are they?"

He glanced around at the sheeting rain, at the steamy mist rolled out where the river flowed, and behind him at the sloping, dense vegetation rising to the trees. "They aren't in the cabin?"

"Would I ask if they—?" Rae popped back into the cabin and reappeared with a yellow slicker. "Sorry to snap. I can just hear it now. Ginny can get Buelah to do anything. She's the type of child who revels in sloshing around in weather like this. They'll both be soaked, darn it."

Dallas looked at the area again. "I'll get my oilskins." He didn't say what he thought, that it was very strange for an elderly woman and a child to leave dinner cooking and go for a walk in the middle of a storm.

With Rae at his side, he retraced his steps to the Land Rover and pulled on his duster and hat. Even if water ran from the brim, it kept it out of his eyes.

"You don't think they'd go out in the boat, do you?" Rae said, swishing in her plastic slicker, turning her head inside the hood. "Can you see the boat?"

"Not from here," he said. "But they wouldn't take the boat out, Rae. Not in this weather. And not when dinner's cooking, right?"

"Right." She rubbed at her cheeks and chafed her hands together. The questions they were both thinking didn't need to be asked aloud. *Where would Buelah and Ginny go? And where did a person start looking?*

"Ginny!" Rae shouted suddenly. She backed away from Dallas and turned. "Buelah!"

Dallas puffed up his cheeks and headed for the Caddy.

The windows were steamed up, but the doors weren't locked. He checked inside. Ginny's purple sweatshirt lay on the front passenger seat. Books scattered the back.

The keys hung in the ignition.

"Hey, Rae." He slammed the door and tramped after Rae, who made her way up the rutted lane. "Rae, hold up. How did they get into the cabin?"

When he reached her, she was breathing through her mouth, and he saw the signs of panic in her eyes.

"How did they get into the cabin?"

She frowned. "Through the door. It wasn't locked. Maybe they decided to go up to the road and look for us."

"We'd have seen them."

"We could have missed them in the rain. Remember? Even you said you couldn't see much."

Pointing out the holes in her theory would be cruel—and pointless—until he could think of an alternative. "I had no idea you'd left the door unlocked, Rae. That isn't smart."

"Don't tell me that now. I wasn't thinking."

"You mean you had too much on your mind, don't you?" he asked.

"It doesn't matter what I mean. Hurry up. Oh, Dallas, hurry."

They made it several hundred yards up the track before Rae stopped. "Something's happened to them."

"No. There's a solution we haven't thought of."

"Quick, back to the cabin. The timer on the oven will tell us something."

"Good idea." And now he had to be the one to do what must be done. "I'm going to put in a call to Nick."

Rae clutched his sleeve. "The sheriff? Oh, Dallas. You do think something awful's happened."

"I don't know what to think. But they're more likely to come strolling up by the time we get back. If they don't, we do need to call the sheriff and get a few extra pairs of eyes down here to help us round 'em up."

"You think they got lost?"

That wasn't beyond possible. "Could be. You start wandering around out there and all the trees look the same. There are acres of trees, Rae. This is a huge estate."

She raced ahead and into the small kitchen inside the cabin. The mouth-watering aroma of roasting meat wafted to greet Dallas.

"Pot roast," Rae said, looking into the oven. She took the lid off a pot on the stove. "Collards. And corn bread batter in that bowl."

The timer went off.

Slowly Rae pushed back her hood. "Buelah wouldn't forget."

"Everyone forgets things sometimes."

"Not Buelah. Not something like meat in the oven."

"They're going to walk through that door."

Rae went onto the porch.

Dallas picked up the phone and called Nick Serb.

"I'm going to start searching," Rae called. "I'm going to range back and forth from about the center point above the cabin to the left. You take the right."

This wasn't a woman who would ever sit back and wait to be looked after. "Sheriff's coming with as many people as he can scare up. I'd like you to stay with me, Rae. No point in losing you, too."

She was already leaning into the rain and striding out in her slippery, insubstantial sandals. Dallas joined her and she didn't protest.

"It's going to get dark," she panted, and he sensed how close she was to coming unglued. "What if an animal attacked them?"

"Not at this time of the year," he told her. "I'd only worry about that if food was scarce. And it won't be dark for hours yet."

"It's already dark."

"Only because of the storm. Gloomy doesn't count."

"*Stop* trying to gloss this over. My God, Dallas, they're gone. They wouldn't just take off in a storm and traipse around."

He wanted to tell her she was right. He said, "You can't know for sure what they'd do. We'll find them, Rae."

Branches whipped against his face. Dallas moved a stride ahead. "Walk behind me and watch for things hitting you."

"I don't care if they hit me!" She pushed his back, urging him on faster. Her sobbing breaths sounded unnaturally loud. They sawed the thick air.

Dallas felt the futility, but at least she was occupied until there were enough men and women gathered to spread out in an organized search.

He stopped abruptly, and Rae thudded into his back. "What is it?" Her voice rose higher. "What do you see?"

Dallas peered in every direction. Dripping foliage, vapor rising in thick, slow spirals from the sodden layer of fallen needles and leaves, visibility almost nil.

"Dallas?"

He faced Rae. Moisture coated her face.

"This is pointless," he told her. "I want you back in the warm. Nick will be here with a small army shortly, and we'll do this in an orderly fashion."

"Could someone have gone into the cabin and taken them?"

"No." He'd already added that to the list of possibilities.

"Yes they could. It's not Buelah's fault; it's mine. I shouldn't have expected her to keep Ginny safe."

"Why not?"

"I'm going back."

Dallas stopped her, and wrapped an arm around her shoulders. "It's going to be okay. Stick with me, Rae. We'll make it through. At least they're together."

"Yes," Rae said, trying to run again, her feet sliding. "Let's hurry. They'll get there and wonder where we are."

Breaking from the trees once more, they held hands and started downhill.

A small figure appeared in the open door to the cabin.

"Oh!" Rae sobbed. "Oh, thank you, thank you. Oh, I could be sick, I'm so relieved."

Dallas didn't tell her he knew exactly how she felt.

Tripping and sliding, her arms outstretched for balance, Rae dashed wildly onward. "You scared us to death," she shouted. "Where have you been? It's awful out here. You must be soaked."

Buelah wore a white cardigan that sagged under the weight of the water it had absorbed. Her blunt-cut hair hugged her head. She hurried forward, squinting while she wiped water from her glasses with a handkerchief that was obviously already soaked.

"You shouldn't have come back," Rae said. "Oh, Buelah, I want to get so angry, but I'm too grateful."

"I wanted you to change your mind and come home with us," the woman said.

At least she was direct, Dallas thought. He didn't like her haggard appearance.

"Ginny and I made a pact. We'd come back and refuse to leave without you."

"You're going to have to leave without me. I've got serious things to accomplish here, and I can't do them if I'm worrying about you and Ginny."

"Rae." Buelah stood in the beating rain, replaced her glasses and couldn't possibly be able to see a thing. "Rae, I didn't know Ginny had gone off the porch." Twigs and pine needles clung to her clothes. Mud caked her feet.

Dallas's gut knotted. He looked toward the cabin, not expecting to see what he so desperately wanted to see.

Rae had grown still. She pushed away her hood, and in moments her heavy, dark hair hung in wet strands around her face.

"I was cooking. She said she was going to call for Wolf and see if he'd come."

"Wolf's with us," Rae said indistinctly. "He's been with us."

Buelah shook her head. "She knew that, but she went outside to call him anyway."

"Ginny isn't here?"

"Rae, hold on," Dallas said, but when he reached for her, she jerked away. "Just hold it. We'll get her."

"Buelah," Rae said. "Isn't Ginny here?"

Utterly miserable, Buelah shook her head. "I've looked as far as I can. I don't know what to do next."

"She's wandered off," Dallas said with fear mounting in his breast. "Kids and trees. They always find so much to explore."

"In the pouring rain?" Rae said. "Not Ginny. She's not like that. She likes those things, but she wouldn't just wander off and worry Buelah."

"She'll be okay, I tell you," Dallas said, watching for approaching lights that would tell him Nick was coming. "We'll find her wandering around trying to get back. Concentrate on how she's going to feel. The poor kid is probably really scared right now."

"I can't bear for her to be scared."

The faint sound of sirens reached them. Nick and Buzz never missed an opportunity to use sirens and lights.

"Hold on, Rae, it'll—" He saw what he should have seen before, should have checked before. "Did you pull the boat away?"

"Huh?" Rae shot around. "Where would I pull it to? It's too much for me to pull. Dallas, the boat's gone."

"She wouldn't get in the boat," Buelah said, her crackly voice wobbling. "You can't even see the water."

"Even if she wanted to, she couldn't get the thing into the water," Dallas said, feeling relieved. "She'd never manage to push it that far. And she'd certainly never manage to get it turned right side up."

"Someone bigger could turn it over," Rae said. "Even I managed that."

"Please do as I ask and stay here," Dallas told her. "Both of you. The sheriff will be here within minutes."

He jogged down to the bank. A smooth mark in the mud suggested the boat had been pushed into the water. He searched around but could see no sign of it. The rest of the area bore a mess of rapidly disappearing footprints and what looked like sets of punctures into the slimy earth.

Dallas walked the riverbank for several hundred yards downstream, then repeated the process in the opposite direction.

Nothing.

He had never felt so helpless, or so deeply horrified and afraid. Not afraid for himself, but for the child he scarcely knew but cared for because he loved her mother.

Heavy inside, Dallas turned back. Covered with mud, Wolf splashed out of the mist over the river. He made straight for Dallas and jumped to plant his filthy front paws on his boss's chest.

For the briefest of moments, Dallas grinned. Wolf had brought Rae's old tennis shoe back again. "Good fella," he said. "C'mon, let's move this along." He thought, *Let's get this done.*

Glory's two new police cars, and the two that had been retired a year ago, convened in a haphazard row before the cabin. Bodies of people he knew spilled out and fell in behind Nick and Buzz.

Rae turned her face toward Dallas.

She wanted him with her.

He broke into a run and arrived neck-and-neck with Wolf. "Child missing, Nick," he said. "Little girl. Ten. Blond hair. Not very big. How big, Rae?"

"She's only about four feet, six. She weighs maybe sixty-five pounds."

"Hear that?" Nick shouted. "Spread out."

"The shoe," Rae said, bending over Wolf.

"He keeps hiding it and digging it up again," Dallas said, distracted. "Or trying to drown it, this time, I guess."

"Dallas."

He glanced at Rae. With her eyes stretched wide, she held up the tennis shoe Wolf had brought in his teeth. "This isn't my shoe. It's Ginny's."

Twenty-five

They had found the boat a mile down-river.

There was no sign of Ginny.

Too numb, too sick, and horrified, and exhausted to do any more but observe, Rae sat with Buelah in the cabin.

Searchlights turned the surrounding area into a blinding stage. Shouts reached Rae through the open door. Shouts. No laughter.

"They're going to find her," Buelah said.

Buelah had said the same thing many times in the hours since the police had first arrived. No reply was expected.

"So many people," Buelah said. "So many good people."

They had come in cars and trucks, and on motorcycles, and even a few on bicycles. "Yes," Rae said. A map and a minutely detailed chart lay under plastic on a trestle table in front of the cabin. These people, mostly complete strangers, had arrived and been dispatched to areas pointed out by a man who had once been a deputy, but who was now too old to hack his way through dense vegetation on slippery, uneven ground, in darkness—even with the aid of searchlights. Searchlights shone past objects, not through them, and once beyond the illuminated sphere, powerful flashlight beams were the best that could be done. Obstacles could lie in a thousand shadows out there. So could one little girl.

Even Tyson LaRose had come, tight-lipped and silent, and quick to take directions. A man who said he owned the paper came, but assured her he wasn't there as a reporter, but to search for the child. Lucy Gordon arrived with Linsay May Dale, who still bore bruises on her face.

Joella LaRose, with Fancy Niel, drove in together, said nothing to Rae, but asked where Tyson had been sent, then set off in that direction. Rae had the fleeting thought that they were an unlikely pair, but trouble could bring people together.

People loved children. They cared what happened to them. Normal people did.

The search had been going on for hours. A small canteen truck used to take meals to shut-ins served hot drinks and sandwiches to weary helpers each time they returned.

Rain continued as if it would never stop. Rae had heard people remark on how high the river was, and how it was flowing unusually rapidly. She didn't remember a summer storm as wild and persistent as this one.

"They're going to say they'll stop looking until it gets light," Rae said. Earlier, while she'd hunted along the river-bank, she'd cried, but there were no more tears. "I heard the bulletins go out. They're already watching for her on the highways and everywhere. They wouldn't do that so soon if the sheriff didn't think something awful's happened to her. But they won't keep people out there in this storm all night. They always stop sooner or later. I can feel the time running out. It's ticking away. That's the way these things go. Hope goes away minute by minute."

"I don't know," Buelah said. She'd changed into dry clothes but continued to appear smaller and more frail than she ever had. "I don't know. I just don't know."

Rae patted her hand. "Go and get some sleep."

"I shouldn't have come back."

"Buelah, this is my fault, not yours." Since Dallas first arrived in Decline she'd acted impulsively every step of the way. And fascination for a man had played a part in keeping her acting impulsively. "I forgot what I'm supposed to do. I won't forget again." If only she was given another chance with Ginny. If only there was still time to find her alive and all right.

"Forgot what?"

"That Ginny's all that matters. She's the reason for everything I do; she has to be."

"You're a good mother," Buelah said. "You were a good mother even when you were still a child yourself."

The assurance didn't bring Rae greater sense of peace with herself. When she'd left Glad Times she'd been strong and determined. Ginny had become the focus of her own young energy, and she'd stayed focused.

She'd come to Glory because she owed it to John to find out why he'd expected to die, and he *had* expected to die. And so far she'd discovered only that Dallas was right; Warren had been cheating the family business.

And she'd become obsessed with Dallas.

She'd gone so far as to tell him she trusted him, and cared for him. He'd made rash declarations, too, but she ought to have learned how men could say whatever it took to get what they wanted, and forgot promises, or put them aside when it suited them.

Ginny was alone out there.

A great tide of emotion rushed at Rae. "Buelah, she's so sweet." Her eyes burned and her throat tightened. "Please let her be okay."

Buelah took off her glasses and squeezed the bridge of her nose. Her face was gray.

"Rae?" Joella LaRose tapped on the already open door. "May I come in?"

Rae nodded, and Joella entered, revealing that Fancy Niel stood behind her. Both women were disheveled and dirty, Rae noted, vaguely surprised. They really had come to help.

"Linsay May Dale's out there," Joella said. "She reminded us about what happened to her on the bridge."

Dallas walked in with the sheriff. At the sight of Fancy

and Joella he looked blank, then frowned even more deeply
and said, "What are you doing here?"

"They've been helping," Rae said quickly.

"It's awful, Dallas," Fancy said. "A little girl like that.
We've got to find her."

He smiled at her briefly, but with wariness still in his eyes.

"Just wanted to tell you we're hopeful, Ms. Maddy," the
sheriff said. "We haven't found any signs to suggest somethin' happened to Ginny."

"Have you found any signs to suggest she's okay?" Joella
asked, sounding disgusted. "I thought they said Dallas's dog
brought a shoe."

Turning red under Joella's scrutiny, Nick Serb said, "Wolf
has a thing for shoes. Everyone knows that. He could have
picked that shoe up anywhere, and . . ." His voice trailed
away.

"Nice going, Nick," Joella said. "You need classes in
comforting frightened people."

"Yes, Nick," Fancy said, "you surely do. Rae here is suffering for her child. You stop playing sheriff, and think before
you speak."

"Sorry," Nick said. "Guess I wasn't—thinking. I'd better
get back out there."

Joella stopped him. "Fancy and I were talking to Linsay
May about what happened to her on the bridge. A kook, that's
what we all agreed. But you never did find him, did you?"

Nick shook his head. "Never can be sure with Linsay May
Dale. Could have fallen off that bridge all on her own, that's
what we're sayin'."

"Or," Joella said, "she could have been attacked. And
since you haven't found whoever did it, you ought to be
wondering if there's any connection between that and the
little girl going missing like this."

Rae fought for her next breath. "And my tire being shot
out. And the snake someone threw at me. You decided it was
hunters, but you never did have any proof of that."

Dallas removed his hat and knocked off moisture. "That's enough talk." He approached Rae and stroked back her hair. "Hang in there. We're doing everything we can."

"Come on back to Sweet Bay with me, honey. I can't bear seeing you stay here and suffer like this."

Fancy Niel's invitation froze everyone in the room.

She looked at each person in turn. "Well, we've got to learn a little kindness in this world." If she wasn't sincere, Rae thought, then she was quite an actress. "Joella here has taught me a thing or two today, I can tell you. There's no wound too deep to heal, is there, Joella?"

"Not a one that's too deep," Joella agreed. "And Warren was Fancy's husband and my brother. We don't think you're like any of his other women. You seem decent enough. So we've decided he'd want us to do what we can for you, and that's what we're going to do, isn't it, Fancy?"

"You've got that right, Joella."

Rae heard their words but couldn't concentrate on anything but the idea that Ginny might have fallen into the hands of a man who could shoot at a stranger, or throw a snake, or even throw a woman off a bridge.

"If he'd wanted to kill you or Linsay May, he could have," Dallas said, with what was becoming his uncanny habit of responding to her thoughts.

"Ransom," Fancy said, nodding her head. "You all remember it was me who first mentioned ransom, mind. Mark my words, there'll be a note. You can be sure whoever did this figures that you know enough people in high places around here to make this disgusting thing worthwhile."

Dallas said, "Fancy, I don't think—" but his sister cut him off by clapping her hands together.

"What about that man?" she asked. "The awful one from Macon who said he was owed money?"

"Les—no, Sam McIver," Joella said. "The man Fancy sent to Tyson's today. He said you and Rae were there when this person talked about wanting a lot of money from Calhoun."

"And he didn't get anything but the price of a motel room so far," Fancy put in. "What if he decided to find another way to get money out of us?"

Rae didn't want to listen to them anymore. She found Buelah's hand and squeezed, and Buelah clung to her.

"She could be trying to get attention," Buelah said, for Rae alone. "It's not like her; but she's been upset, and she surely didn't want to be separated from you after the first few days."

"Ginny loves being with you," Rae told her, while a little hope flared.

"Yes," Buelah agreed, "but she got upset when you didn't come back. And we had that other trouble—you know. Then, when we were coming here, she was excited. I saw her face when you told her you'd like us to go back to Decline and not spend the weekend. She didn't say much, but she thought a whole lot. When we set off from the café in Glory she cried."

"But you brought her back."

"Ginny knew the two of us were doing what you didn't want us to do."

"So you think she may be hiding?" Nick asked. "It's pretty nasty out there. Chances are we'd have at least heard something, and flushed her out by now."

Rae stared up at him and said, "You're losing hope, aren't you?"

"Thanks, Nick," Dallas said. "I'll join you again shortly."

The other man shuffled his boots, making up his mind whether to follow a fairly direct instruction to leave, then walked out.

"He doesn't think she's out there," Rae said to Dallas.

Nobody spoke. Nobody told her she was wrong.

Buelah stood up so abruptly Rae jumped. "I'm going back to Decline," Buelah said. "She doesn't talk about it, but she knows how the two of you got there. She's heard me say how brave I thought you were. Ginny could decide to hitchhike home—just to make us take notice."

Rae argued, but Buelah wouldn't be moved. Within fifteen minutes she was driving the Caddy through the rain, up the track to the road. After Fancy hurriedly extracted an assurance from Rae that they could work on letting go of the past, Joella and Fancy insisted upon following Buelah to the main highway to make sure she was safely on her way.

The night progressed, events turning into a repetitive cycle. Searchers returned. They pored over the chart and were sent back out to another area, or told they must go home and rest. Rae persuaded Dallas to let her make another trip into the woods. She didn't ask to be sent back to the river where a team of professionals from Savannah was combing every inch.

At first light the scene gradually took on a hopelessness that deadened Rae's flesh and bones, and her soul.

No explanation had been offered for how the boat had been righted, but the consensus was that it had floated off as the level of the river rose.

There was still not a shred of evidence to explain Ginny's disappearance. Her shoe had been bagged and removed hours earlier, but no one seemed to think it would yield any valuable clues.

Rae felt hope go out of the collective heart of the searchers, both professional and volunteer. Gradually they drifted in, exhaustion pressed into their faces, flat expressions in their eyes.

The hunt had already moved farther afield. More sweeps would be made of the immediate area, but it was felt that Ginny wasn't there.

"Fresh group's on its way in," Nick Serb said, waiting when Rae and Dallas trudged to the trestle after another useless foray. He patted Rae's shoulder awkwardly. "You get some rest now, y'hear me? Sleep. This is hard. It doesn't get any harder. But think about hundreds of men and women who aren't half-dead on their feet. They're looking for Ginny now. Her photograph's gone out on the wire."

Rae rubbed her eyes and bent over the charts. "Where do I go now?"

"To bed," the sheriff said. "Maybe we should get you a room at the motel."

"No!" He thought she would leave without Ginny? "I'm not going anywhere. This is where I belong, where she knows to come back."

Dallas's arm, sliding around her, sapped rather than strengthened her. Her knees sagged, and he held her at his side. "Of course we're staying here," he told her gently, bending over her. "Let me carry you inside, okay?"

Dimly she registered that he was respecting her dignity in front of Nick Serb, but she shook her head and said, "I'll go in and sit by the window. Buelah should have called by now. Did she? Did Buelah call?"

"Not yet," Nick said. "The storm's taken the roads out in parts. Could have got held up."

"Nick's right," Dallas said.

"No." Rae wiped moisture from the face of her watch and peered at it. "No! She'd have found somewhere to call from, just to make sure I wasn't worrying about her, too."

"Not necessarily," Dallas told her. "She's worried too, re-member?"

"What should I do?" Each breath cost too much, and she felt so sick. "I should go to Decline and look for them."

"The roads are being watched," Nick said. "No point in giving us all one more person to worry about."

"I should go," Rae said again, thinking aloud. "Dallas, I don't know what to do. I don't know if I should go to Decline, or stay here."

"You said before that this was where Ginny would expect to find you. So would anyone else who wanted you. I think you should stay. Come on." Dallas urged her toward the cabin.

Rae looked over her shoulder. "I could take the Jeep and check the roads." Her stomach burned. She hadn't eaten in hours, and couldn't eat now.

"Like I told you," Nick said, "we've got people doing that, Ms. Maddy."

"Rae, come on, sweetheart."

"You're giving up." Panic tore its miserable path to her throat once more. "I can't give up."

"We are not giving up," Dallas told her. "It won't help if you collapse, and you're getting real close."

"I'll have someone watch the cabin," Nick said. "Just in case."

"In case of what?" Rae said.

"In case you need something," Dallas said, "but I'll sack out on the couch, Nick, so don't bother. I'll hear if anything happens."

Rae didn't hear Nick's reply. Leaning on Dallas, she stumbled toward the cabin, dragged up the steps to the porch and into the building.

Dallas closed the door. He said, "Go fall into bed. I'll be right here. All you have to do is shout. Or croak, if that's the best you can manage. I don't sleep heavily."

She glanced at him, at his beard-rough jaw, the dark marks under his eyes. He looked a much older man than he had just the day before, older and angrier, despite the smile he summoned up for her benefit. "I want a shower," she said. "If you want one, you can go first."

"Ladies first." The smile fixed. "If I'm still awake, I'll wait for you to give me the all-clear."

She wanted him to lie with her, to hold her and warm her.

Was that so wrong, to long for a little comfort?

It was wrong. Where was Ginny? Was anyone comforting her? Was she crying, frightened—dead?

"I'll let you know," Rae said. "The bed's made up in the other bedroom."

"The couch will be fine."

He meant the couch would be closer if she called out or needed something. He also meant that he wanted to be alert and in a central location in the cabin.

Rae turned toward her bedroom, and the phone rang. Dallas picked it up before she could get there. "Yeah. Yeah, this is Dallas." He listened, his eyes on Rae, and made assenting sounds until he said, "When?" and, "you're sure?" and, "I guess I should say I'm sorry, but I'm not up for it right now. Maybe it's good news in a way." He whistled soundlessly. "Yeah. More activity than this old town's had in years. I hope this will be our ration for a long time to come. Okay. Later."

She curled her fingers around the doorjamb and held back the urge to shout at him. "Who was that?" Rather than shout, she gave him something close to the croak he'd tried to joke about.

"Buzz. Seems they got called to the motel. There was some trouble there. Nothing to do with us, though. Not really. Nothing for you to worry about."

"Don't treat me like a child, Dallas. I heard you say something about good news."

"Careless of me. It's not good or bad news—for us. Sam McIver ran into some trouble. He must have taken a room there and decided to celebrate the windfall he expected to get."

She didn't understand what he meant.

"Looks like he chose the wrong person to celebrate with. He's dead. They think he was murdered."

Twenty-six

Dallas leaned close enough to the steamed-up mirror to see while he used his fingers to rake his wet hair back.

Clean felt good.

Nothing else felt good.

He'd listened to Rae showering, and listened to her moving around her bedroom, and listened when she called to him that she'd finished.

Then he'd waited a few minutes to give her time to fall asleep before creeping past the bottom of her bed and closing himself into the little bathroom. Her scent soaked the humid air. In the shower, he'd used the soap she'd used, held it beneath the water and watched the drops bounce—and clamped his teeth together. For the only time in his life he wanted to share all of himself with another human being, and to share all that she was, all that she brought with her.

The small, intimate things of life were those things that bound people together, or held them at a distance from each other. Permission and acceptance. Permission to enter the sphere of intimacy, and acceptance of everything that went with that intimacy: disillusionment and joy. Enough trust and you learned to shrug off the disillusionment, and make damn sure the joy wiped out the bad stuff. If you failed the balancing act, then distance was the prize.

He wanted a chance to practice balancing with Rae. He thought they could be very good together.

Just give them that chance.

With a towel secured around his waist and his clothes over his arm, he turned out the bathroom light, tiptoed out, and closed the door.

Gray dawn prodded the edges of closed wooden jalousies.

Unable, unwilling to just walk away, Dallas moved quietly to the foot of Rae's bed and looked at her curled shape beneath the covers. Her hair was a shadow on the pillow. He couldn't see her face.

If he hadn't barged into Decline, and into Rae Faith's life, her little girl wouldn't be missing.

And they would never have met.

Neither idea was bearable.

He drew a deep breath and let it out slowly. Where was Ginny? Sam McIver wasn't in the picture anymore, poor devil.

The aquatic people from Savannah were certain Ginny hadn't gone into the river. They had searched far beyond any point where she might have been carried. The water was much deeper than normal, but not deep enough to take her very far, very fast, they had pointed out.

The shoe? They didn't know yet.

So all they could do was wait.

"You should try to sleep."

Rae's voice startled him. He said, "I thought you already were."

"I can't turn off my brain."

"Neither can I."

"I'm going crazy." She curled into a tighter ball. "Something really terrible has happened. I know it. No news about Ginny, and now Buelah's gone. Where are they? I keep thinking I hear the phone. Then I'm not sure if I wish it would ring."

Because she expected bad news. "Rae, I want to tell you everything's going to be okay."

"You're a good man."

"I'm a selfish man. I want you to be happy."

"Is it selfish to want someone else to be happy?"

He looked at a blade of dusky light across the wall above the bed. "It is if it's because you want them to be happy with you."

She moved, straightened on her side, and pulled the sheet and blanket beneath her chin. "A little while ago I was thinking about how I came here. Why. I thought it was all because of Warren and what he did. He lied. He was kind and good to me, but he lied, then left me."

"He died." Even Warren, for whom Dallas could feel no kinship, deserved compassion. "He was wrong, but he wanted you badly. I can understand that."

"Would you have done what he did?"

"No!"

"Emphatic about it, aren't you? But you've never been in his position, so you can only guess."

The inference disturbed him, but this wasn't the time to argue. "Please get some sleep, Rae. I'll be on the couch."

"Okay." Such a small voice.

He went to the door and turned the handle.

"Have you eaten anything?" she asked.

Once a mother, always a mother. He smiled a little bitterly. Ava Calhoun had never been into worrying about her children one way or the other, except to warn them that they had "standards" to uphold. Tully had been the caregiver, the nurse, the arms that cuddled when a cuddle was needed.

"Dallas?"

"I'm fine." Looking over his shoulder, he started to open the door. "No, I'm not fine. I don't think I've ever been less fine. A few breaks, and I'll bring the business through. It won't be easy. I'll have to make some tough decisions. But that's just what I have to do because it's what I am. It's not who I am. The who is all tied up with you now, Rae. You and Ginny."

She turned onto her back and rested the back of a forearm

over her eyes. "Warren wanted me to get a good lawyer first. I'm just so tired, so tired."

"First?"

"Before I dealt with what's in the safety-deposit box in Savannah."

He narrowed his eyes to see her more clearly.

"Money, and bonds. Stocks. What looks like a fortune to me. All in my name. And a letter from Warren telling me it belongs to me now."

No answer leaped to mind.

"It doesn't belong to me, does it?"

"Rae—"

"I should have told you earlier, but I had to find out for myself. Warren said I should be careful. But most of what's there is yours."

"Is it?"

"It has to be. It wouldn't make sense for him to have all that from refrigeration sales, would it?" She laughed. A mirthless laugh. "My mind is going. He never was in refrigeration sales. So there's our answer. It's yours. Almost all of it."

"Did you think I'd"—he released the door handle and went to hold the railing at the bottom of the bed—"did you think I'd leave you with nothing?"

"The Decline house is in my name. I only paid part of things, but maybe we could work . . ."

"Rae," he said softly, moving to stand beside her feet. "Oh, honey, I don't even want to talk about this now. Let it go, okay? Later will be soon enough."

"I'll take you to the bank and show you. You can help me do what I have to do to give it back."

Why didn't he feel relieved? Triumphant?

"I've never cared about money, except for wanting enough for Ginny. I can support us just fine. I'm not bad at what I do."

Now she was searching for ways to stop thinking that Ginny might not come back.

"You'll never have to worry about things like that," he told her. "Try to rest."

"Would you rest with me?"

Dallas crossed his arms and bowed his head.

The greatest words in the world, yet he couldn't accept because he knew why she asked. Out of fear and need, not love.

Love? When had that become a condition for going to bed with a woman?

This wasn't just "a woman." This was Rae, and she'd changed him.

"Please?"

There was a rustle, and he looked up to see her extend a hand to him.

"I don't think it would be a good idea." It was the best idea he was going to be offered.

"Why?"

She'd already been through too much, and there was too much more to come. He forced a laugh. "Well, I'm an old-fashioned boy at heart. I'm still atoning for a major slip I already made with you. I'll be here for you, Rae. However you want me to be. I won't let myself do anything else I'll regret."

"Okay."

He nodded and looked at the door.

"It's not okay," she said. "The way I want you to be here for me is all the time. Can you do that? All the time, whatever happens?"

The questions were getting tough. "I'd like to be."

"Then do it. I'm too tired to care if I beg. If you mean it. If you care about me, then I'm glad. I care about you—more than I know how to say. I don't want to think of a life without you. I'm desperate, Dallas, desperate, and I feel as if I'm giving up. That horrifies me. I need your strength."

His body turned hot, then cold.

"Anyone would say I'm wrong to tell you this now. They'd say I'm a woman who should only be thinking about her missing child. I am thinking about her. I can hardly bear what I'm thinking. All the things I should say to her. I may never get the chance. But you're all mixed and muddled up with me now, and with how I feel about Ginny. I'm not making the same mistake with you that I may have made with Ginny. I'm going to tell you what I want you to know. It's as if we became us and I don't know how that happened. I'm grateful for you."

"Want to try and explain some more?" Pretty speeches were outside his experience, but he surely wanted to learn fast.

"If what you told me before is true—if you'll be with me however I want—then stay with me. If it wasn't true, or isn't true anymore, you should go. You won't be unkind to leave me then. It would be cruel to stay."

There had already been enough words—too many. He dropped his clothes on the one chair in the room, pulled off the damp towel and draped it over the back, and approached her. "I've had it, Rae. I'm worn out. To hell with timing—I can't fight this anymore."

From beneath her arm she looked up at him in the creeping dawn. "Not out of pity."

"Out of love," he said, and realized he wasn't afraid of the word.

She pulled back the covers, and he climbed in beside her, lay on his back. Lay very still on his back.

"I'm naked," he told her.

"Are you cold?"

He almost laughed. "No. I just thought I should mention it."

"Oh. Thank you."

Dallas turned his head and found her staring at him. "Should we find out if we're good at . . . cuddling?" He couldn't believe the way she made him feel. Aching deep inside. Aching that was so good.

He saw her nod and eased an arm beneath her neck. She scooted closer until she could settle her head in the hollow of his shoulder with her forehead resting against his jaw.

When her fingers touched his ribs, he jumped, and she withdrew quickly. "No," he said, "don't pull away. You surprised me is all."

"I'm surprising myself, but I like it." And she burrowed near, wrapped her arm around him, pressed her breasts against his side. She wore something cotton, something that made a lousy bundling board. "I know what I'm doing inside my head. I'm shutting everything but you out and wishing we could stop everything right here."

"Sounds good to me." It sounded incredible to him.

"If we could stop all of it, we'd never have to face what comes next."

Dallas had the irreverent thought that he might not want to stop what he'd like to have come next. Then he felt guilty—a little guilty.

"Does that make any sense?"

"Perfect sense." Pulling her almost atop him was easy. He rested his chin on top of her head and did his darndest not to let anything come up that would put the lie to his noble intentions. "Are you comfy?"

"Mmm." Her lips softly pressed his neck. "Mmm." Sleepy at last?

Considering the wisdom of the act, he stroked her back, ran his knuckles lightly down the length of her spine. Her nightie had ridden high, and he felt her smooth thighs.

He winced. The battle might be going to the enemy.

One of those smooth thighs rose over both of his legs, all the way to . . . He breathed again, if shallowly. She'd stopped just short of disaster.

"Rae," he whispered.

"Mmm?"

"This is bad timing, but the way I feel isn't going to change. Obviously we've got to get some things sorted out." Like finding Ginny. Please, God, let them find Ginny alive and well. "Rae, I love you."

"Love you, too. Always will."

The declaration wasn't emphatic or ecstatic, but more than he'd hoped for under the circumstances. "Honey, we will be happy again. We will."

She shifted again. This time there was no averting disaster.

Dallas held still, then cautiously raised his head a little to look down into her upturned face.

She was asleep. Or unconscious would be closer. Grinning ruefully, he settled her on her back and braced his head to watch her sleep.

Twenty-seven

The first things Rae noticed were bright slivers of daylight striping the bedroom walls.

Second, there were no voices shouting outside.

And she wasn't alone in her bed.

She rose sluggishly from a netherworld that tried to cling. If she were a drinking woman, she'd assume she had a hangover. Her head ached. Everything ached.

A large, warm, relaxed hand held hers on top of the covers.

She wasn't alone in her bed.

Dallas's hand.

Ginny.

The whole of the previous day, each of its moments, rolled back. It wasn't a dream—or a nightmare. Rae closed her eyes tightly. The phone hadn't rung all night and was silent now because there was no news, and because people knew the oblivion of sleep was as close as she'd get to peace as long as her child was missing.

If they didn't find Ginny . . . alive. Thinking about the other was unthinkable.

And Buelah. Buelah had never called.

She turned her head to look at the man beside her. He faced away from her, toward the window. Beard shadow darkened the angle of his lean jaw. He moved, rolling half toward her, and she saw how his elegant features were stark, yet vulnerable in sleep. But it was a hard face, uncompromising. The vulnerability would dissolve the instant he opened his eyes.

"I'm naked."

Rae recalled Dallas had told her that. She couldn't remember much else of what had been said before she slept.

He was naked. Their joined hands held the covers taught across his belly. The hair on his chest was black and shiny. A muscular man, nevertheless his ribs were clearly defined, and his hipbones.

She looked at the clock. Nine. They hadn't slept very long, but it was time to start again. A call to the sheriff's office first. The sickness in her belly rekindled. Carefully, she began to withdraw her hand.

Instantly Dallas's fingers became a clamp. "Where d'you think you're going, ma'am?"

"I need to make a call to see if there's any word." Rather than look at him, she stared straight up at the ceiling.

"Lie still. The phone's on my side." Without letting go of her hand he contrived to place the call. "Dallas Calhoun. I'm with Ms. Maddy. We'd like a status report, please."

Not more than seconds went by before he said, "I understand that. No, nobody's criticizing your efforts. You've got to expect us to be anxious. More than anxious. We're beside ourselves. This isn't a stranger we're talking about, she's our little girl. And a dear friend."

Our little girl. There was so much confusion in her life.

"Of course I care about strangers. Who is this?" Another brief silence. "Yeah, well, thanks. Please call with any information. Yeah, we'll be here. If we leave, you can reach me on my cell phone." He dropped the receiver back on its base.

"Nothing," Rae said, feeling the start of another slide into hopelessness. "I was exhausted when I went to sleep. Somehow it seemed okay to sleep because I kidded myself Ginny would be back by the time I woke up."

"You're allowed to do whatever it takes to get through this. Come here, you."

She did turn to him then, and looked directly into his gray eyes, dark, dark gray. His lashes were thick and black and perhaps the softest thing about his face. "You broke your nose once, didn't you?"

Several blinks later he said, "Oh, yeah, my nose. Twice. Once when Jesse and I were about ten and built a plane. We launched it off the roof at the back of Sweet Bay. The miracle is that he didn't break anything, and my nose was all I did break. My father informed us that if we tried something like that again, he'd break any bones we didn't break."

"That was a really stupid thing to do."

The flicker in his eyes suggested he was assessing how serious she was. She didn't smile, and he said, "Pretty stupid. Second break was when Tyson and I had a fight over a girl in high school. Now *that* was stupid."

"Who was the girl?"

"That would always be a woman's first question. It was Joella, Tyson's wife."

"Ah."

"Ah," he echoed.

"Do you think about Jesse much?"

His mouth flattened, and she regretted the thoughtless question. He said, "There are a lot of theories about twins. Feeling connected, and so forth. I still feel connected to Jesse. I'll always believe he was the best . . . I miss him. I'll always miss him."

"I'm sorry I—"

"No! No, don't be sorry. The hardest part about losing someone you love can be that people try to behave as if they never existed. It's as if they're afraid they'll upset you by mentioning the name. I can't explain how often I've wished there was someone to talk to about Jesse."

"I wish I'd known him," she said, feeling inadequate.

His sigh went on until he had to be drained. "In a way

you do. We were identical. Sometimes I thought we had two copies of the same mind. Sometimes I still do. It's as if he's here, only—only he's not, and I'm used to it. But no, I'll never forget him."

They fell silent—alone, yet together. She didn't have to tell him she understood; he knew she did.

"I'm going to go search for Ginny," she told him at last, "and try to find out where Buelah is. I can't understand what happened after she left here. She never got to Decline, Dallas."

"I know. But you're not going anywhere. Not until you look as if you could stand up without falling down. I'm going. First I'll bring you something to eat. Then I'll go out and see what's up. Please go with this, Rae. My way. I'll be back just as soon as I have a clear picture of where we stand."

I am in hell.

"Okay?" He rose to brace an elbow and prop his head. "If you get sick, it won't help anything."

"I'm a very strong woman."

"Sure you are. This may be really wrong, and really selfish, but could you tell me what you remember about our conversations before you checked out on me last night? Earlier this morning, I should say?"

Yes. Oh, yes, she remembered every moment of that, too. She hadn't at first, but now she did. "Remind me." Stalling was okay sometimes.

"No, no. I'll settle for whatever you can dredge up."

"We said we cared for each other," she mumbled.

"We did that. What else."

Rae shook her head.

Dallas said, "I told you I loved you, and you told me you loved me, too. You said you always will."

Rae contemplated him without flinching, and slowly nodded her head.

He narrowed his eyes at her, and she was confronted once

more by the evidence of the man's uncompromising side. "I shall hold you to it," he said, throwing back the covers.

Rae looked quickly away, but not before she saw enough to make her more than warm. Some reactions had little to do with being appropriate.

"I told you there's money and—"

"Not now," he said gruffly. "The only way I'll care about that in the near future is if we need it to deal with a ransom demand."

Her stomach rolled so violently she turned on her side and pulled her knees up to her chest.

"Someone at the front door," he said, at the same moment Rae heard the knock. "Stay put. I'll deal with it."

Denim scraped over skin, and a zip closed. Dallas was out of the room amazingly fast, but Rae was almost as fast. By the time voices sounded in the other room, she had shed her nightie and pulled on a T-shirt and shorts.

The sight of Linsay May Dale and Lucy Gordon, hovering on the threshold of the cabin, stopped Rae. She was over-whelmingly conscious that they would know she and Dallas had spent the night here, together. Even if they hadn't slept in the same bed, that assumption would be made.

"I declare, a woman who should be out of her mind over her child, and she's . . . well, you know. She's with a man. Well, what can you expect from a woman like that?"

It didn't matter what they thought. Rae closed the bed-room door behind her and went farther into the room. It did matter, but it shouldn't.

Lucy Gordon cleared her throat. Her frosted hair showed evidence of mistreatment at the hands of the elements. Behind her glasses, her eyes remained aimed at the floor. Her cheeks were pink. "Is it all right if we talk to you?" she asked.

"Of course," Rae said. "Come right on in, please. Thank you for all you did last night."

"Anybody would do the same, wouldn't they, Linsay May?"

"They sure would."

"Would you like some coffee?" Rae asked, praying they would refuse.

"No, thank you." Linsay May peeped up at Dallas and turned not pink, but white. "I guess we came a little early. We don't have to do this now."

"Oh, yes we do, Linsay May," Lucy said. "No time like the present, my mama always said. No use putting off until the day—"

"Not now," Linsay May muttered. "No sermon, please."

"No, well, you gonna tell it, then?" Lucy asked.

Linsay May's brown eyes shifted from place to place as if she feared to look at anything—or anyone—directly. "Maybe this isn't right now."

"It *is* right," Lucy said. "You tell them about the café at Buzzley's, and the telephone call, and the—"

"*Lucy,*" Linsay May moaned. "Hush up. Give me time to collect my wits."

"Rae and I have a busy day ahead of us," Dallas said. "I'm sure there can't be anything that difficult about what you have to say."

"Then you're entirely wrong," Linsay May said. "But then, men usually are entirely wrong, aren't they?"

Silence met her question.

"Yes, well, they are."

Lucy put an arm around her friend's shoulders. "Let me begin. It'll make it easier. This is partly my fault. I probably shouldn't have let you into the archives, Rae. And when I had, I shouldn't have been so quick to let certain people know what you'd been interested in." She shot an accusatory glare at Dallas. "Because of me, other people found out, too—including Linsay May here. She'd already rented you this cabin, but she didn't know who you were."

"Who am I?" Rae asked shortly.

Lucy licked her lips and swallowed. Linsay May wrapped her arms tightly around her slender middle and said, "Lucy only means I didn't know you'd been involved with Warren. That you were involved with him when he died."

"How *did* you figure that out?"

"Me," Dallas said. "Me and my big, careless mouth. I made a call in front of Lucy."

"And Lucy told me," Linsay May said. "Then someone else wanted to talk to me about it."

"Why would that be?" Dallas asked with a softness that unnerved Rae.

"Because"—Linsay May poked at her thick, black hair and sweat shone on her brow—"well, because I had been close to your daddy and this person knew I wouldn't want that to be public knowledge."

Rae wanted to dissolve. She detested people who cheated and lied.

"People know what happened?" Dallas said.

"Only those who were involved," Linsay May flashed back. "You made sure of that, Dallas. The sheriff had to know, and one or two others who helped. It's not common knowledge."

"That's what you want to believe because you think it's worth good money to me to keep it as quiet as possible."

"To keep it from your mama, you mean," she said, flushed now. "That woman's made of spun sugar with a heart of pure poison. We'd all be afraid of the poison if we didn't know how spun sugar cracks apart. That sugar is that woman's pride. Pure and simple, pride. But I've never been indiscreet, no sir. I've done my best to keep the sweetness wrapped around your mama's selfish, poisonous heart."

"That'll do," Dallas said shortly. "Now, if you'll excuse us."

"Oh, Dallas," Lucy said. Her glasses magnified tears that stood out in her eyes. "This is hard for Linsay May. She's tryin' to preserve her own dignity. Allow her that. I should have stopped her, but I didn't. I'm always too weak. She asked me to help her by letting Rae think we wanted to get together as friends with a grudge against men. So I did. But she allowed herself to get carried away. You've got to forgive her for not bein' stronger."

"When I find out exactly what it is I'm supposed to forgive, I'll let you know how I feel about it."

Rae found she needed to sit down and went to the couch.

"You okay, honey?" Dallas asked.

Rae said, "Yes," and caught the glance that passed between the other two women.

"Tell them," Lucy said. "Please, Linsay May."

"I was warned that if I didn't do as I was told, everyone in Glory, and in a lot of other places, would find out where I was when your daddy died, Dallas."

Rae pressed against the back of the couch. The room began to sway. She scrunched up her face, then rubbed it hard. Nothing helped.

"So to keep this person quiet, you pretended to befriend Rae," Dallas stated. "Nasty."

Lucy sighed miserably.

"I didn't have a choice," Linsay May said. "What else could I do?"

"Say no, and come to me."

She faced him defiantly. "You haven't been as willing to help of late, Dallas. Maybe I've been wrong, but I haven't had the kind of luck some people have."

"Unlucky people don't always turn to victimizing people they don't even know. Who told you to do this?"

"You're only going to get mad."

"I already am mad, and getting madder the longer you play this game."

"Don't be so hard," Rae said. "It doesn't matter. None of this is important anymore."

"But maybe it is," Lucy said. "Maybe it has something to do with where that dear little child is."

Rae gripped her bare knees, and curled up her bare toes.

"That's it," Dallas announced, hands on hips, apparently unaware, or unconcerned, that his jeans were only half-zipped and the rest of him was bare. "I want the whole story. *Now.*"

"Fancy asked me to do it," Linsay May said, her face starting to crumple. "I'm sorry. I didn't want to come, but Lucy said I had to."

"Fancy told you to make friends with Rae?" Dallas raised his brows. "Fancy knows about you and Daddy?"

Linsay May nodded. "She said a close friend told her I was, well, she said I was . . . you *know?* When Biff died?" She turned to Rae. "You heard when I was in the hospital."

"Yes," Rae said, humiliated for the other woman.

"I did get attacked on that bridge," Linsay May said, her voice choked. "I didn't make it up like Nick's tryin' to say I did. A man grabbed me from behind. He put a big, nasty-smelling hand over my face and whispered in my ear that he was going to make me pay for what I'd cost him. Then he stopped. He just stopped right there and cussed. Then he pushed me off the bridge. Or threw me off more like."

"McIver," was all Dallas said.

"Because of Warren? McIver thought Warren had given away money that should have been his. He thought he gave it to . . ." Rae stopped herself from saying too much, but Dallas inclined his head, considering.

"I'm sorry I did what Fancy told me, even if I was scared," Linsay May said. "I've never been a mean person, but I panicked, I guess. She said she wanted Rae out of Glory before the whole town found out about her and Warren. Fancy said she wasn't going to be laughed at because of one of Warren's women."

"Please don't think about it anymore," Rae told her. "I guess when Fancy heard about my connection to Warren she wanted to know more about me. She couldn't make herself just come and ask, so she decided to use you. We talked at

Buzz's. I thought it was because you wanted to be friendly. Big deal. I've been wrong before."

"Oh, I can't stand this a moment longer," Lucy said. "It wasn't the meeting at the café. It was what came afterward. Tell them, Linsay May. Oh, please just tell them."

Linsay May raised her chin and said, past lips that trembled, "I was always a good shot. I almost killed your daddy once, Dallas. Fancy . . . she wanted Rae out of town for good, and I was supposed to scare her away."

"So Fancy paid her to shoot out Rae's tires and throw a horrible snake," Lucy said in a rush, and shuddered.

"Yes," Linsay May said, "and because Rae didn't leave Glory, Fancy refused to pay me."

Twenty-eight

Some things had changed at the *Glory Speaker*. But some were exactly the same as Ava remembered from her last visit. That had been years earlier, before computers took the place of typewriters. The old typesetting equipment was gone, too. But cigarette smoke still hung so thick in the air that it stung the eyes, and the employees would still win the prize for the worst dressed people she'd ever seen all in one place.

And Carter hadn't stopped using the rooms above the paper as his getaway or, probably, as a convenient place to take women. Carter hadn't lost his appetite for female companionship. If she'd had any doubt, the way he'd fondled her breast at Tyson's would have snuffed it out.

Ava's breasts tingled thinking about sitting, naked, on Tyson's lap while Carter looked at her, touched her. Despite her embarrassment, she'd seen what he wanted. He was as good as he'd ever been at keeping his feelings locked away behind a cold face, and a colder tongue, but she knew. Yes, sir, she knew he'd never stopped pining for her.

She walked briskly along a window-lined corridor. On either side of her people were about their Monday morning duties. They looked curiously at Ava. She felt them stop to watch her progress toward their boss's private aerie.

Smiling, she wiggled her fingers at them, knowing they would have a good deal to say about Ava Calhoun's visit to

Carter LaRose. Let them talk, there would be more to be said later.

The familiar door stood open at the top of uncarpeted stairs. Some of that classical music Carter knew so much about was playing. Loud. Ava preferred a good song herself. Listening to Engelbert Humperdinck was a real turn on, and she'd never admit it, of course, but she had every recording Elvis ever made and played them when she was on her own.

Whatever she'd expected, it hadn't been to find Carter stretched out on a couch in his bathrobe, and drinking champagne.

He didn't even notice she'd arrived.

She checked for wrinkles in her tight, animal print dress, and peered behind her to make sure the seams in her black stockings were straight all the way to her heels in high, backless gold sandals.

Ava slammed the door shut.

With her hands on her hips, she enjoyed the shock on Carter's face. He got it under control soon enough, but not before she'd seen it, just for a second. She was going to make his day.

"Mornin'," she said loudly. This was going to be short and very sweet. "We've put this off too long, Carter. We're not putting it off anymore."

Carter settled himself more comfortably on the pile of shabby green cushions at one end of a couch the same color and swigged his champagne. He did watch her while he up-ended the glass, and Ava took pleasure in that.

She was going right to the point, so to speak. She would take the bull by the . . . Yes, well, she'd get done what had to be done.

"I've got such a headache," she shouted. "Could you turn that off, please?"

He rested his head on the cushions and watched her through slitted eyes. The music continued to blare.

Ava undid the gold belt at her waist and let it fall to the shabby, mottled green carpet. "You were always the most difficult creature on this earth, Carter LaRose. I guess that was part of your charm." Running her hands over her hips, she sat beside him on the couch and scooted back until her bottom pressed against his side.

Carter drank more champagne and closed his eyes.

"Aren't you going to let me share your celebration?"

He might almost be asleep.

Ava looked around the room but didn't see another glass. She shrugged, picked up the bottle and took Carter's glass from his unresisting fingers.

"What d'you want, Ava?" he said, causing her to jump.

After refilling his champagne, she swallowed thirstily herself before giving it back to him.

His bathrobe hung open. The hair on his chest was as gray as that on his head, thick, too. When . . . It used to be dark brown. She glanced lower. Was he gray down there, too? Darling Biff had stayed dark-haired. Lordy, how that man had loved her. They'd had a perfect marriage, the perfect life together. He'd never given her a moment's doubt that she was first in his life. How she missed him. He'd made her his queen, given her everything she wanted, appreciated her mind as well as her body.

Ava pulled her shoulders back, tucked in her stomach, and gave Carter the profile view of her breasts. She'd sensed how he'd never forgotten how they looked, and that he lusted after them just as much as he ever had.

"You always did like champagne," Carter said. "You were drinking champagne the first time I got inside your pants. You were fourteen."

"That's bunk," she told him defensively. "Guys' shower talk. I'll just bet you told them all that, didn't you? All those pimply little boys."

"No," Carter said. "I didn't tell them. Back then I thought I was in love."

"You *were* in love." They had loved each other. "You know you were. You couldn't get enough of me. In fact, Carter LaRose, you never stopped wanting to get your hands on me—and everything else on me. I saw your eyes at Tyson's. You were thinking about it then."

"Was I?" He offered her his drink. "Finish this up. There's plenty more."

This was going to be easy. But then, she'd expected it to be. Letting her lashes lower, she gave him her lazy, lush look while she finished the champagne in the glass, refilled it, and drank it all down again.

The heavenly buzz began.

"Better?" Carter asked. His face was softer.

"Much better." She'd been a teensy bit unsure how to manage things, but the champagne helped. Do what came naturally, as the wise person said. "It was always you, y'know, Carter. All these years, I've missed you. I'd have come the instant Biff died, only that wouldn't have been seemly."

"Not seemly," he agreed.

"But I'm here now, and we're going to put all those lost years behind us and catch up."

Carter shook his head when she filled the glass and offered it to him.

"You taught me all about sex, Carter. You were such a *big* boy, even when you were *so* young. I've missed you, sugar. Have you missed your sweet peach?"

He turned on his side and pushed a hand beneath his cheek.

Ava huffed, and sipped, and said, "Well, now. You're just going to make me do all the work, aren't you? Just to punish little me for putting you through such hell. You poor thing, you. Ending up with that dull Melvira. It's a good thing you sent her packing. If I'd been you, I'd have wanted her to leave, too. But I'm here now, Carter. And I'm stayin'."

"We'll have to be careful for a while, at least till all these other nasty things settle down, but then we'll start a nice, genteel courtship and—"

"Courtship?" Carter said.

"Not without sex, silly." Playful, the way she'd learned to be playful around strong men, Ava tweaked his robe belt undone and ran her fingers through the hair on his chest. "You know I could never get enough of you. Do you think I could be this close and not want all of it? I'm sure your divorce from Melvira is just a formality by now. And I'm a widow. People will think it's quite suitable. As long as we give them time to get used to the idea."

She expected him to make a move, to touch her.

Carter didn't twitch a muscle.

"Your turn to play hard to get? Why, that's positively cute. I hope you've been eating your Wheaties, lover."

The dress had come from Bloomingdales' catalogue. There had been no time to make a trip to buy what she'd visualized. With Tully's ungracious help in altering a feature or two, all Ava had to do to accomplish the right dramatic effect was undo a single, slippery hook, and let the wraparound dress fall open.

Underneath she wore a black push-up bra that quit pushing just before it reached her nipples, black, thong bikini panties, and a black garter belt with her black stockings. She kicked off one shoe, crossed her legs and let the other shoe hang by her very tippy toe.

If she weren't such a lady, she could go looking for, and find, plenty of people who would love to photograph her like this. She knew because she'd practiced posing in front of a mirror.

She allowed the dress to slip from her shoulders, but didn't take it off. They always said you should leave something to the imagination. Turning sideways, she put an arm each side of Carter on the couch and leaned forward.

He looked, and she smiled.

She bent closer, and he kept on looking. She smiled more widely. "Tell me what you want, sugar."

His eyes rose to hers.

Ava shed her other shoe and climbed to straddle Carter's hips. He remained on his side. But he let her coax him onto his back. Of course he did. She sat on his lap. That was always her favorite thing to do.

Tyson mustn't come into her mind, not now. At least not in that way. Not sex. She would have to forget all about Tyson's dark blond hair, and the darker blond hair on his body, and how smooth and firm his skin was, and his muscle.

"You and I have been coming to this point for a long time," she told Carter. "We've just been marking time, and waiting. I'm all yours now. Anything you want, you get, as often as you want, in any way you want."

He produced a remote control from beneath a cushion and flicked off the music. "Why?"

Momentarily bemused, Ava fingered the tops of her breasts. "Why, it's obvious, darlin'. You've got something I need. And I've got something you need."

"What?"

She swallowed. He was going to make her sweat. Well, so be it, but she'd make him sweat first. The center fastener on the bra parted beneath her fingers, and her breasts swung free. She shrugged out of the dress, and the bra, and lowered herself onto his face, onto his mouth. With two fingers, she fed a nipple between his lips and drew in a hissing breath.

Let him sweat.

Grinding her hips against his made her instantly wet, and instantly desperate for release.

"Do it to me, Carter. Do it, please." She panted, and flipped first one, then the other breast across his face. Her hips moved rhythmically back and forth. "Oh, come *on*, Carter. It's the drink, isn't it. It always made you slow, and me fast. Faster. Damn you!"

She sat up on him and bounced, loving the feel of her heavy breasts responding, moving. And loving Carter's eyes, watching them. But he was too drunk to do anything about it, dammit.

Ava shoved her fingers inside her panties. She closed her eyes and did what little it took to make her come.

Waves, like aftershocks, rippled through her. God knew that since Biff died she'd had enough practice pleasing herself when there was nobody else to do it for her.

She'd have to find ways to be with Tyson. They both deserved it.

"Was it good for you?" Carter asked, sounding amused.

Amused? Glaring, Ava pushed back her hair. "You always did think you were funny. You're not. You're sick."

"Tell me what it is that's going to make me want to be with you?"

Ava smacked him, only lightly, on the cheek and pouted. "That's insultin', Carter, and you know it. All right. You've punished me enough. Now it's my turn. You're going to promise you'll never say a word about me and Tyson because, if you do, I'll say it's a lie, and then I'll tell everyone how you lured me up here today."

"Go on."

"That's it. I'm coming back to you, Carter. And we're going to forget all that nasty stuff."

"Like you fucking my son in his office while I watched."

Heat flamed into her face. "Don't you *dare* use language like that in front of me. I didn't know you were watching."

"But you were fucking Tyson."

"Carter," she moaned. "Why are you making this so painful?"

"Want another drink?"

"I want you to be sweet to me. Just remember that I can get Dallas to do whatever I want. When I'm good and ready, I'll get him to give Tyson that job he wants. Biff left him controlling interest in Calhoun Properties because he knew

Dallas would always defer to me about the important things—things that matter to me."

"Cozy for you. Have you decided to give Tyson up? Because you think I might spill the beans about the two of you—and possibly some interesting family ties?"

"No. I decided to give him up because I want you."

"And you're not using sex to try to keep my mouth shut?"

"It's not like that," she told him, bridling. "I *want* you."

"Stop it." The force with which he lifted her from him winded Ava. He dumped her at the far end of the couch and tightened his robe belt again. "You're sick. Disgusting. You make me feel disgusted that I ever wanted you. Except that I only wanted you for the same reason any other young heap of hormones wants an oversexed female—to get between your legs and get it off as often as I could."

Ava covered her mouth and whimpered, "Carter, no."

"You're pathetic. You're still beautiful, don't worry about that, but there's nothing else about you that any man would want. Pathetic and selfish. When we were kids I dreamed about those tits. They gave me the best wet dreams a boy could beg for. Sometimes I imagined they filled the room and just kept coming for me, and I'd jerk off again and again. That probably makes you proud."

She was going to throw up. "Boys will be boys," she whispered.

"But I'm not a boy anymore, Ava. I haven't been for a very long time. Don't worry, I won't talk about what you've been doing with Tyson. I thought I wanted to humiliate you, to get revenge for the way you made a fool out of me. But it's not worth it. I don't give a shit if Tyson ever goes on board with Calhoun. No, that's a lie, I hope he doesn't. He needs to wash this place off his life. He needs a fresh start, but that's his call, not mine."

"But you said—"

"I said a lot of things because I've been angry most of my adult life. You were engaged to me, or as good as. It was wrong, but I had expectations. You were the richest girl around, and your money was going to help me get where I wanted to go. Just call me shallow LaRose. Then your daddy saw that Biff Calhoun's money added to yours would make a formidable fortune, and you did what he wanted; you married Biff. And you wouldn't have done it if you hadn't wanted to. You wanted to be the richest woman in the county. Hell, probably in the state. I didn't mean any more than that to you, and it hurt me. But it doesn't hurt anymore."

She didn't have to take this from a broken down failure of a newspaperman. Ava stood up, and stood proudly, proud of having a body most men would kill to wind themselves around.

"You're a fool," she told him. "You were always a fool. It doesn't matter if what you say is true. That was then and this is now. And I'm prepared to forget what you just said. Like I've already told you, we need each other. You need me to put some money back in this paper. And I need you to—I need you."

"You need me because you're afraid I'll blow your cover as the cool lady of the manor and let everyone know the only thing you like better than young men is boys. You're also terrified Dallas might find out what you've been up to. The way things are, he thinks he's got to keep you floating on a cozy cloud because you're so *fragile*." Carter laughed unpleasantly. "As long as you've got him buffaloed, he'll make sure you're comfy."

Her heart raced. "I . . ."

"Enough said. You don't have a thing to fear from me. This morning you've given me all the payback I'm ever going to need from you. Get dressed and leave."

"No."

"Do as you're told. Get out. I've got work to do. At least until I find a buyer."

Ava frowned, but immediately massaged the space between her brows. "What are you selling? I told you I have money."

"You want to buy a newspaper?"

No response at all came to mind.

"I didn't think so. But some fool will. I've decided I need a change of scenery."

"You'd never leave Glory." This was ridiculous. And she would make him pay even more than he already had for the way he'd behaved. "Not unless I go with you, and I'm not doing that."

"No, you're not," Carter said. "I'm going to start something new. Why not? I always wanted to try my hand in the big city. I'm a fair journalist. And I may just look up Melvira."

She stared at him. "She left you."

"I don't blame her. I never let her forget about Biff. She wouldn't defend herself. Did you know that? Melvira would never say yes, or no, to having been intimate with him, so I took it as yes. Hell, I don't know anymore. I think I'll give her a chance to make a fool out of me. She deserves the opportunity. I'm going to ask her to take me back."

Ava snorted. "She won't. The whole town talks about how she told you she never wanted to see you again."

"All true. And she probably won't want to see me again. But I'm going to try."

"Carter, you will not treat me like this. Listen to me. I'm going to give you what you've always wanted. We're going to get married. I'll make you the best wife in the world, and we'll set this town on its ear. Everyone will be jealous of us." Every one of those gossipy women would be green with envy. "I'll be Mrs. Carter LaRose, and we'll run the paper together. I'm only sorry we've wasted so much time, but we'll have it all, lover. I'm still your girl."

"You're no girl."

Her skin turned clammy. She hated to sweat. "You can't

talk to me like that. I've just told you I'm all yours, just the way you want."

He found the remote and started the music again. Over the roar of kettle drums, he said, "You can't argue with gravity, y'know. Better get that bra on. Make sure you don't fall down the stairs in those shoes."

The sheriff's office was housed in an ugly square building beside the fire station on Pecan Street—just a block off Main.

Sitting in an uncomfortable straight-backed chair in Nick's office, Dallas began to lose his temper. In the wake of the storm a fresh heat wave festered on the land, and the one window in the room was screwed permanently shut. An overhead fan circulated hot air and flapped papers skewered to a bulletin board.

Rae had assumed a familiar pose: seated on the edge of a mismatched chair with her hands pressed together between her knees. She was completely colorless, and a sheen stood out on her forehead. Her body rocked slightly, and constantly, and her eyes never left the door.

They had spent the early part of the afternoon in Macon on a fact-finding mission before returning to Glory and coming directly to Nick Serb's office.

"I think Les McIver had something to do with Warren's death," she said suddenly. "I'm sure he did. Then he left Macon. Probably left the country."

Dallas didn't want to, but he'd been having some of the same thoughts.

"Why else would he have left without a word to anyone?"

"Sam knew," Dallas reminded her.

"I wonder. I'm not sure he wasn't just guessing because Les was his meal ticket and he couldn't find him. You put him on the spot by asking where Les was, and he came up with something."

Another idea that had occurred to Dallas. "Yeah. We didn't get a whole lot out of the trip to Macon, did we?"

"Better than doing nothing," Rae said distantly. She sprang to her feet and crossed her forearms tightly over her stomach. "Why doesn't Nick come back? There's got to be some news by now. How could . . . even if Ginny could get . . . lost, how could a great big old turquoise Cadillac disappear?"

"Maybe Nick's finding something out." Dallas hoped fervently that there was news of Ginny and Buelah, and that it was good, or at least, not bad. Nick had been called away almost as soon as they had arrived. That had been forty-five minutes earlier.

"Why wouldn't we be able to find out where Les's offices were?" Rae asked. She'd so obviously fixated on the McIvers as a way to keep some shred of sanity while she waited for the only thing she really cared about—the return of her daughter. "You can't run a construction company without an office. And a telephone listing."

"I don't think Les runs your average construction company," Dallas said.

Nick puffed in wiping sweat from his brow. Wet rings circled the underarms of his crisply pressed uniform shirt, and dappled the front. "What a day," he muttered. "And it ain't over yet."

At five in the afternoon, Dallas wondered how much more they could hope to do before they were told to give up again until tomorrow.

"You've got news?" Rae asked. She rubbed her palms on her jeans.

"All kinds of news." Nick plopped into his chair. "Just got a call from Macon."

Dallas and Rae looked at each other.

"Seems we don't just have a murdered McIver. We've got a missing one, too. Next step is to figure out if Sam got on Les's bad side. From what you told me early this morning—Tyson's statement matched—from what you told me, Sam said he was here to collect money for his brother. What if his brother didn't like that? What if he thought Sam was planning to make off with it? Coulda killed him for it."

"There was a big fight, then?" Rae asked. "At the motel?"

"No fight at all." Nick puffed up his chest and pushed out his lips as if cleverly matching puzzle parts. "Sam was taking a soak in the tub. The motel radio was attached to an extension cord and dropped in the water. Electrocution."

Dallas winced a little. "Could have been an accident. He could have liked music with his baths."

"And bubble bath? And some sort of lotion for massage? And"—Nick cleared his throat and turned slightly pink— "and a pair of edible panties, and some, er, pasties set out? And a couple of, er, feathers?"

Dallas squashed a temptation to chuckle. "How do you connect that to Les? Sounds more like Sam had a friend over."

Rae frowned from one to the other of them. "I didn't think he knew anyone here in Glory."

Once more Dallas fought against laughter. "I didn't think so either, honey. But he could have met someone casually."

"Oh." Comprehension dawned on her striking face. "Of course. And she killed him? Why would she do that?"

Nick was ready to expound. "We reckon it was deliberate because the radio was plugged in around the corner from the bathroom when there was an outlet right there. The cord barely reached. Someone wanted to sneak the radio in the water before Sam had a chance to see it coming."

"Logical," Dallas said. "How much money did he have?"

"Fifty bucks. Give or take."

Dallas exchanged another glance with Rae. Exactly the amount Dallas had given him for incidentals, and he doubted the man had come to Glory with a bundle in his wallet.

"He was probably robbed," Nick said. "That's what made me think of Les."

Nick Serb's obscure powers of deduction were frightening. The desk phone rang, and Nick picked it up. A number of grunts and monosyllables later, he set it down again. "I wonder what that means," he said. "We had the boys in Macon sniff around a bit. Last person to see Les McIver—last one they can find—was a barkeep. Les was drunk and nasty. Fighting with anyone who'd pay him any mind. That was weeks ago. They got a warrant to go into his place. His passport's still there. Doesn't look like anyone's been around for some time. And his car's in the lot out back of the apartment building."

"What d'you think?" Dallas asked, not expecting any sensible response from Nick.

"What else did the barkeep say?" Rae asked.

Nick scootched around in his chair. "Said Sam was with Les. And Warren Niel. The guy knew it was Warren because he saw his picture in the paper afterward."

Rae stood up. "How long afterward?"

"Take it easy," Dallas said, standing up beside her.

"Next day," Nick said. "What d'you reckon, Dallas?"

"I think this Les McIver is hiding out," Rae said. "I think Sam wasn't supposed to draw any attention by coming here to Glory, and when he did, Les decided he ought to be stopped."

"With lotion and feathers?" Dallas asked mildly.

"You can hire that kind of person," Rae told him, a little pink herself this time. "But I don't care right now. We came to find out about Ginny and Buelah."

Dallas took her hand and chafed the back.

Nick looked blank, then slapped his forehead. "It's the good policeman mentality, y'know. We're trained not to get too close and personal."

"Damn you," Dallas snapped before he could temper his reaction. "What the hell do you mean?"

"Calm down now, Dallas. There's no news, no sign of either of them. Ms. Maddy's house in Decline is being watched, and Ms. Wilks'. No sign of Ginny or Ms. Wilks. But you know what they say, no news is good news."

Twenty-nine

"What would you do if you heard your husband's lover was in town and parading around as brazen as you please?"

Rae looked into Fancy Niel's violet eyes and saw not suffering, but fury. "I don't think I'd pay someone to shoot out tires and throw snakes." She'd agreed to come to Sweet Bay on the condition that if she encountered Fancy, Dallas wouldn't intervene in any discussion of what Fancy had done.

"There's a name for a woman who messes with married men," Fancy said.

"Fancy." Dallas's voice held a warning.

Rae wasn't above a little sarcasm herself. She said, "Is the name the same for any woman who messes with married men?"

Fancy wouldn't look at her. "I don't know what you mean. I won't apologize. And, anyway, it's the word of that jealous tramp Linsay May against mine." She flounced from the drawing room, and her high heels clicked rapidly on tile in the foyer.

"I'm sorry," Dallas said.

"Your sister's used to getting her own way," Rae told him. "She never expected Linsay May to tell us what happened."

"She's been out of control as long as I can remember. This time she's gone too far."

Rae had other things, more important things, on her mind. "I don't care," she said. "Dallas, I can hardly breathe, I'm so scared. They're gone, aren't they?" She couldn't bring herself to say the word that hovered in her brain: *dead.*

"No. No, I won't believe that. I think we'll hear something soon. Whoever's behind this is making sure we really sweat. They'll want money. Believe me, we'll hear."

"But they've often already killed the person they've kidnapped."

"Please don't give up, sweetheart. We can't give up."

The last two days had been the longest of Rae's life. Even as a kid, when she'd never been certain what would happen next, she'd been cushioned from much of the slow-ticking fear by the optimism that came with assuming grown-ups would somehow change at any moment; at any moment they might make everything better.

Once you were the grown-up, you knew fickle humanity for the volatile force it was, and she'd spent forty-eight hours of abject fear because she was secure in the knowledge that nothing was certain.

"Come outside," Dallas told her. "You've got to try to relax, just a little at least."

He led the way out to the veranda where Tully had set glasses, a bottle of white wine, and a tray of enormous sandwiches on a table between two chairs.

They sat down, and Rae said, "I don't think either of us has really slept in two days." She frowned at the monster sandwiches. "I don't think I'll ever sleep again."

Dallas poured wine and picked up a glass. "I know what you mean. Hang in here with me. Please. And eat something."

"The sandwiches are huge." And looking at them made her feel like throwing up.

"Tully calls them man-sized."

"Hmm." Rae didn't remind him she wasn't a man. Instead she picked up a fistful of wheat bread and smoked salmon and took a tiny bite.

"We'll tuck you up here, Rae."

She just couldn't stay. "I'm going to the cabin, Dallas. Thanks anyway, but I think it's best. How will they go about trying to track down Les McIver?"

"First things first. You stay here tonight."

Dallas Calhoun might never learn that he couldn't automatically push until he got his own way. "I will not be staying here. End of discussion. The cabin is where I want to be now."

"In that case, it's where I want to be, too."

"You've got your own life, and your own troubles. I'm a grown-up. Let me deal with mine."

"You are dealing with it. I think we've got to a point where my troubles are yours, and yours are mine, don't you?"

Rae broke off a piece of crust and rolled it between her fingers. "Do you think they'll come back?" She wasn't a fool. She knew she was searching for comfort, even if no one could give it to her.

"Yes, I think they will." Dallas put a fist to his chest. "I feel it here. You are going to have to tell Ginny about Warren, Rae."

He was trying to divert her again, but she welcomed his efforts. There was rarely a moment when she didn't try to decide how she would tell Ginny about Warren.

Lights among the roses showed off the profusion of blooms in the bed beside the veranda. Rae breathed deeply of the scent and said, "She's going to be confused."

"And we're going to have to tell her the truth about me."

The abrupt flap of a bird's wings caught their attention. The lights picked out bands of black and white across the back of a dove. It's soft coo-cuh-cuh-coo soared out of hearing.

Rae ate another bite of her sandwich.

"We will, y'know."

"What will we say?" she asked.

"That"—Dallas set his own sandwich down—"that I lied to her. Leave it to me, okay?"

Responsibility for Ginny was hers, not Dallas's. "We'll see. I'll do what's best—or as close as I can."

"I'm going to marry you, Rae."

Her sandwich lost any remnant of appeal, and she put it on her plate. "We've got to think our way through everything."

"I already have."

"Give us more time. I can't risk making mistakes with Ginny."

"She likes me."

"Sure she does, Uncle Dallas."

He leaned toward her and offered her his hand, palm up. "Hold on, kid, it's going to be a rough ride. I know that. But it's going to be worth every bad minute to get where we're going."

A great wave of darkness swept over Rae. "If we ever find her."

"Hello, darlings," Ava Calhoun said, arriving behind Dallas's chair and slipping her arms around his neck. "I heard all about Rae's little girl. I'm so sorry."

"Thank you," Rae said politely.

"Children can be *such* a burden. Ask me. I had two of them. Oh, my."

"You had three children, Mama," Dallas said.

Ava blinked and turned her face away. "That's right. I had three. They've all given me their share of heartache, too, I can tell you."

Rae felt sorry for Ava. "They do that, don't they?"

"They surely do," Ava said, abruptly becoming all business. "Dallas, I'm taking a little trip. This has been such a trying summer. I don't have to tell you what I mean."

"No," Dallas agreed, turning to see his mother. "Where are you going?"

"New York," she said airily. "Clara Bolling's going with me. We'll stay at the Plaza and shop. Living in a backwater like this can make a person narrow. I need to spread out a little. After all, Clara and I don't have husbands at home to worry about. We might as well have a little fun. We're going in the morning, and I don't want you to worry about me, darlin'."

"Have fun," Dallas said, watching his mother's silk skirts float as she entered the house again by one of the French doors into the drawing room.

Rae got up. "I think I should go to the cabin. I'll let Nick know I'm leaving now. I don't want to put you out more than I already have. I'll call Buzz and see if he's up for a taxi job. I've got to stop allowing myself to be cut off without transportation."

"You aren't cut off without transportation." Dallas rose, picked up the tray of sandwiches in one hand, and put the other around Rae's waist. "Do you have anything decent to drink? Or should I bring the wine, too."

She prepared to protest, but took the bottle of wine from its bucket instead and went down the steps to the driveway without protest. Arguing with Dallas was a wasted effort, and she'd need her energy when they got to the cabin and prepared for another night of waiting for the phone to ring.

Little more than an hour later, sitting on the upturned hull of the boat that had been returned, and drinking wine, Rae sought a way to do what she didn't want to do: make Dallas go home. He'd brought a cellular phone down by the river and let Nick know he could reach them there.

She rarely drank much, but the wine helped dull the jumping that never left her muscles, her stomach.

"Moon on the water beats rain on the water," he said. "At least, it does now." Since they had returned to the cabin he'd avoided mentioning what she knew filled both of their minds.

"When all this is over and we finally settle down, we'll make sure Ginny never feels she can't come to us with whatever's troubling her."

She was grateful to talk about Ginny again, but *we, us?*

He assumed he could make everything all right. "It's getting late," she said, and found a rock to throw into the water. The river had gone down some, and the sound that came was of a splash followed by rock hitting rock.

"Time for bed?" Dallas asked.

"Oh, yes." Time to be alone with her thoughts again, and just maybe to sleep, if only from desperate exhaustion.

"Let's do it, then."

She looked sideways at him. The moonlight that frosted the water put a glitter in his eyes and dramatic shadows about the distinct bones in his face.

He raised one brow. "Shall we?"

"Shall we what?"

"Go to bed?"

Rae couldn't do a thing about either the way her stomach rolled or an instant shot of trembling excitement.

Physical reflex. Animal instinct. Completely inappropriate instinct.

"I'm going to bed. You should probably go to bed as soon as you get home, too. You've had as little sleep as I have."

"Sleep isn't what I've got in mind. Not immediately."

Coy was something she'd never been. Or stupid. "Dallas, if you're asking me to have sex with you, you aren't being very subtle."

"I'm not being subtle at all."

"And you are asking? Even though my child is out there, somewhere, maybe dead. And Buelah, you're—" she choked, and couldn't finish.

Dallas caught her in gentle arms and held her close. He rested his chin on top of her head. "I don't think I'm asking. I'm taking it for granted. Now more than ever before we need each other. We can stay out here and discuss it all night. Pros and cons. How crass and pushy I am. How outraged you are that I can even think about making love to you. The fact that I'm not going back to Sweet Bay tonight, and if you won't let me into the cabin with you, I'll sit on the porch and sing. I haven't played the piano for you yet. I ought to do that. If I had a guitar with me, I could—"

"Dallas."

"What?"

"You are blabbering."

"Blabbering?"

"Blabbering. Chattering. What's the matter with you?"

"I'm sex starved."

She bowed over her glass. "Isn't it wrong to want to make love because I'm in agony? Because I'm desperate?"

After a moment he murmured, "No. Love is sweet. Love heals."

"Even if it would be loving out of abject fear, and not wanting to think, because I'm giving up?" She gasped, and held on to his shirt.

Dallas held her more tightly. "What about as a kind of offering up? Giving up everything to whatever powers are in control and clinging to someone who loves you—for all the right reasons?"

"I—" He wasn't like anyone she'd ever known. She stood. "Come on. I'm not agreeing to anything, but we can't stay down here all night."

"Don't let go of me," he said, the timbre of his voice changing, growing lower.

He tipped up her chin and kissed her. Rae barely stopped her glass from falling to the earth.

She wanted to lie down, or was it just to stop standing up? Her legs trembled. His mouth was insistent on hers, insistent yet sweet, and strong. The power of that kiss bent her backward. He tasted of the wine, and smelled of clean skin and freshly laundered denim.

He paused and looked at his glass. "It's the little things that get in the way," he said, taking hers and putting them both on the grassy bank.

"We should take them in."

"I don't want to go. It's—clean out here. Open," he murmured, kneading her shoulders and nuzzling her neck. "Can you understand that in spite of everything, for the first time it all feels possible."

She understood him, but couldn't banish her own dread. "There's still so much to deal with. We don't know how much yet."

"We'll deal with it. Kiss me, Rae."

Her mouth opened beneath his, and she felt herself slipping into him. His shoulders were wide and hard under her hands, his hair soft on her fingers, his chest unyielding where it pressed her sensitive breasts.

It all feels possible. "You make me believe it can work, Dallas. You almost make me believe fate will smile and bring back my child, and my friend."

An instant passed, and she felt his subtle switch from patient to urgent. Tension strung between them, and an edge of aggression.

Dallas slid his hands beneath her T-shirt, around her waist, and pulled her even closer. Her pulse speeded, and deepened, and hummed with the force of blood through her veins. She ached.

The kisses went on and on. Rae's mouth felt swollen, but she only sought more. Their breath mingled, loud, and rasping in the night.

It all feels possible, he'd said, yet Rae still knew it was desperation that drove her most strongly.

He put his tongue deeper into her mouth, withdrew. A small, powerful, and perfect parody of what he desired. Automatically Rae raised onto her toes and tipped her hips into his. He was hard, and heavy, and pulsing.

Her breasts responded, her nipples tensing. Heat flashed from her pelvis to her face. Deep in her womb, she throbbed. "Stop! Dallas, stop. We can't."

"We can." The two words came through his clenched teeth.

"But—"

"No. No, Rae. Do it my way, okay?"

She should say that he wanted too much "his way," but she couldn't think properly.

Spanning her ribs, he shimmied her T-shirt up until she felt a warm breeze caress her naked breasts. She tried to look around, but Dallas covered her mouth, bit her lips. If he was in control, that control was fragile.

Breathing heavily, he bent to take a nipple in his mouth, and Rae cried out. His lips and teeth held the tender flesh while the tip of his tongue flickered over the bud with maddening delicacy.

Delicate, but demanding.

He would have what he intended to have.

Her T-shirt passed over her shoulders and head, and she dimly saw it pass, very white, as he tossed it aside.

Naked to the waist, she stood in the arms of a man who could be as dangerous as any she'd encountered. More dangerous. This man could destroy everything she'd worked for so long to secure. But she wanted him, too.

"Your breasts are something," he said, and his voice, breaking the silence, shook her. "You feel every touch, don't you? Down here, too."

Rae gasped when he cupped between her legs and pressed the heavy seam of her jeans into burning, moist flesh. She opened her mouth and moaned, deep.

"You're hot," he said. "Any way I touch you, you're hot. You make me hot."

Rae couldn't form words. She tugged at his shirt, and he fumbled with the buttons until he could struggle free. But he didn't take her in his arms again. He held her shoulders, held her at arm's length and stared at her.

Without warning, he took her nipples between his fingers and thumbs, pulling lightly as if plucking berries. Rae's knees began to buckle, and she hooked her hands over his forearms. Dallas used his intimate hold to bring her to his mouth once more. This time the suckling changed her moan to a thin scream, and he chuckled.

"I can't wait, Rae."

"Not here," she told him.

"There's only you and me." He moved quickly. The snap on her jeans popped open, and the zipper slid down. "It's always going to be this way. I feel it. We're always going to be like wildfire together."

Rae tried to protest. Then her jeans and panties were around her knees, and Dallas's fingers slid inside her. His fingers were inside, probing and withdrawing, and his thumb worked the place that stole her inhibitions.

His right hand was on her and in her. His left hand dealt with his own jeans.

When she was on the brink, begging to be taken over, he paused to kick aside his jeans. Naked in the moonlight, he braced his feet apart and let her look at him. When she met his eyes she saw triumph. He was a confident male animal, confident of his potency and satisfied that she would accept his dominance, at least for now.

Using a foot, he pushed her jeans around her ankles and held them there while she stepped free.

Rae shook steadily, but not with cold. Her nerves, her emotions were flayed. In that instant she hesitated, half turned from him.

Dallas pulled her back. He kissed her, thrust his tongue in and out of her mouth in time to the rhythm of his fingers reaching inside her.

Her climax flowed from his touch, but when she pressed her thighs together, he forced them apart and lifted her until he could enter her. Rae called his name, but heard it from a great distance. They were movement, sensation, light, slick skin, and straining muscle. The wave broke within her again, and he cried out his own deliverance.

They heaved together in the silvered darkness, bound by flesh, and need. Even while she surrendered to the flesh, Rae identified her need—and his. An addiction. The revelation shook her.

The next shudder came from Dallas when he left her body, but drew her close. "My love," he whispered. "I do love you."

"You're wild, Dallas. A wild man."

"Uh huh."

"We're naked and anyone could come strolling along."

"Unlikely."

"I want to go inside." Overwhelmed by the vulnerability of where and how she was, Rae twisted away, saw her shirt and caught it up. "Hurry, Dallas. *Please.*"

"Puritan." He laughed and made a grab for her, but she evaded him. He said, "Don't excite me more than I'm already excited. It's dangerous."

"You should be exhausted. You need to lie down." Rushing to cover herself, she wrenched the T-shirt over her head and picked up her jeans.

"Stop right there," Dallas told her. "I'm not finished, sweetheart."

"Inside," she said, and her voice rose to a squeak.

He shook his head and advanced, slightly bowed, his arms outstretched.

"No, Dallas! You're frightening me."

"Not possible. I could never frighten you. I'm part of you, Rae. You're never going to get rid of me."

Her T-shirt stopped at the level of her hipbones, and she couldn't try to put on her jeans. "Dallas, what are you doing?"

"Hunting the woman I want."

A thrill climbed her spine. "If you do this, it will be against my will." She backed up. *"Dallas."*

He kept coming.

Rae turned to run, headed within inches of the boat, and toppled over the hull.

"Against your will?" Dallas chortled, a wickedly arousing sound. "Actions speak louder than words, love."

He folded over her on top of the boat, cradled her, supported her breasts, and took her fast, with a savage intensity akin to thrusts from a velvet-sheathed dagger.

Enthralled, shocked, Rae slumped in the wake of her own forceful climax. "I'm not like this," she muttered. "I've never done this. Nothing like this."

"Good," Dallas said. "You'll do it again."

Rae didn't resist when he picked her up and carried her to the cabin. She did say, "Our clothes?"

Dallas said, "We don't need them."

Thirty

Wolf's barks reached Dallas through a drugging mantle of sleep and satisfaction. He stirred and slowly became aware of his legs tangled with Rae's, her bottom tucked neatly into the curve of his lap. She sat, in fact, where he'd like her to sit for the rest of their combined lives. And their lives were going to be combined.

Damn dog. Dallas had deliberately left him at Sweet Bay, but he should have guessed the determined animal might find his way to the river. From the sound of it, he was still on the other side, but he'd cross when he had a mind to.

Rae muttered indistinctly. He pulled the sheet over both of them and held still, waited for her to fall deeper into sleep. She wriggled against him and he got hard. Mind over matter didn't seem to work when he was anywhere near this woman.

Wolf kept right on barking.

If he didn't stop, he'd wake Rae.

And if Dallas's renegade hormones didn't quit raging, *he'd* wake her. She'd turned him into something that reminded him of being eighteen again. The mind might get a kick out of that idea, but the body could only take so much.

Easing away from Rae, he slid out of bed. At least he'd found the sanity—between bouts of great madness—to go retrieve their clothes. He put on his jeans and shoes and tiptoed from the room, grimacing at every squeak of the old wooden floors.

The night was still warm. Dallas slipped onto the porch

and down the steps, and set off to follow Wolf's barks. They came not from the river, but from the direction of the track.

The blow to his skull didn't come until Dallas reached the parking area beyond the hedge of shrubs.

When it did come, it sent him to his face on the gravel, but didn't knock him unconscious.

The second impact snuffed out the moon.

Wolf was barking.

Rae pressed her face into the pillow. Poor Wolf must have followed Dallas all the way here.

She smiled, and, at the same time, her eyes filled with tears. Happy tears. Love was really something. She'd never thought a whole lot about it. There hadn't been any reason beyond enjoying the kind of love she shared with Ginny— and with Buelah, in a way. But then there was Dallas and love was a different thing.

A report sounded in the distance. A vehicle backfiring on the highway.

Had she told Dallas she loved him yet?

Wolf wasn't barking anymore.

Rae rolled over, and pushed to her elbows. She was alone in the bed.

A panicky flutter started in her chest. No light showed under the bathroom door. "Dallas?" she called. "Where are you?"

But for the peculiar sounds of silence, she heard nothing. No answering shout.

She dropped back onto the bed. He wouldn't just leave.

"Dallas?" she said, more quietly.

Of course, he'd gone outside because of Wolf. Relief carried a rush of blood through her veins.

Listening hard, she waited for the sound of his returning footsteps on the porch.

The cabin creaked. The night creaked. Subtle shifts in the darkness made her peer, thinking they might take shape.

Despite the heat, she grew cold, and didn't want to move. A sheet covered her, yet she felt conscious of her nakedness.

A draft crossed her face.

"Dallas?" The bedroom door was open. A wedge of fuzzy pallor divided the wall between the window and the corner.

When she could make her fingers work, she inched a hand upward toward the bedside lamp, but paused again, listened again.

A presence.

She wasn't alone in the cabin.

If she put on the light, she'd only help an intruder.

The wedge on the wall grew wider.

There was a tall shadow in the soft gray light on that wall.

She remembered the Sauer. But if it was Dallas creeping back, and trying not to wake her. . . . But if it wasn't Dallas and she spoke again. . . .

Be still. If it's Dallas, it'll be over in a second. If it isn't, maybe it's someone come to steal. Don't move. Please God. Oh, please. Nothing to fear, but fear itself.

The door opened another fraction, but the human shadow wasn't there.

She'd imagined it. Another surge of relief left her weak. She lifted her head . . . and saw something move. Then it was gone.

The urge to scream forced her mouth open.

Sucking air in, rather than pushing it out, Rae inched her hand between the mattress and the wooden bed frame until her fingertips met cool, smooth metal.

"Keep still, bitch."

A man. A stranger.

Rae screamed. She couldn't help it. But the noise she made was little more than a croak.

"Best keep your mouth shut," the voice said. "You're

gonna do what I say. Hear me? Do what I say and you and me'll get along just fine."

Pulling the sheet around her, she kept her hand on the gun, but scooted away from the voice.

"Didn't mind havin' him all over you, did you?" He coughed. "Lettin' him stick it to you out there. In front of God and all the world. Tramp."

"Who are you?"

"Whore."

"Who *are* you?" Dallas would come back. All she had to do was stall long enough, and Dallas would walk through the door. She glanced in that direction. Somehow she'd know he was here and she'd warn him she wasn't alone.

"Lookin' for someone?"

Her heart thundering, her skin an ice-slick film, she looked to her left and saw the intruder. An indistinct form standing beside the bed, beside the place where Dallas had lain.

"Lookin' for him?" He coughed again, and she saw the angle of his elbow when he wiped his face. "He ain't comin' back quick, on account of he's busy chasing that fool dog of his."

"How do you know that?" she whispered. "Who are you?"

"Where's the girl?"

Rae's free hand flew to her throat.

"Where is she?"

"I don't know who you're talking about."

He moved, bent over the bed, grabbed for the sheet and pulled.

Babbling, whimpering, Rae tugged back.

"C'mon, you shouldn't save it all for him. All I want is a little up-close look." He held still. "Do what I want and I'll let you go."

She didn't believe him. "What do you want?"

"Everything I've got coming to me. Everything you and Warren Niel took away from me."

Rae tried to see him. With what light there was behind him, he was a tall, thin, but very real form without a face.

"Tell me where you've put the kid. They stopped searchin', and you're not behaving like you're grieving. You found her, and I want her. She's worth a lot to me."

"Ginny's not here," Rae said. She threaded her fingers around the Sauer and pulled it into her palm. Why hadn't she kept up practicing with it the way Warren had wanted her to?

"I asked you where she was."

If she threatened him, would he run away? She should do it and hope he did. But then she wouldn't know where he'd gone, and she couldn't risk that, not if he was after Ginny.

"Answer me!" He didn't shout, he *screamed*. Shrieked. And then he coughed as if he'd spit out his lungs.

He swayed, and Rae jumped to the floor. The bed was between them. The bed and the man were between her and the door.

Her choice had been to take the sheet or the gun with her. She'd chosen the gun.

Wheezing filled the room. Bending over the bed, he made his way to the bottom. "I gotta have the kid, hear me? I need that kid. She'll give me what I need, what I deserve. You should have stayed where you were. You should've never come here. I thought it would be okay. But you've made my life more hell. I knew what I was doin'; then you and him messed everything up again."

"I don't understand," Rae said, struggling to sound reasonable. "Why don't you explain? I'm sure we can work something out."

"You ever been raped?"

Her legs sagged. She should try to shoot him now.

"I'd say that was rape out there, but you asked for it. You begged for it. Loved it."

"Why do you want to find Ginny?"

"She's my ticket, bitch. She's my ticket out of hell."

"Are you Les McIver?" Of course he was. "You are. You're Les McIver. That's it, isn't it? You want the money you think Warren owes you."

"He does owe me. He owes me for all the years he had what was mine."

"Warren's dead."

"Yeah. A little bird came and told me that. So someone else will pay."

"But, Ginny—"

"Damn you," he roared, coming closer. "Someone will pay to get Ginny back. She's worth plenty to you, and you're worth plenty to that fucker. And he's a rich boy. Someone's got to pay me." His voice rose another notch. "You gotta pay me. You owe me!"

She knew what she had to do.

"I'll do what you say."

"You gotta *pay* me." He was crying. Sobbing out his rage. Stumbling nearer, and nearer.

"Okay, okay. Let's work out how you can get what you're owed."

"Bitch!"

Rae switched on the lamp and braced the gun in both hands. "Don't move." She blinked rapidly to grow accustomed to the light.

"I'll kill you." In his right hand, upraised, he held a knife. "I'm goin' to cut you good, and kill you."

"Stay where you are."

"Always the feisty one, weren't you? I told you to look after me, but you wouldn't. No siree, you wouldn't look after me."

Rae's mouth grew even dryer. The man who stood within feet of her, threatening her with a kitchen knife, was thin and stooped. Lank hair, gray mixed with traces of light brown, fell over his face. His slack, wet mouth hung open between a ragged mustache and beard. She could smell him. Rancid, unwashed.

If she didn't hold on, she'd faint.

"Willie?"

He coughed, and when he coughed his eyes squeezed shut and he wavered. "Yeah," he said when the spasm passed. "Gimme the gun, bitch. No woman was ever any good. That whore Betty left me, and me all but crippled on account of her."

"It's okay," Rae said soothingly. It no longer mattered that she was nude in front of him. All she cared about was making it all end. "Mama must have had her reasons, but it's okay now."

"Smashed my goddamn head and left me for dead, she did. Left me with no one to do shit for me. I come to and you was both gone." A fresh fit of coughing spewed phlegm. "Had to get me a job in the end. Me being sick, too. Had to get me a job as a janitor at the school."

Rae's scalp grew tight. "That's too bad." He thought her mother had been the one to hit him. She wouldn't ask him anything that might anger him. "If you go sit in the other room while I get dressed, I'll—"

"I like you the way you are. Your tits got bigger, a whole lot bigger. Nice ass, too."

Bile burned her throat. "I'll get dressed and take you to Ginny."

"Goddamn lyin' bitch. You'll tell me where she is. You ain't goin' nowhere. Gimme the gun. You ain't got the guts to fire, anyways."

Where was Dallas?

She had to do something. "Okay. How did you find me?"

He smirked a little. "Wouldn't you love to know? I'll tell you one thing. You got enemies, bitch, enemies you don't know about."

At first she couldn't think at all. Then she tried to make names and faces take shape. Nothing fitted.

"Didn't know I had it in me to be clever, did you? Well, good ol' Willie knows how to grab a good thing. Took myself off to Decline, Georgia, right quick. About ready to close in, and you were off again. Cattin' around with your new man. And then, just when I'd have got to you here, the whole thing gets messed up again."

He wanted to talk, wanted to gloat. "But you waited it out, Willie," she told him. "You were too smart for me. I'll take you to Ginny." She had to get him out of the room, out of the cabin. She couldn't be closed in here with him.

"We'll do it my way. Gimme the gun now or I'll cut you."

She leveled the weapon at him. "I'm not giving you the gun. I will give you a chance to get away, though. I'm going to start counting. If you're still here at ten, I'll shoot."

"You ain't got the guts." He dragged a filthy sleeve over his mouth again, and came at her with the knife.

Rae backed up, slammed into the wall and yelled, "Stop."

The knife blade shone. "Just a few cuts. Just so he won't want to look at you no more."

"Then maybe he won't want to pay you for Ginny," she panted, sliding to her knees.

Wildness glowed in his red-rimmed eyes. She saw how his hand shook, how the knife shook. He was weak, probably ill. "Please stop. We'll work something out."

He lunged. Rae closed her eyes and pulled the trigger.

She pulled the trigger again. The impact jolted her whole body.

Hissing, clutching his chest, Willie crumpled slowly, folded forward, then fell like a man felled by a great blow. The knife slithered under the bed.

A bubbling, gagging noise came from the pile of destroyed humanity and old clothes that was what Willie Skeggs had become.

Rae wanted to vomit. She curled over and waited.

His breath escaped in clicking bursts, and a bubbling sound came.

Her teeth chattered, and she shook uncontrollably. Keeping the Sauer trained on Willie, she tore open a drawer and pulled out a shirt and some shorts and struggled into them as best she could.

She ought to call the sheriff.

Willie wasn't moving.

She'd shot him. Killed him. Laughter burst from her. "Killed him again." She wrapped her left arm over her stomach, stepped around him, and giggled. "I killed him again."

Who would believe anything she said once they found out she was a lie? Everything she'd told anyone about herself since she'd left Glad Times was a lie.

He hadn't moved the first time.

Rae giggled again, but crouched and felt under his stringy hair to find the pulse in his neck. No pulse. And she saw the side of his face. His mouth was open, so were his eyes. Open and staring. They would never see anything ever again. Blood trickled from the corner of his mouth.

Dallas would believe her. He knew the story of what had sent her on the road with a baby. Buelah knew some of what had happened, but Rae hadn't told her the really sordid stuff. Dallas would help her figure out what to do. He wouldn't let them arrest her, and lock her away. If they did, Ginny would be alone. She couldn't leave Ginny.

Find Dallas.

Scrambling, she slipped on sandals. She couldn't make herself take her eyes off Willie. The first time she'd killed him he hadn't died. He might get up again this time.

She needed to go to the bathroom.

She needed to be sick.

A knock sounded at the front door, and Rae slapped a hand over her mouth, and looked at the gun.

Another knock came, louder and more insistent, and a voice. "Rae? Rae, you in there? Come on, Rae. Open up." A woman's voice.

She left the bedroom, remembered Willie, and shut the

door. "Coming." Placing the Sauer on a stool behind the front door, she opened up and looked into the distraught features of Joella LaRose. "Joella," she said, disoriented.

"I'm sorry, Rae," Joella said. "I'm so sorry to come like this. I couldn't help it."

Rae glanced over her shoulder, toward the bedroom. When she turned to Joella again, she knew the woman had seen that glance.

"Oh, I'm sorry. I shouldn't have come. This is inexcusable. You're not alone, are you? Dallas is with you, of course."

"What's the matter?" Rae made herself ask.

"No word about Ginny yet?"

She didn't need this. "No."

Joella inclined her head. Her eyes were still frantic. "They'll find her. I'm troubled, Rae, troubled by so many things. I haven't lived a good life. I've been selfish, and taken up with all the wrong things."

"We all make mistakes," Rae said, resisting the urge to check the bedroom door again. "I'd ask you in, but—"

"Forget it. I'll go."

"No. No, not like this. Tell me what I can do to help you."

"Did you know the Werther house used to belong to my family? Warren and I lived there until we were young teenagers."

"I think I heard something about it."

"I never got over what we lost," Joella said. "Tonight I drove over there just to take a look. I've got to stop, Rae. I've got to let go of the past. The house. Warren. I loved Warren."

Rae didn't know how to respond.

"I'll leave," Joella said.

Rae stepped onto the porch and placed a hand on Joella's arm. "We're all trying to deal with something. Seems as if a big, black cloud gathered over this part of Georgia recently." A dead man lay in the bedroom behind her and she could be accused of murder, and both her child and her dearest friend were missing.

But she had to call the sheriff. First she'd persuade Joella to go home; then she'd get Nick, and pray he'd listen to her.

"Will you come up there with me, Rae? I'm afraid to go there again on my own—in the dark. And I want to go inside. Just one last time."

"Joella, it's three, maybe four in the morning."

"I know. I'll be fine. I'll just walk back up there. Don't worry. Give me the key, though. So I can go inside."

"Oh, Joella." Pity overwhelmed Rae, and she pulled the other woman into her arms and awkwardly patted her back. "So much unhappiness. You're right. We've all got to learn to let go and move on." To whatever was ahead.

"I will. But I've got to go into the house first."

Rae stared past Joella at the dark trees standing between them and the big, deserted house. "Just a minute, I'll get the keys."

She'd put the envelope containing Warren's letter and the keys on a high shelf in a kitchen cupboard. She climbed on the counter to reach them. When she rejoined Joella, she locked the front door of the cabin. Dallas didn't have a key. If she hurried, but he still came back before she did, he'd be surprised by the locked door. Maybe he'd even think she'd got angry with him and locked him out. The thought troubled her, but there wasn't time to think of an alternative.

They were well into the trees before Rae stopped and frowned at Joella. "The keys? Why did you come to me for them?"

"We always kept a set at the cabin." She hesitated, and gave a strained little laugh. "I assumed the Parkers did the same, and they did."

"Yes," Rae said slowly. "Yes, they did." Joella wouldn't have any way of knowing Warren had secretly bought the house and left it to Rae.

Getting to the house took much too long. It loomed as a

great, many gabled hulk against the early morning blue-black sky. The grass was long here, too. Rae had only been to look at the place once by daylight. And she'd made one trip to the area the night Ginny had disappeared. On both occasions the desolate property had been as heavily still, and had felt as abandoned as it did now.

"Joella," she said, "this is a bad time to do this. It's going to be impossible to see anything in there."

"There must be some electricity on. They wouldn't switch everything off in case they needed to show the house in the evening. Not that they'll do that now, anyway. It's sold."

Rae's stomach made yet another revolution. When and if she could finally let down, she'd collapse, and it sounded good. "Is it?"

"I only just found out. I guess that's what made me keep thinking about how it used to be when we lived here. Everything was so different back then. Nobody laughed at me when my granddaddy lived here. Fancy Lee didn't treat me like dirt then."

"I thought the two of you had made up."

"Give me the keys," Joella said, her voice sharp. "You'll come in with me, won't you?"

Rae didn't want to go in. She'd almost managed to put the fact that she owned the place out of her mind. It would have to be sold again, and the money would be given back to Dallas.

The door squealed as it opened. Joella went inside and Rae took another check around. She couldn't make her thoughts ordered. There had to be a car somewhere, Joella's car. To the left, between the house and the separate garage, was the wide covered drive-through to gardens at the back.

The shadowy shape of a car showed inside the open garage. Rae frowned.

"There's light, see," Joella said, sounding less anxious. "Just a quick look and I'll drive you back the easy way. Oh, thank you, Rae. I knew you were different from . . . well, I knew you had a good heart."

Rae stepped into a dank-smelling foyer where water stains waved across flocked, umber-colored paper above high, walnut wainscots.

The car in the garage had fins.

She shook her head. Too much, too fast—and for too long. She was losing her mind.

The car had fins. Big, pointy fins.

"That used to be my granddaddy's study over there," Joella said from behind her. "Go look. It still smells of his cigar smoke."

"How?" How would Joella know what her granddaddy's study still smelled like if she hadn't been here for years? "How long did you live here, did you say?"

"We had to—we left when I was fourteen."

"Where did you live then?"

"This is home," Joella said, ignoring the question. "This is where I belong. I've always belonged here, always will."

Buelah's car was in the garage beside this house, Rae thought. And she was inside the house with Joella LaRose, who didn't look, or sound, stable. Where was Buelah?

Where was Ginny?

There was more than one old car with fins in the area.

More 1954 Cadillacs? More than one of only a couple of thousand made?

Rae hadn't seen another one—not quite like that. But it was dark. She couldn't be sure.

She had to get out of here and go for help. What happened to her didn't matter anymore. Buelah and Ginny did matter—and that meant she had to get to a phone.

"Joella, I'd better go back to the cabin." She bowed her head and contrived to appear awkward. "I didn't say where I was going. I'm sure you understand."

"Because you've got company, you mean?"

Rae nodded.

"Who is it?"

She stared at Joella. "Do you mind if I leave you now?"

"Yes."

"Well, I'm sorry, but I've got to."

"Why? Dallas isn't there. You've got time. I want to show you the basement. Warren and I used to spend a lot of time under this big old house. You'll want to see it. We liked it because it's so secret. No windows. No way for people outside to know you're down there."

"I'd like to leave now."

Joella swept open a door beneath the wide, curving staircase and bowed to Rae. "After you."

"No, thank you."

"After you," Joella repeated, and produced a small pistol from a pocket in her full skirt. "Who did you shoot at the cabin, by the way?"

The pattern on the dusty carpet at Rae's feet blurred. She straightened her spine. "I don't know what you're talking about. Why are you doing this? Dallas will find me."

"No he won't. I made sure of that. He never knew what hit him."

Rae clamped her teeth together.

"Just like I made sure that horrible Sam McIver wouldn't make more trouble than he already had. Now I'm going to make sure you're just as quiet as they're going to be from now on."

She should have brought the Sauer. "Shoot me here, then. I'm not going down there. Why should I? To make it easier for you?"

"Because I told you to." Lunging, Joella grabbed Rae by the arm and shoved her hard toward the top of the steps. "Do as you're told. At least in this one thing, do as you're told."

The toe of one of Rae's sandals caught in the frayed rug, and she stumbled forward, forward into the gloomy space that opened beyond the basement door.

She flung wide her arms, cried out, tried to grasp something, anything, to stop her fall.

A blow to the middle of her back sent pain shooting into her head. Her ankles twisted. The next blow came when her hip struck the opposite wall at the top of the stairs; then she sprawled, and rolled, hitting step after step—almost caught her balance, only to have her heel shoot out again, only to feel herself bounced from wall to wall.

At last it was over. It was over, but everything swung. The exposed wooden studs above her, the unpainted concrete walls on either side, the stairs, the long, long flight of stairs down which she'd cannoned—and Joella LaRose's grinning face.

Joella turned out the light in the foyer and climbed slowly down toward Rae, the pistol trained steadily on her. "Owie," Joella said. "We'd better kiss you and make you better."

"Stay away from me." Rae thought the words, but wasn't certain she'd spoken.

"I told you she wasn't nice, didn't I," Joella said, sitting a few steps from the bottom and smiling past Rae. "An opportunist. She's been sleeping with Dallas, just like I said. Now it's our turn to get what we want."

The slightest attempt to move brought agony. Rae moved anyway. She struggled until she sat up, and pulled her knees to her chest. Things moved, she thought with detached surprise.

"Keep it down, Joella. Ginny's asleep."

This time Rae felt herself passing out and didn't have the strength to fight it. She sagged until she lay down again.

The instant before her eyes closed, she looked into the face of Warren Niel.

Thirty-one

More than life . . . More than you'll ever know.
I couldn't . . . couldn't want you more.

The sawing noise inside his head sounded like a fiddle with strings about to break.

Too tight.

Words of some song went around and around.

I love you more than you'll ever know.

"Damn. Aah." Speaking made the strings of pain twang harder. *More than life.*

He did. He did love her more than life. Rae was his one and only love.

He'd never fallen in love before.

Dallas opened his eyes. Not that he could see a thing. He could feel, though. A mess of pointy stuff sticking into his face. More stuff, gritty, in his eyes and mouth.

Something wet slid across the back of his neck.

Dallas waited, and got another gentle, wet lick from a familiar tongue. "Wolf," he said, spitting out dirt. "Hey, boy, give a guy a hand, will you?"

Wolf whined, and snuffled.

"I know how you feel, boy. Geez." Very gingerly he maneuvered to a sitting position. The dog sat beside him. Dallas leaned. The dog leaned back.

He was a fool. A *dang fool.* He'd walked right into a trap.

Wolf got up and loped downhill, away from Dallas.

Dirt in the eyes was the worst. He spat out more debris,

and did his best to wipe particles from his eyelashes with the back of a wrist.

More than life. More than you'll ever know.

For as long as he could remember—about twenty seconds, give or take a second—he'd gotten lines of songs stuck in his brain. Drove a guy nuts.

He loved Rae more than his life.

Someone had slugged him on the back of the head, not once, but twice. He'd been out here because he'd heard Wolf barking and been afraid the dog would awaken Rae.

Rae was alone in the cabin.

Or she had been when he'd left her.

Shee-it. How long had he been out? Moving like a drunk, a drunk wading in four feet of water, Dallas struggled to his feet and staggered down the track. By pressing the heel of a hand to each temple, he could stop his head from splitting down the middle. Almost.

Going slow didn't help. Going fast didn't make the pain a whole lot worse. Dallas went as fast as his rubbery legs would take him. He made it up the porch steps by leaning over and steadying himself with his fingertips on the wood.

Wolf sat outside the door.

Dallas turned the handle.

Locked.

He knocked, pounded, yelled, "Rae! Rae!"

His heart thundered. He hadn't locked the door, and Rae wouldn't . . . unless . . . What if she'd thought he'd left her again? She could have gotten mad enough to lock the door in case he changed his mind and tried to come crawling back.

His own sickly grin wouldn't be an enticing sight. The one part she'd gotten right was the crawling back bit.

Dallas hammered some more.

She wasn't coming to the door, dammit. "Rae! Rae, you let me in, hear? C'mon, Rae. Let me in."

He felt worse, not better. And Wolf just rested his big old

bones in a tired heap like nothing had happened. Dallas shook his head at the dog, and noticed blood on his flank.

"You hurt, boy?" The blood oozed from what looked like a long cut—or a sideswipe from a bullet. Closer inspection showed the wound was mostly superficial with one deeper gouge. The work of a little bullet by the looks of it. And a tattered length of canvas leash trailed from Wolf's collar. "Tied you up to make you bark and get me outside. Then tried to kill you. What did you do, boy, make to tear out the bastard's throat?"

He needed light to look at the dog. And he needed to fix his eyes. And he needed to call the sheriff's office.

And he needed Rae.

"Rae!" Backing up a wobbly few steps, he threw himself at the door, and swore when it cracked under his weight. Not only the lock gave out, but the whole thing, like he was a wrecking ball hurled into a glass house. The hinges flat broke off, and he landed inside the cabin.

His head would never be the same. He closed one eye, then the other, testing to see if things got any steadier if he didn't open them both at the same time. No difference.

"Rae!" He got to his feet, turned on a light, and staggered to her bedroom. He hadn't closed that door either. It was closed now. "Rae, knock it off. I need you."

Throwing open the door, he reached for the light switch at the same time.

The bed was empty.

He walked in and went directly to check the bathroom, and never made it that far. On the floor beside the bed lay a man. Dallas could smell him—like something rotting in the heat of the night. Filthy, with a big, emaciated frame and lank, lightish hair.

Dallas looked at the bed, and at the sheet tangled on the floor, and a drawer open and sagging from the chest of drawers.

The stranger was dead—shot—but he hadn't been dead

for too long. The body was still warm and hadn't stiffened up yet.

Rae.

The facts didn't line up in any order. A dead man. A locked door. Rae missing. And someone had lured him out and tried to kill him—and Wolf. Dallas turned and realized the dog wasn't in his customary spot at his heel. Darn dog had a way of slipping away, but he was hurt.

Searching the rest of the cabin took only minutes. Rae wasn't there. He made for the front door and only stopped because there in plain sight, on top of a stool, rested a gun. From the look of it, Rae had brought the Sauer . . . Nope. That Sauer was still at the Decline house. Dallas had seen it in the study. How many guns did she own? If this was hers, too.

He'd better call the sheriff, not that he had a whole lot of faith in their trusty lawmen.

A cupboard above the kitchen counters had been opened. On the very highest shelf, sticking out on top of a row of cans, was the corner of some sort of packet.

Dallas considered whether or not to touch the gun, and decided mussed fingerprints, or even his own fingerprints on the weapon, would be preferable to having someone use it against him. He shoved the gun into the waist of his jeans.

The packet was a brown envelope. He pulled it down and looked at the front. *Rae.* Nothing more. While he removed the contents, a letter and a set of keys, he picked up the phone and punched numbers.

No dial tone. The phone was dead.

He couldn't take time to search for what would probably turn out to be a cut line. His keys were in the bedroom.

Reading and walking wasn't easy, especially reading, walking, and trying not to curl up and hold your aching head.

The letter was from Warren. To be read after his death. Warren telling Rae what to do, and how to do it. Hire a good lawyer, he told her. Don't go near Glory too soon, he said.

Dallas dropped to sit on the edge of a chair and read the letter to the end.

Warren Niel had bought the old Werther house—with Calhoun money, no doubt—and left it to Rae. That was a little something she'd left out of her grand payback gesture. What else hadn't she told him?

There had been two sets of keys. Now there was one.

"Leave this to me," Joella said to Warren. "You don't have to do a thing."

He'd carried Rae into a huge, unfinished room and stretched her out on an old tweed-covered couch. The walls were of concrete blocks, loaded with dust and cobwebs. Rae felt unreal, disoriented. The man who stood over her, frowning down, was John Maddy, only he was Warren Niel.

He was—wasn't dead. In the midst of a hot night, she shivered, and shrank from him.

"I shouldn't have listened to you." He spoke to Joella, but stared at Rae. "Look what we've done."

"Pull yourself together," Joella snapped. "The only mistake in all this was when you decided to get mixed up with her. She's a nuisance to us, Warren. Dangerous."

Rae ordered her thoughts enough to say, "Ginny? Where is she?" He'd said she was sleeping. "And Buelah? I saw her car."

"Damn garage door doesn't catch properly," Joella muttered. She took a step toward Rae and raised a fist to strike. "You don't get to ask questions."

"No, don't," Warren said in a shaking voice.

Fear trampled Rae's concentration. "They think you're dead."

"Shows how you can't believe what people say," Joella said. "How many people did you tell? About this house and all the other things?"

Rae shook her head. "John?" He'd been *buried.*

"It's okay," he said. "You took a bad fall."

"I was pushed," she told him, testing each limb to make sure nothing felt broken. "I should say, I was pushed, *Warren*. Why me? Why did you pick me to lie to?"

"We don't have time for this," Joella broke in. "The plan's changed. It had to. Things have gotten too messy."

"I never planned to do what I did, Rae," Warren said. "Then I saw you, and . . ." He drew his shoulders up. Thinner than when she'd last seen him, there were dark smudges beneath his blue eyes.

"And?" Rae prompted. "And you decided it didn't matter that you already had a wife? You'd just marry me, and adopt Ginny—supposedly—and it didn't matter what you did to us?"

"It always mattered. At the beginning, when all I could do was try to figure out how to have you, I hardly slept for weeks."

She couldn't believe this was happening. "You want me to be sorry for you?"

He wasn't listening. "Later I got used to what I'd done. I had a wife I didn't love here in Glory. And my business life was here. Then there was you in Decline. It worked, didn't it? Mostly? We were happy."

Rae propped her head on the arm of the couch. "It was wrong. And it was mad. If you thought you'd never get caught, you were mad." She thought of Willie lying dead on the floor at the cabin, and of how she'd squeezed the trigger on the gun. This time there would be no running away from what she'd done. "Sometimes it takes a long time, but we always get caught in the end."

"You do see we're going to have to make changes in your plan, don't you?" Joella said to her brother. The resemblance between them wasn't strong, except for the eyes. Both of them had extraordinary blue eyes.

"There's no reason to change anything," Warren said. "Rae will be a trooper. It's going to work, Rae, honey. We're going to be together again, just like before, only better. I won't be going away anymore."

Joella laughed, very loudly, and the laugh spiraled upward.

Chilled by the sound, Rae swung her feet to the floor and did her best to straighten her wrinkled T-shirt.

"You won't be going anywhere anymore, Warren," Joella said. "Remember? You're a dead man."

Rae recalled what the shock had made her forget: the evidence of Warren's death. "The plane crash," she said. "Dallas told me all about it."

"Dallas?" Warren said.

"He showed me your car, too. He told me it's been there ever since the accident."

"See?" Joella laughed again. "Just like I told you. *Dallas showed me.* She hasn't been mourning your *death,* brother dear. She's been screwing around with your brother-in-law."

"They wrote about it in the papers," Rae said. "Dallas showed me."

"Dallas showed her," Joella echoed.

Rae ignored her. "And there are records that show you radioed in to say you were having trouble. There wasn't any question, so it all said."

"It was my plane and I wasn't anywhere else. That added up to it being me who bought it. Quick and easy."

"It would have been if you hadn't found yourself some extra baggage, then decided you couldn't walk away when you had to," Joella said. "I tried to stop her from coming here, but it didn't work."

Warren looked at his sister. "You tried to stop her?"

"Well," Joella lowered her eyes, "someone had to think clearly."

Another piece of the puzzle slipped into place for Rae. "Did you go to Willie Skeggs and tell him where I was? Did you send him to Decline?"

Joella smiled. "Clever, wasn't I. He'd had a rough time,

poor guy, so I told him where he could get a little money for his trouble."

"Joella—"

"Don't say anything, Warren. I'll make up my own mind what I should and shouldn't do. Forget Skeggs. She's stirred up too much trouble. She's got to . . . We've got to get rid of her."

This was about whether or not to kill her, Rae thought, strangely detached. "Who was in Warren's plane?" She stood up. "Who made radio contact?"

Joella laughed too loudly. "Warren did, of course. Before he jumped out."

"But they'd know if there weren't any human remains, wouldn't they?"

"There were human remains."

"Who . . . No, don't say anything. It was that man Les, wasn't it? Les McIver? You were drinking with him the night before."

"We'd never be able to control her," Joella said.

"Was it Les McIver?" Rae persisted. "Did you kill him?"

"No," Warren said. "It wasn't anything like that. He was diabetic. That's what he told me when he got sick from drinking too much. And then he had a sort of fit and died."

"So you decided you'd pretend he was you, and—"

"We don't need a map of past events," Joella said. "You're very quick. You've got it right. With Warren supposedly dead, we could start again. We could be free of any dangerous connections, and enjoy what we'd worked for. But the idea to make the switch was mine, not Warren's. He couldn't afford to be publicly connected with McIver. There would have been awkward questions. It was best to cover up the death. I decided we could best do that by using it. If I hadn't thought fast, everything could have fallen apart."

"Everything? The fact that he's a thief who has been stealing from his wife's family for years?"

"You lived well on that money," Warren said. "You will

again. I made sure of that. I made sure you could get at it for all of us—once everything quieted down."

She had to give herself time to think. "Dallas will wake up and come looking for me."

The laughter Rae dreaded pealed out again. "Dallas isn't going to wake up, snookums. Dallas has checked out for a time."

There was menace in those words. Rae drove her fingernails into the threadbare piping along the edge of the seat and said quietly, "Dallas is at the cabin."

"Dallas isn't coming on his white horse to carry you to safety," Joella said, "any more than Sam McIver will be asking for more money, or giving us headaches while we wait to see if he's going to shoot his mouth off."

"It was *you* who killed Sam?"

Joella grinned and nodded. "In a manner of speaking. I set him up. Candles and soft music, and bubble bath. You should have seen the idiot drool. Then I—"

"I *know* what you did."

Warren said, "I don't."

"She electrocuted him in the bath," Rae said. "Where's Ginny?"

"Safe," Warren said. "Asleep. The radio fell in the bath. It was an accident."

Rae caught Joella's secret smile. She was secure in her power over her brother. But surely she didn't believe she'd done nothing wrong? "Is Buelah here, too? Did you bring her here so she couldn't let me know whether or not Ginny was in Decline?"

"It was so easy," Joella said. "I dropped Fancy off at the gates at Sweet Bay and let her walk in while I followed Buelah. Doing my good deed. Then all I had to do was catch up with that slug of a car she owns, force her over, and tell her Ginny had been found. She followed me back. End of story."

"We did what we had to do," Warren said. He didn't take

his eyes from her face. "It's going to be fine. Ginny and Buelah are fine. I've waited more than twenty years for this. We'll set up here in my home, and Joella will be our link to the outside world. Not that we'll need much of a link. We'll have each other Rae, forever."

She watched his mouth make the words. He couldn't be suggesting they all become prisoners, hermits hiding in a big old house, waiting for Joella to deliver supplies from time to time. "What's happened to Dallas?" she asked, a fist of fear clenching in her breast. "Where is he?"

"So worried about poor Dallas," Joella said, snickering. "You don't want Dallas Calhoun's leftovers, Warren."

"I'm better than him," Warren said. "His granddaddy took advantage of mine. We were on bad times, and old Calhoun came in and bought up this place for pennies on the dollar. Then he sold it for a bundle. We were driven from our home. Those people had more money than God, but they wanted ours, too."

"Sounds to me as if you didn't have any," Rae said, knowing she trod a skinny line, but unable to keep quiet.

"I married Fancy to get my foot in the door. It worked. They let me sweat my way to signing my name on any lovely check I wanted to sign. I had it made, and I'm not letting go of a cent I earned. Dallas is never getting anything back. I won't give it to him."

"Of course you won't," Joella said, as if speaking to a small child. "You've got a right to it."

Warren said, "Buelah can teach Ginny. And you and I won't have to be apart anymore, Rae."

Rae looked at Joella and saw hatred the other woman made no attempt to hide. "There are formalities," Rae said. "Legal papers to be executed."

"We're going to get Joella's husband to take care of that. He's a lawyer. He's scared of his shadow. He won't have the guts to risk what something like this could do to him professionally if it came out."

"That's right," Joella said. "You look tired, Warren. You go get some rest. I'll stay with Rae and explain how things are going to be."

"She knows. I've told her. We've got this place back, and we're all going to live here together. No one will ever know. They can't ever know."

He paced around the room. A yellow cotton shirt and brown chinos fell in folds from a body that used to be so solid. "They can't know, can they, Joella? That wouldn't do. They wouldn't let us stay here."

"That's right. They can't know and they're not going to. But we've got to change our plans. Listen up, Warren. Listen good. You're not yourself. You've got to let me do the thinking for both of us."

Rae's stomach squeezed, and squeezed.

Joella produced her small, mother-of-pearl-handled gun. "We're going to have it all. Tyson will draw up a new will leaving everything to me. It will be a surprise *find*. We'll get all those documents from the bank. You should have let me do that before she got here, but we can't go back."

"You can't get anything from the bank," Rae told her.

"Because of your signature? Not a thing to worry about. I've got it down. Whoo, Fancy's face will be a sight when Tyson finally reads the will! She's not getting anything."

"No," Rae said. "Warren, don't let her do this."

"Joella won't hurt anyone. She's just talking."

"She wants to get rid of us." Ginny was somewhere in this house, in this basement, and so was Buelah. They all had to get out. "What do you think the gun's for?"

Warren glanced at the gun. but his expression didn't change. "Joella won't hurt anyone," he repeated.

"Warren"—Joella used her patient parental tone—"Warren, listen to me carefully. All these weeks down here have taken their toll. We'll have to figure out a way for you to get out now and then, but we won't worry about that now."

"Not now," he agreed.

"Where's Ginny?" Rae asked. "I want to see her."

"Well you're *not* going to see her," Joella said, advancing. "You're not seeing her. And you're not telling anyone how anything's going to be. Got that?"

As long as they kept talking, there was time. "Where's Dallas?" Rae asked again. "Warren, make her tell us where Dallas is."

"Because you're in love with him?" Joella's grin was a vicious thing. "She's in love with Dallas, Warren. She's not good enough for you. She's cheated on you."

"Stop it!" Warren said. "Stop it. Rae would never cheat on me. We should all be very quiet. Ginny's asleep, and Rae's had a fall."

Joella went to her brother's side and hooked an arm around his elbow. She looked up at him. "You're too good, that's the trouble. When I got to the cabin, guess where she was?"

He blinked slowly, but said nothing.

"She was in bed with him. With Dallas. Weren't you, Rae? You were sleeping with Dallas."

"No," Warren said. "That's not true."

"Tell him, Rae," Joella said, and raised the gun. *"Tell* him."

"Is Buelah all right?"

"I said she was," Warren said. "She's sleeping, too."

"She'll sleep a long time," Joella said. "I made sure of that."

"Joella—"

"No," she said imperiously, cutting Warren off. "We've got things to do before it gets light. You know I'm right. It's all gone too far. We've got to protect ourselves. That means your secret little family is going to have to take a very long nap."

Dallas approached the Werther house obliquely. The only light came from a moon now partially obscured by clouds.

Not a glimmer showed at any of the windows he could see. He emerged from dense trees and ran, head down, toward banks of shrubs.

He needed something for the pain in his head. All he'd taken time to do was grab his shirt. The Jeep had still been in the carport beside the cabin, and as far as he could tell, the only thing Rae had bothered to take was the set of keys to this house.

It didn't make sense that she'd get up and come here.

Unless . . . He squinted to make out what lay ahead, and skirted a line of old hydrangea. No, he couldn't believe Rae was covering her bases, talking about returning what Warren had stolen, but not intending to do so unless she was sure she had someone else to provide for her, and provide well.

But why hadn't she told him about the house? Probably because she had so much on her mind that everything had started to run together.

By dodging around the back of the garage he could access the front of the building via a drive-through to gardens at the back. The pain in his head lessened, and he moved quickly, kept his back to walls as much as possible, and flattened himself to corners, waiting for any sound, any movement.

If someone saw him, they would laugh until they were sick at his apparently ridiculous caution. But the fact was that there was a dead man in the river cabin, and the woman he'd left there, whose bed he'd left a few minutes before he was felled by a silent assailant, might well have come here.

At the corner that would take him to the front facade, Dallas crouched, gathering strength and breath, and looked in all directions. But for the lightest of breezes through leaves, nothing moved.

He prepared to make a rush for the front door, but took one more glance to the right. When he'd made a circuit around the house the night Ginny went missing, the garage had been closed. The door nearest to him was open now.

Keeping low, he covered the distance to the garage and peered inside.

Very little light was needed to identify Buelah Wilks' big old Caddy. He dropped to one knee. Damn if it didn't begin to make sense that Rae and Buelah were up to something together. Could Ginny's disappearance have been a hoax? Why? Hell, *why,* had become the most frequently used word in his vocabulary, but he would find out *why?*

Dallas wasn't a man who took comfortably to the idea of being duped. By the time he made it to the front door, he'd worked up a head of steam that didn't lend itself to the necessary wariness.

The door opened smoothly, and he almost laughed—at himself for being all kinds of an ass. She'd come here and let herself in, and obviously hadn't felt threatened by intruders. Well, if Rae Faith could play games, so could Dallas Calhoun. He would sneak up on her and shock her to her sexy toes. Damn, he loved that woman.

Sending up one's blood pressure like an express elevator was guaranteed to give any headache a boost. Dallas's brain was almost at meltdown.

He closed the door again very gently.

A few seconds didn't do much to help his eyes adjust to the thick darkness. He strained to catch any sound, but didn't hear anything.

When he'd been a kid he'd been here a couple of times to parties given for Warren when his granddaddy still owned the place. The house was big. Choosing where to start looking was a challenge.

He had an uncanny sensation that he felt Rae nearby.

She had really meddled with his mind.

Standing upright again, he started for the first room on his left and entered until he could see anonymous reflections in vast mirrors.

Wherever she was, if she was here, she wouldn't be in a

dark room. Unless she expected him to come and ... *If she's here, find her.*

Four rooms yielded no sign of life. There were as many rooms again on the ground floor. He looked upward to faint sparks of diamond-white light in the crystals of a dusty chandelier.

Making up his mind on a search plan, he climbed the stairs.

Warren was a sick man, Rae decided. Sick of spirit. His will bent before that of his sister, and his weakness spelled nothing but the worst kind of trouble for Rae. The woman wanted to get rid of anyone who could stand in the way of her controlling Warren. She'd do anything to get what she wanted.

Warren sat on a stool with one short leg. The stool rocked each time he moved. His hands hung between his knees, and he trained his eyes on the floor.

"You do see it, don't you, Warren?" Joella said. She swung between wheedling and ranting. Wheedling was back. "I only want what's best for you. There's no other way out. Look at me."

He raised his face slowly.

Joella smiled at him. "I'm going to take care of you. You've had it hard for too long; now it's time things got easy."

"I can't do it." He sounded like a man in a trance. "She didn't do anything to me."

"She has now. She's done what you told her not to do. If she hadn't, we wouldn't have the kid here, or the old woman. And we wouldn't be looking at the possibility that everything could go bad on us. Rae disobeyed you, Warren. She shouldn't have done that."

Warren's blue eyes were dull.

"She shouldn't have slept with Dallas. The two of them planned to use your money."

"No." He shook his head. "No."

"Mama?" From the far end of the long room, from one of two doors, Ginny came running. She wore a pink night-gown Rae didn't recognize. "Mama, you came. Buelah said you would." She darted at Rae and threw her arms around her neck.

Rae hugged her, would not allow herself to cry, and stared directly into Warren's eyes. Pleading? Yes, she was plead-ing—for the sake of the child he'd "adopted."

Ginny smelled like Ginny, like soap, and sunshine. Rae nestled her nose in loose blond hair and held on even tighter.

"I don't like it here, Mama, but Daddy said we had to stay."

"Not for long now, Ginny." Rae challenged him silently. "You and Buelah and I are going to leave." He wouldn't hurt Ginny, or let Joella hurt her. Joella had folded her arms to hide the gun.

"Daddy came for me when I was looking for Wolf. Dad wore those climbing things on his feet to make me laugh. Then Buelah came, but she isn't very well. She sleeps all the time. I think Buelah needs to go to the doctor."

Rae kept right on staring at Warren, willing him to act, to declare himself on her side. When he still didn't speak, she said, "Our girl needs to be in her own bed, Warren. Why don't we see to that—and to getting Buelah back to Decline with us. We'll talk about all this later." When some sign of comprehension showed on his face, she pressed on. "I give you my word I won't make any moves until you and I talk again. On our own."

"See how it is?" Joella said. "Manipulative. You'd never think she just got out of bed with—"

"*That's* enough," Rae said sharply. "This is between War-ren and me."

"I don't like her," Ginny said. "I know I'm not supposed

to say things like that, but she says nasty things about you, Mama. She said Uncle Dallas wasn't my uncle. She said you were his girlfriend, not his sister."

Rae held the sweet-smelling head against her shoulder and put hate in her eyes, hate that came easily. "Dallas isn't my brother," she said. "He needed to find a way to talk to me, so he made up a fib to tell Buelah so she'd say something to help him."

Ginny leaned away. Her solemn features turned Rae's heart. "That's why he fibbed? Why did you fib?"

She deserved this. "I'm sorry. That's not good enough, but it's the best I can do. There are some complicated things I've got to tell you. I hoped to wait until you were a bit older. Not a lot, but a bit."

"Get up," Joella ordered.

Warren stirred and said, "Leave them be."

"For God's sake! You always were spineless, but you used to know it well enough to let me do the thinking." She gave Rae a glimpse of the gun, a warning. "I told you to get up."

Rae got to her feet. "Time to go," she said softly to Ginny. "Come on, pumpkin, up, up, up."

"Time to go, pumpkin," Joella said, her voice sweet. "We've got to do what your mama says, and she says you've got to go."

The hand wrapped around the gun connected with Rae's shoulder hard enough to send her to her knees. Joella shoved her backward, and grabbed Ginny. "Time to go," she crooned, using a hand in Ginny's hair to force her, facedown, on the floor.

Ginny cried out, "Mama! Mama!"

"*Joella.*" Warren shot to his feet. "What are you doing? Ginny, honey, get up."

Joella said, "Leave her where she is." She stood up herself, and propped the ball of one foot on the back of a slim little neck. Holding the gun with both hands, she aimed at Ginny's head.

Ginny whimpered and said, "What's she doing? Why does she want to hurt me?"

Rae made impotent fists. "Me," she said. "Take me, not her. She's a child."

"That might work. I'll have to think about it. You just lie down with Ginny. On your face. That's what I want. Then I'll decide who really has to go."

A sharp sound, explosive sound, came from somewhere deep below Dallas's feet. He'd been ready to call this a wash and go report a body—and wait for Rae to show up.

Gunshot. A second gunshot.

Drawing the Sauer from his waist, he checked the clip again. He'd done so once at the cabin. He slipped downstairs, praying there were no hidden eyes watching him.

At the bottom of the staircase he came to a halt and made a slow circle, trying to probe the darkness.

Another shot sounded, louder this time. Right beneath his feet.

There was a basement down there, a big, big basement Warren had been proud of as a kid.

A smarter man might choose to get the hell out of harm's way. A smarter man who didn't care more than was good for him for a woman who could be in trouble.

As soon as he'd negotiated his way quietly through the door to the basement he saw signs of what he'd expected at every turn in the rest of the house: light.

And he heard voices. Raised voices. A woman shouted, and a man spoke much more softly. The noise wasn't coming from the area at the bottom of the steep steps, but from the room to the right.

Praying that nothing would creak, he made a rapid descent and prepared to advance cautiously.

He looked right, and quit breathing.

He looked into the eyes of his dead brother-in-law, only

Warren wasn't dead. Joella LaRose stood with her back to Dallas, a gun trained on Rae and Ginny, who lay facedown and side-by-side on the bare concrete floor.

Warren's features twisted. Even at a distance Dallas saw the silent fall of tears.

Joella fired into a couch, and laughed when Ginny screamed.

"*Damn* you," Dallas yelled, fury shutting out everything but the man and woman, and the two on the ground. "Drop the gun."

Ginny screamed again, and Rae covered the child with her own body.

Rather than obey Dallas's order, Joella lined up for another shot; this time at Rae's head.

With his eyes on Joella's hand, he prepared to squeeze the trigger.

Warren's sudden bellow shattered the frail stillness of the moment. He opened his mouth wide and let out a bull roar, and threw himself at his sister.

Dallas yelled, "Rae, get away. Get behind the couch."

Above her, Warren took Joella by the throat. They fell, and rolled, and rolled.

Rae crouched over Ginny, then plucked her up as she would a baby and dashed to push her behind the couch. He expected Rae to drop out of sight with Ginny, but she darted back and closed in on the writhing couple.

Sobbing, Joella said Warren's name over and over. When he released her throat, she strained to hold the gun beyond his reach.

"Stay where you are," Dallas told Rae, keeping the Sauer aimed at Warren and Joella. "Stay with Ginny."

"Don't shoot him," she said, bending her knees and creeping even nearer. "No more killing, please."

Warren shifted his grip, and Joella freed her right arm. Instantly she forced the gun toward Warren's neck.

Even if he wanted to shoot, Dallas had no clear line of

fire. Flinching, waiting for the shattering blast, for the lurid blossoming of blood and tissue, he dropped on top of the pair. The impact crushed him into Joella, and her eyes closed. She pulled the trigger, but she'd lost her target, and the bullet went wild.

Holding them both down, he reached for her wrist.

Rae was faster. Slamming to her knees on top of Joella's wrist, she forced the woman's fingers open. The next sound Dallas heard was the unmistakably sickening crack of breaking bones. Joella's.

Screaming, she scrabbled to take her toy-sized pistol in her left hand. Again Rae was faster, much faster. She retrieved the gun and retreated, leaving Dallas to extricate himself and stand, feet splayed, the Sauer steady in two hands, over two people who weren't going to do any more harm.

Joella stayed on the floor, cradling her broken wrist and crying. Warren got up slowly. He said, "My fault. Forgive her," and looked at Rae. "Forgive me?"

She turned away and went to her daughter.

"Is there a working phone—dumb question."

Thunderous pounding sounded overhead. A herd, evidently of humans in boots.

Dallas didn't take his attention from his quarry, but he saw movement to his right, at the edge of his vision.

"It's about time you were here, Dallas Calhoun." Buelah Wilks' crackling voice held nothing but disapproval. "A man ought to make a better job of looking after the people he loves."

"Well, Ms. Wilks," Dallas began. "I didn't—"

Wolf, limping into the room, silenced Dallas. The dog gave his boss a baleful stare before going directly to Joella's huddled form. He pushed his nose into her face and, when she screamed, bared his teeth and lowered his battered rear to sit where he could keep guard over her.

Dallas took pleasure in Joella's shouts to "Get him away. He'll bite me."

"He's got too much good taste," Dallas said.

The stampeding footsteps descended to the basement, and Nick Serb, followed by Buzz and three other deputies, erupted into the room.

"Well, I'll be," Nick said with his customary original turn of phrase. "What have we got here?" Even more original.

Warren said, "I did it. Joella's innocent. I did everything."

"Put the cuffs on him," Nick told Buzz, then looked more closely at his prospective prisoner. "Well, I'll *be*. If it ain't Warren Niel. Ain't it?"

Warren averted his face.

"Yup," Nick said. "Warren Niel, okay. If that don't beat all. And I attended your funeral."

Dallas noticed Tyson standing in the doorway. "Where did you come from?" He wasn't in the mood for pleasantries.

"Wolf went home for help," Tyson said. "Fancy saw the wound and panicked. She thought something might have happened to you."

"My sister was always a razor brain."

"Your sister . . . Oh, what the hell. If you don't know your sister cares about you by now, it's not my problem. She called me. When I got there, I called Nick. Wolf is quite a guy, Dallas. He's got to be out on his feet, but he's still taking care of you."

"Everyone ought to have someone they can trust," Dallas said. "A good dog fills the bill until a good human comes along." He looked at Rae and she smiled. They weren't all the way home in the trust area, he thought.

"Joella!" Tyson's cry silenced everyone. "Joella? You're hurt?" He hurried toward her.

"Best stay back, Tyson," Dallas said. "Joella needs to be checked at the hospital, and she will be. But she's in trouble."

"She's in pain," Tyson said. "For God's sake, Dallas, she needs help."

"If she wasn't hurt, you might be looking at a corpse or

two in this room. She thought it would be useful to shoot Rae and Ginny, and anyone else who might get in her way."

Tyson's jaw slackened. He appeared stunned.

"Hang in there," Dallas told him. "We've got to take this one step at a time, right, Nick?"

"You've got it," the sheriff agreed. Ever the king of understatement, he added, "Your wife seems to be in some trouble, Tyson. We'll be taking care of things."

"We'd better find out what's happenin' here, Nick," Buzz said. He looked at Buelah Wilks, then at Rae and Ginny. "Did you know there's a dead man in your cabin, Miss Rae? Broke the door down to get in and someone shot him."

"Reckon he was going to rob you, Miss Rae," another deputy said.

"Yeah." Nick shook his head. "Two bullets in the chest. Real mess."

Rae drew Ginny close and held her tightly.

Her face white and devoid of makeup, Fancy peered around the doorjamb. She saw Dallas. "Is it safe?" she said.

"Sure," he told her, wanting to be alone with Rae.

"You aren't going to shoot anymore?"

"I haven't done any shooting yet."

She edged through the doorway. "Well, I could just whip you, Dallas. You frightened me out of my wits. I took one look at that horrible dog of yours and I was just sure you were dead. He was bleeding, but all he'd do was run back and forth until we'd follow him. It takes time to drive all the way here from Sweet Bay followin' a dog."

"I'm sure Wolf's sorry," Dallas said.

Rae stared into his face. Surely they could be together now.

"Well," Fancy exclaimed, falling back, covering her heart with one hand, and pointing the trembling forefinger of the other. "Well, would you look at that? As I live and breathe, *Warren Niel.* You aren't *dead.* You tricked everybody, you no-good worm."

"Fancy," Dallas said soothingly. "Let's get you back to Sweet Bay."

"Oh!" She made fists. "Oh, you were always a disappointment, Warren. Oooh, I won't get the insurance money!"

Thirty-two

Rae remembered the way to Dallas's rooms too well. Dressed in an apricot-colored silk running suit Fancy had insisted she borrow, she walked to his bedroom door.

The door was open. With his back to her, Dallas stood in the middle of a deep green oriental rug.

"Tully told me I'd better come here," Rae said, hovering on the threshold. He'd been distant since they had been allowed to leave the Werther house. "Now. That's what she said. *Now.*"

"That's what I told her to say. Tully's real literal."

"It was kind of Fancy to say she wanted us to come here tonight."

"She has her moments. If she hadn't insisted, I would have. She's feeling guilty—she should."

Polite. He was polite, but remote. Downright frosty, if she was honest with herself. "Buelah's asleep. So's Ginny, but I'd like to stay where I'll hear if she wakes up."

"Tully said you'd feel like that. She'll be listening for Ginny and let us know if she needs you."

Rae had fantasized what it might be like if she and Dallas were together and nothing stood between them. Her fantasies had been warm, sensual. She looked at his broad back. His arms were crossed, stretching a white cotton shirt across his shoulders. She would always find that back, or anything else about Dallas Calhoun, sensual, but there was nothing warm about his tone, or his stance.

"I killed Willie," she said, grasping for the first thing that came to mind.

"Someone needed to kill him. He'd already lived too long."

"I thought the police would be asking a lot of questions by now." She almost asked why he'd been in such a hurry to send for her if he didn't even want to look at her. "Seeing him again—it was incredible. Horrible. Like seeing a ghost. Then, after I fired the gun, I expected him to get up again."

"You did? How do you feel now?"

"All right." She felt awful. She almost asked him if he'd rather she left. Instead, she said, "I thought I'd killed him before, remember?" and she hugged herself.

Dallas cleared his throat. He rocked to his toes and looked at the ceiling. "The authorities will go easy on you. Don't worry. Everything's on your side."

Rae said, "I feel sorry for Tyson."

"How come?"

"He still loves his wife."

"Yeah. Love can be a bitch."

Rae took a deep, slow breath. Was he talking about their love. "Can you believe Warren wore crampons that night?"

"I can believe anything about now. It worked to mess up any footprints when he pushed the boat out. Dirty trick. It only served to make us all think Ginny could have drowned."

"You won't want to hear this, but he's not the man I knew anymore."

He raised his shoulders, flexed muscles in his back. "I don't care who he was. He's a sonovabitch who stole, and cheated. He married you when he wasn't free to marry, and adopted Ginny under a false name. Then he used her trust to lure her away. I hope he gets more than a slap on the wrist."

"He will." She no longer felt surprised that she wanted Warren to be punished.

"Joella's going to buy the farm," he commented. "Or as

good as. Lock a woman like that away and she's not going to hold together."

"I guess not." She wanted to ask what he wasn't telling her. "Will Tyson be okay?"

"He's going to join Carter. His father. They're moving away. They've never gotten along, but evidently they've decided it's time they did. I wish them the best."

"So do I."

Dallas faced her, and Rae barely resisted an urge to flee the cold speculation in his eyes. "If I hadn't seen the envelope, and Warren's letter to you, you and Ginny—and Buelah—you could all be dead by now."

She pressed her stomach. It was true, but she didn't want to hear him say it aloud.

"You didn't want me to know about the house."

"I didn't deliberately keep it from you." She hadn't, had she? "There's been so much."

"You didn't hold that out just in case I failed to come through?"

"Come through?" Surely he didn't mean what she thought he might.

"With the kind of security you thought you had with Warren before all this. After all, the property is free and clear of any will, just like anything else he put in your name. You could choose to fight to keep it."

Rae wanted to move, to sit down, or leave. But she couldn't make her muscles work.

"Nothing to say? No vehement denials?"

She cleared her throat. "If you think I'm capable of something like that, why should I deny it? What would be the point?"

He settled his weight on one leg and bowed his head. The room was a study in dark greens. Heavy antiques hadn't been what Rae expected, but they looked right. Dallas looked right here. And he looked defeated. He didn't trust her, but he wanted to. Or he had wanted to trust her.

"Couldn't you have tried letting me be innocent until you proved me guilty?" she asked.

"I told you I loved you," he said. "More than once. I don't know how many times. You never said you loved me, at least not while you were conscious. I noticed, but I didn't say anything. I thought it was implied."

The accusations hurt too much. She wouldn't defend herself to him again.

"What else didn't you think to tell me, Rae?"

The word "Nothing" sprang to her lips. Buying time to think, she walked past him to the windows. Darkness still obscured the scene outside.

"I'm beat," he said. "You must be, too."

"Yes. But you sent for me, so I came."

"A mistake. We'll continue this when we've both had some sleep."

Rae's temper thinned. "Will we? You mean we'll talk when you decide we should? What do you want me to do, go to my room and wait for another summons?"

He combed his hair with his fingers. "I don't want to fight. This night hasn't been any picnic for me, either."

She'd seen the contusions on the back of his head. "I know. I'm sorry I caused that."

"It wouldn't matter. Nothing would be too much if . . . All I wanted was to believe that this time it was right, that you were exactly what I thought you were."

"Perfect?" She took several steps toward him. "Is that what you thought I was?"

"*No,* dammit. Just honest would have been great."

"Forget it." You couldn't plead your case with someone who'd already condemned you. "Let's forget we ever met."

His laugh was humorless. "I don't think that's going to work real well. Just tell me if I'm likely to walk into any more land mines, so I can be prepared."

"None that are any concern of yours."

Dallas narrowed his gray eyes and came close enough for

Rae to hear his breathing. "Want to expand on that? There is something else, isn't there?"

"It's nothing to you."

"Try me."

She would not retreat. Raising her face, she met his eyes. All right. He wanted the truth. "Ginny isn't my child."

His silence went on, and on.

"She was my sister Cassie's. I told you about Cassie. She died when Ginny was born."

He jutted his chin and found his voice. "By that—*thing?* By Willie?"

Long ago Rae had made her peace with a version of Ginny's paternity. "I can't be sure who her father was. It doesn't matter."

"You've passed that child off as your own."

"When I was seventeen and on the run, it seemed the only thing to do. I thought if I said anything to anyone, she'd be taken away from me."

"Wouldn't that have been better for Ginny?"

She stared at him before saying, "For her to be taken away from the one person who loved her enough to make sure she was safe and happy?"

"People would line up to adopt a baby like that."

"Ginny's *mine.*" Panic tightened her throat. *"Mine."* The silly, fussy sweat suit made her too hot.

"She's not yours. You just said as much."

Telling him had been stupid. "Okay, okay." Forcibly calming herself, she made her tone brisk. "There's no need for this. Of course you're right. Technically. I'm going to see to the legalities of her guardianship. She's old enough to speak for herself now, and they take that into account. She'll be given to me."

"When you love someone, you don't keep secrets."

"Not even if you're afraid they won't love you anymore if they find out exactly who you are? And what you are?"

"Who are you? What are you?"

"I'm Rae Faith, child of who-knows-who, from who-knows-where. But I'm a survivor. I'm a fighter who did the best she could."

He took a scrap of paper from his pocket, looked at it, rolled it into a ball between his palms and threw it into a wastebasket. He didn't comment on what she'd said.

"Thank you for everything you've done for me," Rae said. A few more minutes of this and she'd cry. Only she didn't intend to let that happen. "Maybe it was all because of the stress, the extraordinary situation. It brought us together and we thought—*I* thought we might have something more than a casual thing together."

"But now you've figured out it isn't anything more?"

She made a wide circle around him. "I've decided it never was. Don't worry, the house will be signed over to you with everything else."

"I wasn't worried."

"Of course not. You know you can get it back anyway. I want Ginny and Buelah to get some good rest. But we'll take off as soon as they both wake up. You know where to find me."

"In Decline? Is that what you mean?"

"That's what I mean. I paid a good deal toward the house there. We'll work out a payback for the rest."

Dallas kicked the rug with the toe of a boot. "So, that's it. Is that what you're telling me?"

"I'm telling you I'm sorry for the things I should be sorry for. I should have had the sense to know that once the drama was over nothing would be the same. But I'm grateful for your many kindnesses." Memories of other things they had shared must be closed out. "What are you telling me? Anything?"

Their eyes met again, and he shook his head slowly.

She would never forget his eyes, or the lines beside his mouth, or the way shadow underscored his cheekbones.

"Nothing," she said flatly. "Fine." The walk to the door took too long, yet it was over too soon.

Rae closed his door behind her and leaned against the wall outside. Seconds passed before she could gather her wits enough to leave. She broke into a run. Ginny had dealt with too much already, but their bond would never be shaken; Rae didn't doubt that for an instant.

Dallas must just become one more piece of her past. Tears made her gasp. He'd always be the best piece of her past.

"Just like that!" Dallas opened a cupboard built into a corner of his room and found a bottle of brandy and a glass. "You walk out just like that. You're *grateful* for my kindness? *Damn you, Rae*. You're *crazy*. This whole mess is *crazy.*"

He shoved the bottle and glass back and headed for the door. She wasn't going to get away that easily. She wasn't just going to take off without a whole lot more talk. She owed him.

If he chased her, he'd be putting the power into her hands.

"Damn!" She wasn't the type to come to heel. But neither was he the type to beg, or to pretend there weren't roadblocks when he thought there were.

When the door swung open it almost hit him. Rae barged in, and he came close to another collision. "Sorry," she said.

"Forget it. I'm glad you missed me."

"How would you know if I missed you?"

He scrubbed at his stubbly jaw. "If you'd walked into me, I'd probably have noticed."

Her giggle got his complete attention. "I was trying to apologize for not telling you about Ginny. Not talking about the house thing wasn't deliberate."

"Rae . . ." Every word had to count. "I don't blame you for holding back. The story about Ginny, I mean. You spent a lot of years protecting her by being silent. Those things aren't easy to change. I was wrong to say some of the things I said."

Her face was so pale, and her lips. She appeared bloodless. "Some things aren't easy. And you didn't exactly give me reason to think you were on my side—not for some time."

"No. I know. I believe you, honey. Everything you've told me, I believe."

"Thank you." She just stood there, watching him, giving wooden answers.

"That thing you're wearing doesn't suit you." Great. Now he was being insulting.

Rae frowned at him, then looked down at herself and said, "It isn't mine."

"You're really tired, aren't you?" he said.

"Really tired."

"Want me to walk you back to your room?"

"No."

Dallas sank his hands into his pockets.

"I don't think I can walk that far," she said, lowering her eyes. "Could I stay here? With you?"

Words failed him. He never remembered that happening before. His feet wouldn't shift.

Rae coughed. She covered her mouth and made a hiccupping sound.

Dallas watched her suspiciously and asked, "Are you okay?"

"Uh huh," she said through chuckles.

Laughing. She was laughing. "What's so funny? I could use a good laugh myself."

She gulped and turned red. "Us. We're ridiculous."

"Thanks."

"Well, we are. You get huffy with me. I get mad at you and storm off. Then I come rushing back and almost flatten you with the door because you were coming after me."

"You don't know I was coming after you."

"Weren't you?"

There was a time when a man should give in gracefully. "Maybe."

"Just say yes. It won't be too painful."

"I wanted to come after you. I'm male, so I was fighting it. I'd have lost in the end."

She smiled. Her green eyes shone with humor, and so much more. She said, "I love you, Dallas. I really love you. I never loved a man before."

Life rushed into his limbs, and his tongue. He dropped to a crouch and laced his fingers behind his neck, and laughed.

"What is it? What's so funny now?"

He saw her legs in the awful shiny sweatpants that ruffled around her bare feet because the legs were too long.

"Dallas, talk to me."

He knelt before her, wrapped his arms around her waist, and pressed his forehead into her belly. "Nothing's funny, sweetheart. I love you, too. I guess I'm just having the last laugh at everything that tried to get in our way."

Please read on for
a preview of
Stella Cameron's

The Wish Club

Coming from
WARNER BOOKS
in
June 1998

Scotland, Spring 1834. On Kirkcaldy land.

Max was the only name he knew was truly his. Just Max. Nothing more. He'd become Max Rossmara because a good man had rescued a desperate boy destined for a London workhouse, or worse, and given him a family name to call his own. He was nobody, not really, yet he'd been made part of a great family tradition and he was expected to bear its standard high.

Did he really want to call that standard his own?

If he took it up with his entire heart and bore it with the weight of all it meant, might he pay for the shelter of privilege with his soul?

Yes.

Would he do so anyway?

Answering yes again would likely cost him what he loved most.

He scanned the wild countryside he'd come to love so well. Overshadowing the surrounding landscape, Castle Kirkcaldy rose atop its mount, a massive, many-towered, and castellated bastion, harsh against a crystal-blue spring sky.

Presently the home of his father's older brother, Arran, Marquess of Stonehaven, Kirkcaldy had been held by the noble family of Rossmara for generations.

And Max, the boy who had once picked pockets in London's Covent Garden, had been given the right to move about that castle with as much freedom as had he been born there.

In its sharp, gorse-scented snap, the air bore the memory of winter. The breeze tossed his hair and stung his eyes. He turned his back on Kirkcaldy's hill to regard instead the simple croft where Robert and Gael Mercer lived with their children, Kirsty and Niall. She was inside—Kirsty was inside. He knew because he always knew when she was near. And she would feel his presence soon enough, if she hadn't already.

Robert Mercer was also near, watching from the chicken coop, while pretending not to watch, and worrying about his beloved daughter, and what he perceived as the danger of her being hurt by a man above her station.

Max could never hurt his sweet Kirsty, not if there was a choice. And the choice was his unless he allowed that choice to be taken from him.

His boots making no sound, he entered the croft.

The flood of feeling in every part of him grew stronger each time he saw her and he was not fool enough to pretend that those feelings were entirely of the higher nature he'd have sworn to as a boy.

The boy had become a man.

With her back to him, Kirsty bent over the table in what served as the Mercer's rude kitchen. She hummed, and plunged her hands into a bowl of water.

Max walked softly across the earthen floor of the croft until he stood behind her.

Sunlight through the open door made a halo of the fair hair she wore in long braids pinned on top of her head. Curls sprang at the nape of her thin neck. The soft, vulnerable skin there brought Max another rush of emotion, and need.

The stuff of her blue and white checked dress was cheap, but on Kirsty it looked fresh and pretty. Slightly made, she was neither tall nor short, and although she didn't have her mother's red-gold hair there was much about Kirsty that reflected her pretty, fragile mother's aura of sensitive inner strength.

He could not give her up.

Max stopped. He couldn't loosen the fists he'd made, or fight down the swell of tenderness that mixed with anger in his breast.

"Master Max," Robert Mercer had said not ten minutes earlier, doffing his battered woolen bonnet and winding it in work-scarred hands, *"It's no my place t'say as much, but ye'd be doin' me a favor if ye left my lassie alone the now. Ye're no a laddie anymore, a laddie who wants t'play bairns' games. Ye're a gentleman. A gentleman, and kin t'the lairds o' this great estate. My lassie's—my lassie's no for the likes o' ye."*

What Robert Mercer had meant was he feared Max would use his daughter as other men of means sometimes used humble young females. He also meant he'd guessed that a childhood friendship had grown into something more, something so much more, and that he didn't approve any more than Max's own father would approve. Well, what he and Kirsty shared was more than a childhood friendship, but less than Max longed for it to be.

A gentleman? He was a bastard. He was Struan Rossmara, Viscount Hunsgore's adopted son.

"I feel ye sneakin', Max Rossmara," Kirsty said without looking at him. "And I feel ye standin' there, starin' at me."

Of course she did. They'd often confided how they felt close even when they were actually far apart. He hadn't told Kirsty how he sometimes reached for her in the night, and awoke expecting to find her in his arms.

"Ye're troubled." She held her soapy hands out of the water and twisted to see him.

He smiled, easy enough to do when he looked into her startlingly blue eyes. "Not a bit of it, Miss Mercer. Not troubled at all. Only puzzled. Why would a sensible girl of sixteen be playing with a bowl of water for no reason at all?"

She grew a little pink and used a forearm to push strands of hair away from her face. "There's reason for everythin', Mr. Rossmara. Why, if ye'd eyes t'see, ye'd know I was about an important creation."

Her voice, a trifle husky, sounded as if laughter couldn't be far away. "I would, would I?" he said, going to her side and bending low over the water. "Are there kelpies in there? Are you bathing kelpies?"

"Noo," she told him, giggling. "I'm making bubbles. An' dinna laugh, or ye'll have me cryin'."

Max straightened slowly and studied her face. Intelligence shone there and how well he knew it. He was the older by years, yet she'd badgered him to teach her to read, to learn her numbers, to study whatever he studied—and between the two of them she'd often been the quicker to comprehend.

He'd never kissed her. He'd wanted to often enough, but her innocence and her trust in him gave him the strength to resist—so far. Would they never kiss? Never know even that small, exquisite pleasure?

"Whist?" she said, frowning a little. "Ye're thinkin' if ye'll laugh at me?"

He inclined his head and allowed himself the pleasure of staring at each of her features. "I'll never laugh at you," he said. He looked at her mouth and knew he must not kiss her, for if he did he'd surely lose all power to make the decisions, take the actions he must pursue for both of them.

Her gaze didn't waver from his, but she lifted her right hand, the tips of her thumb and first finger touching, and blew softly until a bubble trembled between them. Sunlight stroked its rainbow colors.

Her generous mouth remained pushed out in a soft "ooh."

He felt his own lips part.

"Make a wish," she whispered. "Go on, Max, make a wish and blow t'bubble away."

"A wish?"

"Aye. We should always have somethin' t'wish for. Haste ye, before it pops."

He closed his eyes and blew, and felt minute droplets scatter on his face.

"What did ye wish for?"

"I thought you weren't supposed to tell."

Her smile wobbled a little. "Maybe it'd be all right for the two o' us t'know? If we kept t'secret between us, d'ye think?"

He thought being twenty-two and in love with sixteen-year-old Kirsty was the sweetest, yet the most painful thing in the world. "I think it would be all right."

"Tell me then." The top of her head reached his chin. She'd inherited her mother's light skin and freckles. The end of her nose tipped up just a little. *Tell* me," she begged.

"I wished for time to stand still. Right now. I wished to be standing here with you—looking at you—forever."

Her smile fled and her throat jerked as she swallowed. "I see."

She knew.

"Ye've come t'say ye're leavin' again."

"For a few months. My father, and Uncle Arran, want me to study estate management on the Yorkshire properties."

"Yes." Nodding, she bowed until he couldn't see her face anymore.

He ought to say something about it being time for them to see less of each other, about how she should think about looking for a husband, but he said, "You'll read those books I brought for you? So that we can talk about them when I get back?" And he thought he would die if he ever had to see her with another man and know that man was her husband.

"I'll read them," she said.

He heard tears in her voice now and said, "Will you make a wish before I go?"

Silently she dipped her hand into the water again, swished it around, and raised her joined finger and thumb to blow. Then she closed her eyes tightly and he saw her lips move.

The bubble separated from her fingers and floated toward the roof.

"And what did you wish for, Kirsty?"

Her arms fell to her sides. She pressed her lips tightly together and stood quite still. Her eyes glittered.

"Oh, Kirsty." Not caring who might come, who might see—or that he must find a way to let her go, Max enfolded her in his arms and held her close. "My Kirsty. Please don't cry."

She shuddered, but slowly returned his hug. "I wished for t'same as ye. I want t'stay here like this. I never want it t'end."

"Sounds as if we've one mind, then," he told her. "We ought to form a club for people who think alike."

"Aye, a club o' two." She nudged her sharp chin into his chest. "A club for wishin'."

His smile, the smile she couldn't see, was bitter. A man and a girl could have their wishes, couldn't they? At least they could keep those.

Max said, "A wish club."

DANGEROUS GAMES (0-7860-0270-0, $4.99)
by Amanda Scott

When Nicholas Barrington, eldest son of the Earl of Ulcombe, first met Melissa Seacort, the desperation he sensed beneath her well-bred beauty haunted him. He didn't realize how desperate Melissa really was . . . until he found her again at a Newmarket gambling club—being auctioned off by her father to the highest bidder. So, Nick bought himself a wife. With a villain hot on their heels, and a fortune and their lives at stake, they would gamble everything on the most dangerous game of all: love.

A TOUCH OF PARADISE (0-7860-0271-9, $4.99)
by Alexa Smart

As a confidence man and scam runner in 1880s America, Malcolm Northrup has amassed a fortune. Now, posing as the eminent Sir John Abbot—scholar, and possible discoverer of the lost continent of Atlantis—he's taking his act on the road with a lecture tour, seeking funds for a scientific experiment he has no intention of making. But scholar Halia Davenport is determined to accompany Malcolm on his "expedition" . . . even if she must kidnap him!

ROMANCE FROM JANELLE TAYLOR

ANYTHING FOR LOVE   (0-8217-4992-7, $5.99)

DESTINY MINE   (0-8217-5185-9, $5.99)

CHASE THE WIND   (0-8217-4740-1, $5.99)

MIDNIGHT SECRETS   (0-8217-5280-4, $5.99)

MOONBEAMS AND MAGIC   (0-8217-0184-4, $5.99)

SWEET SAVAGE HEART   (0-8217-5276-6, $5.99)